IN THE MOONLIT ROSE GARDEN, JARED KISSED HER AGAIN AND AGAIN . . .

Maybe, Jared thought, maybe a long time from now he'd be able to ask Heather to marry him. But that was all so far in the future that he didn't even want to think about it, and the present was so bleak that he didn't want to think about that either.

He wrapped her tightly in his arms, pressing her lithe, well-formed body against his own. It might be the last chance he would ever have. But that turned out to be a mistake. It took all of the willpower he possessed to push her away from him and say, "We'd better go back inside . . ."

Heather's lips were throbbing and her whole body sang with pleasure as she stood before him. She watched his eyes sweep over her body, then gaze, overflowing with desire, into her own . . .

Books by Lydia Lancaster

Always the Dream
The Arms of a Stranger
False Paradise

Published by TAPESTRY BOOKS/POCKET BOOKS

Always the Dream

Lydia Lancaster

PUBLISHED BY POCKET BOOKS NEW YORK

Another *Original* publication of POCKET BOOKS

 POCKET BOOKS, a division of Simon & Schuster, Inc.
1230 Avenue of the Americas, New York, N.Y. 10020

ISBN: 0-671-62909-3

First Pocket Books printing June 1987

10 9 8 7 6 5 4 3 2 1

↪ Chapter 1 ↩

HEATHER BAILEY AND Mrs. Allenby looked at each other. Heather's face was lively with interest, and the cook's was a picture of dismay as the raised voices carried all the way from the front parlor to the kitchen. Thatcher Cranston and his daughter, Emma, were going at it hot and heavy, and it wasn't the first time, either, although this seemed, by the volume of their voices, to be the worst quarrel of all. The other quarrels had been more like an ongoing bickering, sometimes more vicious but always stopping short of mayhem, as the staid and proper Emma had endeavored, these five years past, to reform her father's wicked ways.

Secretly, because it never would have done for her to voice her uncalled-for opinion, Heather leaned toward Thatcher's side. While it was true that Thatcher had cut a wide swathe once the year of mourning for his deceased wife had passed, Emma was too strict and unbending by far. But then Emma was the image of her mother, just as Jared, her older brother, was Thatcher all over again. Jared was far too handsome for his own good, and he had all of Thatcher's happy-go-lucky charm. Heather's heart fluttered until she nearly suffocated every time Jared came down from Harvard to aid and abet his father in his dissipation and to cut a wide swathe of his own.

Heather had been with the Cranstons for three years now,

1

having applied for the position of hired-girl-of-all-work when she was fifteen. In the ordinary course of events she would never have considered hiring herself out as a servant, but the circumstances had been extraordinary. Her widowed mother had had the opportunity to remarry. The only hitch was that Caleb Potsby had dragged his feet because Judith Bailey had a nubile daughter who would not only have to be fed but would soon cause him a deal of inconvenience when young men began to haunt his doorstep in pursuit of her.

Moreover, having an eye to his pocketbook, Caleb wanted Judith to vacate the modest house that had been her home ever since her husband had died, and move into his own rooms over the bookstore with him. Caleb owned his own property, while Judith had to pay rent. And the rooms over Caleb's bookstore could not accommodate an extra person.

Outside of being penurious, Caleb was a good catch and Judith favored him. Because his bookshop leaned heavily toward religious works, he was a suitable mate for the widow of a minister. Even so, Judith had been horrified when Heather had proposed striking out on her own so that she would no longer be an impediment to her mother's marriage plans.

Heather answered her mother's protests with cool logic. After all, the work would be only what she had always done, cleaning and polishing, and to her way of thinking she might as well do it where she would be paid for it. And in the process she would get herself out from under her mother's and Caleb's feet. Heather had not been eager to sit at Caleb's table and have him count every mouthful of food she ate. Heather's appetite was hearty.

Emma had been only sixteen when Heather applied for the position at the Cranston home, but she was already a capable mistress of the house. Ordinarily Emma wouldn't have considered a girl who was not only overly young but also entirely too pretty, but Heather was, after all, the daughter of a parson, and as such she could be nothing but moral and pious, which was exactly what Emma demanded in her servants.

Heather had had sense enough to keep the actual state of

2

her piousness to herself. In actuality, she was much more inclined to immerse herself in romantic novels borrowed from the public library than in the Bible. So Heather had been hired, and Judith had married Caleb, and all three of them were content.

It hadn't taken any time at all for Heather to piece together the story of her employers' lives. As a young man, Thatcher had been strikingly handsome, but he had possessed no fortune of his own and had had few prospects. As he and hard work had a natural antipathy for each other, he had looked for a young lady of wealth and found her in Maude Wetherby.

To give him credit, Thatcher hadn't married for money alone. Maude was beautiful, and he had fallen in love with her and entered into the marriage with every intention of being a good husband.

Maude's father, Lucian Wetherby, had amassed his wealth by maintaining deplorable conditions in his cotton mill. But as all of his other offspring had died either in infancy or in early childhood and his wife had followed them shortly after Maude's birth, Lucian had got religion.

To ensure that he would be allowed to join his wife and children in heaven when his own call came, Lucian had sold the mill to a new owner who maintained the same deplorable working conditions. And to ensure that when her call came Maude would be permitted to join the rest of her family in that golden land beyond the Pearly Gates, he had brought her up in his own fanatical beliefs.

Lucian had been well into middle age before Maude was born, and Thatcher had gambled that it would not be too many years before the Wetherby fortune passed into his own hands. It wasn't that he had wished an early demise for his father-in-law; it was simply the nature of things for a man to die when his time came.

Lucian Wetherby had obliged him by dying five years after the marriage had taken place, but that was as far as Thatcher's good fortune went. Maude had been so thoroughly indoctrinated by her father that she had considered any worldly pleasure to be a sin. She had gone so far as to get down on her knees after they had made love and pray for her husband to be forgiven for having enjoyed the act, with the result that he had soon ceased to enjoy it, at least with her. It was a wonder that the union had managed to produce two children, Jared and Emma.

All in all, the twenty years of Thatcher's marriage had been anything but pleasurable. Maude would not tolerate the smoking of tobacco, the imbibing of spiritous beverages, the playing of cards, dancing, betting on horses, or any other worldly pleasure, and her force of will had been such that Thatcher had lost the battle for dominance in his own household. His only consolation had been that his son took after him. His daughter, however, was as much of a dead loss as Maude.

His release had come sooner than he had counted on. Maude had departed this life because of her insistence on eating a portion of fowl that Thatcher had declared to be tainted. Maude had declared that it was not tainted and that waste was a sin when the world was filled with heathens who could be brought to the light by missionaries sent to them with money that was not wasted by throwing away good food.

Heathens or not, Thatcher had refused to eat his own portion, and he had personally removed the children's plates and ordered bowls of bread and milk from the kitchen in substitution. Maude had set out to prove that she was right, and she had died for her pains, of acute food poisoning that no amount of purging by a hastily summoned physician had been able to counteract.

Thatcher had not rejoiced when the wife who had been such a disappointment to him had died. He had only been sorry that he had never been able to teach Maude that life was to be enjoyed, not merely endured against the day of Final Glory. In respect for her memory, he had observed a full year of mourning faithfully, doing nothing of which she would have disapproved.

But once the year was up he had proceeded to make up for lost time. He had paid his dues, and now it was time to reap his reward.

And reap it he did. The finest wines, fat cigars from Havana, parties and balls, gambling, the company of ladies totally lacking in Maude's joyless morals all served to make him a happy and contented man. It had never entered his mind to remarry. He had had enough of marriage and resolved never again to place himself in bondage.

Albany's tailors loved him for the newfound prosperity he brought them with his custom; his liquor bills were the delight of the purveyors of wines and brandies; the butchers and grocers rubbed their hands with glee over the bills he ran up for his table. The players of serious poker, in the back rooms of outwardly respectable saloons, relaxed their poker faces in brief smiles when they saw Thatcher coming, certain of a profitable evening. Thatcher loved to gamble. The fact that he seldom won did not detract from his pleasure in handling crisp and shiny cards and maintaining a poker face of his own even when a face card didn't come his way all evening.

Emma, so exactly like her mother, railed at him ceaselessly for his wicked ways. But Emma was his daughter, not his wife, and where Maude had prevailed Emma failed.

Not, however, for lack of trying. She was after her father night and day to mend his ways, interrupting her efforts only for her own protracted hours of doing good works. She attended church twice every Sunday, morning and evening; she never missed a missionary meeting or choir practice; and she visited homebound parishioners with her Bible in her hand, to read them cheering passages that assured them of life everlasting if their illnesses should take a turn for the worse.

And now, having failed to save her father's soul, she was about to embark on bigger and better things. She and Humphrey Snell, who pastored her church, a young man as serious in his quest to save souls as Emma, had determined that they would set sail together for China as missionaries. After they had been legally and properly married, of course.

The fact that Thatcher refused to give his consent to the marriage, hoping that Emma would come to her senses before she threw her life away, did not deter her. If she had to wait until she was twenty-one and could marry without her father's consent, she would wait. In the meantime, she considered Thatcher's refusal to allow the union as still one more sin on his soul, and she nagged at him without surcease to remove the blot that would weigh so heavily against him when his sins, which were many, and his virtues, which were few, should be placed on the scale for their final balancing.

This afternoon, the controversy between father and daughter had come to a head. For the past several weeks, Thatcher had been in correspondence with his friend, Caldwell Arlington of Virginia. During their Harvard days, Caldwell had admired the more popular and daring Thatcher no end. But, as usually happens with such friendships, their correspondence until very recently had been desultory, consisting of one or no more than two or three letters in a year.

By now Thatcher was not a well man. His years of riotous living had taken their toll on his health. Allen Dunfort, his friend and physician, had warned him that his heart was none too steady. To add to Thatcher's problems, the fortune that he had thought was inexhaustible had dwindled to the point of disappearing because of his extravagance and poor management. Thatcher, in other words, was not only a sick man but a man on the verge of bankruptcy.

And so Thatcher had stepped up his correspondence with Caldwell, angling for an invitation to visit Arbordale, the Arlington plantation. Soft-footed servants, mint juleps, magnolias—and the prospects of closing up the house, which was eating up what remained of his resources, and living as Caldwell's guest were attractive.

There was the additional incentive that Caldwell's only son, Brice, was still unmarried, and Thatcher had a pretty unmarried daughter. If the two should make a match of it, Thatcher could rest easy with the assurance that Emma would be provided for and that she would be in a position to extend help to Jared if he should ever need it. No man likes to contemplate his own mortality, but it was harder when his children had not been provided for.

Besides, he might live for a good many years yet, and living out those years on a Virginia plantation appealed to him. As he remembered it, Caldwell had played a mean hand of poker, and the well of mint juleps would never run dry. All he would have to do was say that his doctor had advised that he live in a milder climate, and Caldwell would insist on his staying for as long as he wished, especially if Emma and Brice were married.

The snag was that Emma would have no part of it. Emma had made up her mind to marry Humphrey Snell and go off to be a missionary, and nothing would budge her. Thatcher did not bring pressure to bear on her about his own insolvency or his ill health. She would simply point out that he had brought it on himself and that if he would give up his tobacco and whiskey and late hours and other dissolute ways, and live modestly within his means, all would be well. Giving up his dissolute ways and living within his means was a prospect that made Thatcher shudder.

"No daughter of mine is going to marry a psalm-singing Bible thumper and take herself off to the ends of the earth without even finding out that there's more to life than wearing out your knees!" Thatcher shouted. "The Chinese are perfectly content the way they are. They don't send missionaries to convert us to their way of thinking, and we should return the compliment by leaving them alone!"

"Father, there is no need for blasphemy!" Emma told him, her own voice as heated as her moral convictions would allow.

"It isn't blasphemy, it's only the unvarnished truth. You haven't the faintest idea of what life is all about, my girl. Just imagine visiting a Southern plantation, the balls, the fox hunts, the very air redolent of roses and romance!"

"The very air redolent of idleness and self-indulgence and sins of the flesh!" Emma retorted. "Aristocrats who think of nothing but worldly pleasure, to the damnation of their souls!"

"You've steeped yourself in too many sermons. The Arlingtons aren't like that at all. They're good Christian people even if they do know how to live graciously, as people are intended to live. How do you know you wouldn't like it if you refuse to try it? You don't even wear the pretty dresses I bought for you, you go around in those drab browns and grays looking like a church mouse. Refusing to look attractive or to enjoy yourself aren't virtues, they're signs of a weak mind!"

"Every time you open your mouth you're condemning yourself to Hades!" Emma told him hotly. "We're put on this earth to do good works, to save our fellow man from damnation and lead him into the paths of righteousness!"

"Balderdash! Look at you, Emma. You're as pretty a girl as was ever born, but what are you doing with the looks God gave you? You pull your hair back till your skin is stretched, you dress like a woman twice your age, you've never read a novel in your life, or gone on a hayride, or danced until dawn. It's a waste, that's what it is, a shameful waste! You are going to Arbordale with me, and you are going to become acquainted with a way of life that you should have enjoyed and would have enjoyed right along if your mother hadn't tainted you with her fanaticism!"

"You will have to carry me onto the train bodily, kicking and screaming. And I promise you that if you go to such extreme measures to force me to accompany you, you will be heartily sorry!"

There was the sound of a door slamming, and Emma stalked off to her bedroom, having had the final word. Emma almost always had the final word because her wind was more sound than Thatcher's. In the front parlor, Thatcher began to swear, having regained his own.

"Glory be!" Mrs. Allenby said. "I've heard more than one altercation between the two of them, but never anything like this! Do you think he'll really shut up this house and take himself and Emma off to Virginia? It'll be hard on me, at my age, looking for a new position."

"There are any number of families in Albany who would jump at the chance to get someone who can cook the way you do," Heather consoled her. If anyone should worry, it was she. The mistresses of houses that needed housemaids preferred to hire plainer girls, girls who would not have beaux and whose minds would be on their work rather than on their mirrors. More than that, young and pretty housemaids put too much temptation in the paths of husbands and sons.

Mrs. Allenby sighed. "Well, now that the storm has passed, I'll get on with supper, although I doubt that Emma will come to the table. She'll be wanting a tray in her room, to drive home her disapproval of her father's plans. And Mr. Thatcher, if I know the signs, is probably already at the port, and by the time the meal is ready he won't be in any condition to appreciate it. But I'm paid to cook, and so I'll cook."

"Never mind, I'll eat enough to make up for both of them. I'm ravenous! Listening to those two go at it always makes me hungry. Umm, apple dumplings! If they don't want theirs, I'll eat them myself."

Although it was in no way a part of her duties, Heather couldn't resist taking a peek into the parlor, where she confirmed Mrs. Allenby's suspicions that Thatcher was indeed already at the port. The glass in his hand was almost empty, and he was in the process of refilling it. If past experience meant anything, by bedtime he would have trouble getting up the stairs.

Heather would be glad when Jared finished his last year at Harvard and returned home to stay, and not only because things were always so lively when he was around. It worried her that Thatcher was drinking so much, and in the last few weeks he had begun to drink a great deal more than usual, as if something was on his mind and bothering him, although what it could be, outside of Emma's always being at loggerheads with him, she couldn't venture a guess. Whatever it was, maybe Jared would be able to persuade him to ease off. When Jared was at home, he acted as a buffer between his father and his sister. Jared never became angry at Emma, and he could usually smooth things over between them. If there was less fighting between father and daughter, maybe Thatcher wouldn't drink so much.

Her mood brightened as she laid the table with a heavy linen cloth and the lovely china and silver that Thatcher had purchased as soon as his year of mourning was over.

It was already well into spring. It wouldn't be long before Jared was home for good, and then things would settle down. Jared probably wouldn't go chasing off to Virginia with his father, the house wouldn't be closed up, and both her job and Mrs. Allenby's would be safe. For all Heather cared, Emma could go chasing off to China and good riddance. As long as Jared was home, that was all that mattered.

Just the thought of Jared coming home made her heart beat faster. The minute he walked through the door, the house seemed to come to life. Always laughing, a joke forever on his lips, his teasing ways made her blood race, and her knees went weak every time she encountered him in the parlor or the hallways.

Her face felt warm as she remembered all the times he'd pinched her where he had no business to pinch her. And sometimes he backed her into a corner and tilted her chin with his forefinger, while he studied her with his eyes wide with feigned amazement, declaring that she was even prettier than she had been the last time he'd been home.

"If I didn't have to slave my life away over all those dull books, I'd give all those beaux of yours a run for their money!" Jared teased her. "Just you wait till I'm home for good!"

"I don't have any beaux, and well you know it! Miss Emma would have me out of this house in a minute!" Heather would retort. "Behave yourself, Mr. Jared, and let me get on with my work. What if Miss Emma caught us like this? The roof would come off!"

"Emma's bark is worse than her bite. I'd see that she didn't sack you, never fear. I like having you around. You brighten the place up. It's a treat to see a smiling face when Emma and my father are fighting most of the time."

She knew that he didn't mean a word he said. No young man in his position would go chasing after a hired girl, no matter how pretty she was, at least not for any respectable reason, and Heather wouldn't stand for any other kind, no matter how fast he made her heart beat. Just because she was a servant didn't mean she didn't have her standards!

She wished real life was like the romantic novels she devoured one after the other. In romantic novels, a wealthy young man would fall in love with a housemaid, sweep her off her feet, and defy every convention in order to marry her, and they would live happily ever after.

But real life wasn't like that. No matter how she felt about Jared, he'd never consider marrying her, not for a moment. Not that he was a snob. There wasn't a snobbish bone in his body. It was simply that it would never occur to him. He'd marry some girl from a wealthy and socially prominent family, and that was that. And if her heart broke a little because of it, that was also that. Her heart would just have to mend again. It wasn't as if she hadn't known all along that Jared would never fall in love with her. She'd probably cry when Jared found the girl he would marry, but she wouldn't die of it. When you knew from the beginning that you couldn't have something, then you weren't so disappointed when you didn't get it.

All the same, it was a crying shame that real life couldn't be more like romantic novels.

Just as Mrs. Allenby had predicted, Emma did not come to the table that evening but asked Heather to bring a tray to her room. Thatcher, however, ate with his usual hearty appetite even if Heather doubted that his taste buds could fully appreciate the delicious meal Mrs. Allenby had prepared. He put away astonishing amounts of roast pork and mashed potatoes and candied carrots, as well as two apple dumplings. He not only drank too much and smoked too many cigars, but he also ate too much rich food, and at his age it couldn't be good for him.

Caleb Potsby, now, would probably live forever. He never touched a drop of any intoxicating substance, he didn't smoke, and he ate sparingly, his eye always on the expense. Even so, Heather wouldn't ask for Thatcher to be more like her mother's husband. She could only hope that Thatcher would decide for himself to cut down.

She ate her own hearty meal in the kitchen, making Mrs. Allenby sigh with envy. "You pack it in like a stevedore and never gain an ounce, while every bite I eat goes right to my hips!" the cook complained.

"Nobody trusts a skinny cook's cooking," Heather told the older woman cheerfully, gobbling up her apple dumpling and eyeing the last one.

"You aren't going to eat that, on top of everything else! My lands, where do you put it all?"

"Right here," Heather said, patting her stomach. The last apple dumpling disappeared. "And I still have room for Miss Emma's, if she hasn't eaten hers."

Her eyes went to Emma's plate the moment she went to pick up the tray. Just as she had hoped, Emma hadn't eaten her apple dumpling. She probably considered apple dumplings worldly.

Emma was dressed for her Wednesday-night prayer meeting. Her dress was proof of her convictions about bodily ornament, a severely cut, unadorned brown, with the plainest of brown hats and gloves to match. The wardrobe against the wall was crammed with beautiful dresses that Thatcher had had made for her, but Emma never wore them unless Thatcher had guests, when he insisted that she dress in a manner to do him credit. But for the last few months, ever since she had got the missionary bug in her head, she had refused to wear them at all.

Wouldn't one think she'd want to look attractive for Mr. Snell, seeing that she was in love with him and intended to marry him? Heather wondered. The Reverend Snell was thirty-two, almost old, but he was awfully good-looking. He had very fair hair and blue eyes and a strong, square chin, and he was tall; and Heather hadn't failed to notice that on Sunday mornings a good many of the young ladies of his congregation looked at him a lot more than they looked at the hymnals or their Bibles. And even if Humphrey was a dedicated man of the cloth, he wasn't blind. If Heather owned clothes like this and had a man like Humphrey Snell, she'd make sure she'd outshine any other female who had eyes for him!

"I expect that my father is drinking again," Emma said, her mouth compressed with disapproval. "If you have occasion to see him before you go to bed, tell him that I will pray for him."

Why don't you tell him yourself, Heather wanted to say, but she restrained herself. Not only wasn't it her place to make such a remark, but Thatcher's reaction when Emma told him she was going to pray for him was well known to her. He either laughed or told her to pray for someone who was in need of being prayed for, as he was not, already having everything he wanted except a daughter who wouldn't aggravate him to the point of frenzy.

"Yes, Miss Emma," Heather said. She picked up the tray and carried it down to the kitchen, where Mrs. Allenby watched her snatch up the scorned apple dumpling and devour it. A few greedy bites, and the dumpling was gone.

"I can't believe you really ate that!" Mrs. Allenby said.

"I'm only doing it for Miss Emma." Heather grinned. "You know how she feels about waste!" For a moment her stomach felt uncomfortably tight, but then she dismissed the idea. There couldn't be too much of a good thing, and it was a long time until breakfast. Emma never stinted on food for the servants—they ate the same food that was served in the dining room—but she thought that eating before bed was an indulgence. The time before bed was supposed to be spent in prayer, not in eating.

Heather and the cook made short work of cleaning up the kitchen. Mrs. Allenby liked to go to bed early, and Heather was impatient to immerse herself in the latest romantic novel she had borrowed from the library. Adventure, peril, romance, and a happy ending! If she were in Emma's place, with all of Emma's advantages, that was how she would make her life. But she wasn't in Emma's place, worse luck, and it didn't look as if anything wildly exciting and romantic was going to happen any time in the near future.

It would, though, someday. It would if Heather had to take life in her own two hands and shake it until it came through with what she wanted. There was more to be had from life than making beds and dusting furniture, and she was going to make sure that she got her fair share. She just didn't know, at the moment, how she was going to accomplish it.

"Heather, if you're going to stay up late reading another of those books, be a good girl and tiptoe back downstairs and take a peek in the parlor before you go to bed. We don't want Mr. Thatcher to fall asleep in his chair again with a burning cigar in his hand. One of these nights we'll all be burned to death in our sleep!"

"Don't worry, I'll have a look," Heather promised. "I'll see that he gets upstairs if I have to push him all the way." If

Thatcher was drunk enough, he'd go docilely, even though she might have to support him. If he wasn't, he would put up an argument, stating that he wasn't going to be ordered around in his own house. Heather would have to remind him that if he didn't come now, Emma would check on him, which would be a deal more unpleasant than letting Heather coax him to his room. If Emma were the one to catch him with the decanter nearly empty, and dozing with a lighted cigar in his hand, the fur would fly!

It was much later than it should have been when Heather reluctantly put her book aside. She had been so wrapped up in the fictional heroine's adventures that she'd lost all track of time. She'd have to get up and face another day's work before she knew it.

She'd heard Emma come in a long time ago and pause at the parlor door and say something to her father that Heather hadn't been able to make out, before she'd gone up to her own room and closed her door. Heather had left her own third-floor bedroom door open so that she would hear what was going on, hoping that Thatcher would come up before she had to go down and coax him up. Then she'd become so absorbed in her reading that she might not have heard him if he had. She'd just have to check to make sure.

She tiptoed down the stairs, avoiding the two steps that creaked. Emma had ears like a cat, and she didn't want her to wake up and discover her pushing Thatcher up the stairs. Fortunately, only the stairs to the third floor creaked. The gas jet in the second-floor hallway had been turned off, but leaning over the banister she saw a streak of light from the half-open parlor door.

She sighed with exasperation when she saw that Thatcher had indeed fallen asleep in his chair. Even worse, his cigar had fallen to the floor and burned a hole in the carpet. It was still smoldering, filling the parlor with acrid smoke. She should have come down an hour earlier. Mrs. Allenby was going to be cross with her, to say nothing of Emma's outrage when she saw the ruined carpet. It wasn't going to be pleasant at all.

Crossing the room, her nose wrinkled against the smell, she stamped on the smoldering place in the rug and made sure that it was completely out before she touched Thatcher's shoulder.

"Mr. Thatcher, sir? Wake up! Here you've burnt a big hole in the carpet, and what Miss Emma's going to say doesn't bear thinking about! You'd better get up to bed. Sir? Are you waking up, sir?"

Thatcher did not respond. Heather felt cold fingers of foreboding run up and down her spine. Now that she looked at him closely, she saw that his eyes were half open and staring but not seeing anything. He really was in a state tonight, and how she was going to get him upstairs without waking Emma she didn't know.

"Please, Mr. Thatcher! It's time to go to bed!" In her desperation, Heather shook his shoulder.

Thatcher's body tilted sideways. Only Heather's frantic grab for him prevented him from falling out of his chair. A scream rose in her throat, but she stifled it. She mustn't panic.

Mr. Cranston was dead. There wasn't any doubt about it at all. On the table at his elbow his glass was still half filled with port, waiting for him to reach out and lift it to his lips and drain it.

It wasn't Thatcher's hand that reached for the glass, it was Heather's. She'd never tasted wine in her life, nor ever thought to, but she knew that it was supposed to be a restorative and calming to the nerves as well, and her nerves cried out for calming.

The port was good, sweet and heavy and with an underbite that warmed her all the way down. It was a pity she couldn't enjoy it. She finished the last drop and replaced the glass exactly where she had found it.

Then she panicked, and her screams echoed and bounced against the walls.

⤳ Chapter 2 ⤳

IT SEEMED UNREAL to Heather that Thatcher Cranston had been in his grave for four days and that Jared, who had come home for the funeral, was already preparing to return to Harvard to finish up the last weeks of his formal education. The next time he came home it would be to stay, and he would be a full-fledged lawyer.

Not only was Jared packing, but Emma was as well.

"It doesn't seem right, you rushing off like this, with Father hardly cold in his grave," Jared protested. "And it certainly doesn't seem right that you should get married without the usual period of mourning."

"Under the circumstances, people will understand. I can scarcely go off to China with Humphrey without being married to him, can I? And if we don't attend this seminar, we will have to wait for several more months, and our work is far too important to be delayed."

The training seminar for missionaries was being held in Boston. Emma had been prepared to miss this one, as Thatcher had refused his permission for her to attend it. But now everything had changed. The church had found a replacement for Humphrey, and China was crying out for missionaries, and the sooner she and Humphrey got started the more souls they would be able to save. Emma's rushing off to attend the seminar and to marry Humphrey before they sailed might not seem respectful to her father's memory, but she had grave doubts about the state of her father's soul when he had died and high hopes of saving other people's souls, so taking advantage of the earliest opportunity to start her missionary work seemed the right thing to do.

"I suppose it wouldn't serve any useful purpose for you to hold off, but all the same, I would have thought that you cared more for Father." Jared looked at his sister with bewildered reproach.

"Of course I cared about Father! I prayed for him night and day, and I will go on praying, trusting in God's mercy as little as he deserved it." Emma's voice was calm, but Heather saw that she was very pale, and she knew that Emma really had loved Thatcher in spite of having been a thorn in his side. She had heard her crying every night behind the closed door of her bedroom, and her heart had ached for her. Heather had done a good bit of crying herself, because she'd been genuinely fond of Thatcher, but it wasn't the same. "I did my utmost to save him, and I'll never forgive myself for having failed."

"Now, now! It wasn't your fault that he wouldn't listen to you. There's no use in blaming yourself. I'm not at all sure that he was so wicked that there was no hope for him. He might have been foolish, especially where his health was concerned, and he did gamble and drink, but he never hurt anybody in his life. All of his sins were against himself. Go to Boston if your heart is set on it, and go to China too, but try to believe that Father is in heaven right now in spite of himself."

"I pray that is true! Thank you, Jared. You couldn't have stopped me, but your agreeing makes my heart easier." Entirely out of character for Emma, she kissed her brother's cheek, while tears spilled over so that he had to give her his handkerchief to mop them away.

Jared left the next morning, and Heather's heart ached to see him go. Thatcher's death had hit him hard, and now he was losing his sister as well. She wished there was some way that she could comfort him. All these past days she had longed to hold him in her arms and tell him that his grief

17

would pass. She remembered her own tearing, unbearable grief when her own father had died, and how she had thought that she would never get over it.

But she was a servant, not a friend, let alone the sweetheart that she wished she could be. She could only suffer for him in silence.

Without Thatcher, and with Jared and Emma gone, the house would seem so empty that she would start at every shadow, expecting to see one or another of them or thinking that she'd heard their voices in another room or their footsteps in the hallways.

She told herself not to be so morbid. While it was true that she would never see Thatcher again, Jared would come back, and the last thing he would need was a mournful face to remind him of his loss.

She tried not to think beyond the immediate future. She knew that Jared would marry someday, and she wasn't sure if she would be able to continue working in the house when that happened. But she didn't have to think about that now. Jared wasn't even engaged, and there wasn't any particular girl in Albany whom he favored. Maybe he wouldn't get married for a very long time, and by then she would have outgrown her romantic notions about him, or maybe Jared would even fall in love with her. There were times, she thought wryly, when it was a good thing you only had to live one day at a time. Didn't the Bible say "sufficient unto the day is the evil therein" or something like that?

Now, helping Emma pack, she came into a bonanza that couldn't help but lift her spirits, even though she was ashamed of herself for being so greedy.

"Not that dress, Heather! Can't you see it's entirely unsuitable for the life on which I'm embarking? No, not the blue either, or the rose, or the green. None of the things from Father will do at all." Emma eyed Heather speculatively. "We're of a size and the same coloring. I dare say you can get some use out of most of them. Any that you don't care to keep for yourself you can donate to the next church rummage sale."

Heather's face turned pink with excitement. "All of them, Miss Emma? You mean that I'm to have all of them?"

"Yes, yes! I just said so, didn't I? Do watch what you're doing, you'll have to refold that gray."

Heather refolded the gray. She folded plain, serviceable petticoats, underdrawers, stockings, all of them, in her eyes, completely without merit. Emma would look like a frump on the ship that carried her to China, with all of the other ladies decked out in finery. But Heather didn't voice her opinion. Emma might change her mind.

I'll probably never go to heaven, Heather thought, a little bit frightened, but not frightened enough not to want to keep every gorgeous garment that Emma had spurned. She'd never realized how sinful she was until these riches had fallen into her lap! Just for insurance, she'd do her best to pick two dresses to donate to the rummage sale. Or at least one.

"These undergarments, Miss Emma? And the hats, and the gloves, and the pretty boots and slippers?" Heather held her breath.

"You'll have to keep the underthings. They can scarcely be shown at a rummage sale." Emma shrugged off the silks and satins and laces as though they meant less than nothing. "There! I can't think of another thing I need to take. I shall write to you, Heather, and I expect you to answer my letters. I will want full reports on Jared's behavior. I only pray that having seen how the error of his ways led Father into disaster, Jared will mend his own."

So the price of all these beautiful things was to spy on Jared! For a moment, Heather was tempted to give them all back, but the temptation was short-lived.

"Yes, Miss Emma." She hadn't promised to tell Emma everything Jared did, she'd only said that she would answer her letters, so she wasn't actually lying. She'd just have to pay more attention to her own prayers to make up for it.

"I will expect you and Mrs. Allenby to take the same meticulous care of the house as you did while I was here to supervise you."

"Oh, yes, Miss Emma!" This was a promise that Heather was more than willing to make and one that she would keep. It made her feel better to realize that she was only half bad.

"And mind that you attend church faithfully." Emma's voice was firm.

"Yes, Miss Emma." Well, she would, even though she hadn't always been all that eager to sit through long and boring sermons. It was the least she could do. Besides, two out of three leaned toward the good side.

Jared was in low spirits when he returned to finish out his last weeks at Harvard. He and his father had planned a celebration to end all celebrations to observe his graduation, but there would be no celebration now. He wouldn't even be able to join friends who were making the most of the occasion. As soon as he was handed his sheepskin, he would board the train to return to Albany and a house empty of both his father and Emma.

To add to his general gloom, it would take some time for all of his father's affairs, which Jared suspected were in a muddle, to be straightened out. That was the reason he wouldn't be able to give Martin Knightbridge assurance of any definite sum toward the enterprise they had determined to set in motion, the building of a motor car that would set them on the road to fame and fortune.

During the course of the euphoria that Thatcher would have experienced while they were celebrating his son's graduation, Jared had been certain that he could talk his father into advancing the financial backing that he and Martin would need. Jared refused to pay heed to the fact that the last time he had broached the subject Thatcher had laughed and said that it would be pouring money down a rathole.

Automobiles, Thatcher had maintained, were nothing but a passing fad, toys for the very rich, who would soon tire of them, and then the whole idiotic notion would die out. A horse, Thatcher pointed out, did not run out of fuel, a horse did not bog down in mudholes, a horse did not fall apart midway in journey. Horses were reliable; automobiles were not and never would be. But when Thatcher was in a good mood, he could be talked into almost anything, provided the company was congenial and the spirits kept flowing.

The trouble was that Thatcher had had no eye toward the

future. The horseless carriage was the coming thing. It was the horse that would soon be relegated to the past. Gasoline machines did not bolt at the opening of an umbrella or the sight of a baby carriage; gasoline machines did not dirty the streets; gasoline machines did not have to rest between journeys, or get the colic, or break a leg. And Martin Knightbridge was a genius. There was nothing he couldn't do with machinery. He already had the plans for an automobile that would run like clockwork so that every thinking man would want one.

Martin Knightbridge, Jared conceded, did not look like a genius. A more unlikely candidate for the category of genius would be hard to imagine. Martin was an obese young man with a face full of acne and a cowlick that no amount of slicking down with water or Macassar oil would keep in place, who labored in his father's farm machinery store sans wages. His father maintained that as long as he provided a roof over Martin's head and three meals a day, he owed him nothing else.

As a salesman of farm machinery Martin was a washout. He had neither the appearance nor the charm to sell anything at all. But as a repairer of machinery, he was in constant demand by local farmers. There was no piece of machinery he could not fix.

Jared had met Martin completely by chance. He had been driving his father's high-stepping trotter during last summer's vacation when Danny Boy had shied and reared, all but upsetting the buggy. The cause of Danny Boy's alarm had been a contraption that gave the appearance of being another buggy, except that clouds of black smoke were erupting from it, filling the air with an acrid reek. A young man had been tinkering with the engine that was emitting the smoke. Martin had lifted a woebegone face to Jared and apologized.

"I'll push it off the road, it'll only take a minute." Martin's plump face had fallen still more as he'd added, "And then I'll have to push it all the way home. I know exactly what's wrong with it, I just can't fix it here."

Always sympathetic to anyone who was having difficulties, Jared lent Danny Boy to haul the contraption back to the rough shed behind Martin's father's store, where Elias Knightbridge had laced his son out roundly for wasting his time on a devil's device when he should have been working. Elias's face had been red with fury, Martin's face had been red with mortification, and Jared's heart had gone out to him.

"B-b-but five dollars will fix it, Father," Martin had tried to explain. "I-I-I'll put in extra time at the store to pay you back . . ."

"Get to work!" had been the answer. "You'll not get five cents from me, much less five hard-earned dollars."

Jared had bid father and son a hasty farewell before leading Danny Boy back to where he had left his buggy, but not before he had surreptitiously slipped a five-dollar bill into Martin's hand. Martin had been too astonished to do anything more than blink.

The next evening, filled with curiosity about whether Martin had managed to fix the contraption, Jared had gone back to the farm machinery store and found Martin in the shed. Not only was the contraption running, it was running smoothly.

Not having the wherewithal to repay the loan, Martin had done the only thing he could and offered to take Jared for a ride. Jared had accepted, considering such an adventure ample repayment, and Jared had been lost.

He had listened, fascinated, as Martin expounded on this improvement and that. All that was needed was money. But Thatcher had turned a deaf ear to all of Jared's arguments, and he had had to return for his final year at Harvard with the partnership unformed.

Jared had had a brief and unsatisfactory session with Mr. Deems, Thatcher's lawyer, after the funeral. The stipulations of Thatcher's will had been clear enough. Two-thirds of all his worldly assets were to go to Jared and one-third to Emma. Emma, Thatcher had stated in black and white, would have received her full half if she hadn't been so pig-headed about throwing her life away trying to convert the mass of Chinese she was convinced only awaited her coming to be led to the light.

Emma, to Jared's surprise, had seemed satisfied with the

terms of the will. When the estate had been probated and the assets gathered together for division, her third was to be given to the Baptist Missionary Fund. If it had been a full half, she would have felt safe easing off on her prayers for the salvation of her father's soul. As it was, she would only pray a little harder.

The trouble was, it was going to take a considerable amount of time to discover exactly what Thatcher had left. Thatcher had been a poor manager and an even poorer conservator. The large and comfortable house that had come to him through his wife had cost him nothing, but he had spent a fortune refurnishing it. He had indulged himself in paintings and other works of art of dubious value, simply because they had pleased his eye. And no one cared to venture a guess on the sums he had lost in gambling. Jared hoped that the lawyer would have it all sorted out by the time he returned to Albany.

After his joyless graduation, Jared returned to find that Mr. Deems had indeed gone a long way toward sorting it all out. The facts stared Jared in the face. There was literally nothing left but the house and its furnishings and a few hundred dollars that would barely cover the outstanding debts Thatcher had run up.

Jared was stunned. There could be no partnership with Martin Knightbridge now. His dreams of fame and fortune dissolved as he stared at the stack of bills Mr. Deems had told him must be paid immediately.

He cast his mind over possibilities. The logical thing would be to start working and bring in some money if he wanted to continue eating. The second most logical thing was for him to let the servants go. Neither of these two alternatives appealed to him. He'd elected to study law because he had to study something; otherwise, there would have been no reason for him to go to Harvard, and he'd enjoyed going to Harvard. But opening up a practice of his own would take time, clients didn't drop like manna from heaven, and what he could earn as an assistant to an already established lawyer would by no means support the house.

The same could be said for finding and accepting a position as a clerk in a haberdasher's shop, or being a door-to-door salesman, or weighing up sugar and lard in a grocery store.

Or he could, as his father had done in like circumstances, look around for a girl with a wealthy father, but considering the misery of his father's marriage, that idea didn't have much appeal for him either. Besides, in light of Thatcher's reputation and his own lack of prospects, any such father would be certain to look on him with a jaundiced eye, even if he could bring himself to marry for money, the very thought of which made him flinch.

Irritably, Jared pushed the offending statements of accounts due and immediately payable aside, and he scowled when he saw that an unopened envelope had been concealed beneath them.

At least this one wasn't a bill. The envelope was the wrong color and the wrong size.

Caldwell Arlington, Bennington, Virginia. Jared stared at the name and address that was inscribed in the upper left-hand corner of the cream-colored envelope. His father's partner in crime when they had both matriculated at Harvard, although Caldwell, being the lesser criminal of the two, had been allowed to graduate, while Thatcher had been asked to leave.

Writing to his father's friend to tell him that Thatcher was dead wasn't something Jared was eager to do, but it would have to be done out of common courtesy. And as he couldn't answer the letter without reading it, he slit it open with Thatcher's ornate mother-of-pearl and gold letter opener.

My dear friend,

My family and I are waiting impatiently for word of when you will be coming. Brice is exceedingly eager to meet your Emma. Not a day passes that he doesn't ask if I have heard from you. My sister Minna is planning all sorts of festivities in honor of your visit, which we insist must be an extended one. This time you must definitely make up your mind to come, because we are expecting you at the earliest possible time.

Brice wishes me to extend his greetings not only to you but to Emma, and to assure her that he is impatient to escort her to all of the parties and balls. Time passes all too quickly, and I can no longer wait with any degree of patience for our reunion and for our offspring to become acquainted with each other.

We will expect Jared as well. No doubt he and Brice will get along famously just as you and I did all those years ago.

There wasn't any doubt about it, the Arlingtons were in a lather to meet Emma. The belated mention of Jared's own name had been an afterthought. It was a pity that he would have to dash their hopes by writing to them that Thatcher could not accept their invitation because he was dead and that Emma could not accept it because she was in Boston learning how to be a missionary.

Blast it all! If only Emma hadn't gone dashing off like that, all fired up about bringing the light to the heathens! If she had been any sensible kind of a girl, she would be at home where she belonged and he and Emma could have been on the first train they could catch.

Spending several weeks at Arbordale would give Jared the breathing space he needed while he sorted out his problems. As there would be no personal living expenses, it would result in substantial savings. Caldwell Arlington was a wealthy man, and as Thatcher's lifelong friend there was a very good possibility that he might extend financial backing to Jared's and Martin's enterprise.

He might still extend it, if he were approached in the right way, but Jared would much rather talk to him face to face. There was nothing like personal contact when it came to striking a deal. It wouldn't be difficult to persuade Caldwell Arlington that extending the money would be the best investment he had ever made, if only Jared could be there to point out to him how impossible it was for the venture to fail.

As far as Jared was concerned, the Chinese did not need to be preached at by Emma. There were more than enough missionaries to go around. It would take someone with more intelligence than Emma possessed to change their thousands-of-years-old beliefs. Emma had the zeal but not the thoroughly grounded education. Jared only knew one Chinese gentleman personally, but he was impressed by Tao Tsiang's intelligence. Tao Tsiang, who kept Jared's shirts and personal linens in a state of pristine immaculateness when he was in Albany, had a quick mind and a lively sense of humor, and Jared suspected that the Chinese man's literacy exceeded his own.

"Too dirty, too dirty!" Tao would say, fingering Jared's shirts with pretended horror. "Lookee here, all black!"

"It's only ink, Tao. And I know you can get it out. No other laundry in Albany can, but you can."

"Cut it out, maybe so," Tao Tsiang would say, scowling while his black eyes laughed. "Maureen, bring scissors!"

Behind her hands, Tao's pretty wife Maureen would giggle. "No find. Scissors lost."

"What to do?" Tao's forehead would furrow and then clear. "I know! I'll make scorch mark on stain so it won't show."

"You can stop with that pidgin English, Tao Tsiang. We both know that you speak the English language better than I do. Just launder the shirts, please."

"If the shirts are to be ready for you tomorrow, I shall have to insist on extra remuneration. Overtime costs more."

"You drive a hard bargain," Jared would protest.

"I too must eat. No man becomes wealthy operating a laundry, and I have many mouths to feed."

Jared had a very good notion that Tao did very well with his laundry. If he had many mouths to feed, he also had many hands to work. Not only Maureen, but his four sons, ranging in age from nine to sixteen, assisted him.

Because of the excellence of his work, Tao did a thriving business, and he lived simply, with quarters over his shop. The last time Jared had dropped in, Maureen had shyly shown him the diamond ring that her husband had given her for their eighteenth wedding anniversary.

"Old American custom, gift for anniversary," Maureen had told him. "I like American customs."

"I consider it an investment. A diamond can always be sold if times become hard," Tao had said, winking at Jared when his wife cried out in protest.

The names of Tao's family never ceased to amuse Jared. His pretty wife, who was as Chinese as Tao himself, was called Maureen. The boys were Michael, Patrick, Danny, and Sean. Tao himself had changed Maureen's name on the occasion of their marriage. Jared had learned the story of his preference for Irish names soon after he had started taking his shirts to Tao's laundry.

"It is in honor of my friend Michael O'Grady," Tao had told him. "Years ago, when I was working on the railroads, I was set upon by a gang of ruffians who thought it would be amusing to cut off my queue. The Irish immigrants who were enticed to this country to do manual labor were also subjected to indignities, and Michael took exception and came to my aid. The ruffians were routed, and my queue was saved."

"Michael must have been a big man," Jared had observed.

"No indeed. Michael was a small man. But then he was Irish, and that made all the difference. An angry Irishman with a shillelagh in his hand makes a formidable antagonist, no matter the odds." Tao had sobered, and there had been grief in his eyes. "Unfortunately, Michael's prowess with his shillelagh did not extend to routing cholera. He died of that disease several months after we had become friends. He died before he had had the opportunity to marry and produce offspring to honor his memory, so I determined to give my own children Irish names and teach them to revere his memory just as I do."

"But you didn't change your own name," Jared pointed out.

"My name was not mine to change. My ancestors would have disapproved. But my wife and children are my own, and so I could do as I pleased with them."

Michael, Jared thought, would indeed have felt honored if

he could have lived to know what Tao had done. Flowers sent to a funeral soon wither and die, but Tao's tribute to his friend would never die, because Michael, Patrick, Danny, and Sean were pledged to give their own children Irish names, the name of the first boy in every generation to be Michael.

All thoughts of Tao and his "Irish" family fled out of Jared's mind as Heather entered the room that had served Thatcher as an office he seldom used. Jared stared, and then he blinked. For a few seconds, he had hardly recognized her. What the devil had she done to herself? Being a man, he couldn't put his finger on it. He only knew that the girl had been transformed.

Actually, the answer was simple. After Thatcher had been laid to rest and Emma had gone off to Boston to learn how to be a missionary and Jared had gone back to Harvard, there had been a good deal less work for Heather to do, and three days after Emma's departure she had had a brainstorm.

The trouble with romantic novels was that there weren't enough of them. It was becoming harder and harder for her to find one at the library that she hadn't already read. And then the idea had hit her. Why shouldn't she help fill in the gap? It seemed to her that writing such novels must be the easiest thing imaginable. All it required was the ability to string words together to make sentences and a lively imagination, which she certainly had in great abundance.

Filled with excitement, she had bought a composition book, a bottle of ink, and a pen and extra nibs, and every evening after her chores were done she put on one of the lovely dresses Emma had given her and dressed her hair in the most becoming fashion she could devise. If she looked the part of a lady novelist, the work would go more easily, she surmised. If clothes made the man, didn't they also make the woman? Then, having put herself in the mood, she proceeded to fill page after page with a plot that was so exciting and romantic that all of the other ladies who were as addicted to romantic novels as she was were bound to adore it.

There was only one stumbling block. Stringing words together to make sentences was easy, but the writing of her novel obliged her to use words the meaning of which she knew very well but the spelling of which eluded her. Therefore she was forever having to run down the two flights of stairs to consult the dictionary that was kept on the middle shelf of the bookcase in Thatcher's office. She could have taken the dictionary up to her room, but neither Emma nor Jared was there to give permission, and she felt that it wouldn't be quite honest to appropriate it for her own use.

"Heather! Is that really you?" Jared demanded.

"I'm sorry to disturb you, Mr. Jared. I didn't know you were in here. I only wanted to use the dictionary for a moment."

Jared noted the inkstains on her fingers, and his eyebrows rose. "You're writing to one of your beaux, I'll wager. What word do you need to know how to spell?"

Heather's face flamed. "I'm not doing any such thing! I just need to find out how to spell *silhouette*."

"S-i-l-h-o-u-e-t-t-e," Jared told her. "I'll write it down for you so you won't forget it before you get back upstairs."

"That can't be right! How could there be an h in it?" Heather protested. "Are you sure?"

"Sure I'm sure. One thing lawyers have to learn to do is spell. They might not be long on brains in other areas, but spelling is mandatory. A misspelled word could get a tort thrown right out of court."

Heather wanted to ask what in the world a tort was, but she didn't want to display her ignorance about anything except spelling. "May I use the dictionary, please?"

"So you don't trust me!" Jared reached for the dictionary, found the word, and showed it to her.

"Well, my goodness! I guess whoever wrote the dictionary didn't know much about spelling either," she said. "He did put an h in it!"

"He should have consulted another dictionary." Jared kept his face perfectly straight. "Isn't *silhouette* an odd word to use in a love letter?"

"I'm not writing a love letter!" Heather said for the second time, her face flushing hotter than before. She had no intention of telling Jared what she was actually writing. There would be time for that when she was rich and famous. This way, with no one knowing, she wouldn't have to be embarrassed if some shortsighted publisher took the notion that her book wasn't worth printing.

Of course, she knew that it would be. The words just rolled right out of her onto the paper without any effort, except for the dratted spelling. All the same, she didn't want Jared laughing at her for taking the notion that she could write a book.

She fled from the room, snatching up the piece of paper with *silhouette* written on it, and in another moment, the word correctly spelled in her copybook, she was hard at work again. The only trouble was that Jared's face kept imposing itself between her written words and her eyes. Beaux indeed! It was a mercy that he didn't know she had no interest in having beaux because she was only interested in him. She would die of humiliation if he ever guessed.

Resolutely, she went on writing. If she were a successful lady novelist, everything would be different. She would be a lady then, not a servant, and maybe she could make Jared really look at her. As a lady, there wouldn't be any social barrier between them; she'd have as good a chance at getting him as any other girl would have.

Drat! She was about to use another word she didn't know how to spell. She paused, wrinkling her brow, and substituted a word that was just as good and that she did know how to spell. She wasn't going to go down to the office again tonight to ask to use the dictionary! Jared's curiosity would be more aroused than ever, and that would never do.

Seated again at his father's desk, Jared mused over Heather's changed appearance. She certainly was a pretty little girl. Whoa! he told himself. She had been a little girl when she had first come here, but she wasn't a little girl now. She was a darned pretty young lady! If he weren't in the financial bind he was in, he'd give serious thought to competing with those beaux of hers. He'd always been fond of her, and he suddenly realized that it wouldn't take any push at all for him to become a lot more than fond.

But he was in a financial bind, and he wouldn't be in any position for a long time to think seriously about any girl. If Heather was still here and still unmarried when and if his money woes reversed themselves, things would be different.

Frowning, he read Caldwell Arlington's letter again, and for the second time he cursed the fact that Emma was so lacking in sisterly loyalty that she had taken herself off to Boston to learn how to become a missionary, not to mention the fact that even if she were still at home she would reject the proposed visit to Arbordale out of hand.

His fingers seemed to turn suddenly numb, and he dropped the letter back on the desk. That had been Heather just now, but with what a difference! She was not only as pretty as a picture, but she'd looked every inch a lady. How old was she now, anyway? She'd been fifteen when she'd come there to work, so she must be eighteen now. She was almost as old as Emma, and now that he had really looked at her he realized that she looked a great deal like Emma. They were the same size and coloring, both of them with chestnut hair and hazel eyes, although Heather's eyes were usually snapping with good humor while Emma's were serious and often accusing. Heather was a lively girl with a sense of fun. What a sinful waste that Heather couldn't have been Emma!

The thought brought him to his feet so fast that the chair tipped over, but he was in such a hurry that he didn't stop to right it. He took the two flights of stairs two at a time, and, out of breath, he knocked at Heather's door. Heather had time only to thrust her copybook out of sight underneath her pillow before he pushed his way inside without being invited. After all, he knew she was decent; she'd been fully dressed, and damned attractively so, only a moment ago.

"Heather, how would you like to be Emma and visit a Virginia plantation?"

Heather looked at him suspiciously, wondering if he had gone mad in the few moments since she had left him downstairs. "Virginia, Mr. Jared?"

"A plantation called Arbordale. Mr. Caldwell Arlington has invited us for an extended visit, or at least he will as soon as he gets the letter I'm going to write him."

"Oh, that Mr. Caldwell Arlington!" Heather knew all about Mr. Caldwell Arlington and the invitation for Thatcher and Emma to visit Arbordale. She would have had to be deaf not to know, after that last quarrel Thatcher and Emma had had just before Thatcher died.

"Certainly that Mr. Caldwell Arlington! He's determined that Emma and his son Brice are going to make a match of it, if his letter is any indication. And none of them has ever seen Emma, and so there's no reason in the world that you can't pretend to be Emma and get away with it."

"You've been drinking!" Heather accused him, wondering if she should scream for Mrs. Allenby to come and rescue her from a man whose mind was demented by too much alcohol.

"How the devil could I have been drinking, when Emma poured out every bottle in the house before she left for Boston? Come on, Heather, say you'll do it! You have no idea how important it is to me. There's this marvelous opportunity I have to make all sorts of money, only I need money to set it in motion, and Mr. Arlington has heaps of money, but I can't talk him into parting with any of it unless I go to visit him, and I can't go to visit him unless you go with me and pretend to be Emma, because it's really Emma he wants and not me at all," Jared said, all in one breath. "I'm not asking you to marry Brice or anything like that. We'll come home just as soon as I talk Mr. Arlington into backing me."

Certainly he wasn't asking Heather to marry this Brice character. Something must be wrong with Brice if he wasn't already married, or at least engaged, Jared thought, with the choices he must have from among all those Southern belles. Probably he was as ugly as sin, or he stuttered, or maybe he was a trifle mentally deficient. Why else would Caldwell Arlington be so anxious to bring in a girl from the North, a girl who knew nothing about him, and try to pull off a match between them? Heather would only have to pretend

32

to like Brice until Jared got the money, and then they'd skedaddle.

"Mr. Jared, you're crazy! It would be wrong. Besides, you already have plenty of money. Why don't you just use your own for whatever this enterprise is?"

"But I don't have plenty of money! I don't have any money at all. My father, as much as I loved him, didn't have any idea how to take care of what he had, and he died broke. He spent all he had, every penny of it, and there was nothing left to leave to me."

Heather was stunned. She'd always thought that Thatcher was rich, so rich that Jared and Emma would be rich too when he died. Poor Jared! It must have been a terrible shock to him to find out that he was poor. He'd always had everything; he didn't know how to be poor. It was different in her case. She'd always been poor, even while her father was alive. The ministers of small Baptist churches didn't receive munificent salaries, and her family had always had to cut corners, so she knew how to manage on almost nothing. But Jared wouldn't know what to do between now and the time when he'd begin to make money as a lawyer, and she suspected that at first he wouldn't make very much; it would take time to get himself established. Heather's heart twisted for him.

"It wouldn't either be wrong either," Jared said. If he twisted words around like this, how could he ever expect to make a living as a lawyer? But he plunged ahead. "Mr. Arlington will get back every penny he puts up, with a whopping big profit, and he'll thank me for it even if you don't marry his son. Just think what an adventure it will be for you! A real Southern plantation—balls, magnolias, moonlight strolls in a rose garden!"

"I wouldn't think of it! Really, Mr. Jared, I don't know what's gotten into you! What is it you need all this money for anyway? And need it so badly that you're willing to lie to get it?"

"Why, Martin Knightbridge's automobile, the one he's inventing."

"They've already been invented." Heather's voice was

severe. For a moment she reminded Jared of Emma, and it wasn't a pleasant sensation.

"But Martin's is better! He's made so many improvements that it'll revolutionize the industry!"

"It isn't an industry," Heather pointed out. There was an advantage to reading as much as she did. She even confiscated the newspaper when the family was through with it, and she read every word. And so she knew that automobiles were as scarce as hen's teeth; actually they were only half invented yet. People called them those crazy gasoline contraptions.

"They're nothing but crazy gasoline contraptions," she said. It would be dreadful if Jared were to lose Caldwell Arlington's money and have to pay it back, when he didn't have any money of his own to pay it back with. It was going to be bad enough for him not to have any money without being in debt as well.

"They aren't in the least crazy! They're the coming thing. In just a few years the roads will be clogged with them. The horse and buggy is a thing of the past, and the ones who get in on the ground floor are the ones who'll reap the profits."

"I've heard you talking to Mr. Thatcher about Martin Knightbridge's automobile. He laughed at the idea," Heather pointed out. "If he wouldn't invest in it, why should Mr. Arlington?"

"My father didn't have the money to invest in it! I thought he did, but he didn't. That's why it's so important to me to make money of my own. You're looking at an impoverished man. Do you want me to be impoverished?"

"Of course I don't!" Heather was shocked. "But how do I know that your contraption will work? Mr. Arlington would lose his money if it didn't work, and then you'd be worse off than ever."

"I'll prove to you that they work! I'll take you for a ride tomorrow morning." Jared's patience was at an end. If the stubborn girl had to have proof, he'd give it to her! Hang it all, Heather not only looked a lot like Emma, but she was beginning to sound like her too.

Heather wavered. She was almost positive that Jared

would never be able to talk her into helping him perpetrate a fraud, but the chance to ride in one of those newfangled contraptions was more than she could resist. She might never have another chance.

All the same, she hadn't promised that she would go to Virginia with Jared if the contraption worked. She'd only agreed to ride in it.

Her excitement was at a fever pitch the next morning. Jared drove her to Martin's in the buggy, and that in itself was something to store up in her memory and cherish forever. She hadn't ridden in a buggy since her father died, and her father's buggy had been old, and so had the horse. But the Cranston buggy was shiny and beautiful, and Danny Boy drew admiring glances from everyone they passed. She pretended that she was Jared's sweetheart and he was taking her out for a ride. Pretending wasn't actually a sin unless you hurt somebody by it.

She preened. She didn't believe that anybody recognized her as the Cranston's hired girl. She was wearing one of Emma's prettiest dresses, her hair was up, and the hat that matched the dress was outrageously becoming on her. She touched her hat with a daintily gloved hand and smiled at the passersby.

Her reaction when she saw the actual contraption exasperated Jared. "It isn't very pretty," she said. What the devil did being pretty have to do with anything?

"Never mind how it looks. Get in." Jared knew how to drive it; Martin had shown him. All the same, he asked Martin to drive along behind them in the buggy, just in case he ran into trouble.

With Jared in place, Martin cranked the contraption. Jared made adjustments inside, the engine caught, and the machine began to shake and then to move. It was noisy and smelly, but it was wildly exciting. Heather gasped as a carthorse shied and reared, and her ears burned at what the driver of the cart said as he shook his fist at Jared to drive home his opinion of the machine. Little boys ran after them, shouting, and dogs ran after them, barking. A white-aproned grocer came out of his store and yelled, "Get that thing off the street before you kill somebody, you gol-danged idiot!"

Jared, standing at the steering lever, was a picture of confidence. "I have to pick up my laundry," he shouted at her over the noise of the engine. Behind them, Martin was having trouble keeping Danny Boy under control. Martin didn't get along very well with horses; it was machinery that Martin got along with.

They pulled up in front of Tao Tsiang's shop, and immediately all six Tsiangs came piling out through the door to stare at this strange monster that had stopped in front of their place of business.

"It is just as I expected," Tao told Jared. "All of your studying has cracked your brain. May I help you to alight, Miss, before the infernal machine explodes?"

"It isn't going to explode, Tao. It's as safe as a horse," Jared told him.

Mike, the oldest boy, repeated Jared's statement. "It isn't going to explode, Pop."

"Of course it isn't going to explode. Are my shirts ready? I'm going on a trip, and I need them."

"They're ready, but if you intend to make your journey in that contraption, I doubt that you will need them, because you will be dead before you reach your destination."

"Aw, Pop, he won't either be dead!" Pat, the second oldest boy, worked up his courage to touch the automobile, and his grin spread from ear to ear. "It's swell!"

"Do not say swell. I do not approve of slang." Tao admonished him.

Maureen edged closer, and now she, too, laid a tentative finger on the contraption. "Maybe it won't explode, but it isn't pretty," she said.

Pretty, pretty! All women were alike!

"Can I have a ride?" Mike asked. "Please?"

"Why not?" Here, at least, was someone with the intelligence to recognize a good thing when he saw it. "Hop in."

Heather scrambled out with Mr. Tsiang's help, and Mike scrambled in. Off they went to the end of the street, where they turned around and came back. Instantly, as Mike scrambled out, Pat scrambled in. The process was repeated until all four boys had had a ride.

"It's swell!" they said. "Pop, let Mr. Cranston take you for a ride!"

"I regret that I am forced to decline the honor. I have responsibilities. One of you boys could have been spared if the contraption had exploded, but I cannot be spared. Sean, fetch Mr. Cranston's laundry. There will be no charge. It is payment enough that all four of my sons have been returned to me unmaimed. Have a nice journey, Mr. Cranston. And you, Mr. Knightbridge, would do well to return to your father's most esteemable establishment and apply yourself to something more worthy than building a machine that will never be of any practical worth."

"Pop, it's the coming thing! Mr. Knightbridge, can I help you when you work on it?" Mike's face was eager. "I won't charge you anything."

Martin, so nervous that his face was stark white so that his acne stood out in sharp contrast, looked at Tao, swallowing.

Tao nodded. "It will get you out from under my feet. But you are not to operate the machine. You are only to hand Mr. Knightbridge his tools, and perhaps you will learn something by observing. Learning is good even when it is of no practical use."

"I will go for a ride," Maureen said in a small but very brave voice. "If I am honored by being asked."

Tao put his hand firmly on her arm. "You will not. You can be spared no more than I. I have no desire to raise four sons without their mother to assist me."

Back in Thatcher's office, Jared faced Heather. "I don't care if you didn't promise to go to Virginia with me if the automobile worked. You implied a promise, and that's the same thing!"

"It isn't either."

"Yes it is! I'm a lawyer, and I ought to know! Oral contracts have to be honored."

Heather wavered. Seeing her waver, Jared pounced.

"Picture yourself floating down a curving staircase, with a

handsome young planter waiting at the foot to escort you to the ballroom! You'll be so beautiful in your ballgown that all the young gentlemen will fall madly in love with you. They might even fight a duel over you. The oak grove at dawn, flashing swords!" Jared suspected that in this day and age it would be pistols, but swords sounded more romantic.

"Pistols," Heather said. She didn't want anyone to fight a duel over her; someone might get hurt. All the same, her eyes were shining. If there were a duel, with pistols, maybe both of the young gentlemen would miss or one of them only be grazed on the arm.

When had the girl become so blasted argumentative? Jared wondered.

"Do you have any more dresses like the one you have on and the one you wore last night?" For an extended visit to Arbordale, she would have to have a suitable wardrobe.

"Lots of them. Miss Emma gave me everything she thought was too worldly for a missionary," Heather said. There were even ballgowns, three of them. "But Mr. Jared, even if I agreed to go, which I haven't, there couldn't be any balls or parties. You're in mourning."

Jared hadn't thought of that. He frowned, taken aback. It would throw a monkey wrench into the machinery for them to be in mourning. If Caldwell Arlington knew that Thatcher was dead, he wouldn't be in much of a mood to talk about investments; and if he knew that Thatcher had died virtually bankrupt, he wouldn't be in any hurry to lend money to Thatcher's son, especially if, as Jared suspected, the primary reason for the invitation was to foster a match between Emma and Brice. Wealth attracts wealth; that was a fact of life that couldn't be gotten around.

Then his face cleared. "My father wouldn't give a hang if I didn't observe strict mourning. And the Arlingtons don't know that he's dead. We just won't tell them."

"That would be lying!"

"No it wouldn't. It would be just not telling them. I'll write, after we come back, and tell them that he died very suddenly. For now, I'll just tell them that he was called away very suddenly and can't visit them this summer, and that's the truth."

Heather pictured herself floating down a curving staircase in one of the beautiful ballgowns that she'd never dreamed she'd have a chance to wear. And Jared was looking at her with such pleading in his eyes that she couldn't bear it. She didn't want him to be impoverished. If he was impoverished, he'd have to let her go, and then she would never see him again, and she couldn't bear that.

"Do you promise that Mr. Arlington won't lose his money?"

"I promise. Heather, you're an angel!"

He kissed her. Heather knew that he didn't mean anything by it, he was just grateful, but still he kissed her. And having him be grateful to her was a lot better than having him not feel anything about her at all.

"I'll write to Mr. Arlington right now," he said.

For a moment, after he'd sat down at the desk and she'd gone up to her room to change into her work dress, Heather was filled with doubts for having agreed to something that, if it wasn't actually wrong, still wasn't right. She was almost a criminal.

And then her own excitement began to rise. For the first time in her life, all eighteen years and three months and fourteen days of it, something wildly exciting and wonderful was going to happen to her.

She wondered what Miss Emma would think of all this, and then she decided that she'd rather not know.

❧ *Chapter 3* ❧

THERE WASN'T ANY doubt about it, riding on a train was the most exciting experience of Heather's life, even more exciting than riding in the gasoline contraption. Dressed in one of Emma's most attractive traveling costumes, she felt like the heroine of one of her own novels.

There wasn't any doubt, either, that she was frightened. This masquerade was not only going to be difficult to carry off, but she'd have to watch every word she said, and she wasn't sure that she wouldn't let something slip that would betray them. She hoped Jared was right and she would only have to keep up the pretense for a few days. In the meantime, she'd absorb everything she could about plantation life, to use in her next novel.

If everything turned out the way it should, it was going to be simply wonderful. Jared would make heaps of money, and she wouldn't have to look for another position and never see him again. And then when she finished her novel and if someone bought it, she'd be a lady novelist instead of a hired girl, and with Jared already so grateful to her for helping her, she could work on making him fall in love with her.

She was getting ahead of herself, of course. The whole thing might fall through, Jared might not get the money, and she might not be able to sell her book. But even if that happened, she was still having a wonderful adventure, something that only days ago she would never have dreamed could happen. She just hoped that Brice Arlington wasn't too impossible, because she was going to have to be nice to him and pretend that she liked him. If he wasn't downright gruesome, she might even flirt with him a little, just to see Jared's reaction. If Jared was even a tiny bit jealous, then she could hope. In the novels she read, a little jealousy went a long way!

That slightly overweight, slightly overaged gentleman seated across the aisle was ogling her again! Heather stifled an impulse to giggle. At any moment the man might wink at her, and then she would have to pretend to be indignant. All the same, it was nice to know that at least one man in the world considered her attractive, even if he himself was nobody she would look at twice. And wouldn't it be exciting if he made advances toward her, and Jared had to reprimand him—it would be just like something in a book!

She was almost disappointed when the conductor came along and announced that the next station was Bennington before anything of the sort could happen. Jared warned her that she was going to have to alight from the train with alacrity because he'd learned that Bennington was no more than a whistle stop. As she passed the man on her way to exit the train, with Jared's hand under her elbow to steady her, she couldn't resist the impulse to look back and wink at him.

The man gaped, his eyes popping, and Heather giggled. No real lady would have done such a thing, but then it seemed to her that real ladies didn't have much fun. Emma was a real lady, and she certainly never had any fun. Emma would have withered the man with a glance, instead of winking at him just so she could giggle at the expression on his face.

Then Jared was on the platform, reaching up for her, and she gasped as she realized that the man might also debark at Bennington, and that would be dreadful! But she was safe, he was still in his seat, and the train was already moving. She didn't have to worry that she would ever see the ogler again.

Her legs felt wobbly. She felt as though the platform were moving. Never having ridden on a train before, she wasn't prepared for the sensation of still being on the train, and the illusion of jerking and jolting under her feet made her feel giddy. Jared grinned at her.

"It's almost as good as being a little drunk. Not too drunk, just drunk enough to feel it," he told her. "I used to feel the same way before I got used to it. Tonight you'll see all the scenery from the train window pass in front of your eyes when you try to get to sleep. Don't let it upset you; it'll pass."

He broke off as a tall, extraordinarily handsome young man approached them. Heather's gasp of consternation at what Jared had just told her turned into one of astonishment as she took in every detail of the young man's appearance.

To think that she'd thought Brice Arlington might be impossible! The reality was not only tall, but his shoulders were broad, and he was dressed in the most perfectly tailored clothing she had ever seen. He held a broad-brimmed planter's hat in his hand, leaving his fair hair uncovered, hair that curled just above his collar in the back. His face was tanned, and his eyes looked startlingly blue in contrast. Heather's heart fluttered and threatened to stop beating entirely. He might have stepped directly from the pages of a novel!

But unlike the heroes of the books she read, this Southern gentleman's face was austere and unsmiling as he greeted them. Heather had the distinct and unpleasant impression that he wasn't one bit glad that they had come.

"Mr. Cranston, Miss Cranston." Brice Arlington inclined his head, but he made no move to raise her hand to his lips as a genuine hero in a novel would have done. "My father and my aunt Minerva are waiting for you at Arbordale. Aunt Minna is my father's sister, she makes her home with us, and she is all aflutter awaiting your arrival."

Whatever emotions he himself might be experiencing, Brice certainly wasn't all aflutter. His manner was correct to the extreme, but there was a coldness underneath that sent a chill through Heather's blood in spite of the hot summer sun.

"And we're mighty glad to be here! I've looked forward to meeting you and your family for a long time." The fib came from Jared's lips as glibly as though it were the gospel truth. His beaming face told Heather that he hadn't noticed Brice's coldness toward them. Or could she be mistaken about the coldness? Maybe this was the way all Southern gentlemen acted. All the same, considering Caldwell Arlington's letters, she had expected a warmer welcome.

"Saul, take care of the luggage. Miss Cranston, allow me to assist you into the carriage."

Brice's touch on her arm as he helped her mount the step into the landau sent shivers through Heather's body. If he wasn't overwhelmed by her, she was certainly overwhelmed by him! And the landau, its top folded back, came up to every one of her romantic expectations, complete with Saul, who was now happily loading the baggage. The elderly black man, at least, was glad to see them.

"We're mighty glad you could come to visit, sir," Saul told Jared. "You and the young lady. Welcome to Virginia, and I hope you'll stay for a good long time."

Was Heather mistaken, or did Brice wince at Saul's words? An instant later Heather couldn't be sure, because the young man's face was impassive again.

"Is the plantation far?" In spite of her youth and abundant good health, Heather was feeling the effects of the long journey. She still felt as though the train was jerking and jolting, she felt gritty and soiled, she needed a bath and a change of clothing, and she was hungry. She even suspected, with disgust, that the hem of her traveling dress was stained from the tobacco juice that had missed the shiny brass spittoons.

But in spite of not appearing at her newly attained best, she still couldn't help but feel a twinge of pique at Brice's disinterest in her. She knew that she didn't look all that bad because of the slightly overweight, slightly overaged gentleman who had ogled her on the train. And there had been two or three others who had looked as if they would have

43

liked to ogle her if she hadn't been in the company of a male escort. Any reasonably attractive female would do well to avoid traveling by train alone.

"Not far at all," Brice answered. "It's only slightly over three miles." Then, as though he were prodding himself to observe the amenities, he added, "I hope that your journey wasn't too uncomfortable."

"Not in the least!" Jared was fairly bubbling over with amiability. "Trains are improving at an amazing rate. They seem to become more comfortable every year. My sister and I enjoyed every moment of it. It was kind of you to extend us the invitation. It will do Emma good to see something of the country. She's never traveled before, and she's most interested in plantation life."

Ever since they had decided to go through with this scheme, Jared had practiced calling Heather Emma at every opportunity. That had been a minor problem, however, compared to coming up with a plausible excuse for this journey to give to Heather's mother. Heather had never failed to visit her mother over the bookshop on her afternoon off, and her absence had to be explained.

It was Heather who had come up with the solution. They would say that Miss Minna felt the need of a companion, someone young and competent, as she was not feeling very well. And Jared, who was going to visit Arbordale anyway, had thought of Heather and suggested taking her along to see if she would suit. A companion from another part of the country would be amusing for Miss Minna, and so the invitation had been extended to her as well.

Jared had charmed Judith Potsby by pointing out that this was a perfect opportunity for Heather to better her position in life. A companion is a step above a servant, and even if Miss Minna might not need her for very long, Heather would have had experience at being a companion and might find another such position in Albany. Having been a companion to a genuine Southern lady would be a wonderful recommendation.

The town of Bennington was so small that they left it behind before Heather could get any impression of it except for a few storefronts and a pretty town square in front of a courthouse and neat, well-kept houses on tree-lined streets leading off the main business street. Compared to Albany, Bennington was little more than a hamlet.

The countryside they drove through was lush with the full green of summer. It was beautiful, but no more beautiful than the countryside that surrounded Albany. Somehow, that disappointed Heather, because she had entertained the notion that being in Virginia would be like being in some exotic foreign country.

Then she sat up straighter and brightened. A farm cart was approaching them from the opposite direction, the negro driver grinning as he saluted them with a nod, and a black woman, also smiling broadly, held on to a toddler while four other children of varying ages leaned over the sides and grinned and waved.

"It's Saturday." It was Jared who explained. Brice seemed not to notice the cart. "They must be going in to town."

"Yes, suh," Saul agreed.

"I hope they have a good time! I hope the children all get sticks of peppermint candy!" Heather said. Her memory of pressing her nose against a case of penny candy while her father held her hand was still vivid. She'd invariably chosen a peppermint stick because they had lasted so long. Those pretty peppermint sticks, all red and white striped, had been the high points of her childhood.

As she leaned dangerously far out of the landau to watch the wagonload of people draw away from them, they broke into song. It was a spiritual, the tones rich and pure and incredibly lovely as the notes hung in the air. Emma would have approved. Heather simply enjoyed it. She'd never seen or heard anything like this in Albany. Virginia was different after all, and she knew that it was going to be every bit as wonderful as she had dreamed it would be.

Settling back, she saw that Brice was looking at her with a peculiar expression on his face. Hadn't she been supposed to smile and wave at the black family? But the expression didn't seem to denote disapproval; rather it seemed almost pained, as though the young man were being torn with conflicting emotions. Heather was puzzled. Everything about Brice Arlington puzzled her.

There was little other traffic on the road. Only two buggies, their occupants also headed for town, approached and passed them. The couple in the first buggy nodded to them; the three people in the second did not, but kept their faces straight ahead, their shoulders stiff. Heather's puzzlement grew. Brice nodded to the first couple but ignored the people in the second buggy by gazing out of the opposite side of the landau. Maybe Brice simply didn't know the people in the second buggy. But wouldn't that be odd, in a place like this, where she would have thought everybody would know each other?

Another farm cart was approaching them. The driver, with a raveled straw hat and patches on his overalls, also looked straight ahead, giving them no salute of any kind. And, to add to the mystery, as he drew abreast of the landau he spat a stream of tobacco juice in their direction. If his aim had been a little more accurate it would have landed directly on Heather's dress. As it was, it spattered the side of the carriage.

"What in the world!" Jared was startled into exclaiming. "That was close. Now why in the world did he do that?"

"I apologize," Brice told him, his voice tight. "Some of our farmers around here are sadly lacking in manners." He let the matter rest there, with no further explanations. Heather stared at him, every sense alert. She was certain that Brice had left a lot unsaid, and just as certain that the majority of farmers anywhere in the world were as polite as anyone else.

Her attention was diverted just in time to keep her from bursting with curiosity. A long avenue of oak trees led to a plantation house just visible at its end, exactly the kind of plantation house she had always imagined, with vine-grown pillars supporting a broad verandah. It was all she could do to keep from bouncing up and down on the seat, something that Emma would never have dreamed of doing.

"Is that Arbordale? It's positively beautiful!"

"That is the Langdon place," Brice told her. There was a

peculiar timbre in his voice, and, more peculiar still, he didn't even glance at the house but kept his face averted as though the sight of it would be too painful to be borne. She glanced at Jared. Jared hadn't even noticed. But up on the driver's seat, Saul's back was stiff, and he flicked the whip and made the horses trot faster as though he wanted to leave the Langdon place behind as quickly as possible.

Heather opened her mouth to ask if the Langdons were friends of the Arlingtons and closed it again. Some instinct told her that that was not a question that Brice would care to answer. But this was more curious still. She had labored under the impression that the plantation families in the South were closely knit, the best of friends.

A feud? Not likely, Heather thought. This wasn't the hill country of West Virginia, but plantation country. Some long-standing enmity between the two families then? One where the families didn't shoot at each other but simply didn't speak?

It was none of her business, she told herself, but being Heather, she could not dismiss it at that. A puzzle was something that had to be solved, or she wouldn't have a moment's peace. Her mind worried at the problem with such intensity that she was jolted into a start of surprise when Brice said, "This is Arbordale. We're just turning into the drive."

Like the lane leading to the Langdon place, this one was also tree-lined, the shade welcome after the heat of the sun on the dirt road. The lawn in front of the house was a brilliant green, and flowerbeds rioted with color. Honeysuckle vines entwined the columns that supported the expected verandah. The house itself was constructed of brick, faded over the years so that the color was soft rather than harsh. Heather drew in her breath and held it. This, at least, came up to all of her expectations. It was the plantation house of her dreams.

Two figures rose from wicker chairs on the verandah, waiting to greet them. Caldwell Arlington was a strapping man, tall and straight, his fair hair, so like Brice's, blended so that the gray was scarcely perceptible. Like Brice, he was deeply tanned. As he came down the steps to meet them, he moved with a grace that belied his years.

Brice was already out of the carriage, handing Heather down, his gesture courtly. But the hand under her elbow was impersonal, almost as though he wished that he was not required to touch her. Jared jumped down lightly, his own hand extended.

"Mr. Arlington, sir! This is a pleasure! You can't imagine how long I have looked forward to this moment! I feel that we already know each other, my father talks of you so often." Jared was pouring on the boyish charm, and his enthusiasm was reflected in Caldwell's eyes.

"Jared, my boy, I'd have known you anywhere! You're Thatcher all over again! It's a crying shame that he wasn't able to come this time, but you're just as welcome as if he were with you."

Heather's admiration of Jared's performance was interrupted as a pair of arms enfolded her, and a tiny, delicately formed lady some years older than her brother stood on her tiptoes to kiss her cheek.

"Emma, my dear Emma! What a beauty you are! I'm so glad you're here! I've longed for a young face to relieve the tedium of my days. My brother and my nephew are good enough company, but they aren't women, and that's the lack! Come, sit down."

She led Heather up onto the verandah, indicated a comfortable wicker rocker, and then picked up a little silver bell and rang it. "Pearl! Bring the refreshments. Our guests have arrived, and they'll be perishing with thirst after that hot drive from town. You and I shall have lemonade, my dear, while the gentlemen enjoy their juleps. I make the lemonade myself. I hope you'll like it."

Miss Minna was a delight, a positive delight. Like Brice, like Caldwell, she might have stepped straight from the pages of a novel. She was tiny and fragile-looking, but every inch of her vibrated with life.

"What a wonderful time we shall have together! I hope you don't mind having your ears talked off, Emma. Once I get started there's no stopping me. Caldwell says that if races were won with words, I'd have a prize collection of gold medals! What a lovely traveling dress! It makes me wish I could travel so I could have one just like it, and don't go thinking that it's too young for me! You're as young as you feel, and I don't feel a day older than you are. Growing old has its compensations, though. I can wear what I choose, and people only hint that I'm eccentric." Minna's voice was silvery with laughter.

Now that Minna had drawn her attention to it, Heather saw that the older lady was dressed in pink, a color that was generally reserved for the young. It looked wonderful on her, giving her face a glow. Heather warmed to her even more. She liked people who knew their own minds and did as they pleased. Life was too short to live it by other people's rules if the rules didn't suit you.

Near them in the other wicker chairs, the gentlemen were talking with easy companionship. At least Jared and Caldwell were talking. Brice was silent, although he was paying polite attention to what the other men said. Leave it to Jared, Heather thought. He'd already brought up the subject of automobiles!

"I've always enjoyed traveling by train, but have you ever ridden in an automobile? Now, that's the coming mode of transportation. It's an experience never to be forgotten. I have a friend in Albany who's about to embark on their manufacture. His prototype is going to revolutionize the industry!"

Caldwell's eyebrows rose. "Industry? I hardly think you could call the building of perhaps half a dozen of those machines across the country an industry."

"But it's going to be an industry sooner than anyone thinks. All that's needed is to develop a really dependable automobile, which Martin has done. I'm sinking every dollar I can spare into it."

Heather almost choked.

"How about Thatcher? Is he investing?" Caldwell wanted to know.

"Right at the moment my father isn't in a position to add to his investments." Oh my, Heather thought, he certainly is good at telling the exact, absolute truth and making it come out sounding like something else entirely! "But as for me, I only wish I had many times as much as I do to put into the venture."

The exact truth again, Heather thought, but how much is nothing times nothing?

Caldwell laughed. "The enthusiasm of the young for every passing fad! I don't doubt that it would be interesting to ride in one of the contraptions, but they'll never replace the horse."

"Sir, meaning no disrespect, but I'm forced to disagree with you. Think of the convenience! Horses have to be fed and stabled and cleaned up after. To say nothing of their skittishness. Runaway horses cause more accidents than anything else I can think of. But an automobile is clean and always ready to go at a moment's notice, you don't have to harness it up, and it doesn't get tired or sick or decide to balk."

Don't push so hard, Heather wanted to warn him. You're coming on too strong. And besides, automobiles do balk, that's how you happened to meet Martin Knightbridge.

She glanced at Brice, and she was surprised to see that he seemed to have no interest in the subject at all. A young man should be interested, if only out of curiosity. But Brice seemed to be a hundred miles away.

Miss Minna came bustling back from inside the house, where she'd gone in search of Pearl, who hadn't answered the summons of the silver bell. "That girl! She's never around when you want her. But here are our refreshments." She was carrying a tray with three heavily frosted mint juleps and two tall glasses of lemonade with sprigs of mint in them. She handed Heather one of the glasses of lemonade before she served the gentlemen, and then she sat down again in her own wicker rocker.

There was ice in the lemonade, and the coldness of the glass felt wonderful as Heather held it in her hand. Lemonade certainly was welcome. It was just what she needed to quench her thirst. She took a sip, and then another, and then her eyes opened wide.

Miss Minna smiled at her, and Heather could have sworn that the older woman's left eye half closed in a wink. It was lemonade, all right, perfectly sweetened, not too sweet and not too tart. But there was something more than lemon juice and sugar in the water. Heather wasn't familiar with the different kinds of alcoholic beverages. The only one she had ever tasted was the port she had drunk when she'd discovered Thatcher dead in the front parlor. But she'd read that mint juleps were made with bourbon, and so she suspected that it was bourbon in the lemonade.

"Do you like it?" Minna asked.

"Oh, yes, it's delicious! I never tasted such delicious lemonade before!" Heather sipped again. It *was* delicious, but she wondered if Caldwell and Brice knew what was in it besides lemon juice and sugar. Miss Minna's innocent expression told her that they didn't.

Heather grinned. What the men didn't know wouldn't hurt them. She already liked Miss Minna, but now she was convinced that she was going to positively adore her.

Minna grinned back at her. "Finish it up, my dear. Your room is all ready, and I know you're tired. Della will bring you hot water and turn down your bed, and you are to have a nice long nap. Saul will have already carried up your bags. He's dependable, even if the girls aren't."

"I'm not tired at all," Heather protested, but the thought of a nap was alluring. And it would be wonderful to wash away the grime that was making her itch. She must look a sight. It was no wonder Brice couldn't spare her a second glance.

The room was large and gave the impression of coolness, with white curtains moving in a breeze at the windows. Miss Minna fluttered around, telling her that the soap was one of her own imported cakes scented with lavender, testing the water in the pitcher and finding it warm enough, instructing young Della, who was no more than fifteen, to turn back the bed and to draw the window drapes to darken the room as soon as Heather was tucked in for her nap.

"I hope you have a good appetite and don't just pick and peck at your food the way some of these silly girls do,"

Minna said. "Elspeth's beaten biscuits and batter-fried chicken and Lady Baltimore cake deserve more appreciation than that."

Heather struggled to keep from laughing. She would indeed have to pick and peck at her dinner, or what amounted to it for her, because if she ate with her usual hearty appetite both Caldwell and Brice would look at her with horror. Jared wouldn't be surprised—he already knew her habit of gobbling up everything in sight—but he'd be mortified. It was important to give the impression that Miss Emma Cranston was a genteel lady and not appear like a ravenous housemaid!

She'd never slept in a tester bed before. She lay gazing up at the canopy, admiring the intricate tatted border, and breathed deeply of the scented air. The windows opened onto the rose garden, exactly as she had imagined they would. But a wry smile curved her lips as she tried to picture herself walking there with Brice under a full moon. If first impressions weren't deceiving, nothing was further from Brice's mind. She couldn't shake the feeling that Brice didn't want her and Jared there.

At least Caldwell Arlington was glad they had come, there could be no mistake about that. But it wasn't Caldwell she was supposed to impress. Jared was supposed to impress Caldwell while she impressed Brice.

There was one perfectly logical explanation for why Brice evinced not the slightest interest in her. She remembered the expression on his face when they had passed the Langdon plantation. Her lively imagination couldn't help but leap to the conclusion that Brice was suffering from a broken romance with a Langdon young lady. It was possible that Caldwell thought that having a pretty young lady as a houseguest would help to mend his son's broken heart, and that was why he had been so eager for Emma to visit them.

If that were the case, Caldwell was doomed to disappointment. She and Jared would be leaving as soon as Jared had persuaded him to part with enough of his money to set the automobile venture in motion. But it might still be fun to give that Miss Langdon some competition, just to prove to herself that she could do it.

Drifting off to sleep, she thought that this Miss Langdon must be a nitwit if she'd had Brice and then let him get away. In Miss Langdon's place, Heather would have held on to him for dear life. But then she would never be in Miss Langdon's place, so there was no use thinking about it. Besides, she preferred a man who smiled more than Brice did.

Jared was always smiling.

⚘ Chapter 4 ⚘

HEATHER AND JARED had been at Arbordale for three days, and so far none of the romantic events that Jared had promised her had been forthcoming. Everything she had ever heard about the South had led her to believe that friends and neighbors would drop by in flocks, that more invitations would be extended to them than they could accept, and that the Arlingtons themselves would be planning festivities to introduce them to Virginia society.

But no one had dropped by and no mention had been made of entertaining guests in the near future. Caldwell was the soul of hospitality, Miss Minna chattered nonstop, Jared was shown around the plantation, and the food was every bit as delicious as Minna had promised it would be. But so far it was just the five of them, she and Jared and Miss Minna and Caldwell and Brice.

Sitting in the rose arbor with Miss Minna, fanning herself with a palm-leaf fan while Minna's fingers were busy with a tatting shuttle that turned out yard after yard of lovely lace edging, Heather was puzzled. It wasn't only the lack of visitors and parties, but the plantation itself, that filled her with questions.

For instance, in a plantation house of this size, why did the household staff consist of only two adolescent girls and

Elspeth? And why did Saul seem to be the only one who took care of the lawns and flowerbeds as well as the horses? She knew that plantation owners didn't have the hoards of servants they'd had back in the days of slavery, but surely only two young girls, a cook, and Saul was cutting it thin?

Pearl and Della were inexperienced, Heather realized instantly. They were nervous when they were serving at the table, and the dust they missed when they were cleaning made Heather itch to do it herself. Emma wouldn't have stood for such slackness for a moment. And there was no way Saul could keep up with all he had to do; he ought to have at least one helper even if it was only a boy.

Now that she was thinking of the strangeness connected with Arbordale, even Minna's constant chatter seemed a little bit strange, as though she was starved for female companionship. She should have had so many friends dropping by that she wouldn't know what to do with them all. And why, when Heather asked about Minna's friends and neighbors, did the older woman always go off on a tangent, talking about something else?

It had happened again just now. Heather had asked, out of a nagging curiosity, if the Arlingtons and the Langdons did much visiting back and forth, seeing that they were such close neighbors. Minna immediately began chatting about the different varieties of roses in the garden. Her grandmother had introduced the damask roses and that deep crimson and the varicolored ones that were her favorites.

"It's a real task to keep them in perfect condition, I can tell you!" Minna said, her tatting shuttle flying. "Saul has to fight aphids and scale and other pests constantly, but then anything worth having is a deal of work. Arbordale is renowned for its roses; that's where it got its name. I hope that Della didn't forget to refill the vases in your room this morning. It's best to pick them as soon after dawn as possible, when the dew is still on them. They keep longer that way."

Heather stopped listening, intent on trying to unravel the mysteries of Arbordale. But she could find no answers to her questions. She couldn't come right out and ask bluntly.

That would have been appallingly impolite, something that Emma would never dream of doing. All the same, it bothered her.

Not having anything to do from morning till night bothered her too. She was used to being busy every minute of the day, and this enforced idleness was driving her into fits. It would have been different if Brice would pay the attention to her that she had been led to expect, but beyond being polite to her, Brice ignored her. There's nothing like romance to make the time pass pleasantly, but there was certainly no romance to be had there.

Here she was, on a genuine plantation, with the most handsome young scion of the South imaginable right within touching distance, but Brice had turned out to be completely untouchable. If she hadn't remembered how those gentlemen on the train had looked at her, she would have examined herself in her mirror to make sure that she hadn't come down with an acute case of instant ugly.

As if thinking about Brice had conjured him up, he came walking down the shell path to the rose arbor.

"Perhaps you would enjoy a buggy ride," Brice said. He was actually asking her to go for a drive with him! But there were lines of strain around his eyes, and Heather wondered if Caldwell had ordered him to ask her. For an instant it was on the tip of her tongue to refuse his invitation if he couldn't at least look as if he meant it.

But she was already on her feet, giving him the benefit of her most dazzling smile, one certain to turn any red-blooded young man to jelly. This was her chance to force him to notice her, and it was just about time, because her ego was in danger of being mangled to the point where she'd never have any confidence in herself as a woman again.

Bother! She must remember her manners. "Won't you come with us, Miss Minna? You'd enjoy an outing, wouldn't you?"

"Oh, my goodness, no! I have entirely too much to do here." Heather had never heard such a bending of the truth. Miss Minna didn't have a thing in the world to do; all she ever did was sit and tat. She didn't even help Elspeth plan the meals, except to ask for some Southern specialty that she thought would be a treat to people from up North, and she must have already turned out enough tatting to edge every handkerchief in Virginia! "You two run along and enjoy yourselves, and don't hurry back on my account."

Minna's smile was pleased and knowing, and her cheeks were pink. Caldwell had done his best to push Heather and Brice together, and now it was clear that Minna was also determined to stir up a romance between them. One thing Heather had especially noticed was that Minna adored her nephew, and that made it seem all the more likely that Brice was suffering from a broken heart and Minna wanted him to mend it with another girl, one who wouldn't end up hurting him.

If Brice was suffering from a broken heart, Heather was sorry. All the same, she couldn't help being piqued at his total lack of interest in her. I'll show him, she thought with a mental toss of her head. I'll talk about Humphrey Snell. I'll tell him how handsome Humphrey is, and lead him to believe that we're on the verge of a serious courtship. That would make him realize that some other man considered her attractive, even if he didn't, and he'd be bound to look at her with a little more interest.

There would be another advantage to pretending that she was interested in Humphrey Snell. If Brice thought that her heart was already romantically taken up with another man, maybe he'd stop acting like a skittish horse that was fighting against being bridled, and then they could get on with enjoying each other's company.

And maybe, if she told him about Humphrey, he would break down and tell her about the Langdon girl or whoever it was who had broken his heart, and her curiosity about that, at least, would be satisfied. She'd ask him, when they passed the Langdon place, if there were any daughters and lead him right into telling her all about it.

To her chagrin, Brice turned the horse in the opposite direction from the Langdon place, and she couldn't think of any way to bring up the subject without being too obvious about it. Moreover, Brice didn't seem inclined to talk about anything, much less about the Langdons, and she could hardly start to natter on about Humphrey without something to lead up to it.

She was reduced to admiring the high-stepping trotter. After she'd admired him, she could mention Humphrey's trotter. She wouldn't have to tell the truth about it, that Humphrey's buggy horse couldn't hold a candle to Cicero, the minister having more important uses for his money than owning a horse that other men would envy him for having.

"My, but your Cicero is beautiful! He's just about the finest trotter I've ever seen," she said. She hoped that Cicero wouldn't forget his manners while she was admiring him. If he did, she would ignore it as a lady should, but all the same it would be embarrassing. She could scarcely say, "Cicero has the shiniest coat, see how it gleams in the sun, and doesn't he have remarkably good bowel movements!"

She stifled a giggle, thinking how Brice's face would turn white with shock if she were to say such a thing. It was almost a pity that she couldn't say it, just to jolt him out of that stiff manner of his. But Cicero didn't forget his manners, and so all she could do was admire his shiny coat and his trot.

"Would you like to try him, Miss Cranston? He's a little high-spirited, but I'll be right beside you in case he gets out of hand."

It was on the tip of Heather's tongue to blurt out that she had never driven a horse in her life. But Emma knew how to drive, and besides, it didn't look as if there were all that much to it. All you had to do was hold the ribbons, and the horse did the rest. And this might be the only chance she would ever get to drive a horse.

"Never be afraid to try something new, Heather." She could almost hear her father's voice. Joshua Bailey had been a smiling man, with dreams in his eyes. If he'd been afraid to try something new, Heather would never have been born.

Joshua's family had been staunch Presbyterians, but Joshua had fallen in love with a Baptist girl. Because he had always dreamed of becoming a minister, he had used a small inheritance from his grandfather to become a Baptist minister, since Judith was as staunch a Baptist as his parents were Presbyterians. His family had never forgiven him, but Joshua had held on to his dreams and became a minister and won the beautiful Judith Amberly for his wife.

Joshua had approved of dreams. If you dreamed of something hard enough and weren't afraid to try to make your dreams come true, then the chances were that you could get what you wanted. Judith had been the practical one in the family, and Heather supposed it was a good thing that one of them had been practical, but she was glad that her father had passed his love of dreaming on to her. There wouldn't be much point to life if you couldn't dream.

All right, so now she was dreaming that she could drive a high-stepping trotter down a road in Virginia, and she could almost see her father nod and smile. But her confidence was shattered almost immediately. Cicero had no intention of cooperating with her dreams. She might have gotten away with it if Cicero had been willing, but the trotter knew when someone who didn't have the faintest notion of how to drive was holding his ribbons, and he wanted none of that kind of nonsense.

Cicero's pace first became uneven, and then he veered toward the edge of the road. Heather hauled on the ribbons, and he veered the other way. Then, for good measure, he started to prance around, tossing his head. Heather pulled back for all she was worth, and he reared.

Brice looked at her with accusation written all over his face. He grabbed the ribbons from her and brought the trotter under control.

"Miss Cranston, I don't believe you've ever driven a horse!" His voice was filled with reproach. "In another minute we would have been in the ditch!"

Heather was more embarrassed than she had ever been in her life, but she lifted her chin. "Well, maybe I haven't, but there's no need to look at me like that! Didn't you ever want to do something you'd never done before?"

"Not unless I had some idea of how to go about it!" Brice's voice was as severe as his expression. And then, to give him credit for Southern gallantry, he softened a little.

"If you'd like to learn, I suggest that you start with Angel. She wouldn't break into a gallop if the bridge under her feet caught fire. She's perfectly steady and placid and ideal for a beginner."

This was more like it! Brice was going to teach her how to drive! Heather's flush of fury turned to one of pleasure. "I'd love that. Thank you, Brice." The ice had been broken. Brice was acting like a warm-blooded human being, and what could be more romantic than being taught to drive by a man as handsome as he was? Unless it was being taught to drive by Jared. Besides, it would give her another chance to flirt with Brice and see if she could crack his shell still further. Not that she intended to try to make him fall in love with her. She wouldn't let it go anywhere near as far as that, because she didn't want him to be hurt again, but it would be gratifying to make him look at her as if he at least admired her.

"Saul will be glad to take you out. He can teach you everything you need to know; there's nothing he doesn't know about horses."

Heather almost choked. Human, my foot! Brice's momentary warmth had subsided, and he was his usual distant, polite self. Drat him! And drat Jared for talking her into coming to Arbordale with all his nonsense about moonlight and rose gardens and romance! So far, Arbordale had been about as romantic as Albany in a January blizzard.

She returned to Arbordale in high dudgeon. Jared and Caldwell were sitting on the verandah. Sitting on the verandah in the late afternoon, with mint juleps in hand, seemed to be the high point of plantation life, and if that was all that plantation life had to offer she might just as well have stayed home! One glass of Minna's lemonade wasn't enough compensation for the boredom of all the other hours of the day. But Jared, at least, seemed to be enjoying himself.

"Well, our sightseers have returned! You look as if you enjoyed yourself thoroughly, Emma. Your cheeks are all nice and flushed."

Heather didn't doubt that they were. A girl's cheeks were generally flushed when she was as mad as a wet hen. She sat down in one of the wicker rockers, picked up her glass of lemonade, and drank almost all of it without pausing for breath.

"My goodness, you must have been thirsty!" Minna said. "I'll get you another, Emma."

Heather gathered her wits back together. "Indeed no, Miss Minna. One is quite sufficient." She had no idea what would happen if she were to drink two glasses of Minna's lemonade, and she wasn't sure that she wanted to find out. Emma had never ceased her lectures about the evils of demon rum, and the fact that the lemonade was laced with bourbon rather than rum wouldn't have been a mitigating factor. Minna never took more than one glass, so one must be harmless, but two might be something entirely else again.

She helped herself to a square of cake iced with boiled frosting and embellished with half a walnut. She smiled at Brice as she nibbled on it. "Do have one of these, Mr. Arlington. Even our Mrs. Allenby in Albany never turned out anything quite this good." There, that would show him that she wasn't in the least miffed because he had no intention of teaching her how to drive. "Jared, Saul is going to teach me how to drive. Isn't that exciting?"

Caldwell Arlington gave his son a hard look that boded an uncomfortable talk once the two Arlington men were alone. Heather's smile became even sweeter. She hoped Caldwell would give the younger man a raking over the coals that he wouldn't forget in a hurry. She'd had just about all of being ignored by Brice that she could take.

Feeling self-satisfied, she excused herself to rest and freshen up before supper.

Caldwell must have found an opportunity to have a talk with his son, because at supper Brice put himself out to be more agreeable to her than he had been in the habit of being. And at a particularly keen glance from his father, he went so far as to mention a country fair that was to be held in the town of Bishop in two days' time.

"Would you like to attend the fair, Miss Cranston? I doubt that it will be as comprehensive as the fairs you have in Albany, but you might find it a pleasant day's outing."

"Jared would love to go to the fair," Heather said before

Jared had a chance to open his mouth. "And I'm sure that Miss Minna would like to go. You do want to go, don't you, Miss Minna?"

That would really show him that she wasn't setting her cap for him! If she'd had any such intentions, she wouldn't have asked Jared and Minna to go along.

Brice looked agreeable. Miss Minna hesitated, looking uncertain. She looked at Caldwell as though she were asking for instructions, but Caldwell couldn't very well tell her not to go, in face of the fact that Heather wanted her to go.

Odder and odder, Heather thought. One would think that Minna would be in a lather of excitement to get away from the plantation for a day, anything to break the monotony.

"All of you must go," Caldwell said heartily. If he'd been engineering to get Heather and Brice alone for an entire day, he covered up his disappointment admirably. "Elspeth will pack a lunch, and you can make a day of it. I'd go myself, but somebody must be here. A plantation doesn't run itself, and I've seen so many fairs that missing this one won't matter."

Minna's face went pink with joy. "The handicraft exhibition won't have anything to match the afghan I crocheted five years ago that took the blue ribbon. I gave up crocheting when I ran out of people to give afghans to. It's a pity it's too late to enter my tatting, but I mustn't be selfish. It will be nice for some other lady to have a chance to win. Do you do any handiwork, Emma? I notice that you didn't bring anything with you to work on. I never go anyplace without my tatting."

Heather confessed that she had never learned to do handiwork, and both Brice and Minna looked shocked. Jared plunged in to gloss over her ineptness.

"Emma spends all of her spare time doing church work. She has a real knack for running things."

That was better. Both Brice and Minna expressed approval. Then Jared had to go and spoil it all by adding, "And she sings in the church choir. She has a beautiful voice."

Emma sang in the church choir, and she had an absolutely wonderful voice. Listening to Emma when she sang a solo was the most enjoyable part of attending church, as far as

Heather was concerned. But Heather's voice was nothing that even her own father would ever have bragged about. She could carry a tune, and that was about all. She could have throttled Jared when Caldwell insisted that she sing for them directly after supper.

"Do you accompany yourself on the piano as well?" Caldwell wanted to know. "Our piano is in tune. I'm going to enjoy this."

Heather confessed that she didn't play the piano. Once again, both Brice and Minna looked shocked.

"No matter." Caldwell's voice was hearty. "Minna will accompany you. She plays very well. She ought to, the money our parents spent giving her lessons! If we've all finished here, shall we adjourn to the parlor?"

They adjourned to the parlor, where Minna seated herself on the piano stool, fingering through pages of sheet music. "Here, let's do this one," Minna said. "It's one of Caldwell's favorites."

The piece Minna had chosen was "Juanita." Heather almost moaned. "Juanita" called for a pure, sweet soprano which she didn't possess. But there was no getting out of it; she had to sing.

She did the best she could, but her performance left much to be desired. Brice's face was carefully polite, and Caldwell had all he could do not to look pained. Jared, drat him, looked as though he was having to smother his laughter.

"I'm afraid 'Juanita' wasn't in your key," Minna said tactfully. "We'll try a hymn, shall we?"

Heather did better with "Rock of Ages." "Oh, Come All Ye Faithful" was almost adequate, and "The Old Rugged Cross" sounded almost good. Then Heather called a halt. She didn't want to push her luck. As it was, she was sure the Arlingtons thought that only a doting brother could call her voice anything to be remarked on.

"That was very nice, very nice indeed," Caldwell said. But then Caldwell was a Southern gentleman; he could hardly have said anything else. Brice evaded having to utter an outright untruth by merely nodding.

Casting a venomous glance at Jared, Heather escaped to her room. She was sitting cross-legged in the middle of the tester bed, in her nightgown and with her hair in two plaits hanging over her shoulders, scribbling like mad in her copybook, when Minna tapped at her door and opened it a crack before waiting to be invited to come in. Unfortunately, the crack was wide enough so that she could see what Heather was doing.

"Are you keeping a daily journal, dear? All young people should keep a journal. It's a great comfort to read back over your life when you get to be my age. I always used to keep one, until I got too old for anything exciting to happen to me."

Heather's face flamed. "It isn't a journal. I'm just sort of scribbling for my own amusement." At Minna's inquiring glance she bumbled on. "Well, that isn't exactly true. I'm actually writing a novel. Only don't give me away, Miss Minna! Jared would laugh at me, and Brice and Mr. Arlington would probably be shocked."

Minna was delighted. "A novel! But that's wonderful! I promise that I won't breathe a word of it. You're right, Caldwell and Brice would be as shocked as they would be if they ever tasted my special lemonade. Is it a nice, exciting, romantic novel? May I see it?"

There was nothing to do but give her the copybook. Minna turned it back to the first page and began to read.

"Oh, this is good! I like it! I've always thought that I'd like to become a lady novelist, only I can't put two words together on paper and have them make sense. More's the pity, because I have so many plots, wonderfully exciting plots, right at the tip of my fingers. You can't imagine what a gold mine of stories this county has, Emma, and all of them true. And I know them all, love affairs and scandals and tragedies and all, from the war right up to the present. I could give you a dozen plots without even trying!"

Heather was all ears. The way Minna had run on about this family and that, this person and that, she didn't doubt for a moment that the older woman could have written dozens of books if she'd had the knack for it.

"I've never tried to write a novel before," Heather confessed. "I haven't the faintest idea if I'll ever be able to sell it. Selling a novel is probably a lot harder than writing one."

"Why, that's no problem at all! I happen to know a book publisher quite well. Dear Miles, we were engaged to be married when I was a young lady. And we would have been married, except that his teeth clicked when he ate, so I jilted him. But the thing is, my dear, that I didn't want to hurt him because he really was a dear man, and so I arranged it so that he thought he jilted me, and he still feels guilty about it after all these years. I never have to spend a penny to buy a book. He sends me all the books he publishes. I get them in the post regularly. He even sends me books from other publishers if there's something he thinks I would particularly like. One word from me and your book will be as good as published!"

Heather was so excited that she felt as though she were suffocating. Her cheeks flamed, and her eyes were shining. "Miss Minna, would you really ask him to publish my book?"

"Of course I will! I can tell right now that this book is better than a lot of books he publishes. I'll be doing him a favor, not the other way around! He'll buy not only this book but every other book you write, and you're going to write a lot of them, because with me to give you all those plots I know, the ideas will never run out. My goodness, I'm going to have to start a journal again! Just think, my plots are going to be printed in black and white! It'll be almost as good as if I wrote them myself!"

"We'll split the money right down the middle, half for you and half for me!" Heather was bouncing up and down, making the bed shake. "We'll be partners!"

"Oh, no, my dear! How would I ever explain it to Caldwell? He'd never allow it. It will have to be our secret. You keep the money. Just seeing my plots in print will be compensation enough for me."

Heather protested, but Minna was firm. And then they were both laughing and hugging each other.

"Partners in crime," Minna said, wiping away tears of mirth. "That's what we'll be, partners in crime, because our menfolk would certainly think what we're doing is a crime!"

Heather didn't doubt for a moment that Brice and Caldwell would think it was a crime. But she had a sneaking suspicion that Jared would think it was funny and egg her on. Jared had a sense of fun and adventure that these Southern gentlemen completely lacked, and he'd be the first to congratulate her when her first book hit print. He probably wouldn't even be shocked by the contents. But she hoped, fervently, that neither Brice nor Caldwell ever came into possession of a copy, or Emma Cranston's reputation would be in shreds.

Minna put her finger to her lips. "Shh! We don't want anyone to hear us carrying on like this, or they'll want to know what's going on. I'd better get to bed, but I know I won't sleep a wink. Just think, we're going to go to the fair, and I'm going to help you write books! Yes, I'm definitely going to start another journal. Exciting things are beginning to happen to me again at last!"

❦ Chapter 5 ❧

HEATHER'S EYES WEREN'T shining any more brightly than
Minna's as the two women took in the sights and sounds
and odors of the country fair. There hadn't been many fairs
in Heather's life. When she was a little girl her father had
taken her to two or three, but after he died her mother had
had so little money and so little time to spare from the
dressmaking that had helped to eke out their livelihood that
fairs had become a thing of the past.

"This is a strictly local affair. I'm afraid you won't find it
as large or as interesting as other fairs you've seen," Brice
told her.

"I think it's just wonderful," Heather answered. She held
to the firm conviction that if you didn't enjoy being where
you were and what you were doing, then it was your own
fault if you didn't have a good time. She even enjoyed being
a hired girl. She'd had to remove herself as an obstacle to
her mother's remarriage, but she had found plenty of things
in the Cranston household to enjoy. It didn't matter where
you were, life was what you could get out of it.

Minna looked at the two young men, and her voice
brooked no argument. "You two run along, I know you're
itching to get to the livestock. Emma and I can look after
ourselves. We'll meet in two hours"—she glanced at the
watch pinned to her bodice—"by the baked goods display.

67

Go on. Men and women never have been interested in the same things, so let's all enjoy ourselves without having to be bored."

Brice hesitated, his natural inclinations doing battle with his duty as a gentleman. "If you're sure you'll be all right . . ."

"Oh, pooh! What could happen to us? Scat! Come along, Emma, the handicraft display is this way." With her hand on Heather's arm, she urged her along as though looking at crocheted shawls and patchwork quilts were the uppermost thought in her mind.

But Minna stopped short of the crocheted shawls and patchwork quilts, and her eyes were sparkling with mischief as she looked back to make sure the men were out of sight.

"Good. Now we can do as we please. And what I please to do is try my hand at the games of chance and skill. That's why I had to get rid of Brice. As dear as he is, he wouldn't approve at all."

"Your nephew doesn't seem to approve of much of anything," Heather couldn't stop herself from saying. "Doesn't he believe in having fun?"

Minna's dimples deepened. "Most children pray 'Now I lay me down to sleep, I pray the Lord my soul to keep.' But I swear that Brice must have had his own version of that prayer ever since he was six years old. It was 'Now I get me up to work, I pray the Lord I will not shirk.' But he's a wonderful young man for all his seriousness. He's kind and gentle, and I've never seen him lose his temper. He's patient and considerate. He has so many good qualities that any girl would be fortunate to win his heart."

Minna looked at Heather anxiously, trying to erase any impression she might have given that Brice was less than perfect because he took life so seriously. She seemed to be as anxious as her brother Caldwell for Heather and Brice to fall in love and make a match of it. Heather was already so fond of Minna that she was sorry that her wish had no possibility of coming true. It galled her more every day that she was here under false pretenses, that she and Jared were taking advantage of these wonderful people for strictly self-seeking motives.

68

She decided that a change of subject would be wise. "I've never gambled, but it sounds like heaps of fun." She'd brought almost every penny of her savings with her to Virginia, because you never knew when you might need money. It wouldn't hurt to risk just a little of it. She was sure that Jared hadn't been improvident enough to come to Virginia without their return fare in his pocket.

"Oh, it is! It's just heaps and heaps of fun! And this time, by gum, I'm going to win something. I've never won anything yet, but then I've never had more than a minute or two to try when Brice wasn't looking. But this time we have two whole hours, and that should be plenty of time. There, I'm going to toss a penny into that saucer. If it doesn't bounce out, I'll win a prize."

Heather's expression was dubious as she looked at the display of prizes. "But what on earth do you want?" The cheap, tawdry pieces of statuary, the pressed glass of an unlikely lurid pink, were nothing that her own heart was set on owning.

"It doesn't matter a fig. I don't care what I win just so I win!" Minna took careful aim and tossed her coin. It bounced out of the saucer. She tried again, and the second penny also bounced out.

"You try," Minna urged.

Heather tried, but with no better luck. She tried again, with the same result. Anyone would think that the saucer was made of rubber so that any coin that hit it would bounce.

"Bother! Let's try tossing hoops over bottles," Minna said. She pulled Heather along with her with all the determination of a bloodhound on the scent of its quarry.

Of the three hoops Minna had paid for, the first glanced off the bottle, the second was wide of the mark entirely, and the third hovered, frustratingly, just on the lip before it fell the wrong way.

"You try now, Emma. Your aim is probably better than mine. Wouldn't you love to have that beaded pincushion? Pincushions are always useful."

Heather looked at the beaded pincushion and shuddered. All the same, she gave it her best try. All three of her hoops tottered at the lip of the bottle before they fell the wrong way. She was rapidly forming the opinion that gambling wasn't so much evil as it was sheer stupidity. You might just as well donate your money to the man running the booth and save time.

"Over here!" Minna cried, her voice filled with enthusiasm. "Here's something we ought to be able to do. A child could throw the ball at that pyramid of bottles and knock them down, I declare!"

Maybe a child could do it, but a grown man who was trying to do it at that very moment failed dismally. The ball struck squarely at the base of the pyramid, and the bottles teetered and leaned, but then they righted themselves, and only the topmost one toppled.

Not to be intimidated by a strong man's failure, Minna wound up her pitching arm and let fly. Once again, the top bottle went over, but that didn't qualify for a prize.

"It's your turn," she told Heather. "Wallop those bottles good!"

Ball in hand, Heather prepared to throw, but she was distracted when a feminine voice called out, "Why, Miss Minna! It's good to see you. I didn't know that you intended to come to the fair!"

The girl was about twenty, with brown hair simply arranged under a modest hat. Her face was plain, but her smile and her eyes were so warm that Heather took an instant liking to her. The girl held out both of her hands to Minna, grasping the older woman's firmly. "I haven't seen you for the longest time! Carl, it's Miss Minna Arlington. You remember her, of course, you've seen her in church."

"Of course I remember her. How could I forget such a charming lady?" The girl's escort was older, near thirty, and his dark eyes and fashionably trimmed hair made him an attractive-looking man, even though he wasn't as handsome as Brice or even Jared.

Minna remembered the social amenities. "Miss Roundtree, this is Miss Emma Cranston. She and her brother are visiting us at Arbordale. Emma, this is Phoebe Roundtree, and the gentleman is Mr. Carl Amhurst. Emma and her brother are from Albany, New York."

"Of course," Phoebe said. "Mr. Arlington spoke of his Albany friends so often that I feel I already know you! He and your father attended Harvard together, I believe. I'm so glad you could come for a visit. I know that Miss Minna must be enjoying your company tremendously."

Minna saw an opportunity that she had no intention of letting pass. "Mr. Amhurst, would you throw a ball? I just want to see if it's possible to knock that pyramid down. Emma, give him your ball. You can try later."

Carl Amhurst was the picture of confidence as his well-muscled arm took perfect aim, and the ball catapulted to its target. The bottles wavered, but only two of them fell.

"There! That proves that they can't be knocked down. Brice must be right, the game is rigged somehow."

"No, ma'am!" The man running the game was indignant. "You have to hit them just right, that's all. To prove that I'm honest, I'll give the little lady a free ball."

Phoebe's eyes laughed. "No, not for me! Give it to Miss Cranston. She relinquished hers for the test. Miss Minna, Miss Cranston, I hope that I'll see you again real soon."

"Phoebe is a lovely girl," Minna told Heather as the two walked away. "And she and Mr. Amhurst make a nice-looking couple. I wasn't sure that it would work out at first, after . . ." Minna broke off, and her lips clamped shut on whatever it was that she was going to say. "Phoebe is our minister's daughter, and Mr. Amhurst works at the bank."

Heather was intrigued. There was more to the story of Phoebe Roundtree and Carl Amhurst than Miss Minna was telling, but a look at Minna's face told her that this was one piece of gossip Minna wasn't going to share with her.

All the same, it was nice to have met some of Minna's friends at last. She'd been beginning to think that the Arlingtons didn't have any friends, and that was just plain silly. In all likelihood, she and Jared would be meeting a lot more of their friends within the next few days, if Jared didn't talk Caldwell into advancing him the money, after which they would leave.

As precarious as their situation was here in Virginia, she almost wished that Caldwell would take a good long time about deciding to let Jared have the money, so that she and

Jared could stay on to enjoy all those parties and balls that
Jared had promised. And there were still all the notes she
had to take on all of those plots Minna had promised her.

She sighted at the pyramid of bottles and drew back her
arm to throw with all her might. But there was another
interruption just as she was on the verge of throwing the
ball. The man behind the counter was beginning to look
pained.

This was an older woman, well into middle age, at least as
old as Minna. She was short and plump and jolly-looking
and pretty, and her face was beaming.

"Minna! I never dreamed that I'd see you here! You're
certainly looking well. I hope you're feeling as well as you
look."

"I feel just fine, Rosie. I've never felt better in my life."
Minna kissed Rosie's cheek, her own face flushed with
pleasure. Once again introductions were made. The plump
lady was Miss Rosamund Becker, and she and Minna had
been friends all their lives.

Heather's heart was warmed. Things were getting better
and better.

And then everything was spoiled when still another
woman appeared beside Rosie. This lady was a good deal
taller and a good deal leaner, and she had never been pretty
at all, even when she was young, and her bony face held no
hint of friendship.

Isobel Becker was Rosamund Becker's sister, and anyone
could see that she was used to holding the whip hand.

"How do you do, Miss Cranston." The greeting was
scarcely civil, and Miss Isobel ignored Minna entirely.
"Come along, Rosamund. At once!"

Willy-nilly, clearly reluctant and casting a look of apology
that was almost tearful at Minna, Rosie was hurried off.
Well, if that wasn't just the oddest thing! Miss Rosie was a
sweet lady, but Miss Isobel looked as if she'd just eaten a
persimmon. Or as if both Heather and Minna had leprosy,
so she wanted to put the greatest possible distance between
them in the shortest possible time.

She looked at Minna, waiting for some kind of explanation, but Minna's face had gone tight, and she said, "Let's go and see the sideshows, Emma. I've always wanted to see a snake charmer. I wonder if the snake is very large?" She nattered on, clearly trying to distract Heather's attention from the strange exchange that had just taken place.

Exasperated because she could find no sensible reason for such strange behavior on Miss Isobel Becker's part, Heather got rid of the ball she was holding by hurling it in the general direction of the pyramid of bottles, not even looking where she was aiming. There was a crash, and she jumped, and Minna's face flushed again, this time with excitement.

"You won! You did it! You knocked over all the bottles! You're going to get a prize!"

Heather couldn't have cared less about the prize, but the proprietor of the booth was looking at her with such an expression of mingled surprise and chagrin on his face that it gave her pleasure to relieve him of one. She'd still be willing to bet that his game was rigged, so it served him right to be done out of a little bit of his ill-gotten gains.

"What would you like, Miss Minna?"

"But it's your prize, you must choose!" Minna acted as though Heather had her choice between diamonds and pearls.

"I'll take that." Heather pointed at a paperweight with an unlikely-looking flower embedded in the glass. It seemed to be the lesser of several possible evils. She accepted the bauble and pressed it into Minna's hands. "But you must have it. I'm sure that you have a great deal more use for it than I do. If you haven't, give it to Brice. Gentlemen always have a lot of paperwork." It would serve Brice right to have to display the dreadful thing on his desk where Minna could see it every time she entered the office he and Caldwell shared.

"Oh, my! I wouldn't dare do that. He'd know I've been gambling."

"But you didn't win it, I did. He can't tell me not to gamble, can he? I'm not his aunt!"

Minna laughed delightedly. "No, he can't, can he? But he shan't have it, all the same. It's going to go right on my bureau, and he can't tell me I can't keep it, because it's a gift from you. Hurry, Emma! I want to see the snake charmer right now, before something happens to stop me."

The lady snake charmer wasn't as young as she might have been, or as pretty, and the snake wasn't as big as it might have been, and it was lethargic. But Minna was entranced. To Minna the snake charmer was young and beautiful, and she risked her life at every performance by letting a huge and venomous snake coil itself around her. Minna had finally gotten what she had always wanted; she'd gotten to see a snake charmer.

Heather wanted to ask Minna about Miss Rosie and Miss Isobel, but something told her that she had better not. It was certain that, although Miss Rosie liked Minna a great deal, Miss Isobel wanted nothing to do with her. It would be cruel to break Minna's spell, and so they went on to marvel over a tattooed man and a woman who had a genuine beard, or so the posters claimed.

Bah! Heather thought. If the beard was real, why didn't the woman simply shave it off and go about living a normal life? Heather tried to decide what she would do in the circumstances. At least she would have a choice, even if she might not choose to join a sideshow as the bearded woman had. Life was filled with choices, and that was a good thing, because if someone couldn't choose for herself, then she wouldn't be able to call her life her own.

Her own choice, to come to Virginia under false pretenses, had been a wicked one. There wasn't a particle of doubt about that. All the same, she wasn't sorry that she had made it. Jared had to have his chance to recoup his fortunes; she couldn't have borne to see him poor and wanting for anything, much less having to find work with some other family and never get to see him again. Even if nothing could ever come of it, it was better to be able to see him than it would be not to see him. She'd do her best to make up for the wickedness later.

There was all the time in the world to be good. What was hard was to wrest some fun and excitement from life before you were too old to enjoy it, and her choice would always be to have the fun and excitement and all the pleasure she could when they presented themselves for the snatching. If her days of being near Jared were doomed to be numbered, then at least she would savor every one of them that she still had.

And then Heather grinned, because a closer examination of the bearded lady gave her a very good idea that the lady wasn't a lady at all. Her hands were much too large to be a lady's hands, and her bosom, as much of it as could be seen beneath the concealing beard, had a definite look of being lopsided, as if one side had slipped.

"The poor, unfortunate lady!" Minna sympathized. "My heart goes out to her!"

"Yes, so does mine. But look, she's smiling at the tattooed man. Maybe they're having a romance, maybe they're in love, maybe they're even married!"

Minna brightened immediately. "I do believe you're right! They most definitely have the appearance of being in love! I feel much better about her now, Emma. What shall we do next? We still have an hour before we have to meet Brice and Jared. I wish we had the whole afternoon."

"Let's do everything that Brice would disapprove of the most!" Heather said wickedly. "We'll see Lady Egypt, and we'll gamble some more. There's a booth where you throw darts at balloons to try to break them. I'm sure we could do that. It looks as easy as pie."

The balloons proved impossible to break. The darts were dull, and the balloons themselves were only blown up partway, but they still had fun trying.

Lady Egypt was fat, her costume was tawdry, and she jiggled when she went through the sensuous motions of her dance. Heather giggled again. Jiggle and giggle, she thought, and that made her giggle harder than ever. She and Minna were definitely having more fun than they would have if Brice's stern eye had been on them. If Brice's stern eye had been on them, they wouldn't have got to see Lady Egypt at all, and they certainly wouldn't have got to gamble.

But three times during their wanderings Minna changed course abruptly, and Heather was sure that she was avoiding someone she knew. Now that Heather was watching carefully, she would have sworn that at least a few people changed their paths in order to avoid them.

If she didn't get some answers to such odd behavior soon, she was going to burst from curiosity. She couldn't ask Minna what was going on, but Jared was clever. He'd find out for her if she told him that she absolutely, positively had to know.

In the meantime, she hoped that nothing would happen to spoil Minna's enjoyment of this outing, an enjoyment that reached almost to the point of delirium when the man with the hanging scale failed to guess her weight by a full six pounds. Minna was awarded an ugly milk-glass vase, which she carried as carefully as though it were Ming. Heather received no prize; the man hit her own weight right on the nose, one hundred twelve pounds. If the scale was right, she wouldn't have to curb her appetite for some time to come. She had a suspicion that the man had misjudged Minna's weight on purpose, because no one had been waiting to be weighed. But after Minna had won, several people gathered around to try their luck. The carnival people had to let someone win once in a while, or nobody would play their games.

Thinking of eating made her hungry, and they drank pink lemonade and ate saltwater taffy and roasted peanuts. Heather would still be able to do justice to Elspeth's packed lunch even if Minna wouldn't. They were having so much fun that it didn't seem like any time at all before it was time to meet Brice and Jared.

Brice's eyebrows shot up the moment he spotted them. "Aunt Minna, you've been gambling!"

"No such thing! They were games of skill, and we were skillful. That is, Emma was skillful. She won the paperweight. I merely believed that the man wouldn't be able to guess my weight. I've always weighed less than people think I do; I have light bones."

Jared laughed, tickled by Minna's logic. "Miss Minna, you missed your calling. You would have made a top-notch lawyer!"

"Now I know why you were so anxious to get rid of us,"

Brice accused Minna. "Miss Cranston, you shouldn't have aided and abetted her. I'd be willing to guess that you didn't even go near the handicraft display!"

"I've seen enough handicraft displays to last me the rest of my life," Minna told him. "Gambling and seeing the sideshows were a lot more fun." She clapped her hand over her mouth, her face going pink.

Brice's eyebrows shot up even farther than they had before. "Sideshows?"

"The snake charmer and the bearded lady and Little Egypt," Minna confessed.

To Heather's surprise, Brice laughed. "Aunt Minna, you're incorrigible! And you are just as bad, Emma, to go along with her. I hope you haven't stuffed yourself with questionable food, as well."

"It wasn't questionable at all. Pink lemonade and salt-water taffy and roasted peanuts. There's no question about what they are."

Minna wasn't nearly as in awe of her nephew as she let on, Heather realized. All she needed was a little encouragement to stand up to him.

All in all, it had been an enjoyable day. The only flaw was the odd behavior of some of the people who had gone out of their way to avoid them. The mystery nagged at Heather all the way home. She wasn't imagining it; she knew that those people had avoided them. And then there was Miss Isobel Becker, who had literally dragged Miss Rosamund Becker away.

On the other hand, Phoebe Roundtree and Carl Amhurst had been more than friendly, obviously delighted to see Minna, just as Miss Rosie had been. The more Heather thought about it, the odder it seemed.

It bothered her so much that she almost, but not quite, lost her appetite for supper. She knew how much it bothered her when she didn't mind that in playing her role of Emma she couldn't ask for second helpings of everything.

⚘ *Chapter 6* ⚘

ANGEL WAS A dappled gray roan, and she was every bit as tractable as Brice had told Heather she would be. It wasn't because the mare was old either. Saul told her that she was only seven, and that wasn't at all old for a horse. And she didn't look like a plowhorse or a carthorse. She was a beautiful animal, sleek and shining. She held her head high, and her trot was beautiful.

"You don't have to be afraid. Angel here's as gentle as a lamb," Saul assured her as he let her take the ribbons. "The only trouble with her is that you can't get any speed out of her at all. This is as fast as she will go, but that suits Miss Minna just fine."

"I didn't know Miss Minna drove," Heather said, surprised.

"Oh, yes, ma'am, Miss Minna drives, and she always takes Angel. Mr. Brice bought Angel especially for her."

But Minna hadn't given any indication that she drove, nor had she suggested driving Heather anyplace, even if just to go in to Bennington to see the sights. She'd even declined to come along while Heather had her lesson, claiming that she had other things to do.

But it was too nice a day to puzzle over something that wasn't solvable. Angel trotted along like an angel, not fast enough to raise any dust. Fluffy white clouds drifted in a sky-blue sky, and there was just enough breeze to alleviate the worst of the heat.

"Saul, does anyone ever picnic over there?" Heather asked, pointing to a patch of woods. "It looks like a beautiful spot, just perfect for a picnic." Heather gazed at the grove directly across a field where a few cows were grazing.

Saul's voice, usually so calm, registered horror. "Oh, no, ma'am! There don't nobody go to that place, not never. It's haunted."

The ribbons went slack in Heather's hands as she stared at Saul, but Angel paid no heed and just continued with her slow, steady trot. "Surely you're joking! There isn't any such thing as a ghost, everybody knows that."

"Maybe up where you come from everybody knows that, but here in Virginia everybody knows that there is ghosts and that that patch of woods is haunted and has been ever since the war."

Still ignoring her task of driving Angel, who still ignored the lack of guidance, Heather kept after Saul.

"Have you ever seen the ghost? And who is he?"

"Ain't a he, it's a she," Saul told her. He was nervous; perspiration beaded his forehead and rolled down his wrinkled cheeks. "And I ain't never seen her, but she's there all the same. Other folks have seen her, lots of times. Miss Gloria Nelson she was. Is, because she's still around, cryin' and sobbin' and lookin' for her lost sweetheart, right in those trees."

Heather's eyes were shining. This was a real story, something that Minna, for some unknown reason, hadn't mentioned when she'd told her all of those other stories. She couldn't imagine why Minna had omitted this one.

"Go on! Don't leave me hanging, tell me all about it," she commanded.

"Everybody hereabouts knows the story. What with Miss Gloria's ghost and all, ain't nobody had a chance to forget it," Saul told her. "It was back during the war, like I told you. Miss Gloria was a cousin of the Arlingtons, and the

Overtons was neighbors. They lived in the first plantation beyond Arbordale.

"When the war broke out, Robbie Overton lit out and went up North and joined the Union Army. That didn't set well with the Nelsons and the Arlingtons, but Miss Gloria went right on loving him. He'd never believed it was right to keep slaves, Robbie hadn't, that's why he went and became what everybody else around here called a traitor."

Heather pulled Angel to a stop. Angel was perfectly willing. Heather wanted to give her full attention to Saul, and she sat with her hands clasped tightly in her lap, not even holding on to the ribbons. It was all right, Angel wasn't going anywhere.

"Well, there was a skirmish not far from here, and Robbie got hisself wounded. The Union boys was licked and took off as fast as they could go, but Robbie was hurt real bad, and he dropped out so's not to hold them back, an' he made his way home. Miss Gloria had a row with her folks because she went to see him, but they didn't turn him in to the Confederates because the families had been friends for so long. They just didn't want Miss Gloria to go marryin' a traitor, that was all.

"But somebody told the Confederates where Robbie was, they never did find out who, and a patrol came a-lookin' for him. Somebody else came lickety-split to warn him that the patrol was on its way. Miss Gloria was there, and she got him on a horse and took him to those woods to hide him while his folks stayed put to try to convince the patrol that Robbie wasn't nowhere around.

"Miss Gloria and Robbie went right to the middle of the woods, but the Confederates found 'em anyway, and they told Robbie to surrender, only Robbie wouldn't. He had his pistol with him, an' he shot at 'em, and they shot back, and a bullet caught him right between the eyes.

"The patrol took Miss Gloria home. It was like she was dead too, as dead as Robbie. She didn't say nothin', and she didn't eat nothin', she just stared straight in front of her. The doctor said it was shock. The state she was in, nobody ever thought she'd git out of her bed in the middle of the night and take her daddy's pistol and go back to the woods, but that's what she did. Went back there, and shot herself right where Robbie'd been shot. An' she's been hauntin' the place ever since, all these years, like I told you."

"Poor Gloria," Heather said, feeling tears sting against her eyelids. "But there aren't any ghosts, Saul. People probably saw things that were perfectly natural. It would have been at night, so they couldn't make out what it was, and they thought it was Gloria's ghost, and that's how the story got started, and like all such stories it kept building up until people began to believe it, and then more people thought they saw something because they expected to see something. Only they didn't see anything at all, only a shadow or an animal."

"No, Miss Emma. It wasn't no shadow, and it wasn't no animal. They heered her as well as seen her, cryin' Robbie's name." Saul's face was set in stubborn lines. Nobody was going to talk him out of believing in Gloria's ghost.

"It was just the wind they heard, or an owl." Heather tried to convince him.

Sam, Saul's old hound, had been resting his head on Heather's lap, but now he raised it and whined. When they'd got into the buggy, Sam had jumped in too. Saul had ordered him out, but Heather had said that he could go with them. She liked dogs, and she especially liked Sam. She hadn't had a dog since her spaniel died when she was seven. Heather had cried herself sick and refused to let her father replace him. When she'd been old enough to have accepted another dog, her father had died. The Cranstons had never kept a dog because Thatcher's wife claimed they were dirty. Now Heather was ready to love another dog, and Sam was it.

"Sam knows! He wants us to get away from this place," Saul said. Without apology, he took the ribbons and set Angel in motion. Angel was perfectly willing. She didn't mind moving, as long as she wasn't asked to move fast. "Dogs know things, everybody knows that, and Sam don't like those woods at all, nohow!"

As Sam never got more than a few feet away from Saul,

Heather wondered how Saul knew that Sam didn't like the woods. All the same, if it hadn't been a bright summer day, she could almost have believed Saul's story, especially after Sam had whined the way he had, looking in the direction of the woods. As it was, she felt a little chill along her spine, even though she laughed at herself. One thing was certain. Her interest was aroused, and the moment she got back to Arbordale she confronted Minna.

"Miss Minna, did you know that the patch of woods at the far north edge of Arbordale is supposed to be haunted?"

Minna dropped her tatting shuttle. "Oh, dear, Saul has been talking! Of course I know that those woods are haunted." She sounded so matter-of-fact, as if ghosts were an everyday occurence, that Heather stared at her, flabbergasted.

"But then why didn't you tell me about it? This is the most exciting story of all!"

"But you couldn't use it, dear. It wouldn't have a happy ending, and books have to have happy endings. Besides, the story is too well known. No matter how much you changed it around, people would know that it was about Gloria Nelson, and not only the Nelsons, but their friends, wouldn't take it kindly to see the story in print. Even Caldwell would be upset, because the Nelsons are connections of ours even if they've left Virginia. They moved to Georgia after the war because of all the disgrace of Gloria loving a Union soldier and killing herself."

"But all that was ages and ages ago! It couldn't matter a fig now, that Gloria loved a Union boy. Everyone would be just dreadfully sorry for Gloria. Besides, I could make it so that Gloria didn't die. She could be saved and get well and fall in love with someone else and live happily ever after."

"People would recognize the story anyway. And in Virginia it still matters a great deal," Minna said firmly. She picked up the tatting shuttle, and once again her fingers flew. "In Virginia, the war was only yesterday." The ribbon of tatting grew. The attic at Arbordale must be stuffed to the rafters with tatting!

"And then, of course, I didn't want to frighten you,"

Minna went on. "The woods are quite close, and you might not have wanted to stay if you'd thought there were ghosts wandering around in the night."

"Oh, Miss Minna, I don't believe in ghosts! My father told me when I was just a little girl that there aren't any such things." It was on the tip of her tongue to add that her father had been a minister, and so he would have known if anyone did, but she caught herself in time. Thatcher had been just about the farthest thing from a parson as anyone could imagine.

The look on Minna's face gave her a start. Why, Minna more than half believed those stories herself, it was written all over her! To make sure, Heather put forth a suggestion.

"It's such a beautiful spot, why don't we go there for a picnic? Couldn't we arrange to go tomorrow?"

"Indeed not! Maybe there aren't any ghosts there, but those woods are filled with mosquitoes, and there may be snakes. If you want a picnic, there are any number of nicer spots."

"All the same, I think we should go there. Wouldn't that help to lay the stories of ghosts to rest?"

"Of course it wouldn't! We'd be going in the daytime, and the ghost is only seen at night. Nothing is going to stop people from thinking that the place is haunted, so there's no earthly reason for us to make ourselves uncomfortable. There's probably poison oak or poison ivy there, as well as mosquitoes." The firm set of Minna's mouth told Heather that the subject was closed.

Heather was disappointed, but she had other, more pressing matters on her mind. Jared hadn't got anywhere at all in trying to talk Caldwell into investing in the automobile manufacturing business. And they couldn't stay here at Arbordale indefinitely, no matter how welcome they were. If Jared wasn't going to get the backing he wanted, he would have to get back to Albany and start looking for some other means of making a living.

More than that, every day they stayed at Arbordale the danger of having their masquerade discovered became more acute. She was bound to make a slip of the tongue sooner or later; pretending that you were someone you weren't was a lot harder than she had thought it would be. And it wasn't impossible that Caldwell might get word that Thatcher had died and that Emma had gone off to Boston to learn how to be a missionary, and then the fat would be in the fire.

She hated the thought of leaving. Things were just getting interesting, and besides, she adored Miss Minna. She'd miss Angel, and Sam, and Saul, and she never would have a chance to see if she could crack that shell that Brice had wrapped around himself.

The prospect of having to find another family to work for wasn't appealing to her either. No other family would be as easy to work for. She might not be able to eat everything in sight, and even worse, she might be put in the same bedroom with another servant and not get to do any writing at all. She was certain that no other employer would put up with her writing a book, while Jared, if he were to find out, wouldn't care at all. He'd just laugh and tell her to go ahead if that was what made her happy.

As a matter of fact, she was beginning to think that neither she nor Jared was going to like what was in store for them, but there wasn't any use in complaining about it. They would just have to make the best of things. It would probably be easier for her than for Jared. She was used to making the best of things, but he wasn't. It was going to be an awful jolt for him to have to learn to live on next to nothing, and she wished she could be there to show him how.

But it hadn't happened yet, and there wasn't any use worrying about it ahead of time. She'd just go on enjoying herself at Arbordale for as long as she could stay.

After supper that evening she had her first moonlight stroll in a Southern rose garden, except that, unfortunately, there wasn't anything romantic about it, because her escort wasn't the handsome young planter but a Jared who was as near to being depressed as she had ever seen him.

"I've dangled the bait under Caldwell's nose until any other man would have snapped it up like a starving shark," Jared told her, his shoulders slumping. "Hang it all, the man simply isn't interested in automobiles! He's as shortsighted as most men with money. And in the meantime, somebody else is going to get ahead of us if we don't get started, because there are bound to be a few men in this country who know opportunity when they see it. The trouble is, I don't know who they are or how to find them."

He broke off, looking contrite. "Poor Heather! You've been disappointed too. I promised you all sorts of things if you'd only go along with me, parties and balls and romance, and so far this place has been as dull as a three-hour sermon. You've been cheated, and it's all my fault. I can't understand what's wrong with Brice! It's obvious that he hasn't any other romantic attachment. He should have fallen madly in love with you before this, you're certainly pretty enough. Any other man would be dancing attention on you, but he hardly seems to know you're alive!"

"It isn't your fault. I should have had better sense than to come." Heather wouldn't let him take all the blame on his own shoulders. All the same, she couldn't keep the wistfulness from her voice. Jared winced, and on impulse, not knowing that he was going to do it, he put his arms around her, drew her comfortingly close, and kissed her. It started out to be no more than that, a kiss to comfort her, but her lips were soft and warm under his, and the starlight was in her hair, and his arms tightened, drawing her even closer, and the kiss turned into one that wasn't in the least brotherly. A tremor went through his body as hers pressed against it.

Damnation, maybe Brice didn't appreciate this girl who was so soft and sweet and pretty and whose heart was as warm as her smile. She was as sweet as honey, and it was his fault that she was being cheated and hurt, and he wanted to go on holding her and kissing her. He wanted to take care of her and protect her and make sure that she was never hurt or disappointed again.

With a start of astonishment, he realized that if Brice had done what he'd been supposed to do and fallen in love with Heather, Jared would have wanted to call him out in one of those jealous duels that had been outmoded years ago. He'd be jealous of any other man who paid attention to her, and he must be the world's greatest fool not to have realized it a long time ago.

Heather was no longer the cute, curly-haired gamine who had come to work at his house three years ago. She'd grown up. She was a woman, and he wanted her. Only he couldn't have her, because without money or prospects he didn't have a thing to offer her. He must have been blind not to have seen beyond her trappings as a servant at least a year ago. He'd just been so used to her that he'd never really looked at her.

It had taken her transformation after Emma had given her all those pretty clothes to make him really see her, and that made him the world's number one fool. And now that he really saw her, now that he knew that he was in love with her, he'd have to watch her walk out of his life simply because of the lack of money. By the time he got on his feet, some other man would have snapped her up.

Cursing the fates that had brought him so low, Jared released her at last. She was staring at him with widened eyes, her lips still half parted, and it took every ounce of his willpower not to take her in his arms again.

"I'm sorry, Heather. I didn't mean to take advantage of you. Put it down to the setting. Roses and moonlight. I just got carried away for a minute."

Heather closed her mouth, and her teeth bit into her lower lip. For a moment there, she'd been as carried away as Jared had been. She'd had the wild, wonderful notion that her dreams were coming true, that, as impossible as it seemed, Jared loved her as much as she loved him. Her whole body flushed hot as she realized how she had seemed to melt right into his body, how she had longed for more and even more. She'd been a woman, a hot-blooded woman who wanted her man, who wanted to give herself without reserve, who wanted the fulfillment that only Jared could give her. All of the love scenes she'd ever read in her romantic novels hadn't prepared her for the reality of being held and kissed by the man she loved, the intensity of the emotions that had flooded over her until she was helpless to resist them.

Only Jared hadn't meant it, not any of it. He'd just been carried away by the setting! All he cared about was that stupid automobile and making more of them and getting rich so that he could marry some girl from his own social level, and then he'd never give her another thought.

Men! Furious, Heather wondered if she would even be able to finish her novel, with all the love scenes and faithfulness that never wavered. As far as she could see right now, it was all humbug, the fevered imaginings of frustrated old maids. Brice didn't notice her at all, and Jared had only kissed her because the setting was right and she happened to be the girl who was there. Any other girl would have done as well.

She wasn't going to be fooled again, that was for sure. If there wasn't a man in the world who was worth loving, then she would write her novels, even if she didn't believe a single word she wrote, and she would be a spinster lady with a dog and a cat who would at least love her for what she was. A dog and a cat wouldn't even care if she was never successful or if she was as homely as a mud fence.

Miss Minna had never married, and she didn't seem to be suffering from the lack. Heather wouldn't either. She'd be dratted if she would! She'd make some kind of a satisfactory life for herself even if she woke up some morning and there wasn't a man left in the world. But even as she thought all this, Heather knew that her life would never be complete without Jared.

"You're a good girl," Jared said, smiling at her with a crooked smile. "You should have slapped my face and screamed for help, and then Brice would have come to your rescue and challenged me to a duel for insulting you, and your trip to Virginia wouldn't have been a waste."

Heather burst into laughter. "I almost wish I had screamed and Brice had come rushing to my rescue! Can't you just picture the look on his face when he caught you making love to *your sister?*"

"Oh my God!" Jared said, and then his laughter joined hers. They were still laughing when they went back into the house. Brice looked at them strangely, Caldwell looked at them tolerantly, and Minna looked at them with curiosity.

"Whatever could have happened in our perfectly ordinary rose garden to make you laugh so hard?" Minna demanded.

"Jared will tell you," Heather said. And she escaped to her room, leaving him to have to come up with some story on the spur of the moment, and it served him right!

It was sheer boredom that prompted Heather to set out the next morning to drive into Bennington. Saul had assured her that she was capable of driving Angel alone, and she hadn't had a chance to explore the town.

She asked Minna to go with her, but as always Minna refused. There had to be some reason why Minna refused to budge from the plantation except for that one trip to the country fair, but no matter how much she puzzled over it she couldn't come up with an answer, any more than she could come up with an answer to why several people had snubbed Minna at the fair. In the excitement of learning how to drive and going to the fair, she'd forgotten to ask Jared to put his mind to it and try to find out the answers for her.

Never mind. She'd try to remember to ask Jared tonight, even if she was still furious with him about last night's episode in the rose garden. At least Sam loved her. The hound jumped into the buggy the moment Saul had Angel hitched up, giving her cheek a slobbering kiss before he settled down with his head hanging over the arm of the seat, panting with excitement to be going with her.

She took a long, hard look at the haunted woods as she drove past. Sam didn't give it as much as a glance, so went Saul's claim that Sam was afraid of the place. Her chin lifted with determination. She was going to explore those woods even if nobody else would go with her! She'd take Sam, and she'd walk all through them. There wouldn't be too many mosquitoes in the daytime, and if there were any snakes Sam would protect her. But not today. Today she was all dressed up in one of Emma's prettiest dresses, and she was going to town.

She was so immersed in her thoughts about the haunted

woods that the horse and rider were almost upon her before she was aware of them. Any horse but Angel would have shied or tried to bolt, the way the beautiful saddle horse came bearing down on them from the opposite direction, galloping like the wind, its hooves drumming on the dirt road and its mane flying.

Angel held her ground, not even deigning to move over and get out of the way. The rider pulled up, and the saddle horse reared, just seconds before there would have been a collision. Heather stared, her eyes wide and her mouth dropping open.

The rider of the magnificent horse was not a man but a young woman. Her hair was a glowing auburn, her eyes were as green and brilliant as emeralds, and she was altogether the most beautiful girl Heather had ever seen.

She controlled her mount with what seemed to be negligent attention, keeping her seat on the sidesaddle with no effort at all. Before all four of her mount's hooves were on the ground again, she was returning Heather's stare, as though she were taking inventory of every detail of Heather's appearance.

"Good morning," Heather said. "It's a lovely morning, isn't it? I'm Emma Cranston, from Albany. My brother and I are visiting at Arbordale."

"I recognized Angel." There wasn't a particle of warmth in the girl's voice, and her face was just as cold. Then, as though she were satisfied, she lifted the reins and touched her horse with her heel, and it was off again, its hooves pounding. She didn't look back, even though Heather turned in the buggy seat to stare after her until she was out of sight around a bend in the road.

Well, if that was an example of Southern friendliness, Heather could do without it. The girl should have introduced herself, she should have said that she hoped Heather was enjoying her visit, and she should have said that she would call on her at Arbordale or asked Heather to call on her.

Instead, she had looked at Heather with dislike and disdain. Her manners had been disgraceful. Heather might be a hired girl, but she had been brought up as a lady, and she would never treat anyone as shabbily as this girl had treated her.

She clucked and said "Giddup," and Angel resumed her slow, steady trot. There was a buggy whip in the socket, but Heather couldn't imagine anyone ever having to use it on Angel. She wouldn't have used it if Angel had refused to budge. She'd seen how the girl she had just encountered had hauled her horse around, with foam flying from its mouth and its eyes rolling, and that was another mark against her. Any person who wasn't kind to animals was a person Heather had no wish to know.

All the same, she was curious about the auburn-haired girl, and she cut her visit to Bennington short. There wasn't that much to see, in any case. What there was of it drowsed in the late morning sun, and the streets were almost deserted. One lady with a shopping basket on her arm came out of a store and looked at her in a startled manner. The lady hesitated as though she were undecided, and then, almost reluctantly, she nodded. Outside of the undecided lady and two old men sitting on a bench in the town square, engaged in a game of checkers, the town might as well have been deserted.

She went in search of Minna the moment she had turned Angel and Sam over to Saul. She scratched behind Sam's ears and gave Angel an extra pat, the memory of the auburn-haired girl's mistreatment of her horse still rankling.

"What a good girl you are, Angel! You're as good as gold, and I love you to pieces. And you're as good as gold too, Sam, but you can't come in the house with me. I'll take you with me again the next time I go out."

As always, Minna was in the parlor with a piece of tatting in her hands.

"Miss Minna, I met a young lady on the road. She has auburn hair and green eyes, and she's almost too beautiful to be true. She was riding a handsome chestnut with a white blaze on its forehead. I introduced myself, but she didn't return the compliment. Who is she, would you know?"

"Of course I know. It couldn't have been anyone but Evelyn Langdon."

Langdon! Of course, Evelyn must be the girl Brice was in love with. She'd thought all along that Brice was suffering from a broken heart, and now that she'd seen Evelyn Langdon she could understand why he didn't know any other girl was alive. It was a shame that men couldn't see beyond a pretty face. For Heather's money, Evelyn Langdon wasn't anywhere good enough for Brice. Any girl who would be so mean to her horse would be just as mean to her husband.

"Are you well acquainted with the Langdons?" She was digging for information, and she should have been ashamed of herself, but she wasn't.

Minna looked at her as though only a moron could have asked such a silly question. "We've been neighbors for generations," she said. Her voice was complacent, but there was a flicker of uneasiness in her eyes. Briskly, she rolled up her tatting and got to her feet. "I must see Elspeth in the kitchen house," she said.

Minna didn't need to see Elspeth in the kitchen house. She was simply making an excuse to get out of being questioned any further about the Langdons. It was obvious that there was a rift between the two families, and that made Heather all the more certain that Evelyn had jilted Brice, although why any girl in her right mind would jilt Brice was more than she could understand. If there had been any jilting to be done, Brice should have jilted Evelyn!

A little shamefaced, Heather took special care in her appearance before it was time to join the others on the verandah that afternoon. Brice would be comparing her to Evelyn, as he must have been doing all along. And now that she had seen Evelyn, she didn't want to be found too lacking. She knew that actually it didn't matter what Brice thought. But she hoped Jared would look at her twice.

She had to bite her tongue to keep from bringing up the subject of the Langdons, just to see what Brice's reaction would be. But that would be unkind. Whatever had happened between them was none of her affair. And it didn't escape her notice that Minna was uncommonly nervous when Caldwell asked her about her drive to Bennington. Heather didn't have to be hit over the head to know that Minna didn't want her to mention the auburn-haired girl.

"Tell me more about that gasoline contraption of yours, Jared," Minna said. The sly old fox! She knew that once Jared got on the subject of automobiles, nobody else would be able to get a word in edgewise. "Isn't it true that they go so fast that they're a danger to human life? I've heard that no one could breathe at such speeds."

Jared laughed. "Why, Miss Minna, horses run faster than automobiles can go, and trains go a whole lot faster. People are just afraid of anything new. I only wish that I had Martin's automobile right here at Arbordale so I could take you for a ride in it and show you how safe they are. Emma's ridden in one, and you can see that she had no ill effects at all."

"Emma, did you really? You actually rode in one of those contraptions?" Minna's eyes were wide. "I thought only gentlemen rode in them."

"It was the most fun I ever had in my life," Heather told her enthusiastically. It wouldn't hurt for her to help Jared sell the idea to Caldwell. She mustn't be spiteful just because he'd only kissed her in the rose garden because the setting was right and she was the girl who had happened to be there. She supposed that, being a man, he simply hadn't known any better. It would never have entered his mind that he was hurting her.

"And weren't you afraid, just a little?"

"Of course I wasn't! And you wouldn't be either. And you should have seen the excitement it caused! Boys were chasing after us, and dogs were barking, and men were shaking their fists at us. I wouldn't have missed it for the world!"

"And what if the contraption had caused a horse to bolt, and someone had been hurt?" Caldwell wanted to know. "Would the excitement have been worth it, Miss Emma?"

"But nothing like that happened."

"Just because it didn't happen that time doesn't mean that it won't happen in the future, unless this crazy fad runs its course and there aren't any more of the machines around to cause trouble." Caldwell was firm in his convictions. "I'm sure you'll admit that you're a great deal safer in a buggy, driving Angel."

Heather was forced to admit that, but she still put up an argument.

"It's lots of fun driving Angel, but you have to admit that it isn't very exciting!"

Jared looked dejected, and Minna looked perturbed because any kind of controversy upset her. Tactfully, she changed the subject.

"Emma, that dress is simply lovely! If I were you I'd wear it tomorrow night. Oh, I'm afraid I forgot to tell you! Guests are coming to dinner. The Barnstables and the Harpers. The Barnstables are middle-aged, but the Harpers are near enough your age so you're sure to enjoy their company."

Well, and well again! They were actually going to have company! Heather's eyes brightened. It would be a far cry from a real party, to say nothing of a ball, but it was a lot better than nothing at all.

"And I've sent out invitations for a ball," Minna went on. "Not a lavish affair, but there will be music and dancing. It's time you were meeting some of our friends and neighbors."

It certainly was, Heather thought, but she'd lay odds that the Langdons wouldn't be among the friends and neighbors she would be meeting. And then she forgot the Langdons as the fact that there was going to be an actual ball overtook her.

What a silly goose she'd been, imagining all sorts of mysteries just because there had been no entertaining at Arbordale since she and Jared had arrived and because one or two people had snubbed Minna at the fair. Other people had spoken or at least nodded. In any community there were families who had had differences and weren't friendly with each other. An imagined slight, an unintended slur, and there was a rift. It might even have been something that had happened two or three generations ago. Ancient history, and not speaking to each other was simply a habit that no one had bothered to break.

She sipped at her glass of Minna's lemonade, savoring it

to the last drop. There would be no more of this kind of lemonade after she got back to Albany and started working for some other family. There wouldn't be any dinner parties or balls either, except those where she'd be doing the serving.

She was going to make the most of this ball, because it might have to last her for a lifetime. She wasn't going to think about mysteries that didn't exist. She was going to dance and sparkle and pretend that she was a Southern belle. Even if she couldn't hold a candle to Evelyn Langdon, she couldn't help but look pretty in one of Emma's ball-gowns.

Brice would be obliged to dance with her, and if she couldn't make him notice that she was an attractive young woman, it wouldn't be because she didn't give it her best try! It would do him a world of good to realize that Evelyn wasn't the only girl in the world, to say nothing of the good it would do her own ego.

Nothing could come of it, of course, but that was all right. Brice would feel better, and she would feel better, and that was all that mattered. She would have a memory to cherish, and she would never regret that there had been no proposal of marriage in a starlit rose garden and no duel under the oaks at dawn.

But if she could entice Brice into the rose garden for just one kiss, it would be a whole lot better. Besides, it would serve Jared right. She would tell Brice that she held him in the highest regard but that it was far too soon to think of a romance between them. Then she would float back to the ballroom with as many stars in her eyes as there were in the sky and be the belle of the ball.

Being the belle of the ball shouldn't be very hard, seeing that Evelyn Langdon wouldn't be there!

∽ Chapter 7 ∽

THE BARNSTABLES WERE exactly the kind of people Heather had always imagined Southern aristocrats to be. Both had white hair and blue eyes, and Mr. Barnstable actually had one of those pointed little beards that Southern colonels are supposed to wear. But no one called him Colonel, and so she supposed he wasn't one.

Pauline Harper wasn't anywhere near as pretty as her husband was handsome, but anyone could see that Aaron Harper adored her. Both of them were intelligent and well read and had a lively sense of humor. They had been married for eight years and had three children, a boy and two girls, who were at home with their nursemaid so that Heather didn't have the chance to see them.

The table looked lovely. Minna knew how to do things right when it pleased her to do it. The damask was snowy white, the china was heirloom Limoges, and the silver and crystal gleamed with the polishing Pearl and Della had been set to do. The two girls had been so painstakingly instructed in how to serve that there was only one accident, when Della knocked over Pauline's wine glass while she was clearing before the dessert was brought in.

"Never mind, Della. Just cover it with my napkin and bring me another. Rub salt in the stain when you take the

95

cloth off, and then soak it in cold water, and it will come right out."

"Yes, ma'am." The frightened tears in Della's eyes disappeared. Pauline Harper was a real lady. Heather shuddered to think how Evelyn Langdon would have laced out a servant who had tipped over a glass of wine. Her warm feeling for Pauline was strengthened, and she decided that in her next novel she would make her heroine just like Pauline.

But as pleasant as the company was, it wasn't lost on Heather that several worry-laden glances passed among George Barnstable and Caldwell and Aaron Harper and Brice. The ladies kept up their inconsequential chatter and pretended not to notice, but Heather was convinced that there were things beneath the surface that weren't being said because of her and Jared's presence.

When, at eleven o'clock in the evening, Caldwell and Brice accompanied their guests outside to see them into their carriages, they remained outside talking for a long time. Jared didn't seem to notice. He'd gone into the subject of automobiles and how they were the coming thing extensively during the evening, and he was still wrapped up in his favorite subject with no thought for anything else.

"Jared, at the ball, don't you dare spend all your time talking about automobiles!" Heather warned him while she and Minna and Jared were waiting for Caldwell and Brice. "There are other subjects of conversation, you know."

"But they were interested," Jared protested. "Did I really monopolize the conversation all that much?" His surprise made him look like a little boy caught in a gaffe, both hurt and embarrassed. "Aaron certainly seemed to realize the value of something new, even if Caldwell has a closed mind."

"I'm sure that they didn't mind, dear," Minna told him, but her voice sounded absent, and she glanced at the mantel clock, listening for her menfolk to come back in. When they did, after a good fifteen minutes, both men looked serious and worried.

Heather was still turning the puzzle this way and that when sleep overtook her. This time she was positive that there was a mystery. It was frustrating not to know what was going on, and she was convinced that something was happening that the Arlingtons didn't want them to know about. Jared had followed her upstairs, but she'd lain awake long enough to know that Caldwell and Brice and Minna were still down in the parlor talking when she finally went to sleep.

In the morning she felt let down, as people often do after a party. Having had company last night only made the usual isolation at Arbordale seem all the more acute. She had never realized how boring it was to have absolutely nothing to do. Given her choice between living a life of idleness and being a hired girl, she would have chosen being a hired girl, hands down.

"Miss Minna, I believe I'll go out for a drive. Wouldn't you like to come with me this time?"

"My goodness, no! It's only two weeks until the ball. I have my hands full getting ready for it. You run along, dear."

Two weeks! Could she and Jared possibly go on getting away with their pretense for another two whole weeks? But they would have to stay now. Minna was so excited by the ball that to insist that they had to leave would be unthinkable.

"I thought we might go into Bennington. I drove through the other day, but I didn't stop."

"Gracious, there isn't a thing in Bennington, it's just a backwater. There isn't even a decent store, just Mr. Thaxter's Emporium."

"Then I'll visit the Emporium," Heather said. "Is there anything you want?"

"Some tatting thread," Minna told her. "I'm forever running short." And no wonder, Heather thought. Minna must use miles of tatting thread every year.

As always, Sam jumped into the buggy when Heather was ready to go. Saul grinned.

"That old dog purely likes you, Miss Emma. You sure you don't mind him going along?"

"Of course I don't mind! He's good company," Heather assured him.

Saul nodded. "One thing about dogs, they don't give you any arguments. And he's good protection, too. He don't look like much, but there ain't nobody going to get near you if you don't want 'em to."

Heather couldn't resist a little teasing. "Why, Saul, Sam's so gentle and friendly that if a burglar came prowling around, he'd lick his hand! Tell me the truth, has he ever bitten anyone?"

"Just because he hasn't doesn't mean that he wouldn't, if it was needful." Saul's conviction was firm. "With Angel between the shafts and Sam up there beside you, you're as safe as if you were tucked up in your bed."

Heather would have been glad to trade a little safety for a little excitement, but as there seemed to be no likelihood of any excitement in this serene countryside, she would just have to settle for the doubtful amusement of Bennington. At least she had the ball to look forward to. Maybe there would be a handsome gentleman of the proper age who would be smitten with her. Aaron Harper would have done if he hadn't already been taken. Heather had an overwhelming desire to flirt. She'd never had a chance to flirt in her life, and if she was going to play at being a Southern belle she had to flirt. Besides, it might make Brice sit up and take some notice of her. So far, he'd made her feel about as attractive as a boiled turnip, and her ego was suffering.

It wouldn't hurt Jared to see that some other man found her worthy of his attentions either. There was nothing she would like better than to have some other gentleman kiss her in the rose garden and make sure that Jared knew it.

In the meantime, she was going to enjoy her visit to Bennington. She would walk up and down the main street and look in all the shops. She would buy Minna her tatting thread, and for good measure she'd buy some peppermint drops, the hard ones that could be sucked on. The peppermint would mask the smell of the bourbon that Minna laced their lemonade with, and she wouldn't have to be so careful not to let Jared smell her breath. Brice never got close enough to her to smell her breath, but Jared might.

She would buy Saul some candy too, she decided, and some tobacco. She'd seen a corncob pipe sticking out of his pocket while he worked around the garden. She wanted to do something for him for being so nice and for teaching her how to drive and for letting her borrow Sam.

It was a lovely day, not much warmer than a summer day in Albany, and there was a breeze that kept it from being uncomfortable. Angel didn't cover the ground anywhere near as fast as Cicero would have, but her slow, steady pace would get them there. The more of the day she used up, the better. She'd look for something to take back to Mrs. Allenby, too, and she'd find something for herself to remember Virginia by.

The main street of Bennington was called Main Street. If it were Heather's job to name streets, she'd certainly think of something more interesting. She expected that men named all the streets. They named them Main Street because it was the main street, or Water Street because there was a bridge over a stream, or Railroad Street because that was where the depot was. Or else they named them after trees. They didn't have any imagination at all.

All the same, Bennington's Main Street was a nice street. Some of the establishments had awnings to provide shade for pedestrians, and there was a horse trough in front of the Emporium. That was another name that lacked imagination. Of course a store was an emporium! If it were her store she'd call it Shopper's Paradise or Merchandise Palace or something like that. But she was glad to see the horse trough. Angel might need a nice cool drink before they started back.

She stopped the buggy near the horse trough, and then she stood for a moment, hesitating. Should she let Angel have a drink now, or should she wait until they were going back? She wished she knew more about horses.

"Miss Cranston, how nice to see you again! We met at the fair, do you remember?"

Heather turned with a smile of delight. "Of course I remember! You're Miss Roundtree, Phoebe Roundtree."

"Are you having trouble?" Phoebe wanted to know. "You look a little concerned."

"I can't decide whether Angel should have a drink of water now or if we should wait till we're starting back,"

Heather confessed. "I don't know much about horses. I never drove one before I came to Arbordale."

Phoebe laughed. Putting her hand on Angel's neck, she said, "I think it's safe to let her drink now, if she's thirsty. She could hardly be overheated, the pace she goes! Yes, she's perfectly cool enough."

Phoebe led Angel to the trough herself, but Angel played with the water more than she drank it, snorting into it and then tossing her head when it tickled her nose. Phoebe laughed again.

"There! You can hitch her to the rail in front of the store, although I doubt that she needs hitching. She'd stand right there all day without moving an inch even if you didn't put the weight out or hitch her to the rail. Are you enjoying your visit to Virginia? Arbordale is a beautiful place. I've always enjoyed going there."

It was on the tip of Heather's tongue to ask why Phoebe hadn't been there since she and Jared had been there, but she thought better of it. Besides, maybe Phoebe and Mr. Amhurst would be at the ball. It was obvious that Minna and Phoebe were good friends, and of course Phoebe would be invited.

At that moment, a thin, proud-looking woman emerged from the Emporium and bore down on them.

"There you are, Phoebe! You're late. I chose the ribbons without you."

It was obvious that the woman was Phoebe's mother, because there was a resemblance, but Heather doubted that Phoebe would ever acquire the haughty, rather sour look that seemed to have settled on the woman's face with advancing years. Mrs. Roundtree looked at Heather inquiringly and waited for her daughter to introduce them.

There was an odd look, almost of apprehension, on Phoebe's face, but she did as required.

"Cranston?" Mrs. Roundtree said, making it a question. Two vertical lines appeared between her eyes, making her look more standoffish than ever. "You're visiting the Arlingtons, are you not? Come along, Phoebe. At once, if you please!" She followed up her order by grasping Phoebe's arm and literally dragging her away. Phoebe cast an apologetic look over her shoulder, her face red with embarrassment.

Heather stood there still holding Angel's bridle, her mouth half hanging open. That had been one of the clearest snubs she had ever had inflicted on her in her life! The woman hadn't said that she was pleased to meet her, she hadn't asked if she were enjoying her visit; she had acted every bit as coldly as Evelyn Langdon had acted when she and Heather had met by chance on the road.

It can't be me, Heather decided. They don't even know me, they can't possibly have anything against me. And it couldn't be because she had "hired girl" written all over her, because she didn't. Besides, no real lady would snub a hired girl in such a manner.

There was one possible explanation. Could it be because she was a Northerner? Miss Minna had told her that here in Virginia the Civil War seemed like yesterday. Of course, that wouldn't excuse the out-and-out rudeness, but it might explain it. Except that she was a guest of the Arlingtons, and as such she should have been accorded courtesy no matter where she came from.

That left only one thing, something that she didn't even want to think about. It had to have something to do with the Arlingtons themselves. Minna had been snubbed in Heather's presence, and now it was all too likely that Heather was being snubbed because she was a guest of the family.

She decided that she wasn't going to worry about it now. She had come into Bennington to enjoy herself, and that was just what she was going to do.

She decided to leave the Emporium until last, and then she wouldn't have to carry her purchases. She set out slowly and walked up one side of Main Street and down the other, taking in all the sights. On one side of the street was a butcher's shop and a seed and feed store as well as the Emporium and a forbidding-looking building that proclaimed itself to be a bank. A brass plaque informed the public that a Mr. John Thaxter was the owner and president. On the other side was the courthouse, with the same two old men playing checkers on a bench in the town square.

One of the old men nodded to her, and the other one nudged him and said something to him. The first one gave the second a disgusted look and, defiantly, nodded to her again. Heather nodded back, giving him her best smile. On second thought, she included the other man in her smile and was gratified to see his face redden.

Definitely, it had something to do with the Arlingtons, and definitely, some of Bennington's citizens liked the Arlingtons and some of them didn't.

She decided to cross the street so that she could walk past the two old men. The first one nodded to her again and grinned, and the second scowled and refused to meet her eyes.

Not to be outdone, Heather reached down and jumped the second old man's checkers, two of them, with one of the first old man's checkers. Her father's one vice had been playing checkers, and he had taught her well.

"There!" Heather said, smiling even harder at the first old man. "You've won!"

There was a small newspaper shop just a few doors down the street, and another thought struck her. In all the time she had been at Arbordale, she hadn't seen a newspaper in the house. She'd been under the impression, from both Thatcher and her father, that no gentleman could do without his newspaper.

On impulse, she entered the shop. There was a rather bare front room, with a desk in front of a wooden barrier that led to a back room where sounds of activity were going on. There was no one at the desk, so she opened the gate in the barrier and went through to the other room.

There was a printing press, banks of type, and a composing table. A young man was setting type, type stick in one hand while the fingers of the other picked the tiny letters from the type bank, darting over all the little compartments so rapidly that Heather marveled. She marveled even more at the wall behind the type bank. It was literally plastered with globs of dried tobacco juice.

She cleared her throat, and the young man turned around. He saw where her eyes were fastened and smiled.

"I'm sorry about that," he said. "I've meant to clean it

up, I just haven't gotten around to it. You see, typesetters have to use both hands, and they can't spare one to hold a pipe or a cigar, and so most of them chew. I don't have the habit myself, the mess was left over from the former owner when I took over the plant. Is there something I can do for you?"

"I was wondering if I could purchase one of your newspapers. Or better still, your latest edition and several recent copies."

"You wouldn't like to place an ad?"

"Only the newspapers," Heather said. What a nice young man! He was a little over medium height, he couldn't be more than twenty-six or twenty-seven, and he had candid hazel eyes that disturbed her until she placed her finger on the cause. There was a sadness in his eyes that had no business being there.

Laying down the stick of type, the young man crossed to the shelves where back copies of the *Bennington Bugle* were stored. "Our latest issue and six recent ones," he said. "That will be fourteen cents. Will that do it, Miss . . ."

"Miss Cranston, Miss Emma Cranston." Heather watched him closely for his reaction, almost holding her breath. "My brother and I are visiting at Arbordale."

The hazel eyes winced, but for whatever reason the young man recovered himself.

"I'm David Inges. I'm happy to make your acquaintance, Miss Cranston."

He didn't look the least bit happy to make her acquaintance, Heather thought. But at least he was polite. He didn't out-and-out snub her. She found the fourteen cents in her reticule and gave him the coins. He thanked her, and she left. He didn't say that he hoped they would see each other again before she went back North.

She put the newspapers in the buggy when she passed it on her way to explore the other end of Main Street. The two old men were gone from the bench in front of the court-house. She hoped that their friendship hadn't suffered a rift because of her.

She passed a combination livery stable and blacksmith shop, its forge cold, and a house with a sign in a front window proclaiming dressmaking, and a hardware store, and almost at the very end of the street there was a pretty red brick church.

She stopped in front of the church, and a lump came into her throat and tears stung her eyes. It was a Baptist church, and it looked just like her father's old church. She blinked to keep the tears from falling. Her father wouldn't want her to cry; he would want her to enjoy seeing this church that brought back fond memories.

The white clapboard house next door must be the manse, and as she stood there a slight, stoop-shouldered man came out of the house and crossed the dividing lawn to the walkway that led to the church door. Seeing Heather, he stopped.

"May I be of assistance to you?" he asked. His voice and his eyes were kind, and Heather saw that he wasn't as old as she had thought at first. "I'm Ephraim Roundtree, the pastor. I don't believe I have had the pleasure of meeting you before."

"No, you haven't. I'm only visiting here." At the last possible instant, she remembered that she mustn't tell him that her father had also been a pastor of a Baptist church. She recovered herself and said, "You must be Phoebe's father. I met her at the fair, and again just now, in front of the Emporium."

The minister's face lit up. "Yes, Phoebe is my daughter. Would you like to see the church, Miss . . ."

Oh, no! Heather thought. Not again! If this kindly man froze up on her when she told him her name and whom she was visiting, she didn't think she would be able to bear it.

"Emma Cranston," she said. In for a penny, in for a pound! And she added firmly, "My brother and I are visiting the Arlingtons at Arbordale."

For a moment, she thought it was going to happen, but then Ephraim Roundtree's face cleared. "Come along inside, my dear. It would be a shame for you not to see it, now that you are already here. We're rather proud of it, I'm afraid. It took years to replace the stained glass windows after the late conflict. They were broken not by the Union Army but by a Union sympathizer. The man barely escaped with his life, but he was old and considered a little touched, and it ended up with him only serving some time in our local jail. The entire interior was finished by local craftsmen, and the pews have been here since before the war."

Heather didn't blame him for being proud of his church. Every inch of it reflected loving care.

"Sit down in this pew and rest a bit. I was just going to collect some notes from the vestry. I'm forever forgetting things. Phoebe tells me it's a good thing that I don't have to remove my head when I go to bed at night, or I'd never find it again in the morning."

Just like her father, Heather thought with a lump in her throat. Searching for her father's spectacles had become a game to her, and he'd made a habit of losing his hat.

"Father? Father, are you in here?" It was Phoebe's voice, and in another moment she entered through the door that Ephraim had left open. "Mother is visiting Mrs. Walson, so I'll fix your midmorning tea for you."

Her father's head appeared around the doorjamb of the vestry. "That will be fine, Phoebe. Why don't you take Miss Cranston to the house with you? I'll be along as soon as I locate those notes."

"Oh!" Phoebe's hand flew to her mouth. "I didn't see you sitting there, Miss Cranston. It's a bit dim in here. Did you have business with my father?"

"Please stop calling me Miss Cranston. You make me feel like an elderly spinster. Call me Emma, and no, I didn't have any business with your father. I only stopped to admire your church, and he invited me inside to see it."

Phoebe's brow was furrowed, and she seemed to be torn with indecision. And then her manners came to the fore. "I'm sure that you have time for a cup of tea! And there are fresh ginger molasses cookies, Father dotes on them. Father, your notes are right on your desk in your office, where you left them last night."

Heather couldn't think of anything she would rather have right then than a cup of tea and a ginger cookie, unless it were two cups of tea and half a dozen ginger cookies. The tea would wash away the lump in her throat brought about by memories of her father, and the cookies would calm her nerves, which had been shaken by her encounter with Phoebe's mother.

The manse was furnished with old mismatched pieces, and she suspected that many of them were castoffs from the homes of the church parishioners, but every surface gleamed with lemon oil and there was the scent of potpourri in the parlor. It was so like the manse in which she had spent her childhood that tears sprang unbidden into her eyes again. She wished she could talk to Ephraim and Phoebe about her father and the church in Albany. Pretending to be someone she wasn't was beginning to wear on her.

Ephraim had followed them from the church, and now he appeared from another room with half a dozen sheets of paper in his hand, looking astonished. "They were right where Phoebe said they would be, and I seem to remember, distinctly, taking them into the vestry! No matter, the important thing is that I've found them. Now, my dear, how are you enjoying your visit to Virginia? Is this your first visit here?"

"Yes, it is, and I'm enjoying it immensely."

"How is Caldwell these days, and Brice? I haven't seen them for quite some time, or Miss Minna, either."

"Cream and sugar, Emma?" Phoebe asked after she placed a tray on a low table. Heather had the distinct impression that the other girl was trying to steer her father away from a taboo subject. Were the Arlingtons members of Ephraim Roundtree's church? Now that she thought about it, no mention had been made of attending church since she had been at Arbordale, and that in itself was strange.

"They're just fine. Miss Minna is in the best of health and spirits." A giggle rose in her throat. She hadn't intended to make a pun!

Her impulse to giggle disappeared when she noticed that Phoebe's eyes kept straying to the clock. There wasn't a modicum of doubt about it, Phoebe hoped that she would leave before her mother returned home. Someone who wasn't watching for just such little signs wouldn't have noticed, but Heather was already alert for little indications that she was a persona non grata. She was certain that both Phoebe and her father welcomed her and liked her, but she was just as certain that the minister's wife would not be pleased to find her in her house.

"Do have another cookie and let me freshen your tea," Phoebe urged. "I know how slow Angel is, but she'll still get you back in plenty of time for lunch."

It was one of the most tactful hints Heather had ever heard, to remind her that time was passing and she should be on her way. She decided to take the hint. She had no more desire to come face to face with Mrs. Roundtree again than Mrs. Roundtree would have to come face to face with her. She regretted having to leave the cookies. Mrs. Allenby was right, she was a greedy pig, and it was time she learned to curb her appetite. But she regretted having to leave Phoebe and her father even more. She would have liked nothing better than to spend the entire day with them.

She saw the absolute relief in Phoebe's eyes when she stood up and said that she must be going.

"I'm afraid Angel is even slower than you think! But I've enjoyed myself immensely, and I hope we will see each other again soon." She wished she had dared to invite them to visit her at Arbordale, but not having the faintest idea of the cause of the undercurrents that she sensed, she didn't. Besides, a guest must never invite someone else to the home she was visiting, at least without asking permission first.

"Yes, that would be lovely," Phoebe said as she walked her to the door. The girl's eyes scanned the street nervously, and she only relaxed when she saw that her mother was nowhere in sight.

Heather patted Angel's neck when she got back to the Emporium. "I'll only be a minute, and I'll give you a lemon drop for being so patient."

There was one other customer in the store when she entered, and the proprietor was adding up her purchases. She was a nicely dressed lady with a little gray in her hair, and she looked at Heather curiously.

"Put it on my tab, Mr. Thaxter," she said.

The proprietor wrote down the sum in a ledger, and the woman picked up her basket and left. She seemed neither friendly nor unfriendly, but neutral. Heather would have laid a fair-sized wager that the woman knew who she was.

Mr. Thaxter, a cold-eyed, stern-faced man in his late forties, regarded her without welcome.

"I'm Miss Emma Cranston. My brother and I are visiting at Arbordale," Heather said defiantly. "Have you any tatting thread, Mr. Thaxter?"

"It will be cash. I don't give credit," Mr. Thaxter said.

Heather's face flamed. The man had just this minute given credit, and he most certainly knew who the Arlingtons were! His tone had been an insult, but Heather's temper was up and she stood her ground.

"Certainly. Do you mind if I look around a bit, to decide what else I might want? For cash," she added pointedly.

She didn't wait for him to answer but began to walk through the store. It lived up to its name, with an assortment of almost everything anybody could want. Pails and scrub brushes were piled in one corner, boots and shoes in another. Sunbonnets hung from hooks on the wall, and shelves displayed bolts of dress material.

At the far end of the store she found a pile of long johns, or union suits as some people called them, along with heavy work shirts. Several kerosene cans were stacked up near the union suits, for no apparant reason except that there was room for them. One of the cans was dented, a dent so conspicuous that she wondered why Mr. Thaxter had it on display. Perhaps he would sell it more cheaply than the undented ones.

She refused to be hurried. She did not like Mr. Thaxter, and she was convinced that he liked her even less, but this was the only place in town where she might find what she wanted, and she was not going to leave empty-handed.

She'd almost given up hope of finding anything nice enough for Mrs. Allenby when she spied a dusty hair container, a little round, squat bowl with a lid with a hole in it through which combings could be stuffed against having a switch of your own hair made up. It was real china and prettily painted with roses. She carried it over and placed it on the counter.

"Will you dust this off for me, please?" She was gratified to see Mr. Thaxter flush at the pointed hint that his stock was dirty. He gave her a baleful look and swiped at it with a corner of his apron. One up for her, she thought.

For herself, she chose a fan. It was an ordinary palm-leaf fan—she could have bought one just like it in Albany—but it would be easy to pack between her clothing, and she would know that it had come from Bennington. She placed it beside the hair container and the tatting thread Mr. Thaxter had placed there.

"Do you carry any candy? And I want some pipe tobacco, the best you have."

She chose lemon drops, peppermint drops, licorice whips, and hoarhound from the glass jars at the end of the counter. It pleased her to insist that Mr. Thaxter put each variety into a separate bag.

Mr. Thaxter looked at the bills she gave him as though he were examining them to make sure they weren't counterfeit.

"It isn't Confederate money, Mr. Thaxter. It's perfectly good," she said.

He made change with deliberate enmity. He was careful not to let his fingers touch her hand when he dropped the coins into it.

"Some people don't seem to care who they associate with. Some people visit folks they hadn't ought to visit, instead of staying to home where they belong."

"If you ever come to Albany, I will make sure that you are accorded the same warm welcome that you have accorded me," Heather retaliated. She stared at him eye to eye, refusing to be the first to look away. For a moment, she thought she would be there for the rest of the day, but she was saved when another customer entered the store. Gathering up her parcels, she left, shaking with fury. How dare he make such a remark! Even if he had a personal grudge against the Arlingtons, it had been uncalled for.

She untied Angel and led her the few steps to the watering trough to see if she was thirsty by now. To humor her, Angel drank a few swallows. Remembering her promise, Heather fished out a lemon drop and offered it to her on the palm of her hand. Angel's lips were velvety as she took it. Heather felt like leading her up the porch steps and into the

Emporium and asking her to drop a calling card right in the middle of Mr. Thaxter's store. But she couldn't do that; it would reflect on the Arlingtons. Besides, Angel probably wouldn't oblige.

Sam opened one sleepy eye as she climbed into the buggy. He was as patient as Angel; he hadn't budged from his spot on the floorboard all the time she had been gone. She fondled his ears and gave him a lemon drop as well. Some animals were a whole lot nicer than some people. She amended that statement. Almost any animal was a whole lot nicer than some people. She had a wicked wish that she would encounter Mr. Thaxter on the street sometime when Sam was with her, and Mr. Thaxter would say something nasty to her, and she'd tell Sam to bite him good and hard. Only Sam probably wouldn't do it. She couldn't picture Sam biting anyone.

Angel needed no guiding; she knew her way home. To calm her anger, Heather put one of the newspapers on her lap and began to read. One item, on the third page, caught her interest. There were only four pages.

No Clue to Missing Girl's Whereabouts

Miss Naomi Thaxter, the niece of Matthew Thaxter, who owns the Emporium, has now been missing for more than four months, and her uncle has had no word from her. An investigation has turned up no leads, and Mr. Thaxter has expressed his conviction that his niece has met with foul play.

Heather forgot about her fury at Matthew Thaxter for his rudeness to her. The newspaper item kindled her interest to fever pitch. A missing girl, right here in Bennington! And if she was Mr. Thaxter's niece, that might account in part for his unpleasant manner, even if it didn't account for his hostility toward her.

She read the article again, without getting any more out of it. Where on earth could a girl disappear to in Bennington? There was no way she could have left town without having been seen. If Heather had been Mr. Thaxter's niece, she probably would have wanted to turn up missing too, but how Naomi Thaxter had managed it was beyond her.

Heather couldn't conceive of anyone meeting with foul play in Bennington. In a town this small, where everyone knew everyone else and everything that took place, it seemed impossible. And why hadn't Minna told her about it, Minna who was a font of exciting stories and who knew everything about everybody?

She laid the newspaper aside and shook the ribbons.

"Darn it, Angel, giddup! Can't you go any faster?" She was in a tearing hurry to get back to Arbordale and ask Minna about Naomi Thaxter.

Angel twitched her ears and didn't increase her pace by one iota. Beside Heather on the buggy seat, Sam was nosing at the bags of candy. Neither Angel nor Sam knew about Naomi Thaxter, and they couldn't have told her about it even if they did know. Angel plodded on at her own slow pace. Missing girls were outside the realm of Angel's interest, and she saw no reason to hurry.

∽ Chapter 8 ∾

HEATHER CORNERED MINNA in the rose arbor the moment she returned to Arbordale. Minna was drinking lemonade and tatting. As it wasn't time for the late afternoon refreshments on the verandah, this lemonade had nothing but water and sugar and lemon juice in it. Nobody could accuse Minna of being a lush.

Heather dropped her parcels on the little wrought iron table and practically waved the newspaper with the story about Naomi Thaxter under Minna's nose.

"You have a full-blown mystery right here in Bennington, and you never told me a word about it!" she accused. "I met the girl's uncle in the Emporium. I can't say I liked him much." She'd decided not to tell Minna about Matthew Thaxter's deliberately rude behavior. And besides, maybe the Arlingtons had never established credit at the store, maybe they had always paid cash. Whatever the reason, she didn't want to upset Minna with it.

Minna's fingers flew even faster as she turned out a long, narrow strip of tatting. "But there isn't anything to tell," she said. "I don't know a thing about it."

"But you knew Naomi, didn't you? You must have known her if she lived in Bennington with her uncle."

"She hadn't lived in Bennington for very long. Actually, she came from Utica, New York. Her mother died, you see, when she was quite young, and then when her father died she was obliged to come to Bennington and make her home with Matthew Thaxter. She kept house for him and clerked in his store."

"Was she pretty?" Heather wanted to know. "How old was she?" She brought herself up short. She was referring to the girl in the past sense, as if Naomi were dead! But the newspaper said that Matthew Thaxter suspected foul play. "And how could anything have happened to her in Bennington? I can't understand it, can you?"

"I most certainly can't," Minna said, her eyes fixed on the lace she was turning out. "I think it's much more likely that she simply ran away. And yes, Naomi was very pretty and very young, only seventeen, a blonde with a lovely complexion and enormous, beautiful blue eyes. She'd been spoiled by her father, and Matthew was strict with her, so she probably just up and left in order to get away from him and have more freedom."

"Did she have any money, anything to live on until she could find some way to support herself?"

"Not from Matthew, that's certain. Matthew is a parsimonious man. Her father left her a little, but only a very little, a few hundred dollars at the most. Matthew put that in his cousin's bank for her, and she didn't withdraw it. She couldn't have withdrawn it without Matthew's consent, and he never would have let her."

"Matthew Thaxter didn't do away with her for her money, then," Heather mused, thinking out loud.

Minna missed a stitch, startled into raising her eyes. "My lands! Wherever do you get such outlandish ideas? Of course Matthew didn't do away with her! It's what comes from being a writer, I suppose. You have entirely too much imagination, Emma."

Heather didn't want Naomi to be dead, but if she were dead, she'd rather that Matthew Thaxter had done it, and would be caught and punished for it, than anyone else. Minna was probably right. The girl had simply run away. Maybe there had been some man in Utica; maybe the young man had come to Bennington and run off with her. If she was as pretty as Minna said, she'd be almost certain to have a young man, and if Matthew hadn't approved of him, the young couple could have eloped.

Sighing because Minna couldn't shed any light on the mystery, Heather went on to other subjects.

"I met David Inges when I stopped in at his newspaper office to buy the newspapers. I thought Mr. Arlington would enjoy reading them."

"I'm sure he will, dear. It was thoughtful of you."

"Isn't Mr. Inges awfully young to own a newspaper? He seemed like a nice man but quite young."

"David is one of the nicest young men I've ever known. I believe he's twenty-eight. He bought out the paper for a song when it was going under, and he's done very well with it. His father is a physician in Richmond, and he advanced the down payment. David has a brother who is also a doctor, so his father didn't object too much when David wanted to move to Bennington and be a newspaper man."

"Is David married?" Heather wanted to know. She was always avidly curious about anyone she met; it was almost as much of a vice as her appetite.

"No, he isn't married. He and Phoebe Roundtree walked out together for a while, but nothing came of it." Minna said.

"Phoebe!" Heather was off on another tack. "I met her father in front of the church, and he invited me to see it and then to the parsonage, where we had tea and cookies."

Minna's fingers tightened on the tatting shuttle, and for an instant they trembled. "Did you meet Mrs. Roundtree as well?"

"Only for an instant, when she came out of the Emporium just as I was leaving the buggy there. Phoebe was there too, and she introduced us, but Mrs. Roundtree was in a hurry so we didn't have time to talk." There was no use upsetting Minna by telling her what had actually happened.

Minna's fingers stopped trembling. "That was a small loss, if I may say something so unkind. Ephraim and Phoebe are much better company." She rolled up her tatting and rose. "I simply must get back to the house. I set Pearl and Della to polishing the crystal chandeliers in the ballroom and then waxing the floor, and if I don't keep after them they won't do a good job."

Heather didn't believe that for a moment. As long as she had been there Pearl and Della had never slacked off; they did just as they were told and the best they could, untrained as they were. Once again, she wondered why the Arlingtons didn't have older, better-trained servants. There were so many things here that simply didn't make sense.

Could it be possible that the Arlingtons weren't as wealthy as Jared thought they were? If that were true, it would explain why Caldwell showed no interest in investing in the automobile manufacturing venture. Poor Jared! But the mystery of Naomi Thaxter's disappearance was still uppermost in her mind.

To that end, she insisted on helping with the work. "I'll see to it that everything is done just as it should be. I'll enjoy having something to do."

But getting information out of the two girls proved to be an impossible task. In the first place, they were covered with confusion because she, a white lady and a guest in the house, was working side by side with them, something so utterly outside of their experience that they were tongue-tied. In the second place, the way their faces closed when she tried to ask them about Naomi told her that even if they knew anything, they weren't about to tell her. They looked at each other uneasily, and worked harder and faster.

"I don' know, Miss Emma. I never heered."

At least she had the satisfaction of seeing the chandeliers raised again, every prism radiating sparks of brilliant color. She stood there admiringly and tried to picture how the ballroom would look with every candle lighted and how the floor, polished to mirrorlike perfection, would reflect the figures of dancing couples.

"You did a beautiful job," she said. "Miss Minna is going to be proud of you!"

The two heads bobbed, and shy smiles broke out on the girls' faces. "Thank you, Miss Emma. We'll git at the floor now."

Saul had come in to raise the chandeliers and make sure that they were firmly anchored.

"Saul, I've left some candy and tobacco for you on the little table in the rose arbor. It isn't much, but I wanted to thank you for teaching me how to drive. You're a wonderful teacher. I don't have a speck of trouble."

"Didn't reckon you would, Miss Emma. Couldn't anybody have any trouble with Angel."

"There's just one thing. Isn't there any way to get a modicum more speed out of her?"

"If there is, I never found it. You'll just have to be satisfied with her the way she is. Important thing is, she's safe. There ain't no way you could handle Cicero, not without a whole lot more practice."

But she wouldn't be there long enough to get a whole lot more practice, Heather thought, sighing. Actually, she and Jared shouldn't even stay until the ball, but Minna's heart would be broken if they didn't.

She wondered if Minna had invited David Inges to the ball. He was young enough and handsome enough to fit her romantic notions about a Southern gentleman paying court to a guest from up North, and he wasn't married. But bother! If Minna had invited him, she would probably have invited some other young lady for him to escort. Emma Cranston wasn't supposed to be courted by any other young man; she was supposed to be courted by Brice. That much had been made very clear, even though Brice had given no indication that he intended to court her.

In her room, she laid out all three of the ballgowns Emma had given her, comparing the respective merits of each. There was a lovely lavender with tiny cap sleeves and a neckline that bared the top of the shoulders, body-clinging in the front and elegantly draped in the back. There was a blue that justified the name of heavenly, so elegant and sophisticated that she would feel like a *femme fatale* in it. And there was a white trimmed with white lace that somehow managed to look both worldly and demure at the same time.

She wished that she could wear all three, but as far as she knew no young lady had ever excused herself twice during the course of a ball to go upstairs and change her gown and reappear in another. Besides, changing would take time, and she didn't want to miss one minute of the festivities. She was going to dance and dance, and maybe she would wear the soles of her slippers right through the way she had read about so often.

Dance! Her eyes widened with dismay. She didn't know how to dance! Her social life had been so curtailed that she had never had the opportunity to learn. The only outside affairs she had attended since she had gone to work for the Cranstons had been connected with the church, and none of them had included dancing.

Oh, my lands, what was she going to do? Miss Emma Cranston would certainly know how to dance. Emma actually did know how to dance. Thatcher had forced her to take dancing lessons before she'd become old enough to defy him. It was utterly impossible for Miss Emma Cranston not to know how to dance.

The ballgowns forgotten, she sped off in search of Jared. If she didn't learn how to dance before the ball, their masquerade would explode in their faces. Was there time? Was it terribly difficult to learn?

Jared was on the verandah, his feet propped up on the rail, reading a book he had borrowed from the well-filled shelves in Caldwell's study.

"Have you ever read any of Mark Twain?" he asked her. "If you haven't, it's time you started. He's the most comical writer ever to see print."

"Of course I've read Mark Twain. Do you think I'm illiterate? My father had everything he ever wrote. Jared, for goodness sake, put that book down and come and teach me how to dance!"

Jared looked at her with blank-faced surprise. "Are you telling me you don't know how?"

"I wouldn't be asking you to teach me if I knew how, would I? And you'd better be a good teacher and I'd better be a fast learner, or both our gooses are cooked!"

"Where?" Jared wanted to know. "And what will we do about music?"

"The ballroom. The girls and I just finished in there half

117

an hour ago. I helped them polish the chandeliers and the floor. That floor is so slippery I'll probably fall on my face! Come along, do! You can whistle for the music."

"And what if we're caught?"

"We won't be. And if we are we'll just say that we couldn't wait to try out the floor."

She turned out to be an apt pupil, even though Jared's whistling left a great deal to be desired. Jared wasn't much of a whistler. He was off-key more often than on, and the tone was far from melodious. But learning to waltz was easy. There was nothing to it at all; it was just one, two, three, over and over, twirling until she was dizzy.

It took longer to learn the rudiments of the polka, but the schottische was as easy as the waltz. There was no way she could learn any reels; they took more than two people, and Jared told her they were complicated.

"We'll tell them that we don't do reels in Albany," he said. "They won't know the difference. Let's practice the waltz again. If you have that down pat, maybe nobody will notice that you never danced before."

This time Jared didn't whistle, he hummed, and that was a great deal better. He had a nice voice for humming, low and full-bodied. Heather gave herself over to the delight of gliding around the floor in his arms. She imagined that the ball was in full swing, that other couples were swirling around her, and that the chandeliers were lighted, casting their soft glow over a scene of enchantment.

The floor wasn't too slippery after all, and Jared held her firmly. There was no way she could fall. She pretended that she was wearing the white ballgown and that Jared was her sweetheart and that sometime during the course of the evening he would take her out into the rose garden and propose to her. She was so caught up in her dream that she could almost believe it was real.

She wanted to go on dancing in Jared's arms forever and forever and forever. She could hear the strains of violins, the tinkle of a harp, the sweet notes of a piano. She felt as though her feet weren't touching the floor, as though she was as light as air. Her body was suffused with a delicious languorous warmth, as though it were melting into Jared's and soon she would be a part of him, never to be separated from him again.

Looking down into her face, flushed with her dreams, Jared felt a wave of longing flow through his body like a tremor. What a tiny little slip of a girl Heather was, as innocent as a newborn kitten, and he'd dragged her into a situation that might turn very nasty indeed if their deception were discovered. And to make it worse, it had all been for nothing. Caldwell wasn't going to invest in the automobile enterprise. All Jared had accomplished was to waste time that he couldn't afford to waste.

If things had gone as he had hoped they would, he'd have been able to ask Heather to marry him. He'd have been able to take care of her, to love her and cherish her all the rest of their lives. As it was, when they returned to Albany he would have to let her go, and she would have to find some other place to work.

He was engulfed in misery. He didn't want her to work for anyone else; he didn't want her to have to work at all. He wanted, he mocked himself, for her to sit on a cushion and sew a fine seam, and feed upon strawberries and cream, or however the old nursery rhyme went. With him furnishing the cushion and the strawberries and cream.

Involuntarily, he drew her closer until their bodies were pressed together in a manner that would have made all of the Mrs. Grundys in the world gasp with outrage. Her eyes were filled with stars, her lips were half parted, and her cheeks were flushed with a dewy freshness.

With a jolt that took every ounce of his willpower, Jared broke the spell. He stopped humming and held her away from him. One more second, and he would have kissed her, and once he had started kissing her he wasn't at all sure that he would have been able to stop. He would have been inspired to say things that he had no right to say.

"You're perfect," he told her. "There's no need for you to practice any more. Let's get out of here before we're caught and have a lot of explaining to do."

Heather came back to earth with a thump. For a few seconds, she scarcely realized that the ballroom was empty, that there was no orchestra playing on the dais at the end of the room, that the candles in the chandeliers were not lighted. When reality flooded over her, she had to stifle a sob.

Jared saw the hurt on her face, and he cursed himself. "You're going to be the belle of the ball," he told her, trying to mitigate it. "You're going to be so beautiful that you'll turn the heads of every man there. I can see you now, with gardenias in your hair, floating down that staircase with Brice waiting for you at the foot to escort you to the ballroom, just the way I promised. If he doesn't fall in love with you on the spot, something has to be wrong with him!"

But he'd better not, Jared thought without voicing the thought. If he does, I'll feel like cutting my own throat.

Heather had herself under complete control now. "He'd better not," she said. "Nothing could come of it. We'd have to tell him the truth about me, and I can hardly see Brice Arlington marrying a hired girl!"

All the same, she was going to flirt with him like crazy. It would serve Jared right for him to worry a little about having to tell the Arlingtons the truth. And she was going to be the belle of the ball if it was the last thing she ever did!

Unlike the picture Jared had painted for her, on the night of the ball Heather descended the staircase with no handsome young planter waiting at the foot to escort her to the ballroom. There was only Jared, whose lips pursed in a silent whistle of appreciation at the vision she made in the white ballgown. Brice was at the door, with Caldwell and Minna, to greet the guests as they arrived. The only thing that fit the picture Jared had drawn for her was that she looked beautiful in the white ballgown, and there were gardenias in her hair, their heady fragrance making her head swim even before she began to dance.

George and Stella Barnstable were the first to arrive, with Pauline and Aaron Harper right on their heels. Heather had expected they would come and so she wasn't surprised. What did surprise her was that Miss Rosamund Becker was the third arrival, without her sister Isobel.

Rosamund was dressed for the occasion in a flaming pink ballgown that smelled faintly of mothballs. Her cheeks were flushed with excitement that Heather suspected came partly from having defied her sister in order to attend the ball. Minna was especially pleased to see her. Probably she had thought Isobel would forbid her to come.

Heather forced her disappointment back when David Inges did not put in an appearance. Either he hadn't been invited, or he had declined the invitation. And, outside of Aaron Harper, who was already taken, there wasn't any young man who was even a reasonable facsimile of a handsome young planter. Not only were all of the gentlemen middle-aged to old, but they were all accompanied by their wives.

There was one good thing, though. There were enough guests so that she could stop suspecting that the Arlingtons were some kind of social outcasts. Just because a few people had evinced a dislike for Minna didn't mean that the Arlingtons weren't accepted and liked by the majority.

There was a little stir as one more couple arrived, and this arrival gave Heather a great deal of pleasure. After having met Phoebe Roundtree's mother and deduced that Bertha Roundtree, like those others, disliked Minna for no apparent reason, she hadn't dreamed that Phoebe would be here.

Phoebe's escort was Carl Amhurst, which was to be expected as Carl had taken her to the fair. Heather noticed that Phoebe, like Rosamund, had a high color, and she wondered if Phoebe had had words with her mother. What a bother it all was! Wondering what at least a few people in and around Bennington had against the Arlingtons was driving her out of her mind. She had decided not to ask Jared to try to find out, not only because it wasn't any of her business but because Jared had enough worries on his mind without her adding one more.

At least Phoebe was here, so Heather didn't feel so much like a fish out of water, being the only young woman. Maybe Ephraim had taken Phoebe's part. He at least had expressed a warm feeling for the Arlingtons.

If there was a scarcity of young men to make this the ball of Heather's dreams, the ballroom at least was just as beautiful as she had known it would be. The candlelight reflected on the polished floor and off the gilt mirrors on the walls. The mingled odor of candlewax and the scent of the myriad of roses that were arranged in vases all around the room made her head swim.

Five black men, produced from Heather had no idea where, occupied the small dais and provided music. It wasn't the orchestra of Heather's dreams, but the rhythm was perfect and there were no false notes, and in this setting they seemed exactly right. She mustn't be greedy. A month ago, back in Albany, she wouldn't have dreamed that even this much of a dream could come true.

She couldn't complain of being a wallflower, either. Whether or not it was worthwhile being the belle of a ball with such a scarcity of handsome young gentlemen, she was still the belle of the ball. Caldwell himself led her out for the first waltz, Brice for the second, and then Jared for a polka. Jared whispered in her ear that he would claim her for every polka and sit out the reels with her.

George Barnstable danced with her, and Aaron Harper, and Carl Amhurst. Brice was by far the best dancer of them all, although Caldwell ran him close seconds. Jared came somewhere in between. The other gentlemen were adequate even if they were old. That didn't matter; they were all extremely flattering, and the important thing was that no one seemed to have an inkling that she had learned to dance only days ago, right here in this ballroom when it had been empty, with only Jared's off-key whistling for accompaniment.

She stifled a giggle as she saw Jared attempt to steer Miss Rosamund around the floor. Rosie's idea of dancing was robust, to say the least, and she was all but unleadable. Her face flushed with pleasure, and Rosamund flirted with Jared as if she were eighteen instead of closer to sixty. Heaven help Jared if Rosamund got into Minna's lemonade!

Carl Amhurst was dancing with her now, while Phoebe danced with Aaron Harper. Heather pulled her attention away from Jared and Rosamund to attend to what Carl was saying.

"Are you enjoying your stay here at Arbordale, Miss Cranston? I can see that your company is doing Miss Minna a world of good."

"Miss Minna and I get along like a house afire," Heather told him. "She's an absolute darling. I only wish that my brother and I could stay longer."

"You're planning to leave soon, then? Phoebe will be sorry to hear that. She's quite taken with you, Miss Cranston."

"I like her too. But we have to get back to Albany soon. I hope I'll get to see Phoebe again before we leave."

"I'll make it a point to drive her out here." Mr. Amhurst was certainly an agreeable young man. Heather wondered if he and Phoebe were going to make a match of it. Somehow, she would rather see Phoebe with David Inges. It was frustrating that Minna had cut herself short when she'd been telling her that Phoebe and David had used to walk out together. She was consumed with curiosity about what could have happened to make them break up. But then she had the habit of being consumed with curiosity about just about everything.

She saw that Phoebe was laughing at some remark Aaron had made. Her face was animated, and she looked almost pretty. But when the number ended and Aaron escorted her back to Carl, the animation disappeared. It was as if a sunny summer day had suddenly lost its light as she accepted Carl's arm to be led out onto the floor again.

Well, maybe Carl Amhurst was in love with Phoebe, but Phoebe certainly wasn't in love with him! Was she still in love with David Inges? Heather could have stamped her foot in vexation. She didn't like not knowing things, and she especially didn't like not knowing things that she would never know.

Supper was served at eleven o'clock. Caldwell, resplendent in his evening clothes, escorted Heather to the laden tables. Brice escorted Minna. And Jared offered a gallant arm to Miss Rosamund. One look at Miss Rosamund convinced Heather that the lady had been into Minna's lemonade, passing over the mild punch that had been provided for the refreshment of the ladies.

Rosie is going to get Jared out into the rose garden before the evening is over, Heather thought, biting her bottom lip to keep from laughing. She had visions of Jared running for his life, pursued by an amorous Miss Rosamund holding up her pink skirts so that she could run faster.

Beside her, Aaron Harper asked, "Is something amusing you, Miss Cranston?"

Heather gulped. It would never do to share her thoughts. "I'm just having such a good time that I can't help smiling," she managed to stammer out. She took a large swallow of punch and nearly choked.

From across the table, Jared gave her a warning look. She resisted the impulse to wink at him. It wouldn't do at all to be caught winking at her brother. What would these nice, gentle gentlepeople think? It certainly was a bother to have to act like a lady every minute!

There was more dancing after they had eaten, and the guests didn't begin to leave until after one o'clock in the morning. Even if there wasn't any handsome young planter to make being the belle of the ball worthwhile, Heather had thoroughly enjoyed herself. She had only one regret. Miss Rosamund had not been able to lure Jared into the rose garden.

Jared hadn't had anywhere near as miserable a time with Miss Rosamund as Heather imagined. He liked Miss Rosamund. She was lively and witty, and it had been fun flirting with her because she enjoyed it so much. He knew that she was a bit tipsy, but that didn't matter. She was old enough to enjoy herself any way she chose.

The thing that puzzled him was where she had got it. She had had only one cup of the very mild punch, and she had taken only one small glass of wine at supper, but he could smell something a good deal stronger on her breath. Bourbon, if he wasn't mistaken. He had a moment's wild fancy that she had a flask stuck in her garter, and he grinned.

He dismissed the puzzle as unsolvable. He knew that Miss Rosamund couldn't have a flask stuck in her garter. What was important was that she was having a good time, and that Heather was having a good time. He was also having a good time, and so he should be happy.

Only he wasn't happy. It took all of his effort to keep a smile pasted on his face. He would be going back to Albany empty-handed, to face a future that was uncertain at the least. Not only that, but he had let Martin Knightbridge down. Martin was depending on him, and he was going to be crushed. Martin's whole life was wrapped up in his automobile, and now he would have to spend his whole life working for his father. It was not a fate Jared would have wished on his worst enemy, let alone an inoffensive young man like Martin.

Nearly half of the guests had left now, assuring Minna that it had been a lovely ball. Rosamund captured Jared's attention by tapping on his arm with her fan, an indescribably silly, flirtatious, antebellum kind of fan that might have been carried by some lady before the Civil War.

"Mr. Cranston, be an angel and fetch me a glass of Minna's lemonade. The pitcher is in the pantry. Minna didn't think lemonade is elegant enough to be served at a ball so she just made some up for the two of us. Make it a large glass, I need it to fortify me on the drive home. All this dancing has given me a powerful thirst."

Saul was acting as barman, presiding behind the punchbowl and tendering the gentlemen more potent libations on request. The elderly man was beaming from ear to ear, important in the jacket he had donned for the occasion.

"Miss Rosamund wants some lemonade?" he asked as Jared passed him on the way to the pantry. "You know where to find it?"

"In the pantry, right?" Jared replied. Someday, if he could ever afford it, he wanted someone just like Saul to work for him. He would even go as far as to try to entice Saul away from Caldwell, except that that wouldn't be ethical even if Caldwell hadn't come up with the money to get the automobile manufacturing business started.

"In the cut glass pitcher," Saul said. Saul's eyes were dancing with merriment. Jared wondered what he found so funny.

He found the pitcher exactly where Miss Rosamund had told him it would be. He poured a large glass for Miss Rosamund, and on second thought he poured a smaller glass for himself. Miss Rosamund was right, dancing was a thirsty business, and a glass of lemonade would hit the spot right now. He tossed it off before he started back to the ballroom with Miss Rosamund's glass.

It hit the spot all right, right on the target. Jared's eyes bulged. And then he began to laugh. So this was where Miss Rosamund had got it! As for Miss Minna, he wouldn't have thought it of her!

He winked at Saul as he passed him on his way back to Miss Rosamund. Saul winked back, his eyes dancing.

Rosamund didn't as much as flicker an eyelid as she took the glass from Jared and drained it.

"There! That's much better! There's nothing like Minna's lemonade, Mr. Cranston. She has a real knack for it. You should try it some time."

"I'll do that," Jared said.

"They're playing a polka. Come, Mr. Cranston. I do enjoy a good fast polka."

She certainly did. By the time the polka was over, Jared was ready for another glass of Minna's lemonade. So was Miss Rosamund. Jared only hoped that it would hold out until the ball was over.

"Mr. Cranston, you are the best dancing partner I ever had! And you aren't bad at flirting, either, even if you are from the North. But don't expect anything to come of it. I value my independence. If you should happen to propose to me before the evening is over, I would have to turn you down. With regret, I admit, but I would still have to turn you down."

"Miss Rosamund, you've just broken my heart. I'll return to Albany a shattered man."

"But you can write to me," Rosamund told him, rolling her eyes at him. "And I promise that I will answer your letters. Just manage to be as outrageously indiscreet in your letters as you can devise! Isobel reads all of my mail, and I'd like to give her something that will be worth her while to read, just to get her circulation going."

"Miss Rosamund, I guarantee that my letters will smolder in her hands, and she'll have to put salve on her fingers," Jared said. "Her circulation will not only get moving, it might run right away with her!"

"Good," Rosamund said. "If you don't keep your word, Mr. Cranston, I shall go to Albany and find you and beat your head to a pulp with my umbrella!"

Jared had a very good idea that Miss Rosamund was capable of doing just that. He would enjoy writing to her. He only hoped that no postal inspector would find occasion to open one of his letters and read it. Spending the next several years behind bars did not appeal to him. But if Rosamund wanted to shock her sister, he was going to see that Isobel was properly shocked. His declarations of passionate love for Miss Rosamund would shock Isobel's hair into standing on end.

They had one more glass apiece of Minna's lemonade, and that left the pitcher empty. It was just as well. The ball was coming to an end while both of them could still stand on their feet.

They enjoyed the last waltz together. Jared wasn't sure which of them was holding the other up. But it didn't matter. As long as they didn't disgrace themselves by falling down, everything was all right.

"Miss Rosamund, are you sure you won't change your mind and marry me?" Jared asked.

Rosamund leered at him. "That all depends on your letters. If they're good enough, I just might decide to abandon my single state."

He would, Jared thought, have to be very careful about what he wrote.

∽ Chapter 9 ∽

Miss Rosamund was the last of the guests to leave, at half past two in the morning. Both she and Minna had sampled Minna's lemonade so often during the course of the evening that they had to exert an effort to appear normal. Every time Caldwell or Brice looked her way, Minna drew herself together and presented a picture of a serene and perfectly sober hostess, but it was a good thing the ball was over because she wouldn't have been able to keep it up much longer.

Waiting on the verandah for Rosamund's driver to bring her trap around, Rosamund tapped Jared's arm with her fan again.

"Where are your manners, Mr. Cranston? Aren't you going to kiss my hand when you bid me farewell? No, not my hand, my cheek! Meaning as much as we do to each other, you simply must kiss me, or I'll stay rooted right to this spot until you do."

Jared was happy to oblige. In fact, he went Miss Rosamund one better and kissed her, chastely, on the lips.

Rosamund gasped and squealed and fluttered her hands, pretended that she was going to swoon, and demanded that either Caldwell or Brice avenge her honor by calling Jared out. In the next instant she changed her mind and demanded that they not lay a finger on him.

"Poor young man, he's so far-flown with passion for me that he lost his head. We'll have to forgive him, it's only his hot-blooded youth that carried him away. But it mustn't happen again, Mr. Cranston, or you'll be called to account. Well, not more than one more time!" Her laughter pealed out, filled with glee.

Caldwell doubled over with laughter, and even Brice looked amused. Minna gave her friend a push.

"Rosie Becker, you go home this minute before you completely disgrace yourself! The very idea, seducing a man as young as Mr. Cranston!"

"You only say that because I'm the one he favors. I don't blame you for being jealous, Minna, but make sure you remember that Mr. Cranston is mine. Just keep your hands off him, Minna Arlington, or I'll forget I'm a lady and scratch your eyes out!"

By now they were all laughing, carried away by Rosamund's antics. Rosamund's driver, Ben, who was even older than Saul, looked askance as he waited for his mistress.

Caldwell raised Rosamund's hand to his lips, a model of a Southern gentleman. Rosamund bridled.

"Now, Caldwell, don't you go trying to undercut Mr. Cranston. I've already given him my heart. Brice, be a good boy and control your father. And Ben, you just turn your head to the front, and never mind what's going on over here. If you're looking for amusement, you'll find plenty when we get home. Isobel will be up in arms because I'm so late, and besides I'm going to regale her with such tales of my revelry that she'll likely have a stroke. And then you'll have to fetch Dr. Cunningham, and that's just about all the excitement you'll be able to stand in one night!"

Heather wondered if Isobel really would be waiting up for her sister. She wouldn't put it past the sour-faced woman. She'd give a good deal to be a mouse in the corner so that she could witness what went on between the two spinster sisters when Rosamund got home.

"Kiss me again, Mr. Cranston. I want to be able to tell Isobel, truthfully, that I was kissed twice."

Ben kept his face carefully turned forward, so that he could say truthfully, if Miss Isobel asked him, that he hadn't seen Miss Rosamund get kissed. But concealed in the darkness of the rose arbor, another pair of eyes witnessed the departure of this last guest, and a heart ugly with bitterness twisted with fury. His enemy, the man he hated, had enjoyed a ball this evening. His enemy, the man he hated, had not yet suffered what he must be made to suffer.

The watcher was well acquainted with Miss Rosamund Becker, and seeing the condition she was in after an evening of unholy revelry, he regretted that he could not bare her disgrace to the entire town of Bennington. It was not only a disgrace, an insult to the Almighty, for a supposedly genteel lady to be intoxicated, but it would serve her right for having accepted the Arlingtons' invitation to their ball.

The man stirred, easing his aching muscles. He had been stationed in the arbor for well over an hour, and he felt cramped and uncomfortable. He'd thought that the ball would be over long before this and all of the inhabitants of the house asleep. He wasn't used to staying up this late, and he would suffer for it tomorrow.

But he had had one piece of luck. Because of the guests, Saul's hound Sam had been tied outside the stable, so that he wouldn't jump all over the ladies and soil their gowns. Sam had barked and lunged against his rope when the skulker had arrived, and he'd kept it up for so long that the man had become increasingly afraid that someone would hear him and come to investigate. But no one had. The stable was a long way from the house, and the music had drowned out the barking.

After a while, when the skulker had remained absolutely still, Sam had quieted down and probably gone to sleep. He'd put up a fuss again when Saul came to untie him and take him up to his quarters over the stable, doing his best to tell his master that there was an intruder on the grounds, but Saul had soothed him and told him that everything was all right, that it was just Miss Rosamund leaving. "Come on along now, you foolish old dog, and stop making all that racket. I got to git some sleep for what's left of the night even if you don't."

Now Saul and Sam were safely inside, over the stables,

Miss Rosamund Becker had left at last, and the others had gone back into the house.

Still the watcher waited, as the lights in the windows went out one by one, and he pictured everyone seeking their beds to enjoy their undeserved rest. He had to be very sure that the entire plantation was asleep before he moved.

Unseen from where the watcher lurked, because Caldwell's study was at the back of the house where it couldn't be seen from the rose arbor, a light still burned. Caldwell, a snifter of brandy in his hand, stood facing Brice, and his face was as flushed with anger as Brice's was white for the same reason.

"I tell you that I have explored the last possibility! My trip to Richmond last week resulted in nothing. John Thaxter has made very sure that no other bank in Virginia will extend me a loan. Burton Langdon has used all of his influence to see to that. He and John Thaxter are as thick as thieves. All bankers are as thick as thieves!

"Why can't I make it clear to you that if we can't get a loan from Thatcher we'll go under? There's no use in asking Jared. I'm sure he'd let us have it if he had it, but his father controls the purse strings, and Jared is going to put all he can possibly scrape up into that automobile venture of his. I'll just have to wait until Thatcher gets back from wherever he's trekked off to and throw myself on his mercy. You heard Jared say that his father wasn't in a position to invest anything right at the moment, but for an old friend he might be able to come up with enough to tide us over.

"Damn it, Brice, if I could present him with the fact that you and Emma are in love and plan to be married, Thatcher would manage to find the money someplace! It would be all in the family then, and he wouldn't be able to refuse."

The muscles in Brice's jaw tightened. "Why can't I make it clear to you that I will not ask a girl to marry me merely to ensure that her father will extend us a loan? I was against this visit from the first, knowing what you were up to. A marriage for gain! If I were as honest as I should be, I'd tell them both why you got them here."

"Now, Brice, you know that I've always wished that you

and Thatcher's daughter would meet each other and make a match of it. I never cared for Evelyn Langdon, but I held my peace when I thought that you were so in love with her that no one else would do for you. But all that is changed now. It isn't as if you'll ever get Evelyn back. There isn't a reason in the world why you shouldn't at least try to fall in love with Emma. The girl is certainly pretty, even if she can't match Evelyn's beauty. And she and Minna dote on each other. It would be bound to turn out to be a happy marriage. You wouldn't be able to help falling in love with Emma once Evelyn begins to fade from your mind."

"Evelyn has nothing to do with it. The entire thing is dishonest, and I'll have no part of it."

"Then you're a fool," Caldwell told him. "You could make that girl happy, and yourself in the bargain. If I were your age I'd fall in love with her myself. You've already lost Evelyn. If you lose Arbordale as well, what the devil will you have left to live for?"

"Right at the moment, I haven't the faintest idea," Brice told him. "But I expect that I'll survive. Arbordale isn't the beginning and end of the world, even if it has been in our family for generations. I'll carve out some kind of a life for myself, and you'll have to do the same, just as other men in our situation have been forced to do."

"This isn't the time for petty ethics!" Caldwell raged at his son. "This is a fight for our very existence!"

"Then it's a fight that's already lost, and it's time to pick up whatever pieces we can find and start over," Brice said. "I'm sorry if losing Arbordale will break your heart, but there's nothing to be done about it. I am not going to ask Emma Cranston to marry me just so you can ask Thatcher for a loan. And I think that you've had enough to drink."

"I might have to accept your mule-headedness, but I'm damned if I'm going to listen to your preaching!" The two men stood glaring at each other until Brice turned his back and left the room.

In the study, Caldwell decided against finishing what was left in his brandy glass. He just didn't want to let Brice see that he was going to take his advice. He sat down at the desk and put his head in his hands.

Gone, all gone! The work and dreams of generations of Arlingtons to go under the hammer, and all because of that unfortunate girl! How any sane person could believe that Brice had anything to do with it was more than he could understand. But the suspicion was there, and now the town of Bennington was divided against itself, as well as half the county. Even some of those who didn't believe that Brice was guilty were afraid to stand up for him for fear of retaliation. They all depended more or less on John Thaxter's bank, and egged on by both his cousin, Matthew Thaxter, and, even more important, Burton Langdon, the bank would refuse to extend loans to anyone who took Brice's side, and anyone who already had an outstanding loan might have it called in.

A few months ago, Caldwell wouldn't have believed that luck could have taken such a turn against him. If it hadn't been for the roof, he probably would have been able to squeeze through. But the roof had needed extensive repairs which had cut deeply into his pocket, and it had been essential to have it done. One good storm might have caused damage that would have been a great deal more costly. The repairs to the roof had taken nearly all of Caldwell's reserve. Plantations depend on credit, on loans from the bank from one harvest to the next. And so Caldwell had been caught when the hailstorm struck. The hailstorm had ruined the larger share of his crops. It had hit other plantations as well, but Arbordale had taken the brunt of it.

If Naomi Thaxter hadn't disappeared, simply disappeared without a trace, Caldwell would have had no trouble asking for an additional loan from John Thaxter's bank. The Arlingtons had done business with that bank since before Caldwell's grandfather's time.

If Brice hadn't brought Naomi Thaxter to Arbordale, if he hadn't bid for her box at the box supper and shared it with her, if he hadn't been kind to the girl, if Evelyn Langdon and her family hadn't been visiting relatives in another state, leaving Brice free to show a little kindness to an orphaned girl simply because he and Minna had felt sorry for her, Caldwell would not be in the bind he was in now.

But Brice had been kind to Naomi. He had been seen

escorting her around while Evelyn had been away, and the silly girl had jumped to an entirely wrong conclusion. She'd done a lot of talking, letting it be known that Brice was in love with her, telling everyone that she had taken Brice away from Evelyn, that they were all but engaged and that their engagement would be announced as soon as Evelyn got back so that Brice could break off with her.

Anybody with a modicum of sense would have realized that the girl was making the whole thing up. Evelyn and Brice had been engaged for nearly a year, and it wasn't likely that he'd break off with her for a seventeen-year-old girl he scarcely knew. Brice was a gentleman, and gentlemen do not go around jilting the girls they're engaged to.

The trouble was, there were plenty of people in and around Bennington who didn't have a modicum of sense. Talk flew, the gist of it being that everyone knew how wealthy young planters behaved, no matter how moral and upright a face they turned to the public. With Naomi, who was as pretty as a picture, throwing herself at him, why wouldn't he take what was offered? It had happened before, more times than they could count. And in every like case, the girl had disappeared, bought off when there had been consequences that were inconvenient.

The larger share of the Arlingtons' friends of long standing didn't believe a word of it. But there were enough who did to make things mighty uncomfortable. Burton and Alice Langdon were largely responsible for that. Burton had never liked Caldwell, even though they had managed to be polite to each other. Years ago, more years than Caldwell cared to remember, he had courted Alice, who had been as beautiful then as Evelyn was now. He had fallen short of asking her to marry him only because he had discovered over several months' time that Alice was snobbish and spiteful and cruel to anyone who was in no position to fight back, such as her servants.

Burton had also been courting the beautiful girl, and he had developed an enmity toward Caldwell because Alice had favored Caldwell over him. When Caldwell had bowed out of the picture and left the field to Burton, Alice had eventually married him. But Burton had still suffered under the belief that he had been second choice.

The friction between the two men had been patched up, at least on the surface, when Brice and Evelyn had fallen in love. Caldwell had always suspected that Burton had countenanced the engagement only because their marriage would merge the two plantations. Burton was an extremely wealthy man, and his place was larger than Arbordale, but he wanted still more.

The talk about Brice and Naomi had given Burton the chance to acquire Arbordale without allowing his daughter to marry Brice. Without a loan from the bank, Arbordale would go under, and as the bank held the mortgage and John Thaxter was Burton's best friend as well as his largest depositor, Burton would be able to pick up Arbordale for a song. There was no need for Evelyn to depend on having Brice for a husband. She could do better looking elsewhere and find someone who wasn't on the verge of bankruptcy. And Evelyn, who was her mother all over again, was in full agreement. Brice's supposed indiscretion had given her the perfect excuse for breaking the engagement.

With people as influential as the Langdons expressing their conviction that Brice was guilty, it was no wonder so many people believed in Brice's guilt as well. Those who didn't believe it and who were staunch in their belief did what they could, but even several of them owed too much to John Thaxter's bank to make too much of an issue of it.

Caldwell's last loan was coming due, and Thatcher Cranston had been his last hope. As it was a substantial sum that was needed, he had wanted it settled that Brice and Emma were going to be married before he asked him for the money. Thatcher would want to insure his daughter's future. But Caldwell knew that Thatcher wasn't an enormously wealthy man, merely comfortably off; it would be expedient to have more than a college friendship to depend on when he asked for such a sum, and for Emma and Brice to hit it off was the exact answer Caldwell had been looking for.

Caldwell was not a selfish man or an evil one. He

sincerely believed that any girl would be likely to fall in love with Brice, and here Brice was, jilted because the Langdons saw an opportunity for profit, and Brice wouldn't budge an inch.

After a few moments of despair, Caldwell rose and squared his shoulders. If Arbordale were lost, it would have to be lost. Like Brice, he would have to make the best of it and contrive some way to go on with his life.

He blew out the kerosene lamp on his desk and made his way through the other rooms to the foot of the stairs. He knew every inch of this house so well that he had no need for light. He had been born here, and he had never had any reason to believe that he would not die here. The thought that in a short time he might never walk these floors again was a stricture in his heart.

He had one thing to cling to. Brice was innocent of any wrongdoing, and he knew it. One day, the mystery would be solved and Brice would be vindicated. It might not be in time for Arbordale to be saved, but at least they would still have their honor.

In her room, Heather lay awake, too excited by the ball for sleep to come easily. She had never before danced an entire night away. She was tired, but it was a pleasant, tingling tiredness that was more a pleasure than a hardship.

She stretched luxuriously in the bed, enjoying the feel of one of the beautiful nightgowns Emma had left behind and the scent of the lavender that permeated the sheets. She promised herself that even after she went back to Albany she would always put sachets between her bed linen to remind her of Arbordale.

It was a shame that those memories wouldn't include a romance with a dashing young planter, but she mustn't be greedy. She had already had more than she could have dreamed she would have—this trip to Virginia, and getting to meet so many wonderful people, and having plots for goodness knew how many more books fall right into her lap because of Minna's stories.

She was sorry Jared was going to have to go back to Albany empty-handed. He'd counted on a loan from Caldwell, and even though he was doing a remarkably good job of hiding how crushed he was, she still knew that he was crushed. It would be hard for both of them, Jared with no money and her having to find some other place to work and never being able to see him again.

But Jared was still young, and his dreams were almost certain to come true because he was smart and well educated. It would just take a little longer. But at least one of her own dreams would never come true now, because time had run out. She never had had that romantic stroll in a starlit rose garden!

As long as she couldn't sleep, she might as well get up and at least look out the window at the rose garden. She would imagine that she was down there with the sweetheart of her dreams, who looked remarkably like Jared but who wouldn't apologize for kissing her. If imagination was all she had, she might as well make the most of it.

The window was open to the sweet-scented coolness of the night. She fastened her eyes on what she could see of the garden that lay below her window, drawing in deep breaths of the rose-scented air to store up in her memory. There was the rose arbor, and there, in the center of a circle of rose beds, was the sundial. And there were plenty of stars. The only trouble was that she wasn't down there, still in her ballgown, being drawn closer and closer into a handsome young planter's arms, while she raised her face for his kiss, a kiss that would burn right through to her soul.

She rubbed her nose, which tickled. Something was wrong with the picture she was painting in her mind. It wasn't supposed to smell like that. There was a definite odor of roses, as there should be, but there was something else that shouldn't be there at all.

Her scalp prickled. There was no mistaking the smell now that she had put her mind to it. She'd smelled burning wood often enough to recognize it.

But there were no fires burning in the house; it was summer, and the fireplaces were swept clean, with paper fans masking the blackened bricks inside them. The fire in the kitchen-house stove would have been out hours ago.

There was no reason for the odor of woodsmoke to lie in the night air. But it was there all the same, and it was getting stronger.

Should she rouse the men? But maybe it was nothing at all. The smell of smoke can travel for a long way. It might not even be at Arbordale. Someone might be burning brush or tree stumps on a neighboring estate.

But that was unlikely. It was getting on toward dawn, but there was still no light in the sky. Nobody would be out before daylight, burning something.

She turned back into her room and sniffed the air. Except for a wisp or two coming in through the window, the air in the room was perfectly clear. She went to her door and opened it and sniffed again. There was no smoke in the hallway, no smoke coming up the stairwell. The fire definitely wasn't in the house.

All the same, the smoke ought to be investigated. There were no fire companies out in the country, and as terrifying as a fire could be in a city or a town, it would be much worse so far from help. It would only take her a few minutes to check the outbuildings, the barn and the stables and the various sheds.

Groping in the dark, she found her robe where Della had left it over the back of a chair so that it would be within her reach in the morning. Finding her slippers took more time; somehow she had kicked one of them out of place when she'd climbed into bed. But then her foot brushed against the missing one, and she put it on, and then she was running down the hallway toward the stairs, pulling on her robe as she went.

Her night vision had always been good, and she was familiar enough with the house by now so that she needed no light to run down the stairs. She snagged her foot in the hem of her nightgown and nearly went tumbling head over heels, but she caught the banister in time, and then she was at the bottom.

The front door creaked when she opened it; the hinges needed oiling, just another of the small signs of neglect that she had noticed at Arbordale. Emma would have seen to it that the hinges were oiled immediately at the first sound of a squeak.

Outside, she paused only long enough to take a deep breath. The smell of smoke was much more pronounced out there. And then she heard a frantic neighing and the plunging of the horses in the stable.

The stable was on fire! She had made a mistake—she should have pounded on Caldwell's door, she should have screamed for Jared and Brice. She opened her mouth to scream now, and she gave it all she had.

"Fire, fire!" Her voice pierced the night like a siren. Would the men hear, or should she run back into the house? But that would take too long. The horses were trapped, and Saul slept above the stable.

She could hear Sam barking now, a frantic sound in his bark as he tried to rouse his master. She had never run this fast in her life. She reached the stable and struggled with the heavy wooden bar that held the double doors closed from the outside, screaming now for Saul, praying that he would wake up. He was old, and the long evening of tending bar had tired him. Bark louder, Sam! she prayed. Jump on him, lick his face, anything!

She got the bar up at last and pulled the doors open. She was greeted by billows of smoke that seemed to be coming from the back of the building. Her eyes filled with blinding tears and she choked. But there wasn't any time, she had to get Angel and Cicero out. She could tell that it was Cicero who was plunging around and screaming. She'd never heard a horse scream in terror before, and it was the most chilling sound she had ever heard. Angel was moving restlessly, and her neigh was worried and inquiring, as though she were asking if Heather was going to get her out.

Heather knew that the plowhorses were out at pasture, but her frantically racing mind couldn't tell whether Caldwell's and Brice's saddle horses were in the stable or not. Unable to see, she had to depend on her ears. They weren't in the stable, thank God for that! If they had been, she would have heard them plunging and screaming as well.

She heard Saul shout, "Miss Emma, get away from here,

get out of there!" He was behind her, in his nightshirt, grasping at her arm and trying to pull her away.

She wrenched herself free from him. "I'm not going to let Angel burn up! You get Cicero, and I'll get Angel!"

Both of the horses were kept in loose stalls. Angel's was closer than Cicero's; she knew exactly where it was. It took her only seconds to grope her way to the stall door and open it and get her hands on Angel's halter. In the stall further along, she could hear Saul struggling with Cicero as he tried to lead the panicked horse to safety.

Angel was frightened too, trembling and snorting, but unlike Cicero, she calmed as soon as she felt Heather's hand take her halter. Brice hadn't known how right he was when he'd told her that Angel wouldn't run if the bridge under her feet caught fire. She didn't try to bolt now or plunge around; she just pressed close to Heather, still trembling with fright, but she followed docilely along when Heather led her out of the stall, talking to her to calm her.

"It's all right, Angel. I've got you, you're safe. There, we're outside now, everything is fine!"

Saul had managed to get Cicero outside, but the trotter was still rearing and plunging around, trying to break loose and run back into the stable as horses will when there is a fire. Their stalls spell safety to them.

Heather let go of Angel's halter and went to help Saul. She grasped the other side of Cicero's halter, but just as she did so the trotter reared again, and her feet were lifted clear of the ground. Still she managed to scream, "Angel, don't you dare move! If you go back into that stable I'll never forgive you!"

Angel didn't move. Angel never moved unless it was required of her, and nobody was requiring it of her now. And then Brice was there, his hair disheveled, his shirt tucked only halfway into his trousers, and with one house slipper on and the other lost somewhere along the way. He grasped Heather around her waist and set her aside without ceremony, and in another few seconds Cicero was under control and tethered firmly to a post.

Now Jared came sprinting, his hair on end, still tucking in

his shirt. Caldwell was right behind him, and in the flickering light of the flames Heather could see that his face was stricken. To Caldwell, it seemed that disasters followed one behind another, so fast that it left him stunned.

"Emma, can you work the pump?" Brice asked her. "If you can fill the buckets, it will save us a pair of hands. Aunt Minna, stand back, there's nothing you can do."

Minna's hair was in a thick plait down her back, and she clutched a dressing gown around her, her lips trembling. "Do you think you can save it?" she asked. If she had been a little tipsy when she had retired to bed, there was no sign of it now.

"Part of it, if we're lucky. Thank God there isn't any wind!" Brice said.

Heather wasn't as sure. She could see where the stable was burning now, at the back and left corner. The flames were spreading rapidly. If she hadn't been restless tonight, if she hadn't gone to the window to look down at the rose garden and daydream, the stable would have been a total loss, and Angel and Cicero would have perished as well. And oh, God, Saul! Saul and Sam, burned to death! She wouldn't have been able to bear it.

The pump had to be primed by pouring water down an opening at the top from a bucket that was always left partly filled beside it for that purpose. It squealed loudly enough to wake the dead until the water in the well began to gush out of the spout as she pumped as fast as she could move her arms. Brice grabbed the first bucket and ran to dash it on the flames, and a second was filled, then a third. The men formed a four-man chain, smoke-grimed, their eyes smarting, their breath rasping in their throats.

Heather's breath was rasping as well, and her arms felt as though they were going to fall off as she continued to work the pump handle up and down. Her nightgown and robe were soaked, but the effort of pumping kept her from feeling cold.

Finally the flames were dying down, and then only wisps of smoke rose from the smoldering wood until that too was completely doused. The entire back side of the stable would have to be torn down and rebuilt, as well as part of one side and the roof. If Heather had discovered the fire five minutes later, the entire structure would have gone.

But there hadn't been any wind, and the house was safe. And, most important of all, Saul was safe, and Sam and Angel and Cicero. Cicero was still prancing and snorting, but Angel stood quietly, regarding the scene with curiosity but with no trace of fright as long as her people were there. She would be perfectly happy to be turned out to pasture with the other horses. The grass was lush for grazing, and she could sleep anywhere, on her feet as well as lying down. It wasn't even raining.

Heather sat on the ground where she was, in a puddle of slopped water. She was too exhausted to move herself to a dry place. She rested her head on her knees, still gasping for breath. Her arms and her shoulders felt as though they had been pulled out of their sockets. She looked up as Brice put his hand on her shoulder.

"Saul tells me that it was you who discovered the fire, and that you were already going in to try to get the horses out when your screaming and Sam's barking woke him up. He says that you brought Angel out. It's a good thing you didn't try to bring Cicero out, he would have trampled you for sure."

And then, to Heather's amazement, not to say the worst indignation she had ever experienced, Brice began to laugh. It was full dawn, light enough for him to get a good look at her.

"Look at you, sitting in a puddle! And your face is all streaked with soot and smoke. You look as though you're made up to take part in a minstrel show! Your hair's in a tangle, your nightgown and robe are soaked, and you look like a ten-year-old gamine!"

Reaching down, he pulled her to her feet. "But you look like an angel to me, even if you're a filthy, bedraggled angel! Losing the horses and the stable would have been a major disaster, and if Saul hadn't got out safely it would have been a blow from which we would never have recovered. We have you to thank that things aren't nearly as bad as they might have been."

"Her nightgown! She's in her nightgown!" Minna gasped. "Oh, my lands, I'm in my nightgown too! Whatever will people think?"

"If anyone were here to see, they'd think that we had a fire to put out," Brice said, amused. But there was no trace of amusement about him a moment later when Saul approached him, his old face drawn with fatigue.

"Mr. Brice, that fire was set. Somebody soaked the stable with kerosene and set a match to it. I can still smell it strong around there to the side where some got slopped on the ground. Sam found it first, he was nosing at it, and when I went to see what he was up to, I smelled it too."

Brice set off at a run, with Jared close behind him. When they returned, their faces were filled with anger.

"Saul is right," Jared said. "We can still smell the coal oil. Mr. Arlington, do you have any enemies, anyone who would want to do you harm?"

Brice and Caldwell looked at each other, their expressions meaningful in a way that Heather couldn't interpret.

"I expect that every man makes an enemy somewhere along the way. Right at the moment, I can't think who might have done this. It's just as likely that we'll never find out."

"Then you'd better do some tall hoping that he won't try something like this again! The next time he might get luckier."

"We're not going to solve the mystery tonight, that's certain," Brice said. "Aunt Minna, we could do with some coffee. And then you ladies had better get back to bed. You haven't had any sleep at all."

They turned as Della came up to them. The girl's eyes were round with excitement and apprehension. "Miss Minna, Elspeth's already got sandwiches an' coffee made. She told Pearl and me to keep out of your way." Elspeth and the two girls slept in a room off the kitchen house, and the commotion had awakened them. "Pearl and me will take it right to the dining room now if you're ready."

Brice put his hand on Della's shoulder and gave it a pat. "Good girl! I'll tell Elspeth that we appreciate her thoughtfulness. You all did exactly the right thing. Thank you, Della. Emma, you'd better get out of those sopping clothes before you eat. Della will send Pearl to your room to help you. Della, have Pearl bring hot water so Miss Emma can wash off that grime."

Jared, his own face begrimed, and sucking on the heel of his hand where he had singed it by coming too close to the flames, stopped sucking at the burn long enough to grin at Heather.

"You sure could use a good scrubbing! But first, tell me how you happened to discover the fire. What on earth were you doing, wandering around outside in your nightclothes at that hour?"

Heather had no intention of telling him, or anyone, that she'd been daydreaming, gazing down at the rose garden from her bedroom window and pretending that she was down there with a handsome, romantic sweetheart.

"My windows were open and I smelled the smoke," she said. It wasn't a lie, exactly. Her windows had been open and she had smelled the smoke. "I thought I'd better look around, just to be on the safe side, that's all."

Brice's face was stern again. "The next time you smell smoke, rouse us men and let us handle it. Not that we don't appreciate what you did, but you might have been hurt. It was foolhardy of you, Emma, to say the least. But never mind, you've done us a great service, and we're very grateful to you."

This was the first time he'd ever called her by her given name with any degree of warmth, and it had taken a near disaster to do it. Not that she could take much comfort from that, because he had already turned back to Caldwell, and the two of them were deep in a low-voiced conversation.

"Come along, Emma dear. We must make ourselves presentable," Minna said, taking her hand. "What a heroine you are! Rosie will be beside herself for having missed all the excitement, but you can be sure that everybody in the county will hear how brave you were. Just imagine you having the courage to go into that burning stable and bring Angel out! I probably would have just stood there and cried."

"No, you wouldn't. People just naturally do what they have to do. They don't stop to think about it, they just do it," Heather assured her. At least that was the way it had been with her.

Looking back over her shoulder to see if the men were following them back to the house, she saw Jared still grinning at the spectacle she made in her sopping and bedraggled nightclothes. She stuck out her tongue at him.

Drat! Wouldn't you know, Brice took that exact moment to look in her direction, and now he was grinning too, his face filled with amusement at her childish behavior. What on earth had possessed her to stick out her tongue, reinforcing the impression that she was nothing more than an urchin?

If she had ever had any chance of making Brice notice her as an attractive, desirable young lady, it was gone now. He'd never be able to look at her without remembering how she had looked tonight. This might have been the most exciting night of her entire life, but it certainly hadn't been romantic!

∾ *Chapter 10* ∾

PHOEBE DROVE THE distance between Bennington and Arbordale as fast as she could urge her father's horse. She was defying her mother by making this trip, and her father was bearing the brunt of it. The Roundtree family had been virtually at war ever since Phoebe had declared that she was going to the Arlingtons' ball, and her father had taken her side against her mother. Bertha Roundtree was firmly convinced of Brice's guilt in the matter of Naomi Thaxter's disappearance, and Phoebe and Ephraim were just as firmly convinced of his innocence and of the fact that the Arlingtons deserved all the support they could get.

It was Mrs. Langdon who persuaded Bertha Roundtree that Brice was guilty. Alice Langdon had made a particular point of cultivating Bertha after Naomi's disappearance, telling the minister's wife that there was no doubt that Brice had engineered Naomi's dropping out of sight. Alice had confided in Bertha that Caldwell Arlington had been quite a rake and a womanizer in his younger days, that she herself had felt compelled to break off with him because of his womanizing habits and because of improper advances he had made to her. She had pointed out that the old adage "Like father, like son" was undoubtedly true, no matter that Brice had the reputation of being entirely proper in his behavior.

Flattered because the wealthiest and most socially influential woman in the county had made her her confidante, Bertha had believed her. But Phoebe and Ephraim suspected that Alice Langdon was merely trying to vindicate the broken engagement between Brice and Evelyn. The Langdons wouldn't want anyone to suspect that the actual reason Evelyn had broken the engagement was that the Arlingtons were in such severe financial difficulties, and so they had grasped the opportunity to put forth a legitimate reason for the breaking off. If the minister's wife believed that Brice was guilty, a great many other ladies would believe the same.

Phoebe had been a happy and contented young woman before Naomi Thaxter came to Bennington. It was true that she hadn't had many suitors besieging her doorstep, because most of the young men had considered her more a friend than a potential sweetheart. But then David Inges had come to take over the *Bennington Bugle,* and they had taken an immediate liking to each other. David had become Phoebe's constant escort, and it had been taken for granted that their engagement would be announced at any time.

Naomi's arrival in Bennington had changed all that. Not immediately, but Phoebe had seen the handwriting on the wall when she'd seen how David had looked at the beautiful young orphan who had everyone feeling sorry for her. It wasn't as though she and David had actually been engaged. David hadn't asked her to marry him, although Phoebe was sure that he would have if Naomi hadn't come between them.

Phoebe could see that Naomi had been spoiled, that she had an inborn conviction that it was her right to take whatever she wanted. As the wife of the town editor, Naomi's social position would take a big upward step, and she would live very comfortably, much more comfortably than staying in Matthew Thaxter's house and having to work at the Emporium.

And David, being a man, hadn't been able to see the calculation behind those big blue eyes and wistful smile. Naomi had awakened all of his protective instincts, and Phoebe had been helpless to combat it.

She had held her head high, refusing to act the part of a jilted girl and to suffer being pitied. But her heart had ached with an ache she had known would never leave her. She had loved David with all her heart, and she still loved him.

When Carl Amhurst had moved to take David's place in her life, she accepted his company as a stopgap to help her over the worst of her heartbreak. Her mother, furious because of David's defection, favored Carl, who was almost as good a catch. Carl attended Ephraim's church, and his position at the bank made him highly eligible. Phoebe had never meant for her relationship with Carl to become serious. Carl was a pleasant companion, and that was all. If either Carl or her mother had hoped that something more would come of it, she would soon have to find a way to break off the friendship before it got out of hand.

And then, just when Phoebe had been resigned to losing David, her heart had filled with a tentative hope again. Evelyn Langdon and her family had gone away for an extended visit to relatives on the occasion of a marriage in the family. And Brice Arlington, stopping in at the Emporium to pick up some things for Miss Minna, had been as sympathetic toward the orphaned girl as everyone else in town. He had already heard a great deal about her, gossip being what it was in a small town, but he found her even more appealing than he had been led to expect.

Naomi's eyes had gone wide when Brice introduced himself to her. "Mr. Arlington! You live at Arbordale Plantation, don't you? I've met your aunt, she's just the sweetest lady! Everyone says that Arbordale is just beautiful!"

Naomi's eyes had gone all soft and wistful, and there had been a quaver in her voice. Phoebe had been there that day, buying a length of dress material, and she had seen it all. She had almost been amused at how easily Brice had fallen into the trap.

"I've never seen a plantation. There aren't any up North," Naomi had said, her eyes growing even more wistful. And of course Brice, gallant Southern gentleman that he was, had taken the bait hook, line, and sinker. How susceptible men were, even the most intelligent of them!

"I'm sure Aunt Minna will invite you to Arbordale, Miss Thaxter. You can expect an invitation very soon."

The invitation, in Minna's beautiful Spencerian handwriting, had arrived the following day, hand-delivered by Saul. Triumphant, Naomi had shown it to everyone who came into the store, her excitement touching everyone's heart.

Matthew Thaxter had been as elated as his niece. He had always labored under a gnawing envy of people like the Arlingtons, born to wealth and prestige, while he himself had had to work hard for all he possessed and in spite of his moderate success could not be considered a member of the upper echelons of society. Naomi's acceptance into that society would reflect on him.

Even more, once Naomi was accepted, it wasn't beyond the realms of possibility that she might do even better than David Inges when it came to marriage. Matthew had been pleased about David, but if Naomi should marry into a plantation family, some young scion she met through the Arlingtons' auspices, it would be even better. He would feel equal, at last, to his cousin John, who owned the bank. The much more successful John had always patronized him, and it had enraged him although he had been able to conceal his rage successfully.

For Naomi, the visit to Arbordale had been like a visit to fairyland. Brice was the knight in shining armor; the horse and buggy which he brought to personally escort her to the plantation was a golden coach. Minna and Caldwell had welcomed her warmly. Minna's heart was soft, and, like everyone else in Bennington, she felt sorry for the girl. They had had tea in the rose arbor, Minna had shown her through the house, and Brice had been attentive to her. Naomi had returned home, again driven by Brice, with stars in her eyes.

The Arlingtons' kindness had extended beyond that first invitation. Naomi had told Minna the story of her life. The pathos of the orphaned girl being forced to fall back on her uncle's charity brought tears to Minna's eyes. Minna had been so touched that she had planned a garden party for the following week.

The party had been held in the afternoon, on Wednesday, the day that the *Bennington Bugle* went to press, so David had not been able to attend. Minna hadn't thought about it being press day when she set the date. And so once again Brice had been pressed into service to fetch Naomi from town and take her home again.

Phoebe had attended the party with Carl. John Thaxter had given him the afternoon off for that purpose, mindful that it was good for the bank to have his teller linked with the minister's daughter.

Phoebe had always loved visiting Arbordale. She was fond of Miss Minna, and she had always liked Brice and respected Caldwell. But her enjoyment of this party was marred when she saw that Naomi was making entirely too much of having been invited.

It was a difficult time for Phoebe. On the one hand, if Naomi set her sights on Brice, hoping to win him away from Evelyn Langdon and dropping David to that end, it was possible that David would turn back to her even if it were only in search of sympathy. Ashamed of her weakness, she knew she would take him back on any terms. On the other hand, Phoebe was convinced that Naomi was doomed to disappointment and that she might even make things difficult for Brice, who had no idea what was going on in the vain girl's head.

Everything Phoebe had feared came true. Naomi, carried away by what she imagined was her great social success and reaching for still more, actually convinced herself that Brice was already in love with her. The other girls her age were agog to hear all about it when Naomi intimated to them that Brice was already on the verge of proposing to her.

"It was love at first sight!" Naomi said breathlessly, her eyes shining. "I knew the minute I looked at him that he was the only man for me, and he felt the same way. As soon as Miss Langdon comes back, he'll break off with her, and then we'll be engaged!"

"Has he kissed you?" The question was as breathless as

Naomi's far-fetched claims, as the girls crowded around her to hear every detail. More than one of them would be glad to see Evelyn get her comeuppance. Evelyn had snubbed them all on more than one occasion, making transparent excuses to decline their invitations to parties. Any girl as beautiful and wealthy and well dressed as Evelyn was bound to be envied and resented by other girls who were less well endowed.

"But what about David?" Phoebe had asked Naomi, confronting her in the Emporium.

"Poor David," Naomi had sighed. "I hate to break his heart, honestly I do, but there's just no help for it. There was never anyone like Brice. How could I even think of David when Brice is courting me?"

"He's hardly courting you. Just because you were invited to Arbordale twice doesn't mean that he's planning on asking you to marry him," Phoebe had tried to warn her. "It's been taken as a matter of course that Brice and Evelyn would marry ever since they were hardly more than children."

"Oh, pooh! Engagements have been broken before. I know that Brice is in love with me, I can tell." And Naomi had gone right on telling anyone who would listen about how romantic Brice was, the tender things he had whispered in her ear, the passionate embraces they had shared. Phoebe didn't believe a word of it, but others did, and the story spread, and even people who should have known better had begun to believe it. After all, Naomi was a beauty, and to the public at large she gave the impression that she was a good deal nicer and sweeter than Evelyn Langdon. There were many who thought that Brice would do well to break off with Evelyn in favor of the younger girl, in spite of the fact that the Langdons were the wealthiest family in the county and Naomi didn't have a cent. Money wasn't everything. If Naomi could make Brice happier than Evelyn would, then Brice should choose Naomi.

Matthew Thaxter went around with a smug smile on his face, being more jovial with his customers than was his habit. Naomi had convinced him that the engagement between her and Brice was all but accomplished. Matthew was so elated that he went so far as to allow Naomi to choose a length of his most expensive fabric, and he engaged Mrs. Betts, the seamstress, to make her a party dress to wear to the annual box supper which was always held at the Oddfellows' Hall to raise money for the school. The box supper was the most important social event of the year. The ladies kept the contents of their boxes and baskets a sacred secret, and the men bid on them, the highest bidder for each box or basket sharing the supper with the lady who had prepared it.

The Arlingtons had always attended the box suppers before Brice and Evelyn had become engaged, although the Langdons had never put in an appearance, sending a cash contribution instead. But this year, as the Langdons were away, Brice put in an appearance with Caldwell and Minna. Caldwell would bid on Rosamund Becker's basket, and Brice would bid on Minna's. Isobel Becker, like the Langdons, never attended the affair, holding that it was demeaning to womanhood, but Rosie always had the time of her life.

David had asked Naomi to come with him, but Naomi had refused him because she didn't want Brice to think that she was committed to David. When she entered the hall, her face flamed with gratification when she saw that Brice was there.

Minna saw her at once and motioned for her to join them, nudging Brice and whispering to him to bid on the girl's basket, because, knowing Matthew's parsimonious ways, she feared that its contents might shame Naomi.

Phoebe, who was there with Carl, looked from Naomi to Brice to David, and her heart ached when she saw David wince as Minna asked Naomi to join the Arlingtons. David had counted on bidding on Naomi's basket, so that he would have her company for at least this little while.

Naomi had been the last to arrive because she had spent so much time primping in front of her mirror in her new dress, a lovely blue that accented the blue of her eyes. The dress had a low neckline to show off the little gold heart locket that her father had given her for her fifteenth birthday, and she looked so fresh and lovely and innocent that she knew she would be the prettiest girl there.

Because she had been the last to arrive, her basket was the last to be put up for auction. David bid a dollar, and Brice, nudged by Minna, doubled it. Minna, unfortunately, had no idea how much David was in love with Naomi, or she would have refrained. David bid three dollars, and Brice bid four.

"Four-fifty!" David said. Again, Minna nudged Brice, and he raised it to five. No such price had ever been paid for a basket in all the years the box supper had been held, and the hall was buzzing.

David dropped out. He would have been glad to bid ten dollars, but even if he had bid fifty and Brice had dropped out, it would have been no victory. Naomi would have hated him for outbidding Brice, and he would be even worse off than he was now.

Naomi glowed. Brice assured her that the fried chicken was the best he had ever tasted, that her potato salad was delicious, that the cake she had baked was light enough to rival Elspeth's best. None of it was true, Naomi wasn't much of a cook, but she didn't know that it wasn't true.

There was dancing, with piano and fiddle music, after the last of the dirty dishes had been packed up. Naomi had never square danced, but the calls were easy and there weren't too many of them to keep sorted out. In another square, Phoebe saw that Naomi was doing very well with Brice pushing and pulling her in the proper directions. The girl was radiant, laughing and sparkling. Brice, Phoebe thought, had no idea what he was doing. It would never occur to him that he was being anything but kind to an unfortunate child.

His kindness extended even farther. Matthew had not attended the affair, and, having bid on her basket, the gentlemanly thing for Brice to do was escort her home. Eyes met and eyebrows rose and heads nodded as the two left the hall together. In Bennington, for a young man to bid on a girl's basket and then escort her home was tantamount to making a declaration of intentions.

Phoebe had wept that night in the privacy of her bedroom. She'd seen the anguish on David's face when David had left early. And she'd been sure that there would not be any happy endings. Evelyn Langdon was bound to be furious when she learned that Brice had been escorting Naomi around, and that would mean trouble for Brice. David was already suffering, and Naomi would be crushed when Evelyn returned and Brice no longer saw her. It was a certainty that Evelyn would see to it that Naomi was not invited to any affair that the Langdons would either give or attend.

Naomi would probably turn back to David then, and David, as enamored of her as he was, would probably forgive her. But he would always remember that he had been her second choice, and his happiness would be marred. For Phoebe, there was no possibility of a happy ending. Until she had seen the hurt on David's face tonight, she had harbored a hope that he would turn to her again, but now that hope was dashed.

On the day after the box supper, Naomi had regaled her circle of admiring girlfriends with stories of Brice's romantic attentions to her when he had escorted her home. The girls lost no time in spreading the story to their parents. It seemed as if the entire town of Bennington was holding its breath, waiting to see what would happen next.

On the second day after the box supper, Naomi had disappeared. She was not in the kitchen preparing Matthew's breakfast, as she should have been, when Matthew had come down. He had checked her room, and her bed was empty. A valise had been missing, along with a few of her clothes and her toilet set.

After every possibility had been explored and nothing could be learned of her whereabouts, Brice had come under suspicion. He had been the logical suspect. David, the only other man in Bennington who could have had any possible motive, had been at home in his upstairs apartment at Mrs. McCartney's home. Mrs. McCartney attested to that in no uncertain terms, because David had kept her awake all night with his pacing.

There wasn't a modicum of proof that Brice had had anything to do with Naomi's disappearance, but fully half of Bennington didn't need any proof. There wasn't any doubt whatever that Brice had toyed with the innocent girl's affections. They'd all seen it with their own eyes. Naomi's descriptions of Brice's passion for her had fallen on many ears eager to believe every word of it, if only because it added excitement to their lives. Everyone knew, they said again and again, how wealthy young plantation owners were, even if butter wouldn't melt in their mouths in the faces they turned toward the public. And Naomi was not only a beautiful girl, but she had virtually thrown herself at him.

When the Langdons returned home and Evelyn lost no time in breaking her engagement to Brice, their suspicions were confirmed. If the Langdons believed that Brice was guilty, that was enough for them. And Bertha Roundtree, the minister's wife, looked sad and shocked as she nodded. She, too, believed Brice was guilty. What more proof could anyone want?

The town split in two. Those who believed Brice was guilty insisted that he had had good reason to spirit Naomi out of town, that he had seduced her and he hadn't dared to take the chance that she wouldn't tell. The Arlingtons had bought her off as any number of similarly unfortunate girls had been bought off, in order to keep Brice's sins from coming to Evelyn's ears.

Not that it had done Brice any good. Evelyn hadn't been home for a day before she heard all about it from those who believed it was their duty to tell her.

Matthew Thaxter ranted and raved, demanding that Brice be brought to justice. His brief dreams of basking in his niece's glory had been thwarted, and not only that, Naomi's honor—and his own—had been besmirched. But you can't arrest a man for having an affair with a girl who knew no better than to let him have his way with her, and so Brice remained free.

David, his face white, had not ranted and raved. Believing as Matthew did, he had gone to Arbordale and assaulted Brice physically. Neither had won the fight. They were evenly matched, both suffered bruises and abrasions, and it settled nothing. Caldwell had wanted to bring charges of assault against David, but Brice had refused, saying that in David's place he would have felt the same way. The Arlingtons had been bewildered and shocked at the tide of hostile feelings against them, and it would have made it worse if they had had David, who was so well liked, arrested.

The search for Naomi went on, but with less impetus as time passed. There was no way of proving that Brice had been away from Arbordale at the time of Naomi's disappearance. He could have driven her to Richmond or some other city and put her on a train, and the Arlingtons would swear that he had never been away from home.

The only tangible punishment dealt out to Brice and his family was when John Thaxter, prodded by his friend Burton Langdon, had refused to extend Caldwell's loan. The Arlingtons were feeling the pinch. They had had to let a good deal of their help at the plantation go, the competent house servants had been replaced with two green girls, and there was only Elspeth in the kitchen house and Saul to take care of the stables and grounds and a skeleton crew for the fields.

It was common talk now that the Arlingtons were going to lose Arbordale, and some people smiled smugly and said it served them right; others claimed that Brice would never have seduced a girl who was so young and innocent and that she had simply run away when she'd realized that Brice had never had any serious interest in her. She would have wanted both to save herself from ridicule and to get away from her uncle. Matthew Thaxter wasn't the easiest man to live with, and he would be even harder to live with once he learned that Naomi had lost her chance to rise in the world and take him along with her.

The most damaging evidence against Brice was that no one could figure out how Naomi had managed to leave Bennington without being seen, unless she had help. And no one except Brice could have had any reason to help her by providing transportation and money.

In her father's buggy, Phoebe urged Reliable on. Her father had given the gelding that name because he was so reliable in all sorts of weather and under all sorts of road conditions. True to his name, Reliable quickened his pace, and now at last Arbordale was in sight.

Saul rose from where he was weeding a flowerbed, his arthritic joints creaking, and came to take the bridle when Phoebe drew Reliable to a halt in front of the house and jumped out of the buggy. She lifted her skirts and ran to the house. They had to do something, they just had to! In her agitation, she didn't bother to knock. She just rushed inside, nearly bowling over an astonished Heather as she was on her way out to ask Saul to hitch up Angel so that she could take another buggy ride to stave off her imminent demise from terminal boredom. The exciting, romantic South, bah!

↦ *Chapter 11* ↤

THEY WERE ON the verandah, out of earshot of the house girls. Phoebe, her face pinched and white, was imploring Caldwell and Brice to do something.

"He didn't do it. David would never do such a thing!" Phoebe insisted. "I know that he came here and fought with Brice, but that wasn't underhanded, that wasn't sneaking around trying to do you a hurt and not be caught at it. But Sheriff Kotter has locked David up in jail anyway. He says that arson is a major crime and that Bennington isn't going to stand for it, and that there's enough evidence to prove that David did it. The damning thing is that David was near Arbordale when your stable was set afire. He was seen, and that's enough for Clarence Kotter. But David didn't do it!"

"You don't have to convince me, Miss Phoebe," Brice told her, his face serious. "I can see David trying to tear me apart again, but not skulking around in the middle of the night setting stables afire."

"Then you'll get him out? You'll go straight to Sheriff Kotter and tell him that David is innocent?"

"Of course I'll go. But I can't promise that it will do any good. Kotter is a stubborn man, and when he gets an idea in his head it would take an earthquake to get it out. I'll do what I can, I'll tell him that I'm certain he's made a mistake, but I can't guarantee you that he'll be reasonable."

"What David needs is a lawyer," Jared said with all the conviction that his education in law had instilled in him. "I'd better go with you. At least I can evaluate the facts. Just because the Barnstables saw David driving in this direction while they were on their way back to town after the ball isn't proof that David set the fire. It's what we call circumstantial evidence, and circumstantial evidence is rarely enough to convict."

"Oh, Mr. Cranston, would you?" Phoebe looked so grateful that Heather felt like crying for her. But she was still puzzled. She didn't believe for a minute that David had sloshed kerosene on the stable walls and set it afire, but why was Phoebe Roundtree, who was keeping company with Carl Amhurst, so upset about his arrest that she looked as though she were being torn apart? And what had Brice meant when he'd said that he could see David coming to Arbordale *again* to try to tear him apart? Apparently David had done it before, but what possible reason could he have had for fighting Brice even once?

There was one way to find out, and that was to ask. And, whether it was polite to ask or not, she asked. This was too intriguing to stick to politeness. She'd burst if she didn't find out.

"Why would anyone think that David Inges would want to burn down your stable? Or what you just said, come out here and fight with Brice *again?*"

Minna gasped, looking so consternated at the questions that Heather almost wished she hadn't asked them. Caldwell ran her a close second, his face a mixture of emotions, none of which bespoke a settled state of mind.

Only Brice looked calm, mixed with a hearty measure of determination. When his father shook his head at him, Brice shook his own decisively.

"No, Father. This has gone far enough. I'm sick and tired of this charade. It's time to bring everything out into the open. Miss Emma, Jared, I'm ashamed to confess that you were asked to visit Arbordale for selfish and underhanded reasons. The fact is that we can't get an extension on our loan at the bank so that we can keep Arbordale on its feet, because I'm under suspicion of having seduced Naomi

Thaxter and then spiriting her away to hide my guilt. Matthew Thaxter and John Thaxter are cousins, and John has taken steps to ensure that no other bank will extend us a loan either.

"I'm afraid my father was so desperate that he came up with the idea of Emma and me making a match of it so that he could ask your father for a loan. I was against the idea from the first, not meaning any slur on your attractiveness, Miss Emma. You are a lovely girl, and under different circumstances I might have fallen in love with you, but I would never ask you to marry me in order to get money from your father!"

Oh, my! Heather's questions had been answered with a vengeance. Brice was under suspicion of doing a despicable thing, and without any doubt her own suspicion that he had suffered a broken romance with Evelyn Langdon was true. The suspicion against Brice would be enough to make a girl as haughty and proud as Evelyn break off her engagement to him.

And now the Arlingtons were in danger of losing their plantation, and David Inges was in jail for setting fire to the stable! How had she ever thought Virginia was dull?

And then her heart went out to Brice. What a dreadful thing to be suspected of having had a hand in Naomi Thaxter's disappearance! His heart must have been broken when Evelyn broke their engagement. And now to face losing his home as well!

Caldwell spoke in his own defense. "It isn't as bad as it sounds. After all, Thatcher and I have toyed with the idea of bringing Brice and Emma together for a long time, way before all this happened. It pleased our fancy to think that you might make a match of it. I would have wanted you and Brice to get married even if there was no question of money involved. But Brice thwarted all our plans when he fell in love with Evelyn Langdon. I didn't revive my old dream until Evelyn broke her engagement to him."

"I'm glad she broke the engagement!" Minna's voice was far more forceful than Heather had dreamed it could be. "I never cared much for her, she's entirely too filled with her own importance, and her breaking the engagement proved beyond any doubt that she isn't good enough for Brice. Any real woman would have believed in him and stood by him, but she turned tail at the first hint of scandal. There isn't any loyalty in her at all!"

Which was exactly Heather's opinion. In Evelyn's place, nothing could have pried her from Brice's side, she would have gone right on loving him, and married him, and not given a hang about the scandal. She would have made her father give Caldwell the money he needed to save Arbordale, and if her father wouldn't agree, she would have married Brice anyway.

Then another thought struck her, and she ached for Jared as well. Their visit to Arbordale was a total loss. There couldn't be any loan from Caldwell because Caldwell didn't have any money, Caldwell hoped to borrow money from Thatcher! Heather could have cried for Jared, just as she felt like crying for Brice. What a tangle everything was! Novels always had happy endings, but she was learning that real life wasn't like that at all.

"I'll get started for town," Brice said. He looked grim, but it was evident that he was going to do his best for David Inges even if the young newspaperman was one of the ones who thought he was guilty of seducing Naomi, and had tried to beat him to a pulp in retaliation. "Are you coming with me, Jared? None of this really concerns you, but we'll appreciate any help you can give us."

Jared jerked himself back from his own bleak thoughts, which were the same as Heather's. All this time wasted, and for nothing! The Arlingtons were just as impoverished as he was; there wouldn't be a penny from them. There was nothing to do but admit defeat, go back to Albany, and resign himself to years of apprenticeship in some other lawyer's office before he'd be able to set up a practice of his own.

"I'm coming," he said.

"David might not be enthusiastic about accepting help from a lawyer who's a friend of ours," Brice warned him. "But the only other lawyer in town happens to be among the ones who think I'm innocent, and he'd be prejudiced against David. I don't believe David is in any financial position to import a good lawyer from Richmond. I don't know how much he can afford to pay you. You might be working for nothing."

"Experience is worth something. Besides, I couldn't accept a fee anyway. I'm not licensed to practice in Virginia; all I can do is offer what advice I can."

"Phoebe, stay here for a while. You're upset, and you need to rest and compose yourself," Minna urged. "Let me bring you a nice glass of lemonade."

Heather nearly strangled. Not Minna's lemonade! She'd wager that Phoebe had never tasted alcohol in any form in her life, and there was no telling how it would affect her. Even if it didn't affect her, she'd be shocked out of her shoes!

She didn't have to rack her brain to find a way to keep Minna from lacing Phoebe's lemonade, because Phoebe shook her head.

"No, I'm going back to town. Mother is already angry with me for concerning myself about David, and I left poor Father trying to calm her. He's probably having a hard time of it."

The minute the two buggies left, Heather rounded on Minna. "Why is Phoebe so concerned about David, when she's keeping company with Mr. Amhurst? I thought she and David had broken off."

Minna fluttered her hands. For once she hadn't brought her tatting with her to the verandah, and with nothing to keep them occupied when she was asked a delicate question, they had nothing to do but flutter.

"It isn't my place to let out secrets that aren't mine to divulge, but it isn't actually a secret; everybody in Bennington knows, so I suppose you might as well know. Phoebe is going with Mr. Amhurst now, but she didn't start going with him until after David had all but jilted her in favor of Naomi Thaxter. If Phoebe and David had actually been engaged, of course, David wouldn't have taken up with Naomi. David is a gentleman. But they weren't engaged, and so he was free to fall in love with another girl. But I'm afraid that Phoebe still loves David, and everything is all at sixes and sevens, and I just can't see how it's all going to turn out."

More and more tangles! Now Heather had to feel sorry for Phoebe too, because Phoebe had been jilted and her heart had been broken. Here she'd thought Phoebe was so serene, and all the time she'd been suffering.

Minna's hands fluttered again, and she suddenly looked stricken. Her face fell, and her eyes filled with tears.

"You and Jared will be leaving, of course, now that you know the whole disgraceful plot to get you engaged to Brice so that Caldwell could ask Thatcher for a loan. You'll probably be on tomorrow's train."

"We'll do no such thing!" Heather was indignant. "My goodness, we wouldn't think of leaving now! People might think that we left because we found out about your troubles and we think Brice is guilty. We're going to stay right here, so that everybody will know that we think he's innocent, and I'm going to tell everybody I see that he could never, never do what they think he did!"

Minna started to cry, and Heather rose to gather her into her arms and pat her shoulder.

"There now! Did you really think we would desert you? What you need is a nice, tall glass of lemonade."

Minna brightened. "I do believe you're right, Emma. We'll both have one. After all, it's always been considered respectable for ladies to have a glass of sherry when they're upset. I just don't happen to care for sherry. I'll go fetch Caldwell—I expect he's gone into his office—and see if he'd like a julep."

Caldwell thought that having a julep now was a fine idea, and while Minna was inside fixing the drinks, Heather questioned him about his situation.

"Mr. Arlington, couldn't you ask some of your friends for a loan?"

"My dear girl, don't think I haven't tried! But our friends in town don't have that kind of money, and our plantation friends were stricken with the same disastrous storm that all but ruined my crop, and they are nearly as financially embarrassed as I am. Running a plantation is fraught with uncertainty, my dear. There are good years and bad years. This happens to have been a bad year. I'm sorry that I got you here under false pretenses. It's going to be hard for you to forgive me, but I hope you will. I meant no harm, I actually thought there would be a good chance that you and Brice would hit it off. Your father always wrote me what a pretty and remarkable girl you are, and Brice deserved somebody better than Evelyn. I wanted to help him get over her by dangling another pretty girl under his nose. And I still happen to believe that he's worthy of any girl's love, even yours."

"Of course he is," Heather said. Inside, she felt miserable. Brice was certainly worthy of her love, but, just as certainly, she wasn't worthy of his! She wasn't even who she was supposed to be. If the Arlingtons knew the truth, they would have every right to throw her and Jared out, bag and baggage.

She wished she could tell Minna and Caldwell the truth right now. Being a liar wasn't anywhere near as easy as she had thought it would be, even if she hadn't meant any more harm than Caldwell had. Her conscience bothered her, and her stomach felt knotted.

But she couldn't tell them until Jared got back and she had a chance to talk to him about it. He had to be prepared. He was going to be horribly embarrassed, and she dreaded to think what Minna would think of her own part in what Brice had so aptly labeled a charade. All the same, Brice had been honest, and now she and Jared had to be honest as well.

The worst part of it was that she didn't want to leave Arbordale now. She wanted to find out how all this came out. She wanted to see Brice vindicated, and she wanted to see Phoebe happy again, and she wanted to meet Evelyn Langdon face to face and tell her exactly what she thought of her. She wouldn't even mind pulling out a few handfuls of that beautiful auburn hair.

Minna hadn't used a light touch with the lemonade. It was a good thing they were only going to have one. She hoped Jared's julep would be as strong when he got back, because he was going to need it when she told him that they had to tell the Arlingtons the truth. Right now she was sorry she had accepted her drink early; she would probably need it once their story was told.

Minna was right, things certainly were at sixes and sevens. Just when things were becoming exciting, she would have to leave. She truly wanted to see how this whole thing would end, but there wasn't a chance of that now, because she was a liar and a cheat.

"No upstart young lawyer from up North is going to come into my jail and tell me that I have to let an arsonist go! I'm sorry for David, and I'm sorry that his young lady is missing, but arson is serious here in Virginia even if it isn't where you come from!" Clarence Kotter's face was red, and he glared at Jared. "I say he's guilty and you say he's innocent, but here in Virginia a jury will decide, and he's going to stay right here until somebody puts up the money to bail him out, or until his trial."

"He has a family, hasn't he?" Jared wanted to know. "Won't they post bail for him?"

"He won't ask them. He says they've already done enough for him and he isn't going to ask them for anything more. So unless you're ready to put up the bail, he stays right where he is."

Jared's face flushed. He'd be glad to put up the bail, but he didn't have it any more than Caldwell and Brice had it.

"But you don't have a shred of evidence to hold him on!" he said. "Just because he was seen near Arbordale on the night the stable was burned doesn't mean that he set the fire. Any competent lawyer would get him off without half trying!"

"I don't have any evidence, don't I?" Kotter snorted. "Just take a look at this! I took a look-see out Arbordale way myself after I heard about the fire, and I found this alongside the road not half a mile from the plantation. Empty, only a few drops left in it, but it's kerosene all right, and I found this can right where David threw it after he doused the stable and set a match to it. Everybody knows that there's bad blood between David and Brice, and that gives David a motive, and this kerosene can is the evidence!"

"Everybody in Bennington must have a kerosene can," Jared pointed out. "People have to have coal oil for their lamps."

"Sure they have to have coal oil for their lamps. So they wouldn't go throwing away their kerosene cans, would they? And go to all the trouble of taking them out into the country to throw them away alongside the road. Not unless the kerosene can had been used to carry the kerosene that set that stable on fire, they wouldn't!"

"I'd like to talk to David, if you don't mind."

"You already heard him say that he doesn't want to talk to you. He's sitting right there in the cell. I can't force him to talk to you, that isn't part of my duties. A prisoner has the right to refuse to talk to anyone he doesn't want to talk to."

"He still has the right to the services of a lawyer, if you're going to be bull-headed enough to refuse to let him go now that you know Brice and Caldwell aren't going to press charges."

"I don't give a hang if the Arlingtons press charges or not. Nobody in my district is going to go around setting fires!"

"I'll have a court order for his release before you can blink an eye!" Jared said. That was a bluff. How was he going to persuade a judge to order David's release unless the judge was a good deal more sensible than Clarence Kotter? He'd got the idea, in the last few minutes, that Northerners' opinions weren't exactly welcomed here in Virginia.

"Now what are we going to do?" Brice asked when Jared joined him outside the building. They had decided that it would be better if Brice didn't go inside, in light of how David felt about him.

"I'm afraid we'll just have to tell Phoebe that our efforts have failed." It wasn't a task either of them looked forward to.

Bertha Roundtree almost closed her door in their faces when she saw who was asking to see her daughter, but Phoebe slipped past her, her eyes frantically searching theirs.

"Did you see him? Did you get him out?" she demanded, her breath catching in her throat.

"The answer is no to both questions. Kotter refused to turn him loose, and David refuses to talk to us." Brice's voice was regretful. "It didn't come as a surprise to me, but I'm sorry all the same."

Phoebe's face paled, but she raised her chin with determination. "Then I'll go and talk to him! He won't refuse to see me, and I'll persuade him."

"You will do no such thing!" Bertha Roundtree exclaimed, her face registering horror. "A young lady can't visit a jail! Think how it would set tongues to wagging. It would be a scandal! As for you, Mr. Arlington, I would be obliged if you did not come to this house again. We can't afford to become involved in such disgraceful matters. We have our position to protect. My husband has to answer to the church council for his actions!"

Ephraim Roundtree appeared in the doorway behind his wife. His spectacles were pushed up on his forehead, and he held a sheaf of papers in his hands. Bertha's shrill voice had penetrated to his study, and when he had heard her use Brice's name he had hurried to see what was going on.

"It will be perfectly proper for Phoebe to talk to David," Ephraim said. "I'll go with her myself, so that no tongues will wag. Fetch your hat, Phoebe. If you and Mr. Cranston would care to wait in the parlor, Brice, we shouldn't be too long."

The minister caught himself just in time to prevent himself from suggesting that Bertha serve refreshments to their guests while they waited. That would be pushing Bertha too far. Things were strained enough between them as it was. But he most certainly intended to see David. David was a parishioner of his, and it was his duty to aid any parishioner who was in trouble. Besides, he had a firm conviction that David was innocent.

Brice, with a discerning look at Bertha Roundtree's face, made haste to decline the offer. "That won't be necessary. Jared and I will walk up and down outside the courthouse until you've talked to David. I regret that we had to trouble you, Mrs. Roundtree."

Bertha sniffed.

Clarence Kotter's permission to allow Phoebe and Ephraim to see David was reluctant, but even a prisoner had a right to see his clergyman. Kotter wasn't supposed to take sides, but like all of Bennington he had formed his own opinion, and he thought Brice was guilty, and that gave David a prime motive for firing the Arlingtons' stable. Not that he blamed David, but it was his clear duty to hold the young man for trial.

Phoebe struggled to conceal the anguish on her face as she held both of her hands out to David.

"David, Father and I both think that you should talk to Mr. Cranston. I've met him. He's a fine young man, and he wants to help you," she said. "He doesn't have anything to do with all the other trouble. He just happens to be the son of one of Caldwell's oldest friends."

David's face tightened, and his eyes were hard. "How could I trust him? He's still a friend of the Arlingtons even if he is from up North."

"But Brice and his father don't think you're the one who set fire to their stable. They aren't going to press charges. The only thing against you is that you were seen driving toward Arbordale that night. David, what on earth were you doing driving around at that time of night?"

David looked a little shamefaced. "I couldn't sleep. I was thinking about Naomi. Not knowing what happened to her is driving me crazy. I had some insane idea that I'd force my way into the Arlingtons' house and confront Brice in front of all their guests. It seemed to me that it was the worst sort of injustice that he should be living a normal life, even enjoying a ball!"

He broke off, looking more ashamed than ever. "The drive cleared my head. I realized it wouldn't do any good, that I'd just be making a fool of myself and embarrassing a lot of innocent people as well. I was just about to turn around and go back when the Barnstables passed me on their way back to town. If I'd turned around just a few minutes sooner, they wouldn't have seen me, and I wouldn't be in jail now."

"Yes, I remember that the Barnstables were among the

first to leave. They aren't used to late hours, and Mr. Barnstable had indigestion from eating too much. Stella Barnstable had warned him about it, but you know how delicious Elspeth's food is, and he wasn't able to resist second helpings of everything."

David ran his fingers through his hair, making it stand up in boyish spikes above his forehead, and Phoebe's heart twisted.

"If I'd turned around right then and followed George back, I still wouldn't be under suspicion. But the Barnstables live right next door to Mrs. McCartney's house, and George is the slowest man in Bennington about unhitching his horse. I knew he'd buttonhole me and ask me a lot of questions about where I'd been at that time of night, questions that I didn't want to answer. As it happened, the Barnstables didn't hear me come back. I allowed plenty of time for them to get into their house and into bed so I wouldn't have to talk to them."

It was perfectly reasonable, but at least half the town wouldn't believe that David had turned around and returned home without setting fire to the Arlingtons' stable. But what was done was done, and there was no use wishing that it had been done differently.

"Talk to Jared Cranston, David. It can't do any harm. He's studied law, and he might be able to help you."

Now David's eyes flashed with anger. "I can't see how you can be so blind where Brice Arlington is concerned! Can't you see that he's the only one who could have had a hand in Naomi's disappearance?"

"David, I've known Brice all my life. Nothing will ever convince me that he had anything to do with Naomi's disappearance! He simply isn't capable of the despicable actions that are being laid at his door. But even beyond that, you have the *Bugle* to think of. How can you keep it going if you're in jail? You've just got it on its feet, and it would be dreadful if you lost it now just because you're so stubborn!"

David spread his hands. Phoebe was right. If there was any possible way he could get out of here, he had to take it. Seeing his answer in his eyes, Phoebe's face lit up in a relieved smile.

"I'll tell him he can come in. Tell him everything you can remember, David. I know he'll do the best he can for you."

David had little to add to what Jared already knew. "It looks bad for me," he said, his eyes clouded with worry as he thought of his newspaper plant standing idle. "Everybody knows how I feel about Brice Arlington, and I was near their place when the stable was fired. I didn't do it, but there's no way to prove that I didn't."

Jared looked a good deal more cheerful. A lawyer has to look cheerful or else people will think his case is weak.

"Where is your coal oil can?" he asked. "And what does it look like?"

David was puzzled. "It's at my place, where it always is. And it looks like a kerosene can. They all look pretty much alike. There's a shed out in back, and mine is right beside Mrs. McCartney's."

Jared turned to Kotter. "Can you spare a few minutes to walk to Mrs. McCartney's house with me? There's something I want to check up on, and I don't want to be arrested for trespassing if Mrs. McCartney catches me prowling around in her shed."

"What do you want to check up on?" Kotter asked suspiciously. But his curiosity was aroused, and he agreed to go with Jared.

The kerosene cans, both of them, were where David had said they would be. Mrs. McCartney, a heavy woman with an opinionated voice, swore that one of them was hers and the other David's, although how she could tell them apart was a mystery.

"I know my own coal oil can when I see it!" Mrs. McCartney said, glaring at Clarence Kotter. "And I know Mr. Inges's coal oil can when I see it! I see them every day, so I ought to know them, and as for you, Clarence Kotter, you'd better let that nice young man out of jail, or I won't vote for you the next time you come up for election!"

"Mrs. McCartney, it's been a pleasure to meet you," Jared said, pumping the woman's hand. "It's always a pleasure to meet someone of such superior intelligence."

"Well, I should hope so!" Mrs. McCartney said.

"Now, if you'll tell me where I can find Judge Eldridge,

I'll be even more obliged to you," Jared told her. He could have asked Kotter, or Brice, but it was more fun asking Mrs. McCartney in front of Kotter.

"Why, he'll be in his office upstairs in the courthouse at this time of day," Mrs. McCartney said. "He doesn't have all that much to do, but he keeps his regular hours just like clockwork. Are you going to get Mr. Inges out of jail?"

"That's exactly what I'm going to do," Jared assured her. He wished he were as sure as his voice implied.

The judge was a plump, self-satisfied-looking man with a sense of his own importance. But whatever his appearance, he heard Jared out, and in a matter of minutes Jared had an order for David's release, on his own recognizance, with the stipulation that he keep himself available pending a hearing and a possible trial.

"Isn't likely that he'll take off," the judge said, pursing his lips. "He has a newspaper to get out. If Clarence Kotter had consulted me, I would have advised him not to put Mr. Inges in jail in the first place. He should have had sense enough to check up on that coal oil can the way you did." Jared had a definite feeling that the judge relished the opportunity to make it clear that his authority exceeded Kotter's.

Jared wasn't officially representing David, and this wasn't officially his case, but he still felt a warm glow of satisfaction. Maybe being a lawyer wouldn't be so bad after all. At least he could be the best lawyer he knew how to be.

❧ Chapter 12 ❧

JARED AND BRICE were greeted by a scene of pandemonium when they returned to Arbordale. Miss Rosamund Becker's trap was in front of the house, and Saul was helping Ben carry valises and boxes and small trunks up onto the verandah. Inside the house, Pearl and Della were scurrying up and down the stairs, while from the second floor, three feminine voices chattered in a frenzy of excitement.

"Saul, what the devil is going on?" Brice demanded. "It looks as if Miss Rosamund has come to stay for the rest of her life!"

It was Ben who answered. "Reckon that's just what she's done, Mr. Brice. She packed up everything she owns, and here we are."

They went inside, and Minna and Rosamund appeared at the top of the stairs. "Pearl, you mind that you spread those sheets good and smooth, with nice, tight, square corners."

"I'll show her how." Heather's voice came down to them. "Don't worry about it, Miss Minna. I'll show her how to make the squarest corners ever."

"Sam, you and Ben carry all those things on up, they aren't going to sprout feet and walk up by themselves! Della, you can start unpacking Miss Rosie's things as soon as they're carried up. Brice, here you are at last! Did you get David out of jail?"

172

"He's out," Brice told her. "What's happening here, if I may ask?"

"I've come to stay." Rosie's voice was bubbling over. "Isobel and I were at it hammer and tongs all morning, ever since Mrs. Dewey told us that David Inges was in jail for burning down your stable. Isobel said he did it, and I said he didn't. Isobel said that she didn't blame him for doing it because you richly deserved it, and I called her an idiot, which isn't any lie. Isobel said that I'd disgraced our name by coming to your ball and that from now on I had to do exactly as she said because she's older. I've been doing exactly as she says ever since Papa died, just because she's older. But this morning it occurred to me that Papa left everything to us equally, and I have as much right to my opinion as she has to hers, even more because I'm always right and she's always wrong!

"Then Isobel said that if I was going to be such a disgrace, taking the part of people who were guilty of God knows what, I wasn't welcome in her house any longer, and I told her that she can have the house and rot in it for all I care, I'll just have a lawyer set a fair value on it and take that much more in cash to make up for it. And here I am."

Jared was awed. How any woman of Rosamund's age could have made that speech without pausing to draw a breath was beyond him. She stood there laughing, her eyes dancing and her face flushed with excitement.

"I knew you wouldn't mind if I moved in with you," Rosie went on before Brice could make a comment. "I've been wanting to get away from Isobel for years, but I thought it was my duty to stay with her because, after all, she is my sister and Papa expected us to live out our lives in the house he left us. But enough is enough! Papa bossed me around up until the day he died, and then Isobel took over. It's high time I started living my life the way I want to live it! Minna and I are going to have a wonderful time together. We always got along even when we were girls. Mr. Cranston, you will represent me, won't you?"

"Represent you in what way?" Jared asked cautiously.

"Why, about the house, of course! And how much I should demand for my share in it."

"I think you'd better see Judge Eldridge. He will advise you about having the house appraised and suggest someone to represent you. I found the judge to be an honest man. That's the best advice I can give you."

"And how much do I owe you for giving me the advice?"

"Why, ma'am, not a cent! I'm more than happy to oblige."

"Well, I should just hope so! You wouldn't be a gentleman if you charged me, you being a guest in this house and all. Besides, we're sweethearts, and men don't charge their sweethearts."

Heather came running down, fairly jumping with excitement. She thought it was simply wonderful that Rosamund had finally gotten herself out from under Isobel's thumb. She had only seen Isobel once, on the day they had attended the country fair, but once had been enough. You don't have to know some people well to know that you don't like them. But Rosie was adorable, and Minna was so happy to have her here at Arbordale that she was beside herself.

Jared and Brice retreated to Caldwell's study, where they found Caldwell. He was sitting at his desk with his head in his hands.

"I heard you say that David is out of jail. I'm glad about that, at least," Caldwell said.

"Does that mean you aren't overjoyed to have Miss Rosamund here?" Jared wanted to know.

Caldwell had the grace to look shocked. "Of course Rosie is welcome here! She'll be wonderful company for Minna. I only hope we'll go on having a home to offer her. The way things look right now, we're almost certain to lose Arbordale."

And then, in spite of his worry about the future, his mouth began to twitch. "I just wish I could have been there to hear what went on between Rosie and Isobel this morning. It's a wonder it didn't end up in mayhem!"

"If it had come to blows, I'd lay my money on Rosie. But I'm glad it didn't come to that, or I might have had to make another trip to town to get her out of jail, and if I didn't succeed she would never have forgiven me. It was hard enough to get David out, with your esteemed sheriff convinced that he's guilty as sin," Jared said.

Now Caldwell's expression was severe. "That young man has caused us no end of grief, letting people know that he believes Brice was behind the Thaxter girl's disappearance. He swung a lot of opinions his way. A newspaper editor is respected, and people listen to him. All the same, I wouldn't like to see him sent to prison for something he didn't do. It was good of you to help, Jared. I'll have to write to your father and tell him how much we appreciate it."

Brice looked at Caldwell commandingly. "You are not to ask him for money! It's bad enough that you got Jared and Emma here under false pretenses."

Caldwell looked ashamed, but still he defended himself. "It wasn't false pretenses at all. I honestly thought that you and Emma would hit it off, and I honestly thought that if you did, Thatcher would be more than happy to advance us a loan that would have been paid back with interest. But I still feel I owe you an apology, Jared. I only hope that Thatcher won't hold it against me when you tell him."

"I'm not going to tell him, Mr. Arlington." Jared felt smugly self-righteous, because he wouldn't have told Thatcher even if Thatcher had been alive. And then it was his turn to look ashamed, because he had to admit to himself that one of the reasons he wouldn't have told Thatcher was that Thatcher would have been furious enough with him for his own attempted fund-raising under false pretenses that he might have thrown him out of the house, bag and baggage.

Another thought made him gulp. "There's no use writing to my father now. He would have let us know if he had returned home. Besides, I only did what anyone would have done. It was nothing at all." If Caldwell wrote to Thatcher and Mrs. Allenby took it into her head to return the letter with a note that Thatcher was no longer among the living, there wouldn't be enough apologies in the world to cover what he had done.

If it hadn't been for David, Jared and Heather would have already been packing to return to Albany, and then Jared would have written to Caldwell to tell him of his father's death, simply omitting the date of his demise. It was suddenly very important to him that Caldwell and Brice think well of him. And it would save a lot of embarrassment all around, especially for Heather. He could bear the Arlingtons' contempt for himself if he had to, but he didn't want Heather hurt.

One thing was sure. He and Heather must leave as soon as possible. He had already pressed his luck too far.

Heather pulled Angel to a stop in front of the house that was now the sole residence of Miss Isobel Becker. It was an imposing house. Two stories tall with an extra story for attic and servants' quarters, it was white-painted brick with black shutters at the windows. A wrought-iron fence enclosed the property, and all of the window shades were even. Heather herself couldn't have brought up a better shine on the windows.

Well, Heather thought, she was here, and there was no use in delaying facing the lioness in her den.

In her haste to depart yesterday, Rosamund had forgotten to pack a few small items, and she had asked Heather to be kind enough to get them for her. There was an outside chance that Heather would be admitted to the house, whereas she and Minna would not. Isobel would, without any doubt, lock the door against them. Caldwell or Brice would have even less chance to gain admittance. Isobel did not allow gentlemen in her house, especially gentlemen she believed to be criminals.

As far as Heather could ascertain, Isobel thought that very few people were to be trusted, in Bennington or elsewhere. Any woman she did not know intimately was likely to be a pickpocket; any gentleman she had not known for years was more than likely a ravisher and murderer of unprotected women. Even some gentlemen she had known from childhood were ravishers of women, as witness Brice Arlington.

"I'd go myself, but I declare that this time I'd smack Izzy right across her sassy face if she said one word against Brice, providing she let me in in the first place," Rosamund had said at breakfast that morning. "And if I did, she would more than likely have me arrested for assault. There's my photograph album, it's on the closet shelf in my bedroom, and there's a box about so big"—she had held her hands to indicate a box the size of a candy box—"that holds some mementoes, and that's on the closet shelf too.

"And I want my bed. Not that my bed here isn't perfectly comfortable, but I'm used to my own bed. You can stop at the livery stable and tell Eli Yeager to pick up the bed with his wagon. I haven't any idea how much he'll charge, but he'll trust me for it."

Heather had stopped at the livery stable first. Eli Yeager had been avid for details. Apparently the entire town already knew that Rosie had quarreled with her sister and gone to live at Arbordale. Heather had not volunteered any information. She had no intention of adding to the gossip by telling Eli anything he didn't already know.

And now here she was at Rosie's former home. Her steps were determined as she opened the gate and walked to the front door, and she twisted the doorbell just as determinedly. The door opened so quickly that she was sure Isobel had been watching her from a front window, concealed by the lace curtains.

"Miss Cranston," Isobel said. Her voice was flat, and there was no welcome on her face.

"If I may come in, and if you'll show me which bedroom used to be Miss Rosamund's, there are a few trifles she wants me to pick up for her. A wagon will be along later to pick up her bed."

"The addle-witted girl means to stay at Arbordale then! I had hoped she would have come to her senses by now." Isobel's voice was harsh.

"Miss Rosamund is in excellent mental health," Heather informed her. "May I please pick up her things?"

Grudgingly, Isobel allowed her to enter the house. She led the way up a carpeted flight of stairs and down a hallway to a side bedroom and watched as Heather located the album and the ribbon-tied candy box. Then she followed her back down the stairs, keeping an eagle eye on her to make sure that she had no opportunity to filch one of the umbrellas from the umbrella stand in the entrance hallway.

Heather wondered if the woman would hold her deceased father's pistol on Eli Yeager all the time he was dismantling Rosie's bed and carrying it down to his wagon. How had Rosie ever managed to survive living with Isobel for all those years? She herself would rather have gone out and scrubbed floors for a living.

She had one more errand to do. Minna was low on tatting thread again; she went through it as though each ball contained only a few feet rather than yards and yards. She expected that Matthew Thaxter would treat her as coldly as he had before, but the store was a public place, and she had as much right to make a purchase there as anyone else. She wasn't about to let him intimidate her.

To her chagrin, not to say surprise, the door of the Emporium was locked. There was no reason for the place to be closed. It was not a holiday, and the store hours were clearly posted on the door.

Exasperated, she rattled the door and then rapped on the glass. It simply wasn't reasonable that Matthew wasn't here at eleven o'clock on a Thursday morning. He didn't go home for his midday meal until the stroke of noon, reopening at one o'clock sharp.

When there was no response to her rattling and tapping, she looked around to see if there was anyone on the street who could give her any information about Mr. Thaxter's whereabouts. There was no one in sight at all, not even the two old men playing their never-ending game of checkers in the town square.

Not only that, but something else struck her as being odd. It was possible that the two old men had had a falling out, being on opposite sides of the fence regarding Brice, but there was more than an ordinary number of buggies in front of the store or waiting a short distance from it. She could almost feel the hairs at the nape of her neck prickle as her intuition told her something was wrong.

One thing was certain. She wasn't going to go away without making some effort to find out what was going on.

She had always been too curious for her own good, but she preferred to call it being interested. And right now her interest was at a fever pitch.

There must be a back door to the store, and maybe it wasn't locked. It wasn't trespassing if you went through a door that wasn't locked, was it? Jared would know, but she was just as glad that he wasn't here to ask, because he might have said that it was trespassing and forbidden her to do it.

Not giving herself time to think for fear that she might lose her courage, she walked around the store to the back. There was a door there to what must have been Matthew's storeroom, but before she could try it she heard voices.

"Is anybody else coming?" She didn't recognize the voice, but then she wasn't acquainted with many of Bennington's citizens. She was certain it wasn't Matthew Thaxter.

"This is all. We didn't dare ask anybody else, we couldn't be sure who might have let the cat out of the bag. Even some who don't say much are on the Arlingtons' side, and it wouldn't have done to let it get out. If the tar's ready, so are we. A good dose of tar and feathers is just what Brice Arlington needs to show him that he isn't above justice!"

Heather had been aware of a strange, acrid odor hanging in the air, but she had been too intent on her prying to give it any thought. Now she sniffed and looked around, and she located its source. There was a black iron cauldron in the corner of the small space behind the store, and the embers of a nearly burned-out wood fire beneath it.

It was tar! They were going to go to Arbordale and tar and feather Brice! She didn't know how many men there were, but it must be a considerable number judging from the buggies along the street. There were enough of them to overpower Brice and Jared. Caldwell would put up a fight, but he was older and wouldn't be able to give as good an account of himself as the younger men. Not only that, but these men would have the element of surprise on their side.

The sheriff! She had to get the sheriff! Clarence Kotter was the only law in Bennington, he comprised the entire law-enforcing force, but at least he would be armed, and he had the authority to put a stop to this. The cauldron of bubbling tar in back of Matthew's store and the gathering of

179

men inside would be proof enough that they were up to no good. Kotter would disperse the men even if he didn't lock them up because they hadn't done anything yet. She didn't know much about the law here in Virginia, but she was certain that even here it was against the law to tar and feather anyone.

She couldn't believe that the door of the sheriff's office was locked, that the shades were pulled down, until she saw the handwritten note that was stuck in the window: "Gone to Greggory's farm, back before sundown." Where was Greggory's farm? How far was it? She didn't have any idea. She only knew that the sheriff wasn't here when she was in such desperate need.

Who then? There was David Inges. He was the only person in Bennington she actually knew where to find. She knew the Barnstables, and George Barnstable would probably help, but she didn't know where the Barnstables lived. And there was Ephraim Roundtree, but Ephraim was not young, and he was frail, and even though he was a minister, the men at Matthew's store might not listen to him if they were as determined as they had sounded.

But David wouldn't help. David hated Brice.

There wasn't time, anyway. The men would be starting for Arbordale any minute. Heather ran again and scrambled into the buggy. If only Angel wasn't so slow!

"Giddup! Drat it, Angel, giddup!"

Angel started off in her leisurely trot, and, beside Heather, Sam panted and hung his head over the arm of the buggy. Heather wanted to scream from pure frustration. And then her frustration won out, and she did scream.

"Darn it all, Angel, I said giddup! Now giddup!" She snapped the ribbons and screamed again. "Get going, I said!"

Angel got going. Angel got going with a vengeance. The buggy swayed from side to side as Angel galloped at breakneck speed. Heather had had no idea any horse could run that fast. They careened around the first bend in the road, and the buggy almost tipped over. Heather hauled on the ribbons, but it had no effect whatsoever.

She shouted, "Whoa!" but Angel paid her no mind. Angel

had heard her the first time, and the order had been to giddup. All Heather could do was hang on to the ribbons for dear life and pray. She was convinced that every hair on her head was standing on end under Emma's pretty hat.

They passed a farm wagon going toward town, and the farmer's mouth dropped open as he swerved his team to give them room. "What in Sam Hill do you think you're doing, you danged fool woman?" the farmer shouted. At least Heather thought that was what he had shouted. There was no time for her to ask him to repeat the question, because Angel was still galloping hell-bent-for-leather.

Heather closed her eyes. She was afraid to look. Beside her, Sam was barking, frantic with excitement, every muscle in his body quivering. They were already more than halfway back to Arbordale. There was the Langdon place, and there was Evelyn Langdon, just emerging from the drive on her magnificent horse.

Angel came within inches of crashing into the horse and rider. Evelyn's horse reared, and Evelyn went off. Heather had opened her eyes because she was more afraid not to look than to look, and now she looked back over her shoulder and saw the haughty Miss Langdon sit up from where she had landed in an undignified heap, her hat askew and covering one of her eyes, while her horse took off across the fields.

Heather hoped that Evelyn wasn't hurt. If she wasn't hurt, then Heather was going to laugh until her sides were sore every time she remembered how Evelyn had looked, sitting there with her hat all lopsided and mad enough to spit. Then she didn't have time to look any more because she was afraid of what Angel might try to run down next.

How could any horse run this fast, this far? It was unbelievable! But Angel showed no sign of slowing her pace. If anything, she was just getting her wind, and she ran faster than ever. There was the turnoff for Arbordale. Angel swerved into it without slackening her pace, and once again the buggy nearly turned over, and now Sam was on the floor of the buggy, flattening himself. Heather had the impression that if he'd known how, he would have put his paws over his eyes.

Saul came running, his mouth agape. He grabbed for Angel's bridle and caught it by the bit, and Heather was sure he was going to be trampled. But Angel had stopped. She was home. There wasn't any need for her to go on running.

Heather leaped out of the buggy, already sprinting for the house. She paused only long enough to cry over her shoulder, her voice filled with accusation, "I thought you told me Angel wouldn't run!" Then she was inside the house, screaming for Brice, for Caldwell, for Jared.

Brice reached her first. He and his father had been in Caldwell's study, going over for the umpteenth time every possibility for raising the money they needed, crossing off one name after another, one financial institution after another.

"They're coming!" Heather cried, throwing herself at Brice with such force that he had to catch her in his arms. "They're coming to tar and feather you! Matthew Thaxter and a lot of other men!"

Then Caldwell was there, and Jared, still carrying the book he had been reading in his room to escape from Minna's and Rosie's chatter for a few minutes. Minna came hurrying from the parlor with her tatting in her hands, and Rosie was right behind her.

Caldwell's face was grim. "I'll get the rifles," he said. "We'll have to hold them off. Emma, you should have gone to the sheriff!"

"I did go to the sheriff, but he wasn't there!" Heather snapped. "Do you think I'm a halfwit? He'd left a note in his window that he's gone to the Greggory farm. And they'll be here any minute. They were ready to leave when I heard them, I only barely got a head start!"

Caldwell looked at her strangely. "Then how on earth did you manage to get here first, driving Angel?"

Amazingly, under the circumstances, Brice began to chuckle.

"I take it this time Angel took it into her head to run," he managed to say, his mouth twitching.

"Well, I told her to get going, but she didn't have to take me so literally! It was like she'd sprouted wings. I was afraid the buggy was going to go right off the road and turn over. I couldn't slow her down for anything!"

"Angel can outrun any horse in Virginia when she takes a notion to move," Brice told her. "It's just that she's only taken the notion two or three times in her life."

"Well, it's a good thing she took the notion this time, or I wouldn't have got here first. But I hope to heaven that she never takes another notion to move when I'm driving her!"

Caldwell had gone back into his study to unlock the gun cabinet, and now he came back with three hunting rifles. He handed one to Brice and one to Jared and kept one for himself. And for the second time that day, Heather couldn't believe what was happening, because Rosie stepped forward and took Caldwell's rifle from him.

"Let me have that. As I remember it, Caldwell, you couldn't hit the broad side of a barn unless your eyes were closed and it was an accident. I know Brice can hit anything he aims at, but how about you, Jared?"

"I can give a reasonably good account of myself," Jared said modestly. He examined the rifle in his hands and nodded. "I only hope I'm good enough not to actually hit anybody."

"In that case, don't shoot unless they rush us," Rosie said. Heather had never seen such self-confidence. "The chances are that you won't have to fire at all. That goes for you too, Brice. You're good, but you're not as good as I am. Let's get out on the portico and form a welcoming committee for our uninvited guests. Minna and Emma, you stay inside. This might get a little nasty, and I don't want you getting hurt."

Heather and Minna stayed inside, but nothing could have kept them away from the front window, where they would have a good view of everything that went on. "Can Miss Rosamund really shoot?" Heather asked Minna.

"Oh, my goodness gracious, yes!" Minna said. "When we were growing up, I mind one time she butted into a contest some boys were having, and she licked the pants off them. It was Caldwell's rifle she learned to shoot with, right here at Arbordale. She was just itching to learn, and so Caldwell said he'd teach her, but it wasn't ten minutes before she could beat him all hollow. Her father blistered her good when he heard about how she put all those boys to shame. He didn't believe that young ladies should make spectacles of themselves doing things that only boys are supposed to do. Poor Rosie had to sleep on her stomach for a week. It was Isobel who told on her, of course. But Rosie went right on practicing, whenever she visited at Arbordale, only she never let Isobel know about it again."

Minna laughed, remembering. "I always had the notion that Rosie never married because no man wanted a wife who was better at everything than he was, and she didn't want a husband who wasn't as good at anything as she was. Rosie was a real tomboy. She learned to swim all by herself, and she could outclimb any boy who ever lived. And she always took first honors at mathematics, and that in itself was almost a disgrace. Girls weren't supposed to be good at figures, but Rosie was a whiz."

Minna wiped tears of merriment from her eyes, remembering.

"I used to be petrified when I had to act as her lookout when she shed her clothes right down to her camisole and drawers to go swimming in the creek. If her father had caught her at it he would have skinned her alive. Caldwell knew, of course, but he wasn't the kind to tattle. He was only miffed because she could swim better than he could. I've always had the idea that he was one of the ones who might have been interested in her, except that she could outdo him in everything, and his pride couldn't stand for that."

It only went to prove that most men were idiots, Heather thought. If she'd been a man, she would have grabbed Rosie up like a shot. Even now, when she was well into her middle age, Rosie was as pretty as anything. She must have been a real beauty when she was young. But just because she'd been able to outdo men, they'd shied away from her.

In her next book, she was going to use the young Rosie for her heroine. It would take the feminine reading population by storm.

Then all thoughts of plotting a book went right out of her head, because the delegation from Bennington was turning into the lane. There were five buggies, with two men in most of them. Heather could see that the iron cauldron was in the second buggy and still steaming, and another of the buggies had what looked to be at least three feather pillows in it.

"That's far enough," Caldwell's voice rang out. Beside him, both Brice and Jared raised their rifles. "I don't recall inviting you to my plantation, and you are not welcome, so you had better turn around and go back to town."

"We ain't aimin' to hurt you, Caldwell Arlington. It's that son of yours we want. Tell him to put down his rifle and turn himself over, and we'll leave without hurtin' anybody else."

"Caldwell told you to skedaddle," Rosamund said, her voice clear and firm. "Now skedaddle!"

"You git inside the house, Miss Rosamund. This ain't no place for a lady!" was the answer. The men were climbing out of their buggies, determination written all over them.

Rosamund's answer was short and to the point. She raised her rifle and aimed it, and a bullet sent a puff of dust up only an inch from the speaker's foot.

"I didn't miss," Rosamund said. "You know perfectly well that I didn't miss, Joshua Remmington! If there are any men among you who don't know that I can shoot, Joshua can tell you all about it. He isn't too old to have forgotten that I could outshoot him or any other boy, back a few years. And I haven't forgotten how!"

The men stopped, uncertain. They had counted on taking the Arlingtons by surprise. Coming face to face with three rifles, one of them in Rosamund Becker's hands, was another story entirely. But Matthew Thaxter wasn't about to give up so easily.

"Come on, rush them! They won't shoot, they wouldn't dare. There's enough of us to take them. Let's get on with it and show them that they can't run roughshod over all decency just because they're rich and think they're better than the rest of us!"

A bullet whistled past Matthew's ear, close enough that he clapped his hand to his head, looking stunned.

"That was only a warning. The next one's going in your kneecap," Rosie said. Her voice wasn't even angry. She might have been passing the time of day. "A man with his

185

kneecap shot off walks mighty stiff-legged, but if that's what you want, I'll be happy to oblige."

Matthew began to back away, and then there was a scramble as men began to pile back into their buggies. The slowest of them yelped with terror as another bullet smacked the ground directly behind his heel.

"That'll teach you not to be a slowpoke, Arnold Carson," Rosie said. "You always were slower than molasses in January."

It was a scene of pandemonium as men cursed and buggies maneuvered, with everyone trying to be the first to get turned around and out of range of Rosie's rifle as quickly as possible. If Rosamund had been a man, they wouldn't have been in such a panic, but Rosamund was a woman, and you never could tell what a woman might do. Women were flighty. The fool female just might take it into her head to nick one of them to make sure they were really leaving.

Rosie handed her rifle to Caldwell. "Well, that's that. I don't think they'll be back. We'll just send Saul into Bennington to let Kotter know what went on out here, and he'll put the fear of the Lord into them," she said cheerfully. "Clarence doesn't like disturbances in his county, and he'll be in a temper because he had to go out to the Greggory place. I expect Lucan thinks that someone's been stealing his chickens again. He gets Clarence out there at least once a month to look for evidence. If he'd mend his chicken coops to keep the foxes out, he wouldn't come up missing a chicken every week or so. Clarence knows that those trips are nothing but wild goose chases, but he always goes anyway. It makes him feel important even if it does make him mad."

Heather had run out onto the verandah to hug Rosie, but Jared, being closer, beat her to it. He picked the little woman up and hugged her until she squealed for mercy.

"Miss Rosamund, you're my sweetheart! You already were, but this clinches it. If I wasn't convinced that you'd turn me down because I'm not good enough for you, I'd ask you to marry me!"

"And if you weren't still wet behind the ears, I'd accept you," Rosie said. "But I'll still be your sweetheart. Every young man needs a mature woman in his life. There's a deal we can teach you that no sweet young thing ever dreamed about!"

"Rosie Becker!" Minna gasped. "How in the world would you know about things like that?"

Rosie leered at her. "You'd be surprised! I may be a maiden lady, but I'm not blind and deaf. It might stir your circulation up a little to pay attention to what goes on even in a town like Bennington, instead of always concentrating on that dratted tatting of yours. Besides, I read."

"What on earth kinds of books do you read?" Minna gaped at her, halfway between shock and laughter. "Nothing from the public library could give you notions like that!"

"Just read the classics, dear," Rosie told her, winking at Jared. "The *Canterbury Tales* by Chaucer, for one, and then there's Shakespeare. Papa kept those books locked up in his bookcase, but I learned how to pick the lock before I was ten."

My goodness, I wonder where I can get copies of those books, Heather thought as Jared's laughter was all but drowned out by Caldwell's. Brice, she noticed, was not laughing. He looked so shocked that Heather's own peals of laughter were directed more at him than at Rosie's outrageousness.

"Rosamund Becker, when are you going to learn to behave yourself and act like a lady?" Minna wanted to know.

"Behave myself, bah! Where's the fun in behaving? Minna, I think it's time we had our lemonade, and I'm sure the gentlemen would appreciate having their juleps a little early. No, Caldwell, don't lock up the rifles just yet. I don't expect those addleheaded idiots to come back, but we might as well have them handy just in case."

In her wildest flights of imagination, Heather had never dreamed of sitting on a verandah on a Virginia plantation, drinking a glass of Minna's extraordinary lemonade with three rifles leaning against the verandah railing. But then she had never dreamed that there could be a woman like Rosamund Becker either.

Rosie winked at her. "Delicious lemonade. Minna has a hand for it, doesn't she?"

Almost choking, Heather nodded. Minna certainly did have a hand for it, and nobody could be more glad of it at a time like this than Heather.

Brice was regarding her with a warmth in his eyes that she had never seen there before. "Miss Cranston, I can't express how brave I think you were to come galloping home so fast to warn us that that mob was coming. Very few young ladies would have the presence of mind to do what you did."

"It was all I could think of to do. I didn't want you to be tarred and feathered. I'll bet it would be a mess to get off!"

"It would indeed. I don't believe there's enough turpentine on the place to do the job," Brice said. "I can't tell you how glad I am that you didn't come to grief when Angel decided to run. If I'd had any idea that she might ever run with you, I never would have let you drive her. It would have been the worst sort of disaster if you'd been hurt!"

"I wasn't hurt, though. Scared, yes. I was scared out of my wits!" Heather admitted. "I just can't understand how a placid creature like Angel could decide she's a race horse!"

"But that's just what she is," Brice explained. "The trouble was that she couldn't be persuaded to run. She won her first race and her second, and after that she decided she didn't want to run anymore. Her owner lost his shirt on her third race. Still, he kept working with her, but nothing he or his trainer could do would persuade her to run again. The entire county was laughing at him, and he didn't care for that either. He swore he was going to shoot her, and so I made an offer for her. I knew she'd make a nice, steady buggy horse for Aunt Minna."

"I'm going to take her a lump of sugar right now," Heather said. "She deserves it."

"I'll go with you," Brice said. He offered her his arm as they went first to the kitchen house to ask Elspeth for a lump of sugar and then to the stable. Their way took them through the rose garden. It wasn't a starlit night, it was full daylight, but when Brice drew her to a halt beside the sundial she thought her heart was going to explode.

"Miss Emma, would you allow me to kiss you?"

She had to nod for an answer, because she was speechless. It wasn't the most romantic setting in the world in spite of the roses. There was still the smell of charred wood from the stable fire, and the sun was so hot that she was perspiring, but it was a great deal better than not being kissed in a rose garden at all.

Brice pulled her into his strong arms and lowered his lips to hers. The kiss was nice, but it didn't cause the burning ache in her that Jared's kiss had.

Finally, Brice pulled away, his face flushed. "I beg your pardon, Miss Emma. I only wanted to express my appreciation to you. I didn't mean to get carried away. We'd better go and see that Angel is none the worse for her run."

~ Chapter 13 ~

HEATHER WAS GLAD to see Phoebe Roundtree that evening when Carl Amhurst drove her to Arbordale to talk to Jared about David Inges. Their presence took the others' attention away from her. Minna had remarked that she looked pale, Rosie had remarked that she looked flushed, and Caldwell had remarked that she should retire early to recover from her fright when Angel had run with her. Jared had looked puzzled, and Brice had avoided looking at her at all.

Carl seemed discomfited by Phoebe's concern for David, but he still tried to assure her that David would not be convicted if Clarence Kotter still insisted on hauling him into court.

"Isn't it true, Mr. Cranston, that it would be virtually impossible to get a conviction on such flimsy evidence?" Carl asked. "I don't know much about the law, but if I were on the jury, I would consider the evidence to be insufficient."

"Ordinarily that would be true," Jared conceded, but his face was more serious than Heather was used to seeing it. Jared was usually smiling and carefree. Even the shattering of his hopes of obtaining a loan from Caldwell hadn't plunged him into the despair that many other men would have felt. He would manage to survive, even if he was prevented from doing what his heart had been set on.

Now, Heather thought he must look the way he would look some day when he was addressing a jury, his hands thrust into his pockets, teetering back and forth on his heels as he spoke, and she was filled with admiration for him. He frowned and shook his head.

"The trouble is you never know what a jury will do. Men have been convicted on purely circumstantial evidence before. David has no way to prove his innocence, except that his kerosene can is still where it's supposed to be, and his landlady is willing to attest that it was never missing. He could have come by another kerosene can; they aren't that rare. And his hatred for Brice is too well known for it to be possible to get together an entirely impartial jury."

"It isn't fair!" Phoebe burst out. "I know David didn't do it, and it just isn't fair that he should be accused and brought to trial!"

"I'm afraid that George Barnstable's testimony will be damaging. If only David hadn't gone out driving near Arbordale that night, there wouldn't be a shred of evidence against him. It will help when Brice and Mr. Arlington attest that they don't believe he's guilty, but I'd be misleading you if I told you it's a certainty that David will get off."

"Miss Roundtree is of far too sympathetic a nature," Carl said. "I'm afraid she'll spend her entire life taking the part of the underdog, and it will bring her nothing but grief. Phoebe, dear, don't look so stricken! David hasn't been convicted yet, and perhaps he won't be. I'd try to get on the jury myself, but everyone would know that I was prejudiced in David's favor, and I would be disqualified."

"I know you would, Carl. It's a shame women aren't allowed on juries! Any woman would know that David didn't do it, just by looking at him." There were tears in Phoebe's eyes, and she tried to blink them away.

Carl looked pained, but he made an effort to hide it. Heather felt a flash of sympathy for him. It must be hard on him to see the girl he loved making such a fuss over the misfortunes of another man, especially a man who had jilted her.

But something else was nagging at the corners of Heather's mind. She sat forward on her chair, her face intense.

"The kerosene can!" she said. "If somebody took their own can to douse the stable, and then threw it away beside the road, then he must have bought a new one to replace it, mustn't he? I mean, everyone has to have a kerosene can. I've never known any household to be without one. Wouldn't it be possible to find out who's bought a new one?"

Jared stared at her. "You're right. But the rub is, how are we going to find out? The logical place for anyone to buy a new kerosene can is at Thaxter's store, but I can't see Matthew Thaxter cooperating with us if we were to ask him. He'd be on the side of anyone who did it, that's for sure. And after Rosie chased him and his party of would-be tar-and-featherers off this afternoon, he'll be all the more disinclined to tell us what we want to know."

But Heather wasn't to be put off. Her face flaming with excitement, she exclaimed, "Matthew Thaxter! How do we know that he didn't do it himself? He hates Brice as much as David does, maybe even more. I wouldn't put it past him to try to burn down the stable, and when the fire was discovered and put out before the stable was completely destroyed, he could have been so furious that he tried to strike at Brice another way, by tarring and feathering him!"

Brice's face was set in grim lines. "I can well believe it of him. He's been trying to turn everybody who will listen against me ever since Naomi disappeared. But if he did fire the stable, he isn't likely to admit that he has a new kerosene can at his house."

"I can find it! I'll look myself!" Phoebe cried.

"You'll do no such thing!" Carl was aghast. "It would be trespassing, and that in itself is an infraction of the law. It is, isn't it, Mr. Cranston?"

"Carl is right," Jared confirmed. "You can't go snooping around private property without a search warrant, and only an officer of the law can get one of those. The best we can do is for me to go to Kotter and ask him to do it."

With that in mind, Jared drove into Bennington on the

following morning, but when he returned Heather knew from his expression that his mission had been unsuccessful.

"Kotter all but laughed in my face. He conceded that Thaxter had brought that mob out here to punish Brice and try to drive him out of the county, but he intimated that he didn't exactly blame the man. He only laid the law down to him and told him not to try anything like that again or he'd find himself in serious trouble. As long as Thaxter and his cohorts didn't actually do any harm to Brice, he couldn't lock them up. But he isn't about to go nosing around for evidence against a man who isn't even under suspicion for setting the fire. The trouble is, he still thinks that David is guilty, and I couldn't budge him an inch."

Minna looked consternated, and Rosie was furious. As for Caldwell and Brice, they hadn't expected anything else. They had known Clarence Kotter for too long to expect him to raise a hand against one of Bennington's leading citizens unless he had positive proof that Matthew had committed a crime. The Thaxters were a power in Bennington, their good will was important to Kotter if he wanted to be reelected, and John Thaxter wouldn't take it kindly if he were to make any move against his cousin. The two didn't get along, but it would still be a slur on the family name.

"I swear I'm going to organize the women of Bennington and march down Main Street campaigning against Clarence Kotter the next time he comes up for election!" Rosie declared. "If I can stir them up, that is. The women around here aren't very interested in women's suffrage or anything like that."

"If you did any such thing, Kotter would lock you up for marching without a permit and for creating a public nuisance," Caldwell warned her. "And he'd probably be right, at that. You women belong at home, not tampering with things that don't concern you."

Heather bridled. If women were allowed to tamper, maybe things would get done! She was absolutely certain that there was a new kerosene can at Matthew Thaxter's house, and just as certain that someone had to find it. If the men wouldn't do it, that left it up to her.

To that end, she managed to get Phoebe aside for a moment before the other girl left, and she asked her where Mr. Thaxter lived.

Phoebe's eyes widened. "Heather, you wouldn't! Didn't you just hear your own brother say that it would be against the law?"

"Better me than you! I have a brother who's a lawyer to get me out of it," Heather said airily. "Besides, it won't matter if I'm caught and disgraced, because I won't be here much longer. But you have to live here, and anything you do reflects on your father."

"Please be careful!" Phoebe begged, but her eyes had lit up with hope.

Heather didn't confide her plan to Minna and Rosie. Minna would be horrified, and Rosie would want to go with her. And if she were discovered in her illegal act, she'd have to run fast, and she wasn't sure that Rosie could keep up with her.

It wasn't in the least difficult for her to get away the next morning. Everyone was used to her taking Angel and trotting around the countryside. Saul only warned her not to tell Angel to giddup again.

"Ain't likely she'll run again for a couple of years," Saul said. "But there ain't any use taking chances."

Heather only hoped that if she had to make a quick getaway, Angel would take it into her head to run again!

She tried to convince herself that she wasn't frightened, but it was uphill work. She'd never done anything like this before, and she wouldn't be doing it now except that the men wouldn't do it. She purely didn't like Matthew Thaxter, and if he was guilty of setting that fire, she wanted him caught and punished. Besides, it would make Phoebe so happy to have David exonerated that it was worth the risk.

Angel trotted along at her usual slow, steady pace. It was hard to believe that the mare had run so fast only yesterday. Remembering her terror, Heather told herself that what she was doing now wasn't anywhere near as dangerous.

She stopped Angel in the center of town, a full block away from the Emporium, and this time she took care to put out the weight. There wasn't a chance in ten thousand that

Angel would budge if she didn't put out the weight, but there hadn't been a chance in ten thousand that Angel would run yesterday either.

"Stay," she told Sam. "Guard the buggy." She felt silly saying it. Who in Bennington would steal the buggy? But she had an equally silly notion that it made Sam feel important to be told to guard the buggy, and telling him couldn't hurt anything.

Once she found the kerosene can, she would go directly to Ephraim Roundtree and persuade him to accompany her back to Matthew's house and witness the fact that Matthew had a new kerosene can. Nobody would doubt the word of the minister.

The whole thing about the kerosene can bothered her. Why had the can that had been used to set the fire been thrown out along the road? Why hadn't the man who had used it simply taken it back home with him, with nobody being the wiser? It didn't make sense. Nevertheless, the can had been thrown away, whoever had had to throw it away would have had to replace it, and Matthew was the logical suspect.

She had to pass Matthew's store in order to reach the street on which he lived, but she waited until a customer went in and she knew he would be busy. Then she walked fast until she was beyond it.

There was a woman sweeping off her front porch steps three houses down from Matthew's house, but Heather slowed down so that the woman had gone back inside before she passed. A quick glance in all directions showed her that no one else was around to observe her except for a little boy playing jacks across the street, and he was so wrapped up in his game that he scarcely glanced up as she passed him on the opposite side. She veered around the side of Matthew's house the moment he looked down at his jacks again.

For a moment, her heart sank when she saw that the back porch was screened in. If it was locked, what would she do? **Resolutely, she pulled at the screen door, and it opened.**

And there it was. A bright, shiny new kerosene can, sitting right there in the corner beside a mop and bucket. It was so new that it still had its cap on the spout, instead of a raw potato stuck on as so many people did after the cap was lost.

Not only that, but when Heather picked it up she saw that it was dented. The dent rang a bell in her mind, and she furrowed her brow and thought as hard as she could. And then she remembered. This was the same can she had seen in the Emporium the first time she had gone into the store, dented on the bottom a quarter of the way around from the spout. She remembered wondering why Matthew had displayed it along with the others unless he'd meant to sell it cheaper because it was damaged.

Heather was elated. It was just like Matthew to replace his old kerosene can with this damaged one that he couldn't have sold for full price. But the question of why he had thrown away his original can still nagged at her.

She didn't have time to think about that now. There must be an answer, and if she couldn't come up with it Jared probably could. After all, he was the lawyer, not she. Right now she had to go and fetch Ephraim, and after he had seen the can he would go with her to the sheriff. When Kotter saw the evidence with his own eyes, David would be all but home free. Maybe women weren't allowed to vote, but when something had to be done that men were reluctant to do just because it might bend the law a trifle, it was women who weren't afraid to do it. Justice was a whole lot more important than the letter of the law.

She was just putting the can back down when the screen door banged open, and a hand grasped her shoulder so painfully that she gasped. How had Clarence Kotter known she was here? He couldn't have seen her, because she hadn't passed his office. She'd land in jail for sure!

"What are you doing here, girl?" She was hauled around to face her captor, and she gasped again as she took in the full, baleful glare not of the sheriff but of Matthew Thaxter. "You have no business here. I'll have the law on you!"

Matthew had seen Heather walk past his store and turn the corner to continue on in the direction of his house. His suspicions had been aroused, because there was no possible reason for the young woman who was a guest at Arbordale to be walking in that direction unless she was intent on mischief. She didn't know anybody who lived on his street, she couldn't be calling on anyone, and there were no stores or shops except on Main Street.

He had been waiting on Mrs. Pennyhurst when Heather had scooted by looking as if she didn't want to be seen, and the heavyset woman had been more than a little miffed when he had hurried her along and all but pushed her out of the store so that he could lock it and rush off to see what that snippy little miss from up North was up to.

And he had been right in his suspicions, because she had been giving his kerosene can a good looking over when he'd surprised her on his own back porch. Rage suffused his face, turning it a mottled red. He shook her, his hands biting into her arms.

"I'll have the law on you!" he shouted again. "You're coming with me straight to the sheriff!" If he could frighten her enough, she would likely take to her heels the moment he let go of her, and then he could get rid of the incriminating can and deny that it had ever been on his back porch. Then it would be only her word against his, and she was not only a Northerner, but she was also a guest of the Arlingtons and therefore suspect on general principles. Everyone would believe the word of an upstanding citizen of Bennington against hers. Enough people depended on him for credit so that he would have plenty of backers.

Heather's mind was racing as if the shaking she was undergoing had rattled her brains into frantic activity. Her thoughts followed amazingly close to Matthew's. He would drag her off to the sheriff and lay charges against her, and then he would come back here and get rid of the kerosene can. He probably had another old can around somewhere, most people did, and this one would disappear.

So she did the only thing she could do. She screamed. Not just one scream, but a series of screams, as high and shrill as she could manage, and that was enough, because she was half out of her wits with desperation, and that gave her all the lung power she needed. She screamed every bit as hard as she had when she'd had to get back to Arbordale before

197

Matthew and his tar-and-featherers got there and she'd had to get Angel moving.

"Help! Help!" she screamed.

Matthew tried to clamp his hand over her mouth, but she wriggled and writhed like a landed eel, and with a good deal more strength, and she went right on screaming.

Her screams brought results even sooner than she had hoped. First the little boy who had been playing jacks came racing into the backyard, and then the woman who had been sweeping her porch steps, her dustcap still on her head and a dusting cloth in her hand. And then two more housewives and a lone man. They all stood gaping while Heather went on struggling with her captor.

"Look!" Heather cried. "Look at the kerosene can! Take a good look at it! It's brand new. And see how it's dented? Maybe one of you saw it in Mr. Thaxter's store! Little boy, I'll give you a dime if you'll run real fast and fetch the sheriff!"

The boy was already gone, streaking out of the yard, his mind swimming with visions of all the jawbreakers and licorice sticks a dime would buy. The women were gaping at the kerosene can.

"You're right. It's dented, and I'd swear it's the same one I saw in Mr. Thaxter's store only a few days ago. But what on earth does that have to do with anything?"

"Mr. Thaxter had to have a new kerosene can, that's what it has to do with everything!" Heather gasped out. "You might as well turn me loose, Mr. Thaxter. I have witnesses now, and you aren't going to be able to wriggle out of it by getting rid of the can, because these ladies and this gentleman have seen it right here on your back porch!"

Instead of letting her go, Matthew gripped her arms tighter, and he began to shake her again, so hard that her head bobbled.

"Little snoop, sneaking little snoop! A Northerner, a friend of the Arlingtons, sticking your nose in where it doesn't belong!"

"Matthew Thaxter, you stop that!" the woman in the dustcap exclaimed. "You're hurting her!"

Matthew's rage sent him beyond hearing, beyond reason. He shook Heather harder. For the first time Heather began to feel genuinely afraid, even though she went on kicking and struggling.

The woman in the dustcap took action. No matter what this was all about, and she was completely confused, a hundred-and-seventy-pound man who stood almost six feet tall had no business laying violent hands on a slip of a girl who could scarcely weigh a hundred and ten. The woman picked up the mop bucket and upended it over Matthew's head, and for good measure she grabbed the mop from where it hung by a nail and started to beat Matthew's shoulders with it.

Matthew let go of Heather to grab the bucket with both of his hands and remove it from his head, but the instant he could see again, he grasped Heather's arm and started to drag her off the porch.

"You're coming with me!" he shouted at her. "We'll see what Clarence Kotter has to say about you burglarizing my house!"

"That's exactly where I want to go!" Heather shot back at him. "Ladies, watch that kerosene can. Please stay right where you are and watch it. You have no idea how important it is!"

The women looked at each other, not sure that this girl wasn't insane. On the other hand, the way Matthew Thaxter looked right now, they weren't sure that he wasn't the one who was insane. Whichever it was, nothing would have moved them from that spot until they found out what this was all about.

Matthew and Heather hadn't even reached Main Street before they met Clarence Kotter, who was striding along as fast as his dignity would allow while the little boy urged him on with cries of murder and mayhem.

"I want this young woman locked up," Matthew demanded. "She's a trespasser and a mischief maker!"

"I'll confess to trespassing, if you'll just come back to Mr. Thaxter's house with me and look at what I have to show you."

"Not that kerosene can your brother was talking about yesterday?" Kotter's eyes narrowed, and a flush of anger stained his face.

"Yes. And it's there, right on Mr. Thaxter's back porch, and there are witnesses to prove it. They're still there, watching it for me so Mr. Thaxter can't go back and get rid of it."

"She put it there herself!" Matthew said angrily. "She put it there to try to implicate me. She's as thick as thieves with the Arlingtons. She'd do anything to get back at me for trying to give Brice Arlington his just desserts for seducing my niece and then spiriting her away to protect his reputation. We all know that Brice was behind Naomi's disappearance. The girl made it perfectly clear to me that he'd told her he was in love with her in order to have his way with her. She was convinced that he was going to marry her, poor innocent child that she was, and she was so much in love with him that she would have let him do anything. The man is a scoundrel, and this girl is just as bad, taking his side and trying to get even with me!"

"She didn't either put it there herself," the little boy said. "I saw her come down the street and go around back of Mr. Thaxter's house, and she didn't have no kerosene can with her!"

"And there's a lady who saw me walking down the street, and she'll tell you I didn't have a kerosene can with me!" Heather pressed her advantage.

The sheriff clamped his jaw. "All right. Nobody can accuse me of not making a thorough investigation. But that doesn't change matters as far as you're concerned, young lady. You're still guilty of trespassing, no matter what you think you found."

Heather didn't say anything more, because she didn't have anything more to say. She just trotted along behind the sheriff. A small, grubby hand reached out and took hers.

"You didn't have no kerosene can, and I'll tell the truth, 'cause my pop says he'll whale the daylights out of me if I ever lie," the little boy told her. "Do I get my dime anyway, even if I didn't get Mr. Kotter there before Mr. Thaxter went dragging you off?"

Heather squeezed his hand and grinned down at him. "You get a quarter," she said.

The little boy looked stunned. Then he whispered, "For that I might even take a chance on lyin', if there's anything you want me to lie about!"

"No, no! Just tell the truth. There isn't anything I want you to lie about, and besides, I wouldn't want you to get the daylights whaled out of you."

Everyone was where Heather and Matthew Thaxter had left them, still crowded onto Matthew's back porch, forming a circle around a plain, ordinary kerosene can, except that the can had a dent in it, and trying to figure out how such a prosaic item could have caused such a rumpus.

Kotter examined the can. He listened to the woman in the dustcap concur with little Johnny Blake that Heather had not brought it with her. He listened to the testimony of another lady and the man that they had noticed that particular can in Matthew Thaxter's store within the last few days.

"Ask him why he had to have a new kerosene can. Ask him where his old one is right now!" Heather demanded.

"It's in the attic," Matthew said instantly. "It wore out, so I brought this one home to replace it."

"Make him show it to us!" Heather insisted.

It was all Kotter could do to prevent every one of them from following him and Matthew through the house and up two flights of stairs into the attic. Nobody moved until they came down again. Kotter was carrying a kerosene can. It was ancient, half rusted through, and covered with dust and cobwebs.

Heather couldn't contain her triumph. "He hasn't been using that up until a few days ago! Any woman could tell you that it never collected all that dust and those cobwebs in such a short time. I'll tell you where Mr. Thaxter's kerosene can is, Mr. Kotter. It's right in your office, the one you found along the road after the Arlingtons' stable was set on fire!"

Matthew clamped his mouth shut. The muscles in his jaw bulged with the effort, and his eyes were burning with hatred as he glared at Heather. If the sheriff and all those other people hadn't been there, Heather was convinced that he would have attacked her again.

"I think you'd better come along with me," Kotter told Matthew. "I have a lot of questions I want to ask you."

"Bitch!" Matthew hurled at Heather, his voice so filled with venom that she flinched in spite of herself. "Arlington-loving bitch! Brice should have married Naomi. He had no right to make love to her and make her all those promises and then not marry her! He made a fool of her, and he made a fool of me in front of the entire town! I wish that stable had burned to the ground, and I wish Brice Arlington had been in it when it burned! But he'll burn in hell for what he did. God's justice will not be mocked!"

As much as Heather despised the man, she felt almost sorry for him at that moment. Still ranting and raving, Kotter forced him to start walking, his hand clamped firmly on Matthew's arm.

"You aren't making things any easier for yourself. You'd better button your lip until you get a lawyer to do your talking for you," Clarence warned him.

"I don't care! I only did what was right! I'll be vindicated. Truth and justice are on my side. Those Arlingtons will be punished! Those Arlingtons with all their money and their Arbordale, thinking they're better than other folks just because they were born rich. I'm as good as they are, and my Naomi was as good as they are and better than that hoity-toity Miss Evelyn Langdon until Brice led her down the garden path! Everybody knows what Brice did, everybody knows that I had the right to strike back!"

Heather tried to close her ears to the near-insane man's ranting as she trotted after him and Kotter and touched Kotter's arm almost timidly.

"What about me?" she wanted to know.

Kotter glared at her almost as balefully as Matthew had done.

"Go home!" he said. "Go home and stay there. And all the rest of you go home too. I'll call you to act as witnesses when I need you."

Heather lost no time in lifting her skirts and taking to her heels. She wasn't totally convinced that Clarence Kotter

ALWAYS THE DREAM

wouldn't change his mind and haul her along with Matthew, and if there was anything she didn't want, it was to be locked up in the same jail with that man. She only paused when there was a tug at her skirt.

"My quarter! You said you'd give me a quarter!"

Heather stopped and searched frantically in her reticule until she found a coin. It was a fifty-cent piece.

"I haven't got a quarter. This will have to do," she said. And at the look on Johnny's face, she added, "For goodness sake, don't go fainting. I haven't the time to stop and revive you!"

Angel and the buggy and Sam were right where she'd left them. Sam opened one sleepy eye and wagged his tail. Heather put her hands on her hips and glared at him.

"A lot of help you were!" she accused him. "Didn't you hear me screaming? Why didn't you come and bite Mr. Thaxter?"

Sam yawned. Heather relented and scratched behind his ears. "I know, I know, you were asleep. And besides, I told you to stay right here and guard the buggy." A fat lot of good his guarding would have done, with him sound asleep. If someone had wanted to steal the buggy, he probably would have gone right on sleeping while it was being driven away. But after all, he had obeyed her. He was a good dog, and it wasn't his fault that he wasn't the smartest dog in the world.

She couldn't coax Angel to run on their way back to the plantation. She couldn't even coax a brisk trot out of her. After cajoling and commanding and even screaming a little, Heather gave up and began to laugh. She was still laughing when she got back to Arbordale.

❧ Chapter 14 ❧

"You IDIOT! You stubborn, willful little moron!" Jared lashed out at Heather. "Don't you realize you could have got yourself in all sorts of trouble snooping around Thaxter's house? Whatever possessed you?"

"Well, you wouldn't do it because you're so finicky about the letter of the law!" Heather defended herself.

"Don't you know that that man is more than half insane with his hatred of the Arlingtons and that his hatred spills over on us because we're the Arlingtons' friends? Don't you realize that he might have hurt you? And it probably never crossed your mind that if Kotter had taken it into his head to arrest you, you would have had to tell him your real name when he booked you, because not to give your real name would be perjury of the worst sort. We'd have been in a pretty pickle if that had happened!" In his anger, Jared caught Heather by her upper arms and shook her.

"Ouch! Stop it, darn it! I've already been shaken enough today, by Matthew Thaxter! Oh, that hurts!"

"Let me see. Good Lord, look at those arms! Damn him, it's a good thing he isn't here where I can get my hands on him! Does it hurt terribly, Heather?"

They were in the rose garden. Jared had drawn her out there to confront her with the enormity of her actions, out of earshot of the others. All the others had done was to praise her until it was a wonder her head hadn't swelled to twice its normal size, telling her how smart she was and how brave she was. What they should have told her was that she needed to have her head examined!

Heather had spent a lot of time in this Virginia rose garden. She had even been kissed in this rose garden. Unfortunately, neither of the kisses had meant a thing, and both of them had been apologized for!

"Of course it hurts, but that doesn't matter. It'll get better all by itself. Jared, why did Matthew throw his own kerosene can away alongside the road? Why didn't he take it back home with him?" That mystery was still driving her crazy.

"I have an idea that he didn't throw it away. I think it bounced out of his buggy or simply rolled out when he went around a bend in the road. He would have been in a hurry, wanting to get back to Bennington as fast as he could. An empty kerosene can is light, and it would have fallen over and then rolled out when Matthew drove over a rut."

Jared grinned as an idea occurred to him.

"I'll bet he was beside himself when he saw that he'd lost the can somewhere along the way. He wouldn't have dared to go back and look for it. It was getting along toward morning, and farmers get up early. He wouldn't have dared risk being seen. He must have really started to sweat blood when Clarence Kotter found it the next day. So he had to replace it, but as mean about money as his reputation has him, he made the mistake of replacing it with an unsalable can that could be identified."

Heather marveled at Jared's logic. Why hadn't she been able to think it all out like that herself? But at least she had been the one to prove that Matthew had replaced his old kerosene can with a new one, and now he was in jail, and David Inges had been exonerated. Phoebe would be so happy, and Heather was more than a little bit happy about it herself.

Now Jared was railing at her again. "I ought to spank you! I ought to blister you good! I thought you had better sense!"

"If I had good sense, I wouldn't be here at Arbordale at all. I wouldn't have come along with you, pretending to be Emma."

"*Touché!*" Jared had the grace to look abashed. "And don't think that I don't appreciate the way you came along with me, even if it did turn out to be for nothing. I'm only sorry that things didn't turn out better for you. Once we saw that Brice was the stuff that girls' dreams are made of, it's a darned shame he didn't fall in love with you the way any sensible man would have. You could have ended up the mistress of Arbordale, and then things would have been wonderful for you even when I had to go back to Albany empty-handed."

Heather swallowed, and it was painful swallowing past the big lump in her throat. Jared wouldn't have cared at all if she'd married Brice! Even if she had known all along that Jared would never want her for himself, it made it worse knowing that he would have been glad if she had married someone else.

Unaccountably, considering the things Jared had just been saying, he drew her into his arms and held her close. "You mean a lot to me, you know. And it's my fault that you're here, caught up in all this mess. I could kick myself for talking you into coming!"

"I wanted to come," Heather reminded him. "I wouldn't have missed it for the world! Besides, the Arlingtons need us here now for moral support. Minna almost cried when she thought we'd leave the minute we found out the truth. It made me feel so guilty! I wanted to confess our charade right then and get it off my conscience, but I didn't think I should until I talked to you about it."

"I'm not looking forward to telling them, you can be sure of that." Jared's voice was rueful. "Maybe we won't have to tell them at all, if we leave soon enough."

"Jared Cranston! That would be dishonest!"

"But we've already been dishonest, so what difference could it make?"

"It makes a whole lot of difference! Besides, they won't feel so guilty when they find out that we were just as bad as they were. It'll make Brice feel a lot better to know that you were just as underhanded as his father."

Jared sighed. "You're right. I'll have to tell them. But I'll make sure that they know it was entirely my fault. I'll tell them that I coerced you by playing on your sympathy, that you only agreed to come because you were afraid that I'd go out and rob a bank, or kill myself, if you didn't help me."

Heather gasped. "Don't you dare! As if you'd ever do either of those things! I'm not going to let you take all the blame. I'm every bit as guilty as you are."

Jared kissed her forehead. He was always kissing her, except that he kissed her as if she really was his sister! She suspected that he actually loved her in a brotherly sort of way, but that wasn't what she wanted at all.

"I'm sorry if I've ruined your life, Heather. I'm afraid you'll never get over Brice, and it's entirely my fault that your heart is broken."

Of course her heart was broken because Brice hadn't fallen in love with her, he thought miserably. Brice was everything any girl could want. He was a handsome young Southern planter, and it made him even more romantic to have been accused of something he hadn't done. The whole situation was the stuff that romance was made of. It wouldn't matter a bit to Heather that the Arlingtons were on the verge of ruin. She'd be happy with Brice even if they had to live in a hovel, and if he knew anything about her at all, he knew that she would make that hovel into a home. She'd never had anything, and so she wouldn't miss not having much of anything now.

That might work in his case as well as Brice's, except that it was Brice she loved. And Jared had a very good idea that what the Arlingtons would consider nothing was still a great deal more than he could offer her. Wealth had a way of being relative. The Arlingtons had always been extremely wealthy, so they would look on having only a moderate amount of money as poverty. And Jared himself had nothing at all to offer, and no prospects for anything better anywhere in the immediate future.

He kissed her forehead again, wanting to do a great deal

more, wanting to tell her that he loved her and that he'd be miserable all the rest of his life if she ever married anyone but him. But he hadn't the right. He didn't want her to feel sorry for him. She had enough troubles of her own without adding that to the list.

"Poor Heather. I wish there was some way I could make you feel better."

Poor Heather! Heather felt like stamping her foot. She didn't want to be poor Heather, she wanted to be dear Heather, she wanted to be darling Heather! But if she couldn't have that, and she couldn't, there was one thing that she just might have.

"Jared, would it be all right if we stayed on for just a little while longer? Minna will be crushed if we leave now, and besides, I don't want to go until we find out what happened to Naomi Thaxter and see Brice vindicated. Something about her is bound to turn up soon. Put your mind to it, you're good at figuring things out, maybe you can think of what could have happened to her."

"I wish I could, but I'm not a miracle maker. But of course we'll stay for a while if that's what you want." Jared couldn't help it, he kissed her again, and not on the forehead this time.

It turned out to be a mistake. It took all of the willpower he possessed to hold her away from him and say, "We'd better get back inside. A good night's sleep will probably make things look brighter."

Heather's mouth was throbbing as she let Jared take her back to the house. Why did life have to be so dratted complicated? If she couldn't have Brice, whom she didn't really want anyway except that she was so sorry for everything that had happened to him that she ached to make him happy, why couldn't she have Jared? She tried to pretend that there had been a lot more in Jared's kiss than there had actually been, but it didn't do any good. He was only sorry for her, just as she was sorry for Brice.

The three men gathered in Caldwell's study again after supper, and Heather and Minna and Rosie were left alone in the parlor.

"I'm so glad that David has been cleared," Minna said. "And it was all your doing, Emma. Now, if you could only find some way to clear Brice's name too, but I'm afraid that's impossible."

"I can't understand why so many people seem to think he's guilty," Heather mused. "I can understand Matthew Thaxter, I think. From the way he was raving, he has it in for everyone he thinks is more fortunate than he is, and he had his heart set on Naomi capturing Brice so that he could gloat about it. And from what he said, Naomi had as much as told him that she and Brice were having a flaming love affair, and of course he believed it because he wanted to believe it. Phoebe told me that Naomi told a lot of people the same thing, although Phoebe said that it was nothing more than romantical wishful thinking on Naomi's part. It had an effect, though. Some people must have believed her, even if they should have known better."

"Some people are always eager to believe the worst of anybody," Rosie said disgustedly. "Usually people like Matthew Thaxter, who are jealous of anyone who has more than they have. It's nothing more than human nature, more's the pity."

"But John Thaxter should be more intelligent," Heather protested. "How can he be a banker if he doesn't have any better sense than that?"

"Sense doesn't come into it. John Thaxter not only resents the slur on Naomi's name because she's family, but he and Burton Langdon are as thick as thieves. And Burton Langdon has had a hankering for Arbordale for a long time. He's always disliked Caldwell because Alice Langdon would have married my brother if he hadn't realized in time that she'd never make him happy. When Brice and Evelyn fell in love, Burton settled for that. At least his grandchildren would inherit Arbordale someday. But when all this scandal erupted, he saw his chance to get his hands on Arbordale right now and get his revenge on Caldwell at the same time. I know perfectly well that he talked John Thaxter into refusing to extend our loan. If John forecloses, Burton will buy Arbordale. The scandal was simply his excuse to talk Evelyn into breaking the engagement, although I doubt that

Evelyn needed much persuasion. Evelyn isn't the kind of girl to want to marry a man who is in financial difficulties. She'll be aiming a lot higher now, and I pity the poor gullible fool who'll ask her to marry him!"

This whole thing made for an unhappy subject, and as if to match Heather's mood, it stormed that night, a fierce storm that sent sheets of rain dashing against the window-panes and shook the sides of the house, with a wind that sent tree limbs crashing to the ground. If she had been afraid of storms, she would have cowered under her bed. Instead, she stood for a long time at the closed window, flinching at every clap of thunder and streak of lightning but too fascinated to turn away.

It was late before she went to bed, and then she slept poorly, dreaming that Matthew Thaxter had her cornered on his back porch and that no one came when she screamed for help. The dreams dissolved into scenes where the Arlingtons were put out of their house, with Minna crying and Heather trying to comfort her without success. She was glad to wake up the next morning.

After breakfast, which neither Brice nor Caldwell could finish because of their dread of what they would find when they rode out to inspect the fields, she and Jared joined Saul and lent their young strength to helping him clean up the debris that the storm had left in the yard. Saul was horrified when Heather set to work, but Jared laughed at him.

"Miss Emma is from the North, Saul. Northern young ladies aren't as delicate as Southern young ladies. Besides, there's no way we could stop her even if we wanted to. She's a headstrong young miss. At least she's right in our sight, and she can't get into any mischief while she's helping us."

By lunchtime Heather had worked up a ravenous appetite. There was nothing like hard physical work to chase the vapors away.

"The cotton is done for," Caldwell told them. "What we can salvage will have to be sold for a pittance. The other **crops didn't fare so badly, we won't go hungry in the** immediate future, but things could hardly be worse."

He looked at Jared with a shamefaced hope in his eyes,

and Jared looked down at his plate with the same shamefacedness. Heather knew that Caldwell was fighting the desire to ask Jared if he couldn't come up with a loan himself and that Jared felt terrible because he didn't have the money to lend him even if Caldwell should ask. But Brice looked at his father sternly, and Caldwell forced a smile.

They were interrupted when Pearl, her face so apprehensive that it was almost comical, came to tell them that Miss Isobel Becker was calling.

Minna's lips tightened, but she was a Southern lady. "Show her in, Pearl, and set another place." As a Southern lady, she was obliged to extend hospitality no matter how little she relished it.

Isobel marched into the dining room, her back stiff. She waved a dismissive hand at Pearl.

"I will not stay. I only came to apprise you that John Thaxter is furious because it was through your offices that his cousin Matthew has been jailed. If you ever had any hopes of obtaining an extension on your loan, it is gone now. Rosamund, you had better pack up and return home. Your friends won't have a roof to offer you very soon, and you have no choice."

Jared fixed the unpleasant woman with a stern eye. "Miss Becker, your sister will scarcely be impoverished and without a place to lay her head even if the Arlingtons lose this plantation. Miss Rosamund will have half the value of the house you live in, and that will support her for a long time to come. We are arranging to have the house appraised, and if you do not come up with her half of the full and fair value, she will take you into court, and she will win her case. You will save yourself a great deal of trouble and inconvenience if you agree to meet her terms."

Isobel's face turned livid.

"I'll fight her through every court in the land!"

"That would be foolhardy, Miss Becker. The case might drag on for years, and the legal costs would be ruinous to you. I myself shall represent Miss Rosamund, at no charge to her. And in the end, you will lose, and all of the costs will be charged to you."

"Now you're my sweetheart again!" Rosie said gleefully. "Isobel, you weren't invited here, so I think you should leave before you wear out your welcome, which you already have."

"I don't think you'll have any more trouble with her," Jared said as soon as Isobel had walked out, giving Heather the impression that she was ready to start foaming at the mouth.

Even Brice and Caldwell finished their meal with a better appetite than they had started with. Maybe they had lost the war, but they had won at least one skirmish!

Heather wasn't allowed to work in the yard again after they had finished eating. Her hands were blistered, and Jared put his foot down. He would help Saul. She was to find something else to do to amuse herself.

As she had done so often, Heather settled on the one activity that was available to her. And as always, Sam jumped into the buggy and settled down beside her once Saul had hitched Angel up, cautioning her to drive carefully because he didn't know what condition the roads would be in.

"Don't want you gettin' bogged down in the mud," Saul told her. "Haven't hardly got time to go and tow you out!"

The roads weren't as bad as Saul had been afraid they would be. They were a bit soggy, and Angel plodded through standing puddles, but there was no danger of getting bogged down. The air was wonderfully fresh and cool in the wake of the storm, and there wasn't a cloud in the sky. Heather breathed deeply and settled her mind to trying to work out a snag in her book plot. Beside her, Sam hung his head over the arm of the buggy seat and panted as if he enjoyed the freshness as much as she did.

She had to finish her book. If Jared couldn't afford to keep her on as his hired girl, she had to earn some money as quickly as possible so that she wouldn't have to go to work for someone else.

It was comforting to know that, because of Minna, there was a publisher who would at least read her book, but her honesty wouldn't settle for letting him buy it just because he was Minna's friend. It had to be good enough to sell enough copies so that he wouldn't lose money on it. She would make that very clear to him in the letter she would send with the book. If it wasn't good enough, the sooner she found out the better. Like Jared, she would have to make other plans.

Here and there across the road, small branches were down, littering the way, but most of them could be driven over without trouble. But there, just ahead, a much larger branch barred the way. Heather pulled Angel to a stop and climbed down to examine it. If she used all of her strength, maybe she could move it. She didn't want to turn back so soon, she'd hardly got started, and there wouldn't be a thing in the world for her to do until it was time for everyone to gather on the verandah for their late-afternoon refreshments.

She was struggling with the branch, putting both her arms and her back into the task, when Sam's head came up, and then, before she could order him to stay where he was, he was out of the buggy and streaking across the field toward the woods that Saul had told her were haunted by Gloria Nelson's ghost. She caught a glimpse of the rabbit that Sam was chasing before it disappeared in the tall meadow grass.

"Sam, you come back here!" Heather dropped the end of the branch and used all of her lung power. "Come back here this instant!"

Sam paid no heed to her. He kept going, his nose to the ground. After all, he was a hound, even if Saul never had the time to take him hunting.

Exasperated, Heather set off after him. Saul would be upset if she returned without him, and especially upset if she had to tell him where Sam had gone. Saul was afraid of these woods, and she didn't want to worry him.

Actually, the idea of entering the woods was exciting. She'd been wanting to explore them ever since she had heard the story of Gloria Nelson and Robbie Overton. As long as no one else would cooperate with her on an exploration jaunt, she had intended to ask Jared to come with her before they left to go home.

This might be the only chance she would ever have, she

thought. For all she knew, right at this moment Jared might be confessing to Caldwell and Brice, and when she got back she would find that she and Jared would be on tomorrow's train heading north.

By the time she reached the first trees, her shoes were wet and muddy, and in spite of her care in holding them up, her skirts were sodden from brushing against the tall meadow grass, still soaked from last night's storm. In the woods, birds were flitting from tree to tree, chirping and calling.

The patch of wood was dense, and there was considerable underbrush because it had been neglected for all these years. If the old superstition that it was haunted ever died out, Heather supposed that someday it might be used for a wood lot; but superstitions die hard, and she supposed that Caldwell hadn't been able to persuade any of his workers to come here and cut wood for plantation use, especially when other wood was available.

Now where was Sam? Heather stopped, looking around and calling. The underbrush would make it hard for her to find him if he didn't choose to answer her calls, and right at the moment it seemed he did not choose.

Cautiously, taking care not to snag her skirts, Heather went forward, her mind once again on the tragedy that had taken place there. Where had Gloria ended her life? There would be no indication of the spot. Heather might be walking across it at this very moment, and the thought made her skin prickle.

Her skirt caught on some briars, and she stopped to extricate herself, breathing a sigh of relief when she saw that it wasn't torn. The way things were right now, the clothes Emma had given her might be the only ones she would have for a long time, and it would be a pity to ruin even one dress.

She listened, but she heard nothing except the birds and the buzzing of insects. Whatever Sam was doing, he was being very quiet about it. Maybe Miss Gloria's ghost had got him.

She laughed at herself, but even to her own ears the laughter sounded uneasy. This was ridiculous! There were no such things as ghosts, and even if there were, this was early afternoon, and it was a bright, sunshiny day, even if very little of the sun managed to penetrate through the trees. As far as she'd ever heard, ghosts only walked at night.

Nevertheless, she wished Jared were with her. He'd laugh and tease her out of her qualms. But he wasn't with her. Only Sam was with her, but where in Sam Hill was Sam?

"Sam!" she called again, and then held her breath to listen. She heard nothing, and the hairs at the nape of her neck began to prickle. It was as if Sam had entered the woods and dropped into a deep hole.

She forced herself to go on. Sam might be in trouble. What if he'd been caught in some hunter's trap? Ridiculous again! No hunters came into these haunted woods to set traps, and even if some hunter had been that brave and Sam had been caught, he would be making enough racket to raise the dead.

She wished she hadn't thought of that. Darn it anyway, where was that dog, why didn't he answer her or come running back to her? It wasn't like him to run off like this and leave her alone.

There was a dead tree just off to her right, a huge tree, stretching its bare limbs like a specter. Could that be the place where Gloria had shot herself and the tree had died in grief for her passing?

She shook herself. Her imagination was running wild. But well it might in a place like this! This deep in the woods there was hardly any light at all, and it would be the easiest thing in the world to get lost in there. Pictures of herself wandering for hours, of still being trapped there when darkness fell, made her gather up her skirts and try to run. There was no use denying it, she was spooked. She wanted nothing more than to find Sam as quickly as she could and get out of there.

And then she saw a tree that had fallen in last night's storm. There was a blackened place on its trunk where it had been struck by lightning, and the wind had done the rest. Part of its roots were exposed, and on the other side of the roots and the hole they had left, Sam was digging.

"Sam, stop that nonsense and come along this minute! I don't like it in here!"

Sam raised his head and whined, and then he started digging again. And then, to Heather's horror, he raised his head and howled. The sound sent chills up and down her back.

"What is it, Sam?" Her voice was hardly more than a croak. "Is something there? Did you find something?"

She was torn between going around to the other side of the hole to investigate and taking to her heels. Had Sam uncovered a nest of snakes? But snakes wouldn't make him howl like that; if he was afraid of them, he'd just run.

And snakes weren't blue, were they? She'd never heard of a blue snake, even a very faded blue like the blue she could just glimpse from where she was standing. And snakes would move if a dog unearthed them, and this blue wasn't moving.

She took a reluctant step forward, and then another, although her every instinct told her to pick up her skirts and run as fast as she could in the opposite direction. She leaned forward. She didn't want to look, but her eyes wouldn't cooperate. They refused to close.

It was cloth. Not just a piece of cloth, it was attached to something. It was part of a dress. There was still a bit of rotting lace adhering to it. And it wasn't just a bit of rotting, faded dress with a bit of rotting lace still adhering to it; the dress was on someone. Heather's hand flew to her mouth, and she felt sickness flood through her until she was afraid she was going to suffocate.

She had found Naomi Thaxter.

Now she ran, and Sam ran with her. She would have run as blindly as any panicked horse, crashing into branches and tree trunks, except that she had a death grip on the loose skin of Sam's neck, and Sam avoided all the obstacles in their path, making for the open meadow, and the safety of Angel and the buggy, as fast as he could go with Heather hanging on to him.

They had gone a long way into the woods, but they left

them a good deal faster than they had entered them. They burst out of the shadows and raced across the meadow. Sam broke loose from Heather's grip and raced on ahead to leap into the buggy. He was panting heavily when Heather got there, but not any harder than she was panting.

Gathering up the lines, she turned Angel around. "Giddup! Drat it, Angel, go! Get moving!" Heather screamed.

Angel trotted along, not in the least perturbed by Heather's screaming. She might never have run in her life, except that Heather couldn't forget the one day she had run.

But then, she supposed that it didn't matter. There wasn't any hurry, as there had been the last time. Naomi wasn't going anywhere. She would still be there where Sam had unearthed her when Heather reached Arbordale and gave the news.

Saul wasn't in sight when she pulled up in front of the house, but that didn't matter. Angel would stand where she was until he came to take her away. Heather forgot to pick up her skirts this time, and she tripped on the verandah steps and fell face first, jarring all the breath out of her. Struggling to her feet again, not even feeling the scrape she'd sustained along her right arm when she'd flung it out to break her fall, she rushed into the house and threw open the door to Caldwell's study without knocking.

The men, in a huddle around Caldwell's desk, looked up, startled at her bedraggled appearance and white face.

"Emma! What on earth is wrong? You look as if the devil has been chasing you!" Jared exclaimed.

"We found her!" Heather gasped. "Sam chased a rabbit into the haunted woods, and he found her!"

"Emma, don't tell me you think you saw the ghost?" Brice stood up and came to her, patting her shoulder to try to calm her. "I wouldn't have thought that you were susceptible to superstition. You've been listening to Saul's stories, but you should have taken them with a grain of salt."

"Not the ghost! I wish it had been the ghost! Brice, I think

217

I found Naomi Thaxter. A tree had fallen, and Sam was digging there, and I saw a blue dress, and a body, and then Sam and I ran like anything!"

Brice's face paled. "Can you tell me exactly where it is?" he asked, his face filled with urgency.

"Yes, no, I don't know! But wait, there's a tree, a huge dead tree, and the fallen tree is near that, and it must be in the very center of the woods. Just let me catch my breath, and I'll go back with you and help you find it." She didn't want to go back there and see the pitiful remains again, but she had to offer.

"You'll do no such thing! You're shaking like a leaf. You are to go straight to bed!" Brice told her, his tone brooking no argument. "I can find the dead tree and the fallen tree from there."

In spite of her protests, Heather was led away with Minna on one side of her and Rosamund on the other, while Pearl scurried ahead of them to turn down her bed and Della ran to the kitchen house for hot water to wash her scrapes and bruises.

"After all this time," Minna said, her face as pale as Brice's and Caldwell's had been. "And the poor girl is dead!"

Now Heather's hysteria took over full force. "I should certainly hope so, because somebody buried her!" she cried, and then she broke into a flood of tears and cried and shook as though she would never be able to stop.

Her clothing was removed, warm water and gentle hands soothed her, a clean, sweet-smelling nightgown was pulled over her head, and she was tucked into bed. Minna left the room and returned not with her special lemonade but with a tot of brandy.

Between her gasping sobs, Heather drank it, and then at last she was able to take a deep breath and stop crying.

"I'm s-s-sorry! I had no idea that I'd go to pieces like that. But it was horrible! And somebody killed her, somebody had to have killed her, or else she wouldn't be buried there in the woods. I expect she was buried there because nobody goes there, because the place is haunted, and whoever killed her thought that her grave would never be found."

"I expect that you're right," Rosie said. She looked perturbed as she added, a sudden thought striking her, "My lands, Minna, those woods are on your property! It's going to look bad for Brice!"

❦ *Chapter 15* ❧

"I WON'T GO into details," Brice said. His face was grave. "As you know, the body has been there for a good many weeks. But there isn't any doubt that it's Naomi Thaxter. She wore that same blue dress at the box supper, and there was a little gold locket that she told me her father had given her for her fifteenth birthday. It was the only piece of jewelry she owned, and she was very proud of it. Also, there's a satchel buried with her. It's obvious that she had been planning to go somewhere."

If she had packed joyfully, filled with anticipation, it made it doubly tragic, because the only place the young girl had gone had been to her death and a lonely grave in the haunted woods.

"We'll have to send for the sheriff," Brice went on. "I'll send Saul just as soon as we've had a drink." Caldwell and Jared, who had gone with him in search of the grave, both nodded. Jared looked a little green.

"If I were you, I wouldn't send for Clarence Kotter at all," Rosamund said. "Don't you know how bad it's going to look for you, Brice? You were already under enough suspicion without the poor girl's body being found on your land! You should just cover it up again and leave things as they are."

Heather had come down in her dressing gown and slippers, mindless of the proprieties at a time like this. As terrible as it was to admit it, she wished she hadn't discovered Naomi's body. It might have remained where it was for years, until no trace of it was left, and then Brice wouldn't be in danger.

Not only Brice, but Jared too, looked at Rosie with shock.

"We can't do that, Miss Rosie," Jared said. "A crime has been committed, and an investigation must be got underway. It would be breaking the law not to report what we've found, as well as aiding and abetting whoever it was who actually killed the girl."

"Nobody's going to look any further than Brice," Rosie asserted. "You know as well as I do that he's the one who will be arrested. Now that Naomi's body has been found on Arlington land, he'll be tried and convicted and hung, and there won't be a thing we can do about it. The real killer isn't going to come forward and confess just because the body has been found, you can be sure of that!"

"It will just have to be faced," Brice said heavily. Heather could have burst into tears again, but tears would serve no purpose. If something wasn't done, Brice was sure to be railroaded. John Thaxter and Burton Langdon, the most influential men in the county, would be out to nail him. Not only would Mr. Langdon like to see Caldwell Arlington plunged into grief, but it would make it all the more sure that Caldwell wouldn't be able to obtain a loan from any institution, and then he would be sure to get Arbordale when the loan was called in.

Brice and Caldwell had many loyal friends who would stand up for Brice and insist that he wasn't the murderer, but besides Mr. Langdon and Mr. Thaxter there was David Inges. David's newspaper, the *Bennington Bugle,* would be sure to be biased against Brice, and that would swing a lot of opinions.

Heather's mind was racing. There just might be a way! It was a long chance to take, but it was barely possible that it might work, if only these stiff-backed, law-abiding, sickeningly moral men would go along with the idea that had just popped into her head.

"Maybe there is something we can do. Maybe we can flush the real murderer out," she said.

All five pairs of eyes looked at her for signs of delirium brought on by her unnerving experiences.

"But there is!" she insisted, standing her ground. "Nobody knows yet that the grave has been found. The murderer hasn't the least idea that he isn't still safe! There was no proof until the grave was found that Naomi didn't simply run away. But if we could make him return to the site of the grave, and we were watching, then we'd have him, because nobody but the murderer could know where Naomi's body is!"

"And just how are we to accomplish that?" Caldwell wanted to know, although there was a sudden, pitiful trace of hope in his eyes.

"Jared could do it." Heather was still thinking as fast as she could. She had never lacked for imagination, and now it was working overtime. "He could let it be known that he's bought that piece of woodland from you and that he's going to build a vacation place there, a lodge. Yes, that's it! He can say that it's already settled and that in just a day or two men will be hired to go in there and start clearing. He can say that the lodge is going to be built on the exact spot where Naomi's buried, there by that big dead tree!"

She had their undivided attention now, and she rushed on, pressing her advantage. If she didn't make them agree to her plan right now, they might decide against it, being men. And they just had to agree, because it was the only chance Brice had!

"We'll be waiting and watching, and whoever comes to move the body will be the one who killed her!" she urged.

Jared's face was alight with interest. "You might have something there, Emma. We'd have to have reliable witnesses, but there are enough men who believe in Brice's innocence so that it shouldn't be hard to find a few who would lie in wait with us. There's George Barnstable, for one, and Aaron Harper. And the minister, Mr. Roundtree. I think we should try it! We don't have anything to lose, and it just might work!"

Minna and Rosie came to hug Heather, and she felt like

cheering. For once, men weren't being unreasonable and stuffy, they weren't insisting that just because a woman had been the one to have an idea, it wasn't any good.

"Do it!" Minna urged. "Tell them, Rosie!"

"Emma, you're a wonder! How in the world did you think of such a clever scheme?"

"It wasn't hard for Emma;" Minna declared. "Our Emma is wonderfully talented. Just think how she figured out about Matthew Thaxter's kerosene can. If only Jared is as good an actor as Emma is an imaginer, everything should work out just the way it ought to!"

"I'll go into town tonight and talk to Ephraim Roundtree and Mr. Barnstable and Aaron. I'm sure they can be trusted not to breathe a word, and if by some inconceivable chance the grave should be discovered before we can put our plan into action, we will at least have witnesses who will testify that we had no intention of letting it go unreported." Jared hoped that would be enough to mitigate the seriousness of their offense, at least.

There was only one good public place to eat in Bennington, the dining room of the Bennington Arms Hotel. Jared arrived at the height of the noon hour. He was shown to a white-clothed table, and he ordered the best meal the hotel could provide, and then he looked around at the other patrons for likely prospects.

The two men at a table near the front window looked as though they might suit his purpose. Jared smiled at them and approached them.

"You look like substantial businessmen," he said. A little flattery wouldn't hurt. He introduced himself, although he thought it was probably superfluous. The fact that he was a guest at Arbordale made him notorious, and he surmised that there were few people in town who wouldn't recognize him on sight or at least be able to make an accurate guess about his identity.

"You gentlemen might be able to help me," he said. "I'm going to need some workmen by tomorrow morning, and I was wondering if you might know of any men who are available."

"What kind of work?" the more heavyset man asked with a trace of suspicion. A Northerner who was a friend of the Arlingtons wasn't exactly to be trusted.

"Clearing trees and brush. Mr. Arlington has been kind enough to allow me to purchase that tract of woodland on the edge of his property, and I intend to build a house there. It will be an ideal retreat from the stress and strain of business."

The two men looked at each other, their faces showing incredulity.

"You won't find anyone who will be willing to go into those woods and do any clearing for you," the second man said decisively. "That patch of trees has a bad reputation. I'm afraid you've been cheated, Mr. Cranston. I guess Caldwell Arlington didn't tell you that those woods are haunted."

Jared knew what they thought. They thought Caldwell was so desperate for money that he'd cheated a friend.

"I'll pay top wages. As for the ghost that's supposed to walk there, no intelligent man believes in such nonsense."

"I don't believe in such nonsense, but there's plenty who do," he was told. "And you won't find anybody in this entire county to do the work, I can tell you that right now."

Jared frowned. "Then I'll just have to accept Mr. Arlington's offer to have his own people do the work. I didn't like to ask him to take them away from their other tasks, but it seems that I have no alternative."

He made his voice sound enthusiastic as he continued.

"The spot I've selected is ideal. Perhaps you know it. There's a dead tree, a huge thing, it's a wonder it hasn't fallen down of its own accord long since. That will have to come down first. Three or four of Mr. Arlington's hands have said they'll go in and do the work, for double wages. I expect they're holding me up, but I'm determined to get the foundations in before I return to Albany, and the clearing will start tomorrow morning."

"If you're crazy enough to want to build in those woods, you're lucky to get men to do the work for even double wages," they told him. "Down here, we have better sense than to build in a spot like that." The implication was clear.

Jared was a Northerner, and so it was to be expected that he didn't have good sense.

He had planted the seeds, and now all that was needed was to wait for them to sprout. He had no doubt that the story of his madness would be spread all over Bennington before another two hours had passed.

He returned to his table and ate his meal with every appearance of a young man who had nothing pressing on his mind. When he finished, he called on Ephraim Roundtree again.

"There's no guarantee that the plan we've concocted will work, but we have to grasp at straws. I hope that you won't be too uncomfortable waiting in the woods with us to-night."

"The discomfort doesn't matter. The important thing is that you have given your word that you will notify Clarence Kotter about the grave if your plan doesn't work."

"If the plan doesn't work, I'm not going to be too enthusiastic about facing your esteemed sheriff," Jared said. "He'll take a dim view of our not having reported the grave as soon as it was found. I'm just sorry that at least part of his wrath will fall on you for going along with us in this plan."

"I'll face Mr. Kotter with my guilt more easily than I'll be able to face my wife." Ephraim's voice was rueful. "I'll have to lie to her, you know, to get out of the house for so many hours at night. If I told her the truth, she'd insist on going directly to the sheriff, and nothing would stop her. If the plan fails, I'm afraid I'll have to live with her displeasure for some time to come."

And that, Jared thought, remembering Bertha Roundtree, was putting it mildly. He gave Ephraim full credit for bravery above and beyond the call of duty.

The two men clasped hands, and Jared set off to alert George Barnstable and Aaron Harper. They had already promised that they would come, and now he had to tell them that the trap was set.

The three men arrived at Arbordale while the sun was still streaking the sky with its last afterglow. They came in separate buggies within fifteen minutes of each other.

Heather was furious. All six of the men flatly refused to

let her go with them. In fact, both Brice and Caldwell had been so shocked at her proposal to accompany them that she would have laughed if she hadn't been angry enough to spit instead. She was the one who had discovered the grave, and it was her plan, so naturally it was her right to be in on the capture.

"I never heard of anything so outrageous!" Caldwell exclaimed. "A young lady to lie in wait in the woods while we try to apprehend a killer! Minna, Rosamund, I charge you to make sure that Miss Emma stays in the house!"

"You should let me go, you know." Rosamund was as annoyed as Heather. "I'm the one who'd be sure to bring the miscreant down if he tries to run."

"You will stay here!" Caldwell ordered. "I don't know what's gotten into women these days!" His sense of masculinity was outraged. Women were the weaker sex, to be cherished and protected. That was the way it should be, and always had been, and always would be if he had anything to do with it.

The men walked to their destination, although it was a considerable distance. They couldn't risk leaving their conveyances anywhere near the woods to alert the man they hoped would come to remove Naomi's body.

The waiting was more miserable than Jared had dreamed. The woods were black this far away from the open meadow, and it was eerie enough to harbor an actual ghost. But it wasn't apprehension about specters that bothered Jared and the others. With full nightfall, swarms of mosquitoes and gnats had come out, tormenting them by biting them on every exposed inch of their skin. Their hands and faces and necks smarted and burned and itched from the assault. If he had all the money in the world, nothing would persuade Jared to build a house there.

He had never realized how hard it was to wait. Every minute dragged as they crouched in the underbrush, trying not even to breathe. Any sound might alert their quarry that he wasn't alone, and he might get away before they could lay their hands on him.

Jared became so cramped that his legs were in agony, and he winced to think how much worse off Ephraim and

George must be, men of middle age who lived sedentary lives. Caldwell wouldn't fare quite as badly—he had always been active, and he was physically fit—but he was still too old to be indulging in such an activity.

From their place of concealment they had no glimpse of the sky, and so they couldn't judge how much time had passed. Jared tried to count off the seconds, to see how long one minute would be, and he was appalled by the result. It would be better not to count.

Surprisingly, after Jared had despaired that their ruse had worked, Ephraim was the one who laid a cautionary hand on his shoulder.

"He's coming," Ephraim whispered. All six men tensed, holding their breath. Jared heard it then, a rustling of the underbrush as something passed through it, something too large to be a rabbit or even a fox. And then there was a soft, muffled oath as whoever it was ran into a low branch.

Only Brice was armed. They had decided that if the killer actually put in an appearance, they didn't want to risk shooting each other in the darkness and confusion. Brice would not fire unless it was absolutely necessary. It was hoped that Brice's being armed would make their prey surrender on command.

The man was close now but still unseen. Whoever it was must be wearing dark clothing, because Jared's eyes had adjusted enough so that he could have seen a lighter patch in the darkness.

They remained crouched where they were, not moving a muscle, and in another moment they could make out the man's shape. He was advancing cautiously, and he was carrying something. He stopped where the exposed roots of the downed tree had revealed Naomi's grave.

At that moment, while they waited for their quarry to start his gruesome task, Heather was almost at the edge of the woods. She had waited and waited at the house, going out onto the verandah to strain her eyes into the darkness and to listen for any sound of approaching footsteps. Minna and Rosie had gone to bed, telling her to wake them when the men got back, whether they had caught the murderer or not.

After what had seemed eons of time, she had left the house and started walking toward the woods, taking to the meadow as the men had done. She would explode right out of her skin if she waited any longer. It couldn't do any harm if she met the men on their way back, to find out that much sooner if the trap had worked. She wouldn't enter the woods if she didn't meet them coming back. She'd just wait in the meadow, close enough so she couldn't miss them when they emerged.

She had crossed almost halfway across the meadow when a damp nose nudged at her hand, making her stifle a scream while her heart almost pounded its way right out of her body.

"Sam, darn you! You followed me! And you scared me out of seven years' growth!"

All the same, she was glad of Sam's company. It was a comfort to have him beside her. She took a firm grip on his neck skin so that he couldn't run on ahead of her and told him to be quiet. She wished that he wore a collar, but Saul had a stubborn notion that being collared would be an insult to Sam's dignity. A collar would accommodate a leash, and a leash spelled enslavement, a thing that Saul could not tolerate even for a dog.

"Not a sound, Sam, do you understand?" Heather whispered, tightening her grip on his neck. "Be as quiet as a mouse!"

The woods loomed dark and forbidding in front of her, and a shiver went through her from her head to her toes. She wouldn't go in there at night for all the money in the world! Maybe the place wasn't haunted, but it looked haunted in the dark, and now there would be enough new evil connected with it to keep the legend going strong for another fifty years!

Where were the men? What could possibly be taking them this long? She slapped at the mosquitoes and gnats that buzzed around her face, but there was no fending them off. She was being eaten alive. And to add to her misery, she was deathly afraid of stepping on a snake in the tall meadow grass. She could only hope that if snakes weren't afraid enough of her to get out of her path, they would be afraid of Sam.

She dared not go any farther. Another few steps and she would be among the first trees, and the idea made her hair stand on end. She was beginning to regret that she had come at all. The men would be furious with her, she'd have to suffer their scolding, and besides she was being consumed by the fiery stings of the insects. Let them come! she prayed. She didn't want to have to cross the meadow alone again in the dark, even with Sam with her. But the men had brought a lantern so that they could have light on their return journey, and there were enough of them to send any snake slithering for its hole.

But still no one came. There wasn't a sound or a glimmer of lantern light. She and Sam might have been the last two living creatures on the face of the earth except for the mosquitoes and gnats and the snakes that she was convinced were there even if she couldn't see them.

In their hiding place deep in the woods, Jared and the other men were as silent as Heather, their bodies tense as they strained their eyes and ears.

And then Jared sneezed. He couldn't help it. A gnat had flown up his right nostril, and the sneeze was automatic and completely involuntary. There was a startled curse from the darkness only a few yards away from where they waited, and then there was a thrashing and crashing as their prey took to his heels.

Brice took off, sprinting in pursuit, with Jared right behind him. Brice launched himself at the man, while Jared shouted for him to give himself up.

The man whirled as Brice closed in on him, his arms lifted, and Jared shouted out a warning as the shovel the man was carrying descended directly at Brice's head. Jared made the longest leap he had ever attempted and sent Brice sprawling. He took the full force of the blow on his own shoulder. The shoulder went numb, leaving him astonished and in shock.

The others lost precious time as they crowded around, wanting to know how badly Jared was hurt. Brice had dropped his rifle when Jared knocked him out of the way, and now he groped for it in the dark, while the others set off after the man who had now got a considerable head start on them.

The running man burst into the open, and, seeing Heather standing there, he struck out at her, sending her to her hands and knees. Heather's reaction was automatic. With the breath knocked out of her, she wasn't even thinking as she reached out, grasped an ankle, and hung on for dear life, all the while struggling to draw in enough breath to scream.

The man kicked at her and struck at her again, cursing in a frantic, hate-filled voice. He broke free, and Heather's ribs felt as though they were broken where he had kicked her in her side. The long breath she drew sent stabs of pain fanning out all around her rib cage, but she used it to good advantage.

"Sic him, Sam! Get him!"

Sam hardly needed the command. Violence had been committed against the girl he loved, and he was after the perpetrator. He leapt and clamped down on the man's arm and hung on, impossible to dislodge. Heather found another breath, a little less painful than the first.

"Hang on, Sam! Hold him!"

And then the men were there, bursting out of the trees, Jared still holding his shoulder but running with the others.

"There, there!" Heather screamed. "There he is!"

Sam was reluctant to relinquish his prisoner. He'd caught the man who had knocked Heather down, and he didn't want to let him go. It took a sharp command from Brice to make him relax his hold, and he sat down, whining his protest.

Brice and Aaron Harper had a firm hold on the man now, while he cursed and struggled as George Barnstable moved in to help them. Caldwell, muttering words that weren't suitable for a lady's ears, was fumbling for matches in his pockets. If Emma was shocked, he thought viciously, it was her own fault for being where she had no business to be after he had given her strict orders to stay at home.

He found the matches in a pocket he was sure he hadn't put them in, and in another moment he managed to light the lantern they had brought and held it up so that the light fell on the captive.

"Carl Amhurst!" he burst out. It didn't seem possible. Carl was one of the most respected and well-liked young men in Bennington. He was Phoebe Roundtree's constant escort, and everyone believed that their engagement would be announced at any time. Carl had never had anything to do with Naomi Thaxter. They had never gone out together. He had never seen her except in Phoebe's company.

"Why?" Brice burst out, voicing the stunned question for all of them. "In the name of God, why?"

"Go to hell!" Carl snarled. "Damn you, you can all go to hell!"

Now Ephraim came out of the woods, carrying something. "Look at this," he said. "It's a blanket. He came prepared to carry the remains away. As far as I'm concerned, this is definite proof of his guilt. Carl, won't you tell us why you did it? What possible reason could you have had? Naomi never harmed anyone in her life. You scarcely knew her!"

A sudden thought made him break off, and when he spoke again his voice was filled with distress.

"I'll have to tell Phoebe. It will be a shock to her, a very great shock. And to my wife as well. I don't understand any of this. It doesn't seem possible!"

"From what I've seen of your daughter, she'll bear up under it," Jared said in a half-strangled voice. He was nursing his shoulder which, unfortunately, wasn't numb any longer. It throbbed like crazy, and pain shot from it in all directions. But he didn't think it was broken.

The light from the lantern was attracting still more insects. They slapped at them, and Caldwell said, "Damned pests! Sorry, Reverend. I didn't mean to offend you, but they are damned pests!"

"One advantage of being a minister is that we can let other men do our cursing for us," Ephraim said with dry humor. "I would have had to say that they are winged demons, which wouldn't have come near to expressing my true feelings. I suggest that we make our way away from here. It's late, and we still have a great deal to do tonight."

They certainly had, Jared thought glumly. They had to take Carl into Bennington and turn him over to Clarence Kotter, a task he did not relish in the least. Kotter was not going to take their evening's activities kindly. But if they had told him about Naomi's grave, Jared had no doubt at all that Kotter would have come rushing out here. The entire population of Bennington would have known about the discovery within hours, and Carl wouldn't have been able to betray himself by coming to remove Naomi's body. All the same, Kotter might very well bring charges against the lot of them for withholding vital evidence.

Now he directed his attention to Heather, and his face went white with anger in the lantern light.

"What the devil are you doing here? I ought to shake the living daylights out of you! You might have got yourself killed!"

"Mr. Amhurst would have gotten away if I hadn't been here!" Heather had her breath entirely back by now, and she didn't hesitate to use it in striking back at Jared for his unjust accusations. "Sam and I caught him for you, so don't you dare yell at me!"

"I'll yell at you if I want to! Of all the stubborn, reckless girls who ever lived, you're the worst! First snooping around Matthew Thaxter's house, and now this! Why can't you ever do as you're told?"

"And what gives you the right to tell me what to do just because you're a man?"

Brice intervened. "Emma has a point, Jared. If it hadn't been for her, we wouldn't have discovered Naomi's grave, and if it hadn't been for her, Carl would have got away before we had a chance to see who he was. We owe her a debt of gratitude that can never be repaid. And right now we have more important things to do than quarrel among ourselves. Carl must have brought a horse and buggy to take Naomi's body away. I wonder where he left it?"

It was Jared who found the missing horse and buggy, left close against the edge of the trees a considerable distance away from where they had entered the woods earlier that evening.

Caldwell took charge. "Reverend, you can drive the buggy

back to Arbordale, and Jared will ride with you because his shoulder is hurt. Emma, get into the buggy with them, and I don't want to hear any arguments! The rest of us will walk."

Heather opened her mouth to argue and then closed it again. There wasn't anything to argue about. She didn't want to walk back through the meadow grass. She hadn't stepped on a snake on her way, and she wanted to quit while her luck still held.

"Such a reckless girl!" Minna scolded while she poked and prodded Jared's shoulder and placed cold compresses on it. "If I'd known what you intended to do, I would have locked you in your room!"

"If I'd known what she intended to do, I would have gone with her!" Rosie declared. "Emma, I'm really put out with you! Why didn't you tell me so I wouldn't have had to miss out on all the fun? On second thought, I don't relish being eaten alive like you were. Minna, where's the calomine lotion? Everyone who was out there needs to be slathered with it!"

It was Ephraim who set off for town to rouse the sheriff. "I think it's better that I do it," he said. "He isn't as likely to clap me behind bars as he would the others, and I hope that by the time you have to face him his ire will have cooled off a little." The minister had had a hard night, and it promised to become even harder before he could seek his bed and rest.

Heather thought of her cool, clean sheets with longing, but the night was far from over. The party that had walked arrived at last and stopped only long enough to bolster themselves with one stiff bourbon before they set off after Ephraim with Carl Amhurst, his hands bound behind his back, in tow. In spite of his shoulder, Jared insisted on going with them. Maybe he could bluff Clarence Kotter out of throwing them all in jail.

Minna and Rosie went back to bed, but as enticing as the thought of her own bed was, Heather didn't follow them. She compromised by dozing off and on in a chair in the parlor, keeping her ears strained for the arrival of the men when they returned.

She had dozed off again when she heard them enter the

house. She jumped up so fast that she knocked into a table and sent a vase crashing to the floor. She was holding the broken pieces in her hands, looking stricken, when they entered the parlor.

"See what I've done! I know Miss Minna set a lot of store on this vase!"

"Damn the vase," Caldwell said, mopping his brow. "It's only china. Ah, there's the bottle! I could use one more drink after coping with that knothead Kotter. Jared, you did a good job of talking him into being satisfied with having Amhurst behind bars."

Heather's eyes were wide. "Was he really going to arrest you?"

"He was fit to be tied." Jared grinned. "And actually, he was right. I had to remind him that sheriffs are elected and that a lot of people wouldn't be pleased if he locked up a minister, as well as the men who solved the crime for him."

The *men* who solved the crime for him! If that wasn't just like a man, to take the credit when it was a woman who'd solved the crime for them! She was all ready to tear into Jared with a reminder of just who had discovered Naomi's body and just who had thought of the idea of setting a trap for the killer, when Brice intervened.

"Emma, may I speak with you if you aren't too tired?" Brice's face was very serious. He drew her outside and into the rose garden. The stars had faded, and it had begun to rain. It was still only a sprinkle, but the sprinkle increased even as they stood facing each other in the midst of the drooping roses.

Brice didn't seem to realize that it was raining. He put his hands on Heather's shoulders and looked down intently into her face.

"Emma, I couldn't speak before. I had no right, not only because of the shameful way that you and Jared were invited here under false pretenses, but because it wasn't even certain that I'd have a home to offer you. But now things have changed. I've been exonerated, and we'll be able to get a loan somewhere to keep Arbordale afloat. Emma, will you marry me?"

Heather's breath stopped as he kissed her. Her knees went weak, her blood pounded in her ears. It had happened at last, she had been proposed to in a Virginia rose garden by a handsome young planter!

But there any resemblance to her romantic dreams ended. When Brice let her go, some of the calomine lotion from her face had transferred to his, and she knew that her own face must be streaked like a clown's. There wasn't any starlight, and it was raining hard now, and both of them were drenched, their hair plastered to their heads, their clothing plastered to their bodies.

Besides, romantic setting or no romantic setting, she didn't want to marry Brice. How was she going to manage to refuse him without hurting him? He'd already been hurt enough; the thought of hurting him still more made her feel like crying.

And so she did what girls who found themselves in her predicament almost always do. "Brice, thank you for asking me. I'm terribly honored." She was darned if she was going to say that this was so sudden. That phrase made her giggle every time she read it in a romantic novel. "But we ought to think it over. We really don't know each other that well, and marriage is a very important step. You're all excited right now about having caught the real murderer, and you're grateful to me because I helped you a little. Maybe by tomorrow morning you'll have thought better of it."

And maybe by tomorrow morning she would have thought of a way to refuse him without hurting him too much.

Brice looked crestfallen, but he kissed her again, tenderly and gently.

"I won't change my mind, but I realize that you need a little time to think it over. I shouldn't have rushed you like this, without courting you first. I'm almost certain that your answer will be yes when you've had time to get used to the idea. I love you very much, you know."

They went back into the house. The others were still in the parlor, and Heather started to apologize because they were dripping water all over Minna's carpet.

"Father, Aunt Minna, I've asked Emma to marry me," Brice blurted out, to her horror. "She hasn't said yes yet, but I have every hope that she will."

Before Heather had time to think of a thing to say, Minna had enfolded her in her arms, and on her other side Rosie had her arms around her as well.

"Of course she's going to say yes!" Minna exclaimed. She was so happy that she was crying. "Caldwell, isn't it wonderful? Brice and Emma are going to be married!"

Caldwell's eyes held a suspicious glint of tears. He raised his glass of brandy in a toast.

"Nothing could make me happier! I only wish that Thatcher were here on this joyous occasion. It was always our hope that Brice and Emma should fall in love and marry. It cut me to the core when Brice let Evelyn Langdon turn his head and got himself engaged to her. I never did care for that girl. I was hoping against hope that Brice would see through her before it was too late, that's why I didn't write Thatcher about the engagement. Then we could still have got Brice and Emma together and hoped for the best. This is wonderful! Jared, aren't you going to congratulate Brice and wish your sister happiness?"

Jared lifted his glass. The brandy tasted bitter to him, like gall. It had happened, just as he had been afraid it would happen. Brice had finally come to his senses and fallen in love with Heather, and Heather would marry him. Jared's toast was more to the death of any hope that he might have had than to the newly engaged couple.

"We'll have an engagement ball!" Minna exclaimed, almost delirious with excitement. "Heather will be the most beautiful bride Arbordale has ever seen! I can hardly wait to start planning it. I'm going to start right now! Rosie, come along, we must leave the young sweethearts alone. You and I are going to start on the guest list!"

Heather opened her mouth and closed it again. What had happened? It seemed that she was engaged whether she wanted to be engaged or not! Minna and Rosie were hugging each other now, Caldwell came to kiss her cheek, and Brice was beaming. Even Jared was smiling, as if he couldn't be more pleased.

"Off to bed!" Rosie was pushing and tugging at her. "Look at you, you're soaked to the skin, and we're all exhausted. Minna, calm down. We'll start the guest list tomorrow, and I promise that this will be the most fantastic engagement ball that ever was! Brice, have a little consideration for your bride-to-be and let her get cozy and warm and get some sleep. We can't have her getting sick now, it would spoil all the fun!"

With no volition of her own, Heather was urged up the stairs, undressed, and tucked into bed, the two excited ladies patting at her and kissing her cheek a dozen times in the process. How on earth was she going to tell them tomorrow that she wasn't engaged at all, that it was all a mistake, a misunderstanding? Their hearts would be broken. Brice's heart would be broken.

She should tell them right now, but she didn't have the heart. And Rosie was right, she was cold and exhausted, and she needed time to think how to do it without shattering them. Right now, Minna and Rosie were as tired as she was, and they weren't young. They needed a peaceful night's sleep before she broke it to them.

Why did life have to be so complicated? How had she ever gotten herself into a mess like this? Now she'd have to get herself out of it, but for the life of her she couldn't think how.

✑ *Chapter 16* ✑

HEATHER AWAKENED IN the morning feeling radiant. Something wonderful had happened, but it took her a few seconds to remember what it was.

And then she remembered. Naomi's murderer had been caught, and Brice had been exonerated.

On the heels of that thought another one made her hand fly to her mouth, and she gasped with dismay. Naomi's murderer had been caught, and Brice had asked her to marry him, and even though she hadn't said yes, she was engaged.

She closed her eyes again, wincing. She didn't want to hurt Brice, and she didn't want to hurt Minna and Rosie, and she didn't want to hurt Caldwell. It occurred to her that if she were a sensible, practical girl, she'd settle for what had already been settled for her. Almost any other girl in the world would give her eyeteeth to be in her shoes, engaged to the most handsome young planter in Virginia, about to become the mistress of Arbordale.

If she left Virginia with Jared, nothing lay before her but finding another family to work for. She would still go on hoping and dreaming that some day Jared would ask her to marry him, but that would be so long in the future that she shuddered to think about it. And what if he never asked her? If she had a grain of sense in her head, she'd take what she could get.

She opened her eyes again and looked reality in the face. There was no way she could marry Brice. Not only because she didn't love him, but Brice thought she was Emma, and she wasn't Emma. There was only one thing for her to do. She must get up, go downstairs and join everyone at breakfast, and tell them the truth. That would fix everything. She wasn't Emma, and Brice wouldn't want to marry her, and that would be the end of it.

The image that confronted her from the mirror made her burst out laughing. There were a dozen angry red mosquito bites on her face, three or four of them scabbed over where she had scratched at them in her sleep. There were even a few traces of the calomine lotion clinging to her skin. A more ludicrous-looking bride-to-be could scarcely be imagined. But that was all right, she wasn't a bride-to-be, and so she didn't have to look beautiful.

She was the last one down, dreading to face what had to be faced immediately because this charade had gone on long enough. All three of the men rose to their feet when she entered the dining room, and Brice hurried to hold her chair. She unfolded her napkin, and her fingers toyed with it nervously, rolling up one corner and then unrolling it.

Pearl placed a plate loaded with ham and eggs and grits in front of her. She picked up her fork, but for the first time in her life her appetite deserted her. She looked wildly at Brice, and then at Jared, and then back at Brice again. Minna and Rosamund, who missed nothing, looked at her oddly.

"Emma, what on earth is the matter?" Minna wanted to know. "I declare, you look like a child who's been in the cookie jar and expects to be punished! You haven't had second thoughts about marrying Brice, have you? Oh, dear, that would be dreadful! Here it's taken all this time to get you two together, just as Caldwell and I dreamed, and you just can't go changing your mind!"

Heather dropped her fork. It fell to her plate with a nerve-jangling clatter. There wasn't any point in putting it off.

"Jared, we have to tell them," she said. "Will you do it, or shall I?"

"Tell us what, Emma?" Minna wanted to know. They were all staring at her, their faces filled with puzzlement.

"That I'm not Emma. That's the first thing we have to tell you. I never was Emma Cranston. My name is Heather Bailey, and I'm the Cranstons' hired girl. Jared, help me!"

Jared's face had turned a deep red, but he rose to the occasion. "You're right, Heather. It's past time that we should tell them. Emma couldn't come, you see, because she's in Boston learning how to be a missionary, and then she's going to marry Humphrey Snell, who used to be our minister, and they're going to go to China and convert all the Chinese. So I had to persuade Heather to come with me and pretend to be Emma, because it was really Emma you wanted."

He was getting hopelessly bogged down. He lifted his coffee cup, took a long swallow, and searched for words. It wasn't easy, with all of them staring at him as though he were speaking Sanskrit and they didn't understand a word he was saying. Their faces were blank with shock. He concluded that they hadn't had time for the shock to turn to anger.

He plunged ahead. As long as he was being honest, he might as well be completely honest.

"To put it bluntly, I needed money. From you. I hoped to get a loan from you so that Martin Knightbridge and I could start our automobile manufacturing business. Mr. Arlington, I'm ashamed to tell you that my presence here has been nothing but a farce. And I'm even sorrier to tell you that my father is dead. He died not long before we came here, and he didn't leave his affairs in good order. In fact, he left next to nothing, so I was desperate, and I concocted this despicable scheme to pass Heather off as Emma, to give me the excuse for coming here so that I could persuade you to make me a loan. And I'm sorry."

For an electrified moment there was silence in the dining room. And then Rosie began to laugh. After a few seconds of hesitation, Minna joined her, and then Caldwell. Caldwell laughed so hard that he had to daub tears out of his eyes with his napkin.

"A scheme worthy of Thatcher Cranston! How well I remember the way he was forever concocting some scheme or other, all of them disreputable, but it added spice to life, and I never held it against him when his schemes landed me in hot water right along with him!"

Now he daubed at his eyes again, and his face was sober. "Thatcher dead! I can hardly believe it. I never knew a man more filled with life, more overflowing with vitality. We hadn't seen each other for years, but I'm still going to miss him more than I can say. His death must have been sudden, Jared, because we'd been corresponding right before you accepted our invitation to visit us. What carried him off?"

"Being filled with life and vitality," Jared said. "My father enjoyed the best that life had to offer. Unfortunately, he enjoyed those things too much. Rich food, heavy wines, fat cigars. Emma did her utmost to reform him, but even she couldn't make him have any concern for his health. He simply died in his chair one evening, and it was Heather's misfortune to be the one to find him. But he was a contented man, Mr. Arlington. He did what he wanted to do, and he enjoyed every minute of it. I don't blame him for spending all he had. It was his to spend any way he saw fit. The only rub is that it left me in a bind. Don't blame Heather for any of this. I talked her into helping me with my scheme, and she only agreed because of the softness of her heart."

"I wanted to come! Jared mustn't take all the blame. I was dying to see a real Virginia plantation and have a real adventure just once in my life! I'm just as guilty as he is, and I'm sorry, Brice, I never dreamed that it would turn out like this. We were going to leave the moment Jared got the loan from your father, and he would have paid back every penny with interest, so we didn't think it was so terribly wrong. We never meant to cheat anybody."

She told herself that things were bad enough without her bursting into tears, and then she burst into tears.

"But it was wrong, because I let you fall in love with me,

and I didn't have any right to do that! Of course I don't expect you to marry me now. Jared and I will leave just as soon as we can pack, and I'm sorry we've caused you all this trouble because I love all of you so much and I'll miss you all my life!"

Minna had risen, and now she came and drew Heather to her feet and put her arms around her, and Rosie was on her other side with her arms around her too.

"Indeed you're not going to go rushing off! Why, in your place I would have done exactly the same thing. We're not at all angry with you, are we, Caldwell?"

Caldwell opened his mouth, but before he could get a word out Rosie beat him to it.

"Jared Cranston, you're a scoundrel!" she said, her voice filled with admiration. "You're an unmitigated scoundrel, but I never had any use for ordinary, milksop, holier-than-thou men. That's why I never married, you needn't think that it was lack of opportunity that kept me single! I'd grab you like a flash, if only I were five years younger!"

"Why, Miss Rosamund, you don't have to be five years younger. Maybe I'll accept you anyway!" Jared said.

"Rosie, behave yourself! Jared, Emma . . . oh, bother, you aren't Emma, what did you say your name is? Heather, that's it! You can't leave now, we won't hear of it. We have to celebrate Brice not being under suspicion any longer, and you're the one who made it possible, and so you have to stay and celebrate with us. Isn't that right, Caldwell?" Minna demanded.

Caldwell was daubing at his eyes again. "Just like his father!" he said. "He's Thatcher all over again. What was that you said, Minna? Of course they must stay. I only wish that Thatcher could be here with us to enjoy all of this. He would have appreciated the irony of our double deception and laughed himself to . . ." Caldwell broke off, choking, and reached for his coffee cup to wash down the lump in his throat.

Heather looked at Brice. He was the one who really mattered. She'd done a dreadful thing to him, and he had every right to want her out of his house at the earliest possible moment. He must despise her, and she didn't blame him a bit.

Brice was looking at her intently, his eyes holding hers. "Were you still just playing a part last night when I asked you to marry me?"

"Yes . . . no . . . I mean, I was still pretending that I was Emma, only I wasn't actually thinking about it. But then this morning I remembered that you thought I was Emma, and I realized that you wouldn't have asked me to marry you if you'd known I wasn't Emma." There, that should do it. She wasn't Emma, so Brice hadn't actually proposed to her, and now she wasn't engaged anymore. Just to make sure, she plunged on.

"I'm only a hired girl, you know. You couldn't possibly want to marry a hired girl."

"Wait a minute, Heather," Jared broke in, his face flushed. Darn him, why didn't he know enough to keep his mouth shut now that she'd fixed everything? "What's all this about you being only a hired girl?" He looked around at the others and proceeded to make himself clear.

"Heather is a lady. Her family lacked material wealth, but you Southerners have had a lot of experience with genteel poverty. Heather's father was a highly respected clergyman. The only reason she came to work for us in the capacity of a servant was to clear the way for her mother to remarry. She was only fifteen, too young to find any other kind of work. And although her formal education was cut short, she educated herself by reading. Her character is flawless. If you knew my sister you'd realize that Heather's character had to be flawless, else Emma would never have taken her into our house. And so if Heather's only reason for thinking that she can't marry Brice is because she's a hired girl, her reason just doesn't hold water."

Heather could have choked him.

"Then it's settled," Brice said. He was still struggling with shock. His own honesty made it hard for him to understand how anyone could have embarked on a scheme such as **Jared and Heather had concocted. He himself would never** have considered doing such a thing under any circumstances.

But Heather was very young, and Brice had had experience with Jared's powers of persuasion. A girl so young and romantic-minded could be talked into anything by a man with Jared's silver tongue. The blame for Heather's deception could be laid squarely at Jared's feet.

He had asked this girl to marry him, and he was a gentleman. A gentleman did not jilt the girl he had asked to marry him. The fact that Heather was a hired girl did not enter into it. He hadn't needed Jared's hot defense of her to know that Heather was a lady. And she had been the instrument of having suspicion removed from him. He owed her more than he could ever repay.

Beyond that, Heather was not only very pretty, but she had a sweet nature and a lively intelligence. Evelyn Langdon was beautiful, and he had been convinced that he'd loved her, but he was aware that Evelyn was never sweet unless it served some purpose of her own. Evelyn was essentially selfish, and she was a snob. She had broken their engagement at the first hint of scandal, but he knew perfectly well that Evelyn would not have broken the engagement if Arbordale had been financially solvent. Evelyn was a law unto herself. She wouldn't have cared what other people thought if there had been enough money involved.

Any love he had ever felt for the beautiful girl had died when she had sent her engagement ring back by messenger, without even the courtesy to face him in person. George Barnstable had told him that Evelyn had met another man in Atlanta, a man considerably older but whose fortune was solid, and that plans were already underway for her to return to spend the winter with relatives there. He wished her godspeed and hoped that she would never come back. He was only sorry for the man and hoped that he had the strength of character to handle the girl who was determined to snag him.

Minna had never liked Evelyn, and that in itself should have warned him. But Minna doted on Heather, and Miss Rosamund thought she was wonderful, and his father was as fond of her as Minna was. And there wasn't any doubt that Heather loved them all, even if she had been playing a part.

Heather was looking at him now with her eyes still

swimming with tears. "It's settled?" she asked, her voice choking.

"It's settled. Aunt Minna, will you fetch my mother's engagement ring? You've been taking care of it, haven't you?"

"I put it away safely when Evelyn sent it back." Minna pursed her lips. "But maybe Emma, I mean Heather, would prefer another ring. A girl doesn't want a ring that was given to another girl first. I have a very nice ring, the one Mr. Hanover gave me all those years ago when I became engaged to him. He refused to take it back when I made him think that he'd jilted me. We can save your mother's ring for the next generation, when you have a boy who'll want to give it to his intended."

Heather's cheeks flamed, and Brice gave his aunt an admonishing look. Sometimes Minna was a trifle lacking in delicacy. It was a little early to be talking about children, before he and Heather were even married!

Seeing Brice's look, Rosie laughed. "Brice, don't be such a fuddy-duddy! You aren't that old yet, save it till it will be expected of you! Heather, of course you're going to marry Brice, and of course you'll have children, and of course you'd rather have Minna's ring. Oh, my, I envy you the children you'll have! That's the only thing I've missed by remaining single. If I could have had children without being married, I would have!"

"Miss Rosamund!" Caldwell choked, shocked right to his socks.

Rosie laughed again. "You can be a fuddy-duddy if you want to, Caldwell. You're old enough. But thank heaven I never will be! Heather, eat your breakfast. We have an engagement ball and a wedding to plan, and you're going to need your strength."

Now Rosie fixed her eyes on Caldwell, fairly pinning him to his chair.

"Engagement balls and weddings cost money, Caldwell. And Jared doesn't have any, and neither do you. I've been waiting for quite some time for you to become desperate enough to demean yourself by asking a woman for money, but I'm sick and tired of waiting. You can have whatever you'll need, both to bail Arbordale out of its trouble and to see Brice and Heather married with all the pomp and circumstance an Arlington wedding should have."

"Rosamund! Your suggestion is outrageous!" Caldwell spluttered. "Besides, you can't possibly have enough for my needs."

Rosamund helped herself to another piece of ham from the platter Della had left on the table. Her eyes were sparkling with mischief.

"Because I'm only a woman, you mean? An unmarried lady who has only what her father left her? Let me tell you something, you egotistical male! My life has been pretty darned boring. I never had a lick of fun while my father was alive because he wouldn't allow it, and after he died I never had a lick of fun because Isobel wouldn't allow it. And so I amused myself by playing with my inheritance. I gave my lawyer and John Thaxter fits, and that was a large part of the fun. But the upshot of it is, I have more money than I know what to do with. Investments can be fascinating, and I made sure not to make any bad ones, even though John Thaxter kept telling me that I'd end up without a penny. He called what I did gambling. I called it plain common sense."

Rosie decided that she had room for more scrambled eggs. Her eyes were sparkling with merriment as every other pair of eyes around the table looked at her with stunned incredulity.

"You can tell John Thaxter to sit on his money till it grows mold, Caldwell. You aren't going to ask any banker for money and pay their exorbitant interest rates. Just tell me how much you need, and don't be afraid to make it enough!"

Heather's face was flaming with excitement. Rosie was just too much! She'd certainly told these men off; she'd struck a blow for all womankind, and Heather loved it.

But then her excitement died. She was still engaged! Now what was she going to do? A mouthful of scrambled eggs stuck in her throat, and she half strangled before it went the rest of the way down.

Desperately, she blurted out, "I can't marry Brice! I have the wrong name! Everybody thinks I'm Emma Cranston

of age. We're going, and that's that. It's a shame that we'll have to wait until after the wedding has taken place. We won't be able to go until next spring now. We can hardly leave Heather here unchaperoned. But once we get there, we're going to do just everything! We're even going to eat escargots."

"Escargots?" Minna asked.

"Snails," Rosie said complaisantly.

Minna paled. "I will if you will," she said.

Heather felt a tearing regret that she wouldn't be able to go to Paris with Minna and Rosie, but her regret that she still seemed to be engaged to Brice was even more tearing. Wouldn't anything make him back out of the engagement? She'd just have to put her mind to it and think of something so outrageous that he'd be sure to ask her to let him off the hook.

Brice had to be the one to break the engagement. The only way to keep him from having his heart broken all over again was for him to realize that he could never love a girl like her. He'd be relieved when she didn't hold him to his promise to marry him, and they could still be friends.

Maybe she could add some smoldering love scenes to her novel and let him read the pages, and he'd be so shocked that he'd break their engagement then and there. But, of course, she had no practical experience to write those scenes. She had to think of something else. She was a writer, wasn't she? She could come up with all sorts of ideas, given time. For the moment, she contented herself with glaring at Jared. If he'd kept his mouth shut about her being a lady, it would have been all over by now.

The entire town of Bennington turned out to attend Naomi's funeral. All of the business establishments were closed, and people came in from miles around the surrounding countryside. The two old men who played checkers in the town square arrived early and sat in the third pew from the front. Heather was glad that they had patched up their differences. Probably neither of them had anyone else to play checkers with.

Matthew Thaxter was also there. He had posted bond and

was out of jail awaiting trial for arson. Clarence Kotter came in on his heels, obviously keeping an eye on him to make sure that he wouldn't disappear before he had paid for his crime.

Naomi's closed coffin was banked with so many flowers that the wood couldn't be seen. Minna and Rosamund and Heather had stripped Arbordale's garden, and other families had done the same with theirs.

When the mourners gathered at the graveside, Heather pushed her way to a place beside Phoebe and put her arm around her. Phoebe needed her support, because David was standing directly across the open grave from them. His face was pale, showing the ravages of his grief.

"Thank you, Emma." Phoebe's forced smile was tremulous. Phoebe still thought that Heather was Emma Cranston. Heather would have to tell her the truth at the first opportunity. "Poor David! He'll never get over it. He'll grieve for her all the rest of his life."

And you'll grieve for him, Heather thought, and the thought made her rebel. She was sorry that Naomi was dead. Even if the girl had been empty-headed and wildly imaginative and had caused so much trouble with her entirely fabricated tales of the wild romance between her and Brice, she hadn't deserved to die in such a dreadful manner. But all the same, Phoebe had had David first.

"He'll need his friends. He'll need you," she said.

"Maybe he won't even want me around." Phoebe's voice was filled with despair. "Maybe he'll just want to be left alone."

"Phoebe, don't you dare give up without a fight!" Heather's whisper was fierce. "You lost someone too, or at least David thinks you did. You were all but engaged to Carl, and you need comforting as much as David does. It will do him a heap of good to comfort you, and who knows what might come of it?"

"But I never loved Carl! It would be the same as lying!"

"Phoebe, I swear that in a minute I'm going to shake you! Go on, go to him! You don't have to say right out that you loved the man. Just look pitiful and let things evolve from there. Men like nothing better than to provide a shoulder for a woman to cry on. It makes them feel strong and superior."

When Phoebe still hesitated, Heather gave her a push, and a moment later she had the satisfaction of seeing David try to smile, and seeing both of his hands enfold Phoebe's.

It was a relief to get out of the black dress, one of Minna's that had been hastily altered to fit her, when they got back to Arbordale. A little breeze had sprung up, and they all sat on the verandah to take advantage of it. Minna and Rosie were fanning themselves with palm-leaf fans. Heather would have gone up to her room to get her own, but she didn't have the energy. Funerals took all of the starch out of you.

The men were talking about Carl Amhurst's refusal to confess. Carl had taken his stand. He swore that he'd been searching for Naomi's grave for some time, convinced that she had met foul play. He said that he'd wanted to get the credit for finding her body. He insisted that he had located what he had thought was a grave in the haunted woods the day before the bad storm and that he had gone back, at night, prepared to make sure, his only reason for being there with a shovel.

"The trouble is, we can't actually disprove his claim," Jared said, frowning. "If only we could find a motive! I'll be ashamed that I chose law as my profession if I see that man go free when I darned well know he's guilty!"

"Well, he certainly didn't have any motive in Bennington," Heather said, thinking aloud. "But Naomi came from Utica. If it were up to me, that's where I would start looking."

She broke off when she realized that everybody was staring at her. "She's done it again!" Jared exclaimed. "That's exactly what I'm going to do, I'm going to start looking in Utica!"

"Minna, for goodness sake, bring us our lemonade," Rosie said. "I'm perishing in this heat, and the funeral was so depressing. Jared, do you have enough cash to get yourself to Utica and back and stay over for as long as it will take?"

"Yes, ma'am," Jared said. He did, but just barely. He hoped that Mr. Deems would have unearthed a little more before he had to make the return trip. But he wasn't yet reduced to borrowing from a woman, even a woman like Rosie. It was different in Caldwell's case. Rosie was a family friend, a loan for the plantation was a business deal, and besides Caldwell was more desperate than he was. Jared could always get a job.

"And while you're back there, you might as well ferret around and find somebody else to back your automobile manufacturing venture," Rosie said.

"Why, Miss Rosie, I was just about to ask you to back it," Jared teased her. "After all, what are sweethearts for?"

"This sweetheart will think about backing your venture when you've proved that you can build a machine that people will buy," Rosie said. "I didn't get rich by backing fly-by-night schemes. Besides, if you don't have the brains to find another backer, your enterprise will be doomed from the start. It takes brains to build up a business, and as far as I've seen, Heather has all the brains between the two of you."

"You're not my sweetheart anymore," Jared said sourly. But his grin belied his words. Rosie had a point. Finding another backer was exactly what he was going to do, because he had no intention of going through life suspecting that he didn't have any brains. He would be on tomorrow's train, and he didn't intend to come back before he had accomplished both of his missions. He just hoped that he wouldn't run out of money before he could do it.

❧ *Chapter 17* ❧

EMMA WAS FURIOUS. She had been furious for well over a week, and her fury was growing by leaps and bounds.

It wasn't bad enough that her idol had proved to have feet of clay, that Humphrey had crumbled right before her eyes. Any man might feel a few qualms about going to China now that the news of what was being called the Boxer Rebellion was on everyone's lips. She wouldn't have expected it of him, but she would have managed to forgive him. It was the other thing that had prompted her to pack up and leave Boston, determined never to lay eyes on Humphrey again.

At first, she had thought that their plans would only be delayed while things settled down again in China. It wouldn't hurt to wait, Humphrey had argued. They could serve the Lord better if they were alive than if they were dead. Martyrdom was all very well, but he believed that he could save more souls if his head was still attached to his body. And he had argued that he had no right to take Emma into danger, that he had a responsibility toward her, that he considered it his duty to keep her safe.

Emma had insisted that she was not afraid. She had been ready to brave hoards of huge Chinese bandits with sharp swords for the opportunity to save just one soul. And

Humphrey had almost come to the point of seeing things her way.

But then Humphrey had been invited to speak at one of Boston's foremost churches, and the ladies, married and unmarried, had fallen under the spell of his golden good looks. He had been invited everywhere, and, to Emma's chagrin, not all of the invitations had included her.

Another church, about to lose its pastor, had invited him to speak, and the upshot had been that Humphrey was offered the pastorship, which he had accepted.

Humphrey, Emma decreed, was a traitor. He had chosen comfort and a goodly measure of material wealth over doing the Lord's work in foreign fields. Emma, raging, had tried with all her might to be accepted to be sent to China even though she would not have a husband now. She had come up against a stone wall. For a single woman to go to China at this time was unthinkable. Actually, she had been told, it would be unthinkable at any time. It was all very well for a woman to be a missionary, but she must be a missionary in conjunction with a husband who would be the actual missionary and she only his helpmate.

Emma had gone home to Albany, still furious, and had found the house empty except for Mrs. Allenby. Jared, Mrs. Allenby had told her, was off visiting the Arlingtons in Virginia.

Not only was the house empty except for the cook, but Emma soon learned that everything was at sixes and sevens. Mr. Deems, when she called on him for an accounting of her father's estate, informed her that there was pitifully little left. If that was the case, what was Jared doing in Virginia? He should be here, setting up a practice and earning a living.

Even more unsettling, it took her no time at all to learn that Jared had taken Heather to Virginia with him. How like Jared it was to ignore unpleasantness and go rushing off to enjoy himself on a Virginia plantation! And how like him to be so feckless as to take a young girl with him! Even if he had taken her for the purpose of seeing if she would suit the Arlingtons as a companion for Miss Minerva, the girl's reputation would be ruined and Jared's name would be blackened. Emma hoped fervently that Heather had suited. If she stayed on in Virginia as Miss Minerva's companion, maybe word of Jared's indiscretion would never sift back to Albany. Emma had enough to contend with without that.

She had set off to bring Jared home where he belonged, leaving so precipitously that she had had no time to send a message that she would be arriving. It seemed that every unattached gentleman who had been riding in her car had nothing better to do than to ogle her, despite her mourning clothes. An unescorted woman would be safer in China. At least the huge Chinese bandits would have had designs not on her virtue but only on her life.

She had put the obnoxious gentlemen in their places with no trouble. Emma could freeze the most determined of mashers with a single glance. But still the trip had been hot, and the red plush seats had become harder with every mile. By the time she descended from the train in Bennington, her temper had not improved.

The station agent came to attention when she marched into his tiny office, leaving her bag on the platform. It didn't occur to her that it might not be safe to leave it unattended. Nobody, even in Boston or Albany, would dare to steal her bag, much less anyone in a town the size of Bennington.

"I wish to hire a conveyance to take me to the Arlington plantation," Emma said, her voice crisp and brooking no nonsense. "Immediately, if you please."

"Yes, ma'am," the station agent said, shifting his cud of tobacco from one cheek to the other, his eyes bulging.

"Get rid of that disgusting tobacco before you speak to me!" Emma said.

The agent looked wildly in the direction of the spittoon, but something told him that it would not be wise to spit in the presence of this lady. He took the only alternative and swallowed his cud. "Yes, ma'am," he said. Fighting against sudden queasiness, he ventured to ask, "Are the Arlingtons expecting you?" It didn't seem reasonable that they could be expecting her. Ben Stump, the station agent, prided himself on being the first to know everything that went on in the county.

Emma fixed him with a frigid eye. "No, they are not. However, I will be welcomed. I am Miss Emma Cranston, and my brother is a guest at Arbordale."

"Now, ma'am, that can't be right. Mr. Cranston's sister is already at Arbordale, so you can't hardly be Miss Emma Cranston, begging your pardon, ma'am. Not unless Mr. Cranston has two sisters named Emma, and that don't hardly seem likely."

Emma was stunned, but only for a moment. That Jared! What was her scoundrel of a brother up to now? How dared he pass Heather off as his sister, and how dared Heather go along with the deception? The sooner she got to Arbordale and got all this cleared up, the better.

"Fetch the conveyance," Emma said. She said it in a manner that sent Ben Stump scuttling, whether she was Miss Emma Cranston or not.

The livery station in Bennington didn't amount to much. It was kept mostly for the convenience of outlying farm and plantation families who might need a place to leave their horses and carriages if they intended to stay in town overnight. But Eli Yeager had a buggy that he occasionally hired out to townspeople who didn't own one of their own.

Eli was so intrigued with Ben Stump's story of two Miss Emma Cranstons that he drove her himself, leaving his livery stable in charge of his twelve-year-old son. His curiosity was doomed to disappointment, however. Emma's lips were clamped in a straight line, and she did not open them during the entire journey. Eli got the impression that it was just as well that she wasn't in a mood to talk.

When the buggy pulled up in front of the plantation house, Emma didn't wait for Eli to assist her to alight. She jumped down by herself, only ordering him to place her bag on the verandah.

A negro girl answered her sharp rap, looking at her curiously. The girl's cap was askew, and out of habit Emma ordered her to straighten it before she demanded to be taken to Jared immediately.

Della straightened her cap, almost tongue-tied. She wasn't used to being spoken to so crisply. Miss Minna always spoke softly, and besides, Miss Minna wouldn't have noticed that her cap was crooked.

"I asked to be taken to my brother, and stop twisting your apron!" Emma said impatiently. "Are you rooted to that spot, or can you move?"

Della's eyes grew even rounder. "Mr. Jared ain't here, ma'am. He's gone to Utica, New York. I'll fetch Miss Minna."

Emma looked up as light footsteps rounded the curve of the staircase and Heather came into view. Heather, looking like a picture in one of the dresses Emma had given her!

"Who is it, Della?" Heather asked. And then, "Oh! Oh, my goodness! Miss Emma! What on earth are you doing here? I thought you were in Boston learning how to be a missionary!"

"That is quite obvious, or else you would scarcely dare to be here, pretending to be me," Emma said. "Why isn't Jared here, what is he doing in Utica, and what are the two of you up to? Don't stand there as if the cat has your tongue, answer me!"

Heather was struck nearly as tongue-tied as Della. Emma here! It wasn't possible! But it wasn't Emma's ghost either, anymore than there was a ghost in the haunted woods.

She was saved from stammering out an answer as Minna, with Rosie in tow and with her everlasting tatting in her hands, came hurrying from the parlor. "Did I hear someone arrive? Oh, yes, I can see that I did! How lovely to have a visitor, Miss . . ." The last word was a question.

"Miss Emma Cranston, whatever this girl has led you to believe!"

"So you're Emma! I should have guessed. My, you do look quite a lot like Heather, don't you? I'm sorry Jared isn't here just now, he's gone rushing off to Utica, you know, but he'll be back in a few days at the latest. Della, find Pearl and prepare a room. Have Saul carry in Miss Emma's luggage."

"There is no need for Saul to carry in my luggage. There is only one small bag, the girl can carry it easily. I did not come for an extended visit."

"What nonsense! After we've waited all these years to meet you, of course you're going to stay for a good long time! It will only take a moment for the girls to have your room ready. You'll need a rest after your journey. Isn't it nice that you aren't in China after all, but right here for Heather's and Brice's engagement ball!"

It was all too much for Emma. Jared not here, and Heather passing herself off as herself, and now it seemed that Heather was engaged to Brice Arlington. Emma was so confused that she didn't know whether she was coming or going. Moreover, she was exhausted and dirty and hungry. And she began to cry.

Two pairs of soft, urging arms were around her instantly; two voices rose to hurry the house girls on; two pairs of soft, insistent hands urged her up the stairs and into a large bedroom that was furnished with a tester bed. Four capable hands removed her hat, took her gloves, ushered her into a comfortable armchair.

"Now, now, you go right ahead and cry! Train travel is a dreadful thing. I've never enjoyed it, although I expect that I'll have to get used to it once Heather and Brice are married and Rosie and I start jaunting all over the world! Just cry yourself out, and then you'll have a nice long nap, and then everything will sort itself out for you and you can begin to enjoy your visit."

Emma allowed herself to be undressed, to be assisted into a tub of warm, scented water, to be tucked into the wonderfully soft bed. Della pulled the drapes across the windows, and the room was plunged into a cool, soothing gloom. Emma's eyes closed the moment her head touched the pillow. She had just been through several harrowing days, first Humphrey, then finding out that Jared was at Arbordale, and on top of all that finding out that her father had left the two of them virtually penniless. Her world had turned upside down, and she had no idea how long it would take her to right it again.

When she opened her eyes two hours later, she felt

completely refreshed and ready to cope with anything that had to be coped with. She was only humiliated that she had broken down and cried. Except when her mother and then her father had died, it was the first time she had cried since she'd been seven years old and her favorite china doll had been broken.

At the time, her heart had been as broken as the doll, but Emma had learned something that served her well. When something is irretrievably broken, you accept your loss and go on from there. And that, she determined as she rose from the bed, was exactly what she was going to do now.

Della appeared the moment Emma's feet touched the floor, as though she had been waiting just outside the door to hear the first signs that Emma was stirring. Della looked at her nervously, her eyes frightened.

"Your name is Della, isn't it?" Emma asked. "Don't look as if you're scared out of your wits, I'm not going to bite your head off. I'm sorry I spoke so abruptly to you before, I was simply tired and in a bad mood."

Della's hand went to her cap, and Emma laughed. "Your cap is perfectly straight, child. If you knew how much more attractive you look when it's straight, you'd always keep it that way. Being neat and tidy is a sign that you're aware of your self-worth. If you have a good opinion of yourself, other people will too."

"Oh, I never knew *that!*" Della said. "I'm going to tell Pearl so she can keep herself neat and tidy too!"

"That is a very good idea. Later, if I stay long enough, I'll show you other ways to build up your self-esteem. Doing your work properly is one of them. If your work is sloppy, you won't feel good about yourself, and other people won't feel good about you."

"Yes, ma'am!" Della said. "I sure am going to try!" She began looking through the things Emma had brought with her. There were only three dresses, including the one Emma had been wearing. "Ain't you got nothing but black? Black's awful hot for summer."

"I am in mourning," Emma explained. She might have added that she was doubly in mourning, because Humphrey was as dead to her now as her father.

Although she scorned being waited on, holding it to be a worldly indulgence, it was handy to have Della pull the laces of her corset tight and button the long line of buttons down the back of her black poplin, the lightest of her black dresses. But she was startled when she sat down at the dressing table and started to pull her hair back into its uncompromising bun.

"Oh, no! Let me do that! It's part of my job, and I won't feel good about myself unless I do it," Della said.

Emma's smile was approving. The girl was bright and eager to learn. But she had second thoughts when she saw what Della did with her hair. She didn't look like herself at all. Della arranged little curls over her forehead and at the sides. It was positively worldly!

But she didn't want to puncture Della's self-esteem, and just this once it wouldn't matter. All the same, her cheeks flushed as she stole another glance at herself in the mirror. It would never do for a missionary, of course, but she wasn't going to be a missionary now.

She followed Della down to the verandah where everyone had gathered for their late-afternoon refreshments. Two gentlemen rose to their feet. Both of them were handsome, although the older one had gone gray at his temples and was more heavyset than the younger. Emma's eyes were drawn back to Brice, and she hardly heard Minna and Rosie urge her to sit down in one of the wicker rockers.

"Miss Emma, you look beautiful!" Heather exclaimed. "I know, it's your hair! I'll bet that Mr. Snell likes it this way too."

"Mr. Snell has not seen my hair dressed in this fashion," Emma stated, accepting a rocking chair.

"Then Della must have done it. She's awfully clever with hair. And Mr. Snell will like it when he sees it, I know he will."

"Mr. Snell is not going to see it," Emma informed her, keeping her voice as even and free of emotion as she could manage. "Mr. Snell is still in Boston. He has decided to accept a church there."

Heather's mouth formed a round O of astonishment.

"My goodness! Then you aren't going to go to China to be a missionary after all? Do you think you'll like living in Boston?"

"I will not be living in Boston," Emma said. "I will be living in Albany, as I always have."

"But how can you live in Albany if Mr. Snell is living in Boston?" Heather was completely bewildered. "I thought married people always lived together."

"We are not going to be married." Emma's voice was firm. "Having discovered Humphrey's true nature, I broke our engagement immediately and returned home, only to find the house empty except for Mrs. Allenby. It is I who should be asking the questions. Would you care to explain yourself, Heather?"

"What am I thinking of?" Minna exclaimed. "You haven't any lemonade! Isn't ice a blessing in weather like this? Saul takes the greatest pleasure in shaving it so that the gentlemen's juleps are well frosted, but I prefer chunks in the lemonade. I like to hear them clink against the sides of the glass, it sounds so cool. Would you like a sprig of mint in your glass, Emma? We always use it, we grow it ourselves."

"Mint would be very nice," Emma conceded. It was an indulgence, but it was so very hot.

"You aren't going to marry Mr. Snell?" Heather was incredulous. And then her eyes widened with alarm. Oh, no! Minna had already gone to fetch Emma's lemonade! She jumped to her feet so fast that her chair rocked wildly, and took off at a sprint to the pantry.

"Miss Minna, for goodness sake, don't put any bourbon in Emma's glass!" she gasped. "I don't know what she'd do if she tasted whiskey in her lemonade! The least would be to give us a lecture that would make our ears drop off, and she might even pack up and leave tomorrow!"

"Tut," Minna said. "What a fuss you're making. Of course I wasn't going to put any bourbon in Emma's glass. Do you think I'm addlewitted?"

Heather sighed with relief. "She mustn't suspect that ours is laced," she warned. "We'd better not get close enough to her so that she can smell our breath."

She broke off as a horrible thought leaped into her mind. She wouldn't dare drink laced lemonade either, now that she was engaged to Brice. What if he kissed her and smelled it?

A wicked little thought made her grin. Maybe she ought to maneuver Brice into kissing her this afternoon while the bourbon was still on her breath. Then, all covered with guilty confusion, she could tell him that she always drank, that she drank a good deal, that she loved to drink! He'd be so horrified that it would be the easiest thing in the world to make him break the engagement. Like Minna, she could make him think that jilting her was all his idea, and then she wouldn't have to have a guilty conscience about it.

She shook a mental finger at herself. The idea was tempting, but it was also underhanded, and not only Brice would be hurt, but Minna and Caldwell and Rosie. Even Saul would be hurt. Saul thought she was a real dyed-in-the-wool lady, and for him to think that she was a secret tippler would rock him to the foundations of everything he believed in. She had made a commitment, and now it was up to her to live up to it. She was darned if she was going to say she had made her bed and now she had to lie in it. She didn't want to think about lying in bed with Brice. If she had to lie in bed with anyone, she wanted it to be Jared.

Maybe something will happen to get me out of it, she thought, but she didn't have any real conviction. She would end up lying in bed with Brice and wishing that he were Jared, and she could have choked herself for having let herself be carried away just because she'd been proposed to in a Virginia rose garden.

She wished she could confide her dilemma to Emma. Emma was so level-headed, she'd know just what to do. But Emma would also be shocked and give her a long lecture about thinking before she acted, and tell her that it had been the height of wickedness to allow herself to become engaged to Brice when she didn't love him.

As for telling Emma that it was really Jared she loved, that would be even worse. Emma would jump to the conclusion that Jared had toyed with her affections, and she would berate him, and then Jared would think that she was trying to force him to marry her, and she wanted him to marry her because he wanted to, not because Emma told him that he had to.

Back on the verandah, Emma sipped her cold drink appreciatively. It was delicious, and the sprig of mint gave it a tang that she could learn to make a habit. She would have to watch herself, it would be all too easy to let herself be caught in the trap of such gracious living. Having assuaged the worst of her thirst, she fixed Heather with commanding eyes.

"I'm waiting for you to explain this masquerade. I cannot conceive what possessed you to do such a thing! Of course, Jared was behind it, I know how persuasive he can be, but even so, I can't imagine you entering on such an outrageous deception!"

Caldwell came to Heather's rescue. "Perhaps you'll allow me to tell the story," he said. And he proceeded to do so, with a few interruptions from Minna, who was determined to defend Heather, and one short, terse statement from Brice apprising her that he had wanted no part in his father's deception, which had been fully as bad, if not worse, than Jared's and Heather's.

Emma spared Brice an approving glance. "I'm glad that you, at least, did not approve of such underhanded schemes! And no matter if Jared and Heather didn't mean any harm, it was still a dishonest thing to do. There is no excuse for dishonesty, no excuse at all."

Caldwell bowed his head in acknowledgment of his own guilt, but then he spread his hands and chuckled. "But you see, both of the deceptions worked out for the best. Jared and Heather have been of invaluable help to us. It's thanks to them that Brice is no longer under suspicion and Arbordale is safe. If we hadn't given a ball for them, Miss Rosie wouldn't have come to the ball and broken with her sister, and she wouldn't have realized how desperate our situation was and offered me the loan that will save our family home. And here are Brice and Heather, engaged. As much as I agree with you that there's no excuse for dishonesty, in this case I'm heartily glad that both Jared and I were dishonest!"

"Even so, as soon as Jared gets back from Utica, I am going to take him firmly in hand!" Emma's voice was firm.

There was a twinkle in Caldwell's eyes. "And how do you propose to do that, Miss Emma?"

"For one thing, the sooner he gives up the notion of starting an automobile manufacturing business, the better. Such contraptions are clearly the invention of Satan. If the Lord had intended for men to invent gasoline machines for transportation, He wouldn't have provided us with horses!"

"That's a good thought," Rosie said. "Only, haven't you ever stopped to think that He didn't provide us with wheels at the same time He provided us with horses? Men had to come up with wheels all by themselves. He provided us with good rich land, too, but we had to come up with plows. And he provided us with the brains to invent wheels and plows, and so how do we know that He didn't mean us to come up with gasoline machines as well?"

Caldwell's laugh rang out. "She's got you there, Miss Emma! Rosie, it's no wonder you've made yourself a rich woman!"

Emma's face flushed. "Nevertheless, Jared is not in a position to venture on such a risky enterprise, and I shall do my utmost to persuade him to apply himself to something more practical. He is a qualified lawyer, after all."

She had no idea how attractive she looked with her face flushed. Brice looked at her, bemused. And then it was his turn to flush. He had actually been on the point of speculating about what might have happened if he had met the real Emma before he had met the false one. Heather was everything he wanted, and such thoughts had no place in his mind.

Heather, immersed in her own thoughts, noticed nothing. She wouldn't have missed this Virginia adventure for the world, but as much as she'd enjoyed it, she'd ended up in a pretty pickle, allowing herself to be trapped into becoming engaged to Brice.

"Heather, why don't you and Brice show Emma the rose garden?" Minna asked.

All three of them rose, and Heather remembered just in time not to walk too close to Emma, as Emma would smell the bourbon on her breath. She had enough trouble without that.

༄ *Chapter 18* ༄

Ben Stump looked at the only passenger to alight from the train, the second stranger to arrive in Bennington in two days. Yesterday, it had been Miss Emma Cranston, demanding to be driven to Arbordale where there was already a Miss Emma Cranston. Today, it was a tall lantern-jawed man of middle age, who carried a valise so that it was obvious that he intended to stay at least overnight. Like the second Miss Emma Cranston, this stranger confronted him, but only to ask directions to the sheriff's office.

"You'd be meaning Clarence Kotter," Ben ventured.

"If Clarence Kotter is the sheriff, that's who I mean."

"You got business with Kotter?" Ben's curiosity was aroused. Ben was the most curious man in Bennington, which was why he knew so much more than anybody else before they knew it.

His question was awarded with a noncommittal stare. Untalkative cuss, Ben thought, but it didn't matter. Clarence was a talker, and Clarence would tell him just as soon as Clarence knew.

In Kotter's office, the stranger was as laconic as he had been with Ben Stump. He disliked traveling, his digestion was delicate at best, and the swaying of the train had tied his stomach in knots. If this turned out to be a wild goose chase, he'd probably come down with ulcers.

"I'd like a look at your prisoner."

"Why? You can't be some fancy lawyer Amhurst sent for, or I'd know about it. He couldn't have sent for a lawyer without me knowing it."

The stranger didn't bother to acknowledge such an obvious statement. He walked back to the cells and looked at Carl.

"That's him," he said. "He's five years older, but I'd know him anywhere. Been a long time catching up with you, Martin. Too bad we couldn't have done it sooner. I hear you killed little Naomi Thaxter. Afraid she'd remember you, were you?"

Carl seemed to crumble in front of Kotter's eyes. If he had had any hope that he could be found innocent of Naomi's murder, that hope was gone now.

"You mean he ain't Carl Amhurst? His name is Martin?" Kotter demanded.

"Martin Ross. Teller in the bank in Utica. Five years ago he killed Judson Pether on a Friday afternoon after the bank was closed, cleaned out all the cash, and took off. The murder and robbery wasn't discovered until Monday morning, when the bank didn't open. Now I got a question. Do I take him back to Utica with me, or do you keep him for killing Naomi? I should've asked that smart young lawyer who pointed me to him, but it didn't cross my mind."

Clarence was at a loss for words. The stranger didn't seem to notice.

"I'll check in at the hotel till somebody else figures it out." He had to have some bicarb of soda right now.

Clarence clapped his hat on his head and set out in long strides for Ben Stump's office. This needed some talking about, and with Ben he could talk all he wanted.

Jared stood in front of Tao Tsiang's laundry, every muscle in his body so tense that he could feel them ache. On the street in front of the laundry, Tao sat as straight as a ramrod beside Martin Knightbridge as Martin drove the laundryman up and down the block, while his sons raced alongside, shouting and cheering them on.

"Look at it go! It's a marvel! It's the miracle of the age! Go to it, Pop! Mother, isn't it wonderful?" This last shouted back over Michael's shoulder to where Maureen waited with Jared.

Maureen took her hands away from her eyes and risked a peek. "Oh, yes, it is wonderful! When are they going to stop?"

The automobile turned around at the end of the block and came back. Out of breath, Patrick panted, "It's your turn now, Mother. You go!"

Tao Tsiang looked at his wife benevolently as he alighted. "It is safe, I believe. You may try it if you wish." Having tested out the safety of this gasoline contraption himself, and having changed his former opinion about its safety, he did not wish to deny Maureen the pleasure of having a ride in it.

Maureen looked terrified but at the same time filled with excitement. All four of the boys assisted her into the seat of the machine that made a noise like a dragon. She immediately put her hands over her eyes again. Martin put the machine into gear, with Jared hovering to crank it again if it should stall, heaven forbid. His prayers were granted. The automobile did not stall. He'd known that it wouldn't, but it never hurt to have a little extra insurance.

The automobile advanced down the street, with three small boys chasing after it and shouting, a mongrel dog nipping at its tires, and people standing in the doorways of shops and stores staring after it with varying expressions on their faces. A mother swooped a little girl up into her arms and shrank back against the wall of a building, her eyes wide.

Maureen's hands came away from her eyes, and the beam on her face was like sunshine.

"Isn't it everything I said it was? Isn't it wonderful?" Jared demanded of the laundryman. He held his breath, praying again.

"There is a small chance that it might become a success," Tao Tsiang conceded, although with caution.

"You know that it's going to be a success! Why, this is the easiest machine to start that's ever been devised, and Martin has made improvements in the gears, and it backs up as easily as it goes forward! And I'm offering you the chance to make the investment of your lifetime. Isn't that so, boys?"

The idea of giving Tao Tsiang the opportunity to make the investment of his lifetime had come to Jared out of nowhere, during a sleepless night after he had had a long interview with Mr. Deems. The lawyer had managed to come up with only a few hundred more dollars from Thatcher's estate, but he had offered not only advice but a job. The advice had been to accept the job.

Working for Mr. Deems as his assistant, doing all the dull research and paperwork, wasn't exactly enticing, but it held the attraction of coming into the practice after Mr. Deems retired. An established practice was nothing to be sneezed at, even if he had to wait for two or three or more years, doing nothing in the meantime to arouse Mr. Deems's ire. He had the idea that doing nothing to arouse Mr. Deems's ire would be the hardest part.

Actually, he had no choice. Mr. Deems had apprised him of Emma's return, and he must start earning some kind of a living immediately. Now he himself must get back to Virginia and collect her, but however practical he was being about his immediate future, he was not ready to give up his dream.

Tao Tsiang had money. How much, Jared had no idea, but he had a very good idea that it was a considerable amount. And so here he was, watching Maureen bounce up and down on the seat of the automobile and clap her hands, while Michael, Patrick, Danny, and Sean cheered her on and Tao Tsiang looked on fondly.

"What do you think of it?" Tao Tsiang asked his wife as his four sons jostled each other for the privilege of helping her down from her perch.

"It is very exciting. I like it. But it isn't pretty," Maureen said.

Jared looked at her blankly. "Pretty?" he asked, sounding stupid. Women! Heather had made that same comment. What did being pretty have to do with an automobile?

"I think red," Maureen said. "Red is a happy color, it is the color of weddings and rejoicing."

Tao Tsiang looked at Jared. "I have observed that in this backward country men are too often influenced by their wives. So if the wives would like the contraption to be pretty, it would be wise to make it pretty."

Jared looked at Martin. "Can you paint it red and make it pretty?"

Martin scratched his head. "I expect I can, but for the life of me I can't see why!"

"Make it pretty," Jared told him. "And red."

Two days later Jared alighted from the train in Bennington and accosted the station agent.

"I take it my sister arrived safely?"

"Yup. Eli Yeager drove her on out to Arbordale. You're the one who went off to Utica and found out about Carl Amhurst, ain't you?"

"Yup," Jared said.

"He's still here," Ben volunteered. "They ain't figured out yet which state should hang him. You goin' to help 'em decide?"

"If they ask me," Jared said. "Is Eli's buggy available?"

"Yup." Ben would have known if it wasn't. "You want it right now?"

"Yup," Jared said.

They were all on the verandah when the hired buggy drove up with the liveryman driving. As he had been with the second Miss Emma Cranston, Eli was disappointed that he had gained so little information from his passenger. Not knowing what the Arlingtons had given out about the existence of a second Miss Emma Cranston, Jared had decided that it was the better part of discretion to keep his mouth shut.

"So you're here at last," Emma said. "You have a great deal to answer for, Jared, a very great deal."

Jared grinned a sheepish grin.

"Now, Miss Emma, don't go spoiling Jared's arrival," Caldwell admonished. "After all, everything turned out for the best. I expect that you've already heard from the town crier that a man from Utica is in town and has identified Carl Amhurst as a man who's wanted back there for another murder. Now we know Carl's motive for murdering Naomi Thaxter, and it's a certainty that he'll hang."

"Caldwell Arlington, we ladies don't want such an unpleasant subject discussed during our relaxation hour!" Rosie said. "Save it until you gentlemen are alone. I want to hear something more interesting. Jared, did you make good use of your time while you were away, outside of going to Utica?"

"If you can call finding a position with an entirely inadequate salary making good use of my time, I did." Jared grinned at her. "And for good measure, I found a backer for the automobile manufacturing business. Tao Tsiang, a Chinese gentleman who owns Albany's most prestigious laundry, saw the opportunity to make himself a wealthy man, and the enterprise is already underway."

"I knew you could do it! You wouldn't be my sweetheart if you couldn't do a simple thing like finding a backer. And, by the way, you have made your first sale."

Jared looked at her, uncomprehendingly. Rosie preened herself.

"I've decided that I need amusement while Minna and I have to wait around for Heather and Brice to be married. Learning to drive will be fun."

Caldwell's mouth dropped open, and his face turned a deep red with shock and indignation.

"Miss Rosamund, that is outrageous! You are a woman, a lady! Even if you could learn to drive such a contraption, it would turn this country upside down to see a woman driving!"

"Good. What this country needs is a good turning upside down," Rosie said. She rocked and fanned and took another sip of Minna's lemonade. "Don't you worry about me being able to drive the thing. If a man can do it, I can do it! Jared, you told us that there's one of the contraptions completed and that it's reliable. Can you get it here?"

"Miss Rosamund, surely you aren't serious!" Emma gasped.

Heather's eyes were sparkling. "Of course she's serious! And I think it's a wonderful idea! I'm going to learn to drive it too!" She looked at Brice out of the corner of her eye, waiting for his reaction. "I'll be the first lady novelist in the country to drive an automobile. It'll be wonderful publicity for my books. It'll help sell so many that I'll be famous!" If this didn't make him change his mind about wanting to marry her, nothing would.

Brice was beyond speech. When he did manage to open his mouth, Rosie told him to shut it again.

"If Heather wants to learn to drive the automobile, she's going to learn to drive it. Don't be a fuddy-duddy, Brice."

"Just think how people's eyes will pop when they see Miss Rosie and me driving an automobile!" Heather said.

"It's Isobel's eyes I want to pop." Rosie laughed. "I want them to pop right out of her head!"

"Heather, you are not to learn to drive an automobile!" Brice's voice was firm. "I have no control over Miss Rosamund, but as my fiancée, for you to make such a spectacle of yourself would be unthinkable. Besides, it wouldn't be safe." He was actually glaring at her.

Heather seized her opportunity and glared right back at him. "I am going to learn to drive the automobile!" she said. Now they could have a good, raging quarrel, and the engagement would be broken.

Emma shattered the opportunity for an immediate, engagement-breaking quarrel.

"Just see what associating with you has done to the girl," she accused her brother. "You've put all sorts of ridiculous notions into her head."

I certainly have, Jared acknowledged, but silently. I put the notion into her head that she might end up married to a handsome Virginia planter, and I wish I'd never done it! He felt like popping Brice in the nose for telling Heather that he wouldn't allow her to learn to drive. As he couldn't do that without offering an explanation that he wasn't prepared to give, he only took Heather's side.

"It's perfectly safe, and I don't see any harm in it. And as Miss Rosie just said, you aren't married to Heather yet. I'll send word to Martin to get the car here. Miss Rosie, you're going to have the time of your life!"

"Outrageous!" Caldwell spluttered.

"Watch your temper, Caldwell," Rosie said, taking another delicate sip of her lemonade. "It's all settled, so there's no use working yourself up into a stroke."

Martin Knightbridge was an unhappy young man when he arrived at Arbordale with the automobile. There had been all the work of shipping it to Richmond by train, and then hiring a wagon large enough to accommodate it, along with a man to drive the team, to get it the rest of the way to the plantation. Martin himself had ridden in the wagon bed with his precious machine, sweating blood that something would happen to it every foot of the way.

"For Gawd's sake, don't drive over any potholes!" he'd entreated. "I don't want it jounced."

"Wouldn't think of it," the teamster had replied with perfect good humor, and then he had proceeded to hit every pothole between Richmond and Arbordale.

At Arbordale, Jared had to threaten Rosie with mayhem to keep her out of Martin's way while Martin checked every nut and bolt. Minna was content to do her observation from the verandah, a safe distance away in case the contraption exploded.

"Are you sure you can make it run?" Rosie asked Martin for the tenth time.

Martin raised a sweat-drenched face and glared at her.

"Of course I can make it run! What's going to be hard is to teach you how to drive it!" Martin was not in the least happy about entrusting his brainchild to a woman, and he took no pains to conceal it. Only the fact that Rosie had already bought it had made him agree to it at all. But if she wrecked it or ruined it, the fact that she had paid for it wouldn't mitigate his feelings in the least. This automobile was Martin's baby, he had given birth to it, and he was as protective toward it as any mother toward her child.

"Pish tush," Rosie said. The two words expressed her opinion of men's opinions admirably.

Brice was an interested spectator. Because he was a man, Martin didn't mind him hovering over him to learn the function of every part. If the automobile was to be a permanent part of the Arlington household, the more Brice knew about its workings, the better.

"Brice is changing his opinion about automobiles," Jared told Heather. "Now that he can see for himself how safe and reliable they are, he'll withdraw his objections to your learning to drive. Besides, Rosie is on your side."

Yes, she was, worse luck! Every single time she tried to shock Brice into breaking their engagement, Rosie or Minna backed her up and Brice backed down. It was a good thing that engagements lasted for so long, because it was beginning to look as if it was going to take a good long time for her to persuade him to break theirs.

Maybe, when she started learning to drive, she could be so reckless that he would put his foot down and they'd have that last, crucial quarrel.

There was only one trouble with that. If she was reckless enough to cause an engagement-breaking quarrel, she might wreck Rosie's car, and that wouldn't do at all. Even worse, she might get hurt, and Brice would never break his engagement to a girl who was hurt. It wouldn't be the gentlemanly thing to do.

"Just wait till he drives it himself," Jared said. "He'll be a convert. That is, if Rosie doesn't reduce it to a pile of trash first."

Rosie did not reduce the automobile to a pile of trash. To Heather's delight and Martin's astonishment, she proved to be an apt pupil. Steering was no problem for her at all once she got the hang of it, and she took to adjusting the knobs and controls like a duck takes to water. She had the feel for it. The only thing she balked at was the cranking.

"There ought to be an easier way to start it," she told Martin. "Cranking is downright dangerous. A body could break an arm."

"I'm working on that. I just haven't got it figured out yet," Martin told her sourly.

"Well, work on it harder. When you've thought it out and put it into practice, I'll give this one to Brice and buy the new, improved model."

"Don't hold your breath waiting," Martin muttered under his breath. Rosie chose to ignore him.

Exactly two days after the automobile arrived at Arbordale, the peace and quiet of Myrtle Street, where Isobel Becker now resided alone, was shattered as Rosie drove the automobile past the house to the end of the block, turned it around, and drove back again. Angel trotted alongside, with Jared at the ribbons and Martin in an icy sweat, prepared to leap in case Rosie came to grief and the automobile went out of control and he'd have to rescue it before it crumpled itself against the trunk of a tree.

The noise and the smell didn't bother Angel. She had been led around and around it until she had become accustomed to it. Saul, who had done the leading, had been a great deal more frightened than Angel had been. All of Heather's assurances that the contraption was safe had failed to convince him. Only Angel's acceptance of the contraption had finally allayed his fears, but only to a degree. He'd trust an animal above a human any time. On the other hand, Sam refused to get in it, so Saul didn't know what to think, except that he thought that he wished the contraption had never been brought to Arbordale.

Beside Rosie, Heather bounced up and down with excitement. It was all right to bounce. Brice wasn't there to see. Brice and Caldwell had refused to have anything to do with the antics. Minna sat between Jared and Martin in the buggy, not quite daring yet to ride in the contraption itself, but refusing to miss all the fun.

Rosie passed Isobel's house again. When there was no reaction from inside, she turned around and passed it for the third time.

Isobel appeared in the front window, pulling the lace curtains aside so that she could determine the cause of the unnerving racket. Isobel's face paled when she saw her sister driving the outlandish contraption, then it flushed an alarming red, and then she snapped the lace curtains back **together and yanked down the window shade with such** force that it came off its roller.

Rosie was laughing fit to kill as she proceeded to Main

Street to give the rest of the town something to shake up their digestion. A team of horses pulling a cart reared; the few pedestrians scattered, running for their lives. A cat leapt onto the grocer's leg and scrambled the rest of the way up to cling with piercing claws to the grocer's neck while he cursed and tried to dislodge it.

Clarence Kotter came running from the jail. Jared pulled up beside him.

"They can't do this!" Clarence spluttered. "They're disturbing the peace! I'll have them behind bars!"

"And David Inges will write up the story in his newspaper and point out that you persecute ladies, and that you're against progress." Jared grinned. "You want to remember that there's an election coming up."

Having sufficiently astounded and outraged the citizens of Bennington, Rosie turned around and drove back to Arbordale. Heather scrambled out of the automobile and ran to throw herself into Jared's arms.

"Oh, that was fun! That was more fun than I ever had before in my life! Wasn't it wonderful, Jared? Did you see Isobel's face, did you see the expressions on all those faces on Main Street? This will cause more talk than Carl Amhurst's being caught! Rosie's famous!"

"*Infamous* is the word that will be used." Jared held her close for a moment, aching to kiss that shining face. But Brice was approaching them from the house, with Emma beside him, both of their expressions disapproving.

"I hope that now that you've got this nonsense out of your systems, things will settle down around here," Brice said. "I'm only surprised that you got back safely."

"Be a sport, sport," Rosie said. "Get in. I'll teach you how to drive."

Brice hesitated, but only for a moment. Then he got in. It was his duty, after all. He was the one who would have to keep this contraption in running order. All the same, a slight flush of excitement colored his face.

"When I've mastered the essentials of running this contraption, I'll take you for a ride, Miss Emma," he said. "That is, if you would care to go." As an afterthought, he added, "Heather has already had a ride."

They all attended church on Sunday morning. Ephraim Roundtree obliged them by preaching a sermon that all progress is not to be deplored, and he even hinted that Rosie had not committed a sin by driving down Main Street in an automobile. Heather could tell that not all of his congregation agreed with him. But even those who disagreed were mollified when Emma sang a solo.

Emma's voice rose, pure and sweet, into the calm Sunday morning air. The listeners were enthralled. Heather was gratified to see that David Inges was smiling at Phoebe as Phoebe sat in her place in the choir. She was even more gratified when she saw that Miss Evelyn Langdon, no doubt driven by curiosity about this newest arrival at Arbordale, had also attended church. Evelyn, to Heather's delight, looked more than a little disgruntled as people nodded and expressed their enthrallment with Emma's voice. Miss Langdon's nose was out of joint. She had met her match, and she knew it.

Heather even went so far as to say, "Good morning, Miss Langdon," in her own sweetest tone as they were leaving the church. "I noticed that you enjoyed the solo."

Evelyn flushed and looked daggers at her, and Heather's day was made. Now, if only she didn't have to marry Brice, everything would be wonderful.

∾ *Chapter 19* ∾

"I HOPE JARED is almost ready to start back," Heather remarked as she pulled Angel to a stop in front of the Bennington Arms on Main Street. Brice had been drafted that morning to drive Minna and Rosie to Clarkson, the nearest town of any size, to shop for things for the ball that could not be obtained at the Emporium.

The Clarkson expedition had dropped Jared off in town to confer with Clarence Kotter and the gentleman from Utica. It had been decided that Carl Amhurst was to be tried for Naomi's murder here in Bennington, and after he had been tried and convicted, he could be taken to Utica if Utica insisted on trying him for Judson Pether's murder. The gentleman from Utica did not think Utica would insist. Murder trials cost money, and Martin Ross, alias Carl Amhurst, could only hang once.

Heather had to come into town to pick Jared up, and Emma had decided to come with her. She had been helping Minna and Rosie write out invitations to the engagement ball for the last several days, and she felt the need of air and relaxation.

Minna herself had penned the invitation to the Langdons. "I'll never be this happy again to have an invitation refused," Minna had said. "It's giving me the greatest pleasure to send them the invitation, but it'll give me a whole lot more pleasure to read their note of regret. Rosie, you're a bad influence on me. I'm becoming almost as wicked as you are!"

"About time, too!" Rosie had said wickedly. "When I think of all the years I wasted being good, it makes me sick. Now I've got to be just as wicked as I can to make up for all that lost time. We both should have started years ago. Think of all the fun we've missed!"

It had taken all of Minna's and Rosie's and Heather's persuasion to talk Emma into leaving off her full mourning for the ball and wearing the lavender ballgown. Lavender was half-mourning, so it was almost proper. She wouldn't dance, of course, that would be totally unacceptable, but she would be able to enjoy watching, and she was certainly enjoying the preparations. Jared said that Emma had missed her calling, that she should have been a general, the way she turned the entire household into troops and ordered them around and had everything moving like clockwork.

Since Emma's arrival, there wasn't a speck of dust to be found anywhere in the house, the furniture gleamed with lemon oil, the hinges had all been oiled, and she was even busy compiling a cookbook of Elspeth's recipes. But, for all her managing ways, she seemed softer than she had used to be, more tolerant. She was still even wearing her hair in the attractive way Della had fixed it the first day she had arrived.

Now the two girls settled down to wait for Jared to come out of the hotel. Heather didn't mind waiting. The moment they got back to the plantation, Emma would find a dozen things for her to do. And Angel didn't mind waiting. They would have brought Cicero instead of Angel, because Emma had been driving Cicero since her arrival, but at the last moment the spirited trotter had cast a shoe, and they'd had to use Angel instead.

Emma waited quietly, her gloved hand stroking Sam's head, which rested in her lap. Sam had taken a liking to Emma, and, surprisingly, Emma had taken a liking to Sam.

"I wish I could stay on for a little longer," Emma said. "Della and Pearl are coming along beautifully, but they're still only half trained. And I would like to finish the cookbook, and there are so many ways to improve the church activities! I've given Phoebe and her father some of my ideas, and I know they'll carry them out the best they can, but it would be better if I could be here to help them."

"I'll try to help them," Heather said. She didn't know how much good she would be, but she'd try if it would make Emma feel better.

"Of course you will try. But you need a great deal more experience than you have in running a house, too. There's more to it than just dusting and making beds. You must be alert for any sign of slacking off by the servants, but you must remember that their rights are important as well. Their time off is not to be infringed upon, and if extra work is needed, extra help must be brought in."

"Yes, Miss Emma." Heather couldn't get out of the habit of calling her Miss Emma, even if they were equals now.

"But mind that you don't overstaff. There is still a need for economy at Arbordale, and you mustn't abuse Miss Rosamund's generosity."

"I won't, Miss Emma," Heather promised.

"You have enough clothing to last you for a long time, so no outlay need be made there."

"Oh, yes, I have far more than I need! But everything is actually yours, Miss Emma. You must take everything you need back to Albany with you, now that you aren't going to go to China to be a missionary."

Now Emma was scratching behind Sam's ears, and Sam made delighted noises in his throat. "Nonsense! I gave the things to you, and you must keep them. You can consider it my wedding present to you, as I won't be able to give you anything else."

Heather wished that Jared would hurry. She felt awful, sitting here letting Emma tell her what to do after she was married to Brice, when she knew very well that she wasn't going to marry Brice at all. She was being so deceitful that she hated herself, but for the life of her she couldn't think what to do about it at the moment.

"It doesn't seem fair for me to keep everything," she said.

"You ought to at least take back half of the things you gave me."

She broke off as a man burst out of the jailhouse across the street. It was Carl Amhurst. He was alone, and he was getting away. Heather didn't know what had happened to Ben Stump, who was supposed to be guarding the jail while Clarence Kotter was at the hotel, but she had a feeling that it wasn't anything good.

Carl looked up and down the street, which was deserted at this hour when everyone was home having their midday meal. He spotted the horse and buggy and sprinted toward it. With one frantically urgent arm, he wrenched Emma out of her seat and sent her sprawling in the dust of the road with Sam on top of her. Sam, who had been dreaming of chasing rabbits, seemed to keep on running all the way down.

Heather was next. Before she could make any move to try to defend herself or even scream, she was sent tumbling after Emma and Sam. She landed on her hands and knees with a force that rattled her teeth and sent shock waves through her body.

"Bitch!" Carl snarled at Heather. His hatred for the girl who had found Naomi's grave and who had concocted the scheme that had tricked him into betraying himself twisted his face, and Heather flinched more from that than from the jolting she had received. And then her heart seemed to stop as Carl pointed a gun at her, his face murderous as he came within a hair of pulling the trigger before he changed his mind, grabbed up the ribbons, and urged Angel into motion.

Sam got up, shaking his head in confusion. He nuzzled first at Heather and then at Emma as the two girls struggled to their feet.

Heather drew a deep breath to replace the one that had been jolted out of her, straightened her hat, and screamed.

In the buggy, lashing at Angel and cursing, Carl couldn't believe his bad luck. He had heard Jared tell Clarence Kotter, when Jared had stopped in at the jail to pick up the sheriff, that he was going to meet his sister and Heather in front of the hotel after they had eaten, and so Carl had known that the horse and buggy would be there.

He'd counted on the street being deserted at this hour, except for two helpless young women who would supply him with an escape vehicle drawn by one of the fastest horses in the county. The way Ben Stump spent so much time in the sheriff's office telling Clarence everything he knew, Carl knew that Emma drove Cicero, and it had never crossed his mind that with Cicero unavailable Angel would be between the shafts.

It was the only chance Carl would ever have, and it was a good enough chance that he had been eager to take it. Tricking Ben Stump into getting close enough to the bars of the cell so that he could get his arm around his neck and overpower him for the key had been easy; Ben wasn't the most intelligent man in the world.

With a gun from the sheriff's office in his possession and Cicero pulling the buggy, he would have had a good head start before anyone was aware of what had happened. Once he was out of town, there was a network of country roads and patches of woodland where he could lose himself.

He would find a place to hide until nightfall, and then he would rob some farmhouse, leave the inhabitants bound and gagged, and be many more miles away before daybreak. He'd been convinced that he'd get away free and clear. With a little money in his pocket and a good fast horse, he'd be able to make it to Richmond. Then a train, and another city.

It had been the worst sort of luck when Naomi Thaxter's father died and Naomi had come to make her home with Matthew Thaxter. Naomi had been only twelve when he knew her back in Utica, but he hadn't been able to take the chance that she would recognize him. They had lived on the same street, and she'd known him well. He had had everything going for him here in Bennington. There was his solid position in John Thaxter's bank and the certainty of marrying the minister's daughter, thereby establishing an unassailable identity as an upright citizen who would never be connected with the murder and robbery in Utica.

Most of the proceeds of that robbery were safely banked in Richmond under an assumed name. He would never have to worry about money in his old age. He would live a good life, lacking for nothing.

Now, because of that girl from Albany, he would have to start all over. He could have shot the girl. He had wanted to shoot her. The only thing that stopped him was that he hadn't wanted to waste a bullet. He might have need for a fully loaded gun later.

But now luck had turned against him again. Instead of being behind one of the fastest horses in the county, he was behind the slowest. Livid with rage at this turn of fate when everything else had gone just as he had planned, he lashed at Angel with the buggy whip, cursing her in a voice so vicious that it all but strangled him.

Jared was just leaving the hotel when he heard Heather scream. He had left Clarence Kotter and the gentleman from Utica still at their dessert, not wanting to keep Heather and Emma waiting.

It took him only an instant to see the reason for Heather's earth-shattering screams, and then he was running, sprinting faster than he had ever dreamed he could sprint. It took him only a few seconds to catch up with the buggy, because Angel was balking, outraged at having a whip used on her. He hauled himself up while it was still in motion, however slow a motion.

He stopped when he was confronted with the muzzle of a gun pointed right at his head. It hadn't occurred to him that a buggy thief would be armed, and now that he saw who the buggy thief was, he liked it even less. But that didn't deter him from grasping Carl's arm and hauling him out of the buggy with him.

To be honest, he hadn't planned on being a hero. He'd already been in the process of hauling the buggy thief out of the buggy when he'd been confronted with the gun, and his arm didn't have time to get the message from his brain.

Reflex action made him twist as the two men fell, so that Carl was on the bottom. Carl's elbow cracked against the road with numbing force, and the gun went flying.

Heather and Emma crashed into each other and almost went down again themselves as both of them raced to retrieve the gun before Carl could get his hands on it. They both reached for it at the same time, and it was a miracle that it didn't discharge as they struggled for possession before they realized what they were doing.

Emma let go first, her face white. And then Heather, her face equally white, also let go. The gun was on the ground again, almost within reach of Carl's groping fingers, and Heather snatched it up just in time and backed away, holding it with both of her hands and marveling because it was so heavy that it took both of her hands to hold it.

Where was everybody? Why didn't somebody come? Only seconds had passed, but it seemed like an hour to Heather. Furious at the lack of assistance for Jared as he fought to subdue a man whose desperation had doubled his strength, Heather opened her mouth and screamed again. Jared was going to be hurt. Jared was going to be killed. Why didn't somebody come?

Angel had stopped, her ears laid back because she hadn't been in the least appreciative of being whipped. She looked back at the struggling men and bared her teeth.

"Bite him, Angel!" Heather screamed. Realizing what she had just said, she had a hysterical impulse to laugh. Some horses bit people, but Angel certainly couldn't be depended on to do it. She tried again.

"Sic him, Sam! Sic him!"

This was a direct order, and Sam knew what to do about that. With a joyous yelp because he knew what was expected of him, he threw himself into the fray. It was only unfortunate that in the tangle of flailing arms and legs, his teeth made contact with the wrong arm. Jared's grip on Carl was broken, and a cry of startled pain burst from his mouth.

"Give me the gun!" Carl was on his feet, taking advantage of this break in his favor. He advanced toward Heather, his eyes blazing with an insane light.

Heather backed away from him, holding the gun even tighter. It wobbled because her hands were wobbling. She'd never seen a look like that on a man's face before. There was a look of madness about Carl that turned her blood to water.

"Heather, shoot him!" Jared shouted. "He's insane. He'll

kill someone else if he gets hold of that gun! Don't let him get it, don't let him get near you, shoot!"

Heather willed her finger to pull the trigger, but her finger seemed to be frozen. She had never handled a firearm, and the idea of shooting a man, even a man like Carl Amhurst, boggled her mind.

Jared was on his feet, nursing his bitten arm, but he would be too late even if grappling with Carl again might bring him down. Carl was almost upon Heather. All he had to do was take another step and he'd wrest the gun from her, and there would probably be a blood bath right here on Bennington's Main Street.

And then Emma's hand reached out and closed over Heather's, just as Heather's finger finally began to press down against the trigger. Emma's finger pressed against Heather's, the gun discharged, and Carl staggered back and clutched at his shoulder. But with a superhuman effort, he stayed on his feet and started to make a last, desperate lunge for the gun.

Sam, feeling his disgrace, now had a clear target in the man he had been supposed to sic in the first place. He corrected his error. He made a flying leap and crashed into Carl's back, boring him to the ground, his teeth clamped firmly on Carl's arm.

And now, when it was all over, people were coming, running, calling out in alarm and excitement. Clarence Kotter was there, cursing fit to curl Emma's hair.

"I'm going to kill Ben Stump!" Clarence fumed. "I'm going to choke the living daylights out of him! Mr. Cranston, are you all right? It looks like you've been shot!"

"Bitten," Jared said sourly. "Sam needs a pair of spectacles. It's Amhurst who's shot. Heather got him."

"No, no, it wasn't me, it was Emma! I mean it was both of us!" Heather looked down at the gun she was still holding as if she'd never seen it before. Her hand opened with revulsion, and the gun dropped to the ground. "Emma helped me. She deserves all the credit!"

"I didn't feel that I had any choice." Emma's face was still white with shock. "But if that man dies, I don't know how I'll be able to live with my conscience."

"If that man dies, it won't make a particle of difference," Clarence told her. "He's going to die anyway, so what's the difference if it's at the end of a rope or from a bullet fired in self-defense? Will one of you call that dog off so I can see how bad Amhurst is hurt? Somebody go fetch Doc Cunningham, and somebody go see what's happened to Ben Stump. I hope Amhurst didn't kill him, because I want to kill him myself!"

Sam wasn't anxious to relinquish his prize. This was the second time he'd caught this man, and this time he wanted to make sure that he stayed caught. But at Heather's tugging, he finally removed his teeth from Carl's arm so that Clarence could turn Carl over.

Now, after it was all over, Heather began to shake. She was shaking so hard that her teeth rattled. She'd thought that Jared was going to be killed, and if he'd been killed she would have wanted to die too. Jared was her life. Without him her life wouldn't be worth living. Even if he didn't love her, it didn't make any difference. If she couldn't marry him, she would never marry anyone.

She knelt in the dust of the road without a thought for the damage it was doing to Emma's pretty dress, put her arms around Sam, and hid her face against his warm fur until she had her emotions under control. Then she rose and told him to get into the buggy and guard it even though there was no one for him to guard it against now.

Someone had unlocked the jail cell and let Ben Stump out. Ben's face was red with indignation.

"It wasn't my fault! He told me there was a rat in his cell, a big, rabid rat! And when I went to look, with Clarence's gun so I could shoot it, he grabbed me and got the gun! Anybody could have made the same mistake. He sounded real scared of that rat that wasn't there!"

Ben paused for breath and then began to back up as Clarence advanced on him. Still he went on trying to vindicate himself.

"He gagged me with a piece of my own shirt!" Ben said indignantly. "See here, it's all torn and ruined. By rights you owe me a shirt, Clarence."

He backed up faster as Kotter continued to advance. His

throat worked so that his Adam's apple bobbed up and down.

"It's all right about the shirt, I'll bear the loss myself." And then he turned and ran for his office at the depot.

A moment ago, Heather hadn't been sure that she would ever be able to laugh again. Now her laughter joined that of the others, and she laughed until tears came to her eyes. It didn't matter that her laughter was hysterical, it was still laughter. And when Jared came and put his arms around her, held her close and patted her shoulder and said, "There, there, it's all right now, everything's all right. If that bastard had hurt you, I would have killed him!" it was more than all right. She only wished he would go on holding her and patting her forever. The viciousness in his voice when he said he would have killed the bastard if he'd hurt her was music to her ears.

Emma broke the spell. "Jared, I know this has been an upsetting experience, but there is no need to blaspheme!"

At least she had the grace to hug both Jared and Heather. "But I'm so glad that you're both all right that I'll forgive you this time!"

The shoppers arrived back at Arbordale late in the afternoon, the carriage laden down with their purchases. Rosie had had a field day. Without Isobel to restrain her, she had bought everything that had taken her fancy, whether it was essential or not, just for the pleasure of spending her own money as she chose to spend it.

"That dreadful man is going to live to hang!" Rosie said the moment she alighted from the carriage and hurried to join the others on the verandah. "Ben Stump waylaid us and told us all about it. Carl Amhurst has confessed at last. He was afraid he was going to die, and so he thought it wouldn't make any difference. Minna, for heaven's sake, hurry and fix our lemonade! This is going to take a lot of telling, and talking makes me thirsty."

At last the story of how Carl Amhurst had enticed Naomi to her death was out. Heather could hardly restrain herself from asking Rosie to talk faster.

Rosie drained half of her glass and went on, relishing the

ALWAYS THE DREAM

mesmerized audience. "He pushed a note under Matthew Thaxter's kitchen door, where Naomi would find it when she went home before Matthew did to fix Matthew's supper. The note told her to pack a few things for a short trip and to meet him at one o'clock in the morning around the corner from Matthew's house. Only of course he didn't sign his name, he signed Brice's. He said that it would avoid a lot of trouble if he and Naomi were to elope. And of course Naomi swallowed it hook, line, and sinker. I can just imagine how thrilled she was when she thought she was running away to marry Brice! The poor child, it's heart-breaking, but at least Carl is going to pay for his crimes, thanks to Heather and Jared and Emma."

She took another sip of her lemonade, savoring it this time. "Poor Ben! He's all in a muddle. He's all set up in self-importance because he was part of all the excitement, but at the same time he's disgraced because he let Carl trick him, so he doesn't know whether to be happy or sad."

Brice's eyes were fastened on Emma. "Miss Cranston, are you sure you're all right? Shouldn't you be in bed? Did the doctor give you something to calm your nerves when he patched Jared up? You're dreadfully pale. Maybe we should call Dr. Cunningham to come out here and make sure that you aren't suffering any delayed ill effects."

"I'm perfectly all right." Emma's cheeks flushed pink under Brice's gaze. "I only did what anyone would have done, given the same set of circumstances."

"That isn't true at all! You were incredibly brave! It's hard to believe that a delicate girl could do what you did. Most girls would have fainted on the spot."

Aren't I delicate too? Heather wanted to ask. But she didn't, because she wasn't delicate, and Brice knew it. Her resolution hardened. This had gone on long enough. She could at least do as much for herself as she'd done for Phoebe Roundtree. She'd refused to let Phoebe just sit back and let David Inges get away from her. And here she was, just sitting back and letting Jared get away from her. If she didn't do something right away, she'd end up married to Brice, and she couldn't let that happen.

Go on, do it! she ordered herself. After all, what did she

288

have to lose? She wasn't going to marry Brice no matter what, so she might as well make a good stab at getting what she really wanted.

"Jared, will you come out into the garden with me?" she asked.

Jared looked at her, puzzled. Brice hadn't even noticed that Heather had spoken, he was too concerned about Emma.

"What is it, Heather? You look a little green around the gills. Is it that delayed reaction Brice was talking about? Maybe you had better get a little air."

He held her arm solicitously as they walked out to the rose garden. He was still looking at her in a worried manner. "You aren't going to faint, are you?" he asked.

Heather savored his alarm. "I'm not going to marry Brice," she said.

Jared looked even more alarmed. She was suffering from delayed shock! Of course she was going to marry Brice. It was all settled. There was even going to be an engagement ball in a few days' time! What did she mean, she wasn't going to marry Brice?

"What do you mean, you're not going to marry Brice?"

"I mean I'm not going to marry Brice."

"But it's what you always wanted! It's just like all those books you read, all those romantic stories you thrive on!"

"I know, but it isn't my story, Jared, can't you see? If it was my story, it would end here, and I don't want my story to end here, I want it to be just beginning! I don't want to live at Arbordale and be the mistress of a plantation. I don't want to have to learn how to tat and have to be a lady every minute, always afraid that I'll slip up."

"You could learn not to slip up," Jared told her, trying to fight down the sudden hope that flared in his heart.

"That isn't the point. I'm not going to marry Brice because I don't love him! And he doesn't love me either. He only asked me to marry him because he was grateful that I found Naomi's grave and figured out how to trap Carl Amhurst. He was carried away, just as I was almost carried away for a moment. I never meant to let him think I was going to marry him, it just sort of happened. I'd be miserable if I married him, and he'd be miserable if he married me. It's Emma who's supposed to marry him."

"But Brice and Emma hardly know each other! Emma's only been here for a few days!"

"It only takes a few days, if a man and a woman are right for each other. You'd have to be blind not to have noticed how they keep looking at each other. You must have noticed, even if you are a man and men hardly ever notice anything."

"No, I can't say that I have," Jared confessed.

"Of course you didn't notice, because they almost never look at each other! They work so hard not to look at each other that it sticks out like a sore thumb. Any woman knows what that means, even if you men are so obtuse that you can't see your noses at the ends of your faces!"

"I can see my nose at the end of my face if I look at it cross-eyed," Jared said. He was beginning to feel light-headed. He crossed his eyes, and Heather stamped her foot.

"Stop trying to be funny! This is serious, darn it! Brice is falling head over heels in love with Emma, and she's falling head over heels in love with him, only they can't do anything about it because of me. They can't even admit it to themselves because they're so dratted good! So I'm going to let Brice off the hook, and it'll be a narrow escape for both of us!"

She meant it. Jared could tell that she meant every word of it. And she might be right, but all the same the situation posed a lot of problems.

"Good Lord! What will be done about the engagement ball?" That was a stupid thing to be worrying about at a time like this, but it was the only thing Jared could think of at the moment. The rest was just too much for him to assimilate so quickly. "It's too late to call it off. All of the invitations are out, and they've been accepted."

"They'll have the ball, it just won't be an engagement ball. It'll be a celebration ball, because Brice has been exonerated and Arbordale is safe."

"You're perfectly right." Both Heather and Jared jumped when Minna spoke at their elbows. They had been so wrapped up in their discussion that they hadn't noticed that she had followed them out into the garden. Rosie was right beside her, as always. The two women seemed to be attached to each other by an invisible cord. "It won't be an engagement ball, it'll be a celebration ball."

"You heard?" Jared wanted to know.

"Of course we heard! There's nothing wrong with our hearing!" Rosie said tartly. "And it's been just as plain as Heather said that Brice and Emma are attracted to each other and that Heather wasn't happy about marrying Brice. We were just wondering if we'd have to do something about it ourselves, if Heather didn't get around to doing something."

"And you'll back me up all the way?" Heather asked.

"All the way." Minna's voice was firm.

"That's all I wanted to know. You two scat. I want to talk to Jared about something else, alone."

Minna and Rosie scatted, grinning at each other like two Cheshire cats. Jared couldn't imagine what else Heather could want to talk to him about. She seemed to have covered everything already.

"Jared, on the night of the ball, will you do something for me?"

"Of course I will. What is it I'm going to do?"

"I'm going to float down that curving staircase in that beautiful blue ballgown, just like a real Southern belle, and I want you to be waiting for me at the foot to escort me to the ballroom."

"That's an easy promise for me to make," Jared said. He was definitely feeling dizzy. "Brice probably won't be in any mood to be waiting for you at the foot of the staircase if you've told him you aren't going to marry him."

"And then we'll waltz and waltz."

"And then we'll waltz and waltz."

"And then you're going to ask me to walk with you in the rose garden. And while we're in the rose garden, you're going to ask me to marry you." Heather held her breath. This was it. If Jared said he wasn't going to do any such thing, at least she would have tried. And even if he did say that he wasn't going to do any such thing, he needn't think he was going to get away from her! She'd still have all the time in the world to catch him once they were back in Albany.

"I'll be happy to," Jared said fervently. "But do you have any idea in the world what you'll be letting yourself in for? You'll have to live in a dingy flat because I have to sell the house to raise money for the automobile manufacturing enterprise. Mr. Tsiang can't do it all. And half the money from the house will have to go to Emma. Now that she isn't going to go to China and be a missionary, she's entitled to half."

"The flat won't be dingy. I'll decorate it in the Bohemian style, lots of bright cushions and beaded curtains. It'll hardly cost anything. Bohemian is very popular, even the best houses have Bohemian rooms. We'll just go them one better and have the whole flat Bohemian."

Bohemian would be fine for a writer of romantic novels, but Jared wondered what Mr. Deems would think of it for the new assistant at his stodgy law office. On second thought, he didn't give a hang what Mr. Deems would think of it. He'd be living in the flat, not Mr. Deems.

"It will probably be a long time before the automobile business begins to pay off," he warned her. "There's even the possibility that it won't pay off at all. I think it will, but it's still a gamble. It might fall flat on its face."

"And there's a possibility that my books will never sell," Heather said. "But you'll get to try to make the automobile venture go, and I'll get to write my books, and everything won't be ending, it'll be just beginning. Jared, we'll have fun! It'll be exciting! Sink or swim, we're going to enjoy every minute of it!"

Jared was inclined to think that they would.

"I still don't see how you're going to manage Emma. She'll be coming back to Albany with us. Romance doesn't flourish very well over such long distances, no matter what your romantic novels have led you to believe."

"Emma isn't going to come back to Albany with us. Minna and Rosie will insist that now that she's finally here at Arbordale, she absolutely has to stay for a long, long visit. You can trust Minna and Rosie."

"It does seem like a dirty trick to play on Minna and Rosie," Jared said. "Just think how Emma will keep tabs on them, putting a crimp in their mischief!"

Heather laughed. "I'll put my money on Minna and Rosie," she said. "Any time they aren't gadding about the world watching can-can girls, they'll be more than Emma's match!"

"Are you sure about all this, absolutely, positively sure? About marrying me and taking your chances?"

"Certainly I'm sure. And it's all going to happen just the way I said it would."

"Then why do I have to wait for the evening of the ball to propose to you? Why can't I do it right now?"

"Because I'm not going to be cheated out of being proposed to in a starlit rose garden," Heather told him. "The time Brice proposed to me doesn't count. It was already dawn, and it was raining, and there wasn't a star in sight."

"If you say so," Jared said. And then he kissed her.

The garden spun in circles around Heather. It hadn't been that way at all when Brice had kissed her. That had been a nice kiss, a very nice kiss, a proper kiss . . .

Drat proper! She didn't want to be kissed properly, she wanted to be kissed the way Jared was kissing her now. She wanted to take wing and fly. She felt as though she were already flying. Her blood felt like warm honey, her bones were melting, even her hair and her fingernails tingled. And she wasn't in the least embarrassed as she thought of being married to Jared, of sharing the intimacy of man and wife, the way she'd been embarrassed when she'd thought about it with Brice.

This was Jared, her Jared, and loving him and being loved by him was the way things were meant to be. It was part of some wonderful, mysterious plan, and it would be a sin to be embarrassed.

And it was going to be like this all the rest of her life. There wouldn't be a starlit rose garden again for a long time, but she wouldn't need a rose garden. Jared's arms were all the rose garden she would ever need.

They drew apart at last, breathless, looking at each other as if they had just discovered each other. And then Heather smiled and put her hand in his.

"Let's go back and break the news to them," she said. "I hope Minna has extra refreshments ready. Something tells me that a nice tall glass of Minna's lemonade is just what I need right now!"

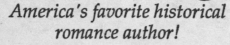

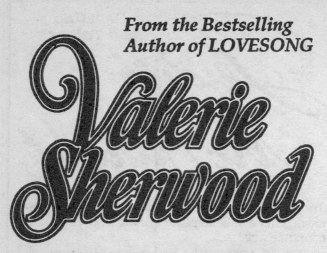